P9-DHN-581

While Paris Slept

While Paris Slept

RUTH DRUART

GRAND CENTRAL PUBLISHING

NEW YORK BOSTON

This book is a work of fiction. Names, characters, places, and incidents are the product of the author's imagination or are used fictitiously. Any resemblance to actual events, locales, or persons, living or dead, is coincidental.

Copyright © 2021 by Ruth Druart

Cover design: Albert Tang. Handlettering: Joel Holland. Photograph of man and railroad: Library of Congress, Prints & Photographs Division, FSA/OWI Collection, [reproduction number, LC-DIG-fsa-8d24426]. Photograph of Eiffel tower: Shutterstock. Cover copyright © 2021 by Hachette Book Group, Inc.

Hachette Book Group supports the right to free expression and the value of copyright. The purpose of copyright is to encourage writers and artists to produce the creative works that enrich our culture.

The scanning, uploading, and distribution of this book without permission is a theft of the author's intellectual property. If you would like permission to use material from the book (other than for review purposes), please contact permissions@hbgusa.com. Thank you for your support of the author's rights.

Grand Central Publishing
Hachette Book Group
1290 Avenue of the Americas, New York, NY 10104
grandcentralpublishing.com
twitter.com/grandcentralpub

First Edition: February 2021

Grand Central Publishing is a division of Hachette Book Group, Inc. The Grand Central Publishing name and logo is a trademark of Hachette Book Group, Inc.

The publisher is not responsible for websites (or their content) that are not owned by the publisher.

The Hachette Speakers Bureau provides a wide range of authors for speaking events. To find out more, go to www.hachettespeakersbureau.com or call (866) 376-6591.

Library of Congress Control Number: 2020933679

ISBNs: 978-1-5387-3518-3 (hardcover), 978-1-5387-3517-6 (ebook)

Printed in the United States of America

LSC-C

Printing 1, 2020

To Jeremy, Joachim, and Dimitri:
my inspiration for this story

And in memory of my grandmother Diana White

"Let us sacrifice one day to gain perhaps a whole life."

—*From* Les Misérables *by Victor Hugo*

While Paris Slept

Part One

Chapter One

Santa Cruz, June 24, 1953

JEAN-LUC

Jean-Luc lifts the razor to his cheek, glancing at his reflection in the bathroom mirror. For a split second, he doesn't recognize himself. Pausing, razor held in midair, he stares into his eyes, wondering what it is. There's something American about him now. It's there in his healthy tan, his white teeth, and something else he can't quite identify. Is it the confident way he holds his chin? Or his smile? Anyway, it pleases him. American is good.

With a towel wrapped around his waist, he wanders back into the bedroom. A black shape outside catches his eye. Through the window, he sees a Chrysler crawling up the street, coming to a halt behind the oak tree out front. Strange. Who would be calling at seven o'clock in the morning? He stares at the car, distracted, then the buttery smell of warm crêpes wafting up the stairs calls him to breakfast.

Entering the kitchen, he kisses Charlotte on the cheek, then ruffles his son's hair in way of greeting. Glancing through the window, he sees the car is still there. He watches as a lanky man extracts himself from the driver's seat, craning his neck, peering around—like a pelican, he thinks to himself. A stocky man emerges on the other side. They walk toward the house.

The doorbell cuts through the morning like a knife. Charlotte looks up.

"I'll go." Jean-Luc's already heading that way. He slips the chain from the lock and opens the door.

"Mr. Bow-Champ?" Pelican Man asks without smiling.

Jean-Luc stares at him, taking in the dark navy suit, white shirt, and plain tie, and the arrogant look in his eyes. The mispronunciation of his name is something he usually lets go, but something pricks his pride this morning. Maybe it's because the man is standing on his doorstep. "Beauchamp," he corrects. "It's French."

"We know it's French, but this is America." Pelican Man's eyes narrow a fraction as he sticks a shiny black shoe across the threshold. He peers over Jean-Luc's shoulder, then his neck clicks as he turns, cocking his head to one side, looking at the car port where their new Nash 600 is parked. His top lip curls in one corner. "I'm Mr. Jackson, and this is Mr. Bradley. Mr. Bow-Champ, we'd like to ask you some questions."

"What about?" He adds inflection to show his surprise, but his voice sounds false to his ears—an octave too high. Muffled sounds of breakfast reach out to the doorstep: plates being stacked, his son's light laughter. The familiar noises echo around Jean-Luc like a distant dream. He closes his eyes, clutching at the vanishing edges. A seagull screeching calls him back to the present. His heart beats hard and fast against his ribs, like a trapped bird.

The stocky man, Bradley, leans forward, lowering his voice. "Were you taken into County Hospital six weeks ago after a car accident?" He stretches his neck, as though hoping to gather information about the life inside the house.

"Yes." Jean-Luc's pulse races. "I was knocked over by a car rounding the corner too fast." He pauses, taking a breath. "I lost consciousness." The doctor's name, Wiesmann, springs to mind. He fired questions at Jean-Luc while he was still coming around, feeling foggy. "How long have you been in America?" he asked. "Where did you get the scar on your face? Were you born with only a finger and a thumb on your left hand?"

Bradley coughs. "Mr. Bow-Champ, we'd like you to accompany us to City Hall."

"But why?" His voice comes out as a croak.

They stand there like a blockade, hands behind their backs, chests thrust forward.

"We think this would be best discussed at City Hall, not here on your doorstep, in front of your neighbors."

The veiled threat tightens the knot in his stomach. "But what have I done?"

Bradley rolls his lips together. "These are just preliminary inquiries. We could call the police in to assist, but at this early stage we prefer... we prefer to get the facts straight. I'm sure you understand."

No, I don't, he wants to scream. *I don't know what you're talking about*. Instead, he mumbles assent. "Give me ten minutes." Closing the door in their faces, he returns to the kitchen.

Charlotte is sliding a crêpe onto a plate. "Was it the postman?" she asks without looking up.

"No."

She turns toward him, a thin crease across her forehead, her brown eyes piercing him.

"Two investigators... They want me to go with them to answer some questions."

"About the accident?"

He shakes his head. "I don't know. I don't know what they want. They won't say."

"They won't say? But they have to. They can't just ask you to go with them without telling you why." The color drains from her face.

"Don't worry, Charlotte. I think I'd better do what they say. Clear things up. It's only questioning."

Their son has stopped munching and is looking up at them, a tiny frown on his forehead.

"I'm sure I'll be back soon." Jean-Luc's voice rings false in his ears, as though someone else is uttering these words of comfort. "Can you call the office; tell them I'll be late?" He turns to his son. "Have a good day at school."

Everything has gone still, like the hush before a storm. Quickly he turns and leaves the kitchen. Normal. He must act normal. This is only a formality. What can they possibly want?

Ten minutes. He doesn't want them ringing the bell again, so he hurries into the bedroom, opening the drawer in the wardrobe, glancing at his ties coiled like serpents. He picks out a blue tie with tiny gray dots. Appearance is important in a situation like this. He takes his jacket off its hanger and walks back down the stairs.

Charlotte is waiting in the kitchen doorway, her hand over her mouth. He takes it, kissing her cold lips, looking her in the eye. Then he turns away. "Bye, son," he shouts toward the kitchen.

"Bye, Daddy. See you in a while."

"Catch you later, crocodile." His voice cracks, missing the right note again.

He senses Charlotte's eyes on his back as he opens the front door and follows the men to their black Chrysler. He takes a deep breath, forcing the air down into his abdomen. Now he remembers hearing the storm break in the middle of the night; can feel the earth thick with water, starting to evaporate already. Soon it will be humid and hot.

No one speaks as they drive past familiar houses with large, open lawns reaching out to the sidewalk, past the paper shop, the baker, the ice-cream parlor. This life he's come to love.

Chapter Two

Santa Cruz, June 24, 1953

CHARLOTTE

I stare out the kitchen window, though the black car vanished many minutes ago. Time feels frozen. I don't want it to move forward.

"Mom, I can smell burning."

"*Merde!*" I grab the pan from the stove and throw the blackened crêpe into the sink. My eyes water as smoke fumes swirl up. "I'll make you another."

"No thanks, Mom, I'm full." Sam hops off the stool and darts out of the kitchen.

As I glance around, the remnants of the disturbed breakfast fill me with panic. But I have to pull myself together. Slowly, I climb the stairs, going into the bathroom. I splash cold water on my face, then slip into the dress I wore yesterday and go back downstairs.

Sam bounces up and down at my side as we walk to school. "Mom, what do you think those men will ask Dad?"

"I don't know, Sam."

"What could it be, Mom?"

"I don't know."

"Maybe it's about a burglary."

"What?"

"Or a murder!"

"Sam, be quiet."

He immediately stops hopping around, dragging his feet instead. A pang of guilt shoots through me, but I have more important things to worry about.

When we get to the school gate, the other mothers are already walking back home.

"Hi, Charlie! You're running late today. Coming over for a coffee later?" Marge's voice rings out from the group.

"Sure," I lie.

After dropping Sam off, I dawdle around the gate to give the others time to get ahead. When I see they're far enough in front, I walk home slowly, loneliness threatening to engulf me. I'm half tempted to join them for coffee, but I know I won't be able to hold myself back from blurting something out. There's a chance that no one saw the car come for Jean-Luc this morning, but if someone did, I'd need to have a story ready. They'll want to know all the details. Yes, it's best to avoid any contact.

Once home, I go from room to room, plumping up the cushions on the couch, washing up the breakfast things, rearranging the magazines on the coffee table. I remind myself that there's no point worrying, it won't help anyone; after all, he's only been taken in for questioning. I should do something practical to keep my mind occupied. I could mow the lawn, save Jean-Luc the trouble.

I pull on my gardening shoes and drag the lawnmower out from the garage. I've seen Jean-Luc pull the string on the side to get it started, so I give it a tug. Nothing happens. I pull again; this time something inside spits, but quickly dies. Now I pull harder and faster. Suddenly it's whirring away, pulling me with it. It stinks of gas, though I quite like the smell.

The rhythm is soothing, and I'm disappointed when the job is quickly finished. I put the mower away and go back into the house.

Maybe the living room could do with a cleaning. As I take the vacuum cleaner out from under the stairs, I remember that I did this only yesterday. Defeated, I slump to the floor, the thick vacuum pipe still in my hand.

The past is flooding back. Jean-Luc never lets me talk about it. In his pragmatic way, he told me to leave it behind, where it belongs. As if it were that simple. I have tried, I really have, but I can't help my dreams when I'm fast asleep, where I see my mother, my father. Home. These dreams leave me with a yearning for my family that casts a long shadow. I have been in touch with them; I wrote once we'd settled down and found somewhere to live. My mother wrote back; a short, curt letter saying that Papa wasn't ready to see me yet. He still had some forgiving to do.

I wander into the kitchen and stare out the window, willing Jean-Luc to come back. Released from questioning, suspicions unfounded. But there's only the empty street.

The distant sound of a car engine sets my pulse racing. Leaning forward so my nose almost touches the window, I peer out. *Please, God, let it be him.* My stomach plummets when I catch sight of a familiar blue hood rounding the corner: Marge from across the road. I watch her struggle with shopping bags while one of her twin boys chases the other around the car. She glances over in my direction. Quickly I back away to the side of the lace curtains. Secrets and lies. What does anyone really know about their neighbors' lives?

I have no desire to run into anyone today. If someone saw the black car, all the mothers will know by now. I can imagine them hypothesizing, getting excited. No, I need to get away and distance myself. I could go shopping to another town, where I won't bump into anyone; somewhere large and anonymous, like one of those big supermarkets.

I grab my purse, take my keys off the hook by the front door, and get in the car before anyone can see me. As I drive north along the coastal route with the window down, the wind blows through my hair. I love driving fast; it gives me a sense of liberty and independence. I can pretend to be anyone I want to be.

After half an hour, I spot a sign for Lucky Store. Turning left off the highway, I follow the arrows till I see a parking lot packed with station wagons. I spot one of those burger places and a merry-go-round. Sam would love it here; maybe we should bring him one Saturday and make a day of it. Normally I avoid these large supermarkets, preferring to shop locally, where I can ask the grocer for his crunchiest apples, or the butcher for his leanest cut. They always take their time to pick out the best produce for me, appreciating that I care.

I don't feel comfortable in this massive supermarket with its endless rows of brightly displayed food. Housewives in full skirts and smart heels with waved hair push enormous shopping carts piled high with jars and tins. It fills me with a nostalgia, a yearning for home, for Paris.

Chicken, I tell myself, that's what I'll cook tonight, lemon chicken. It's Jean-Luc's favorite.

Two packs of chicken breasts, a pint of milk, and four lemons look lost and forlorn at the bottom of the cart when I reach the cash register. I feel embarrassed, but I couldn't concentrate on what else we needed for the week.

The cashier looks at me strangely. "Do you want help bagging, ma'am?"

Is she being sarcastic? I shake my head. "No thank you. I can manage."

My stomach rumbles loudly as I put the solitary brown paper bag in the trunk. I didn't have any breakfast. Maybe I should get a burger, but the mere thought of it turns my stomach. Instead I drive home, praying Jean-Luc will be back.

I park the car in the drive and hurry to the front door. It's locked. He can't be there. Why would I think he would be? He'd have gone straight to work anyway. I know he'd have been worried about being late as it was.

It's already three o'clock. Sam needs picking up from school in thirty minutes. Maybe today it would be better to be late than early. Early means I'll have to exchange banter with other moms. He could walk home alone—some of the children do—but I love picking him up; it's my favorite time of the day. When I was a girl in Paris, all the mothers came to pick their children up, ready with a baguette filled with a row of dark chocolate squares. It feels like a family tradition to be there waiting for him at the end of the day. But today, for the first time, I'll be five minutes late. That gives me twenty-five more minutes to kill.

I put the chicken in the fridge and wash my hands, scrubbing my nails with the old toothbrush on the windowsill. My father's voice rings in my head. "Clean nails are a sign of someone who knows how to look after themselves," he'd say whenever he caught me with dirty nails. "Like shoes," he often added. "You can tell a person by their nails and their shoes."

"Not in America," I'd tell him now if I saw him. "In America they look at your hair and your teeth."

As I put the toothbrush back, I look out the window, trying not to get my hopes up. The street is empty. My stomach rumbles again. I feel a little light-headed. I should eat something sweet. Lifting the tin from the top shelf, I wrap a cookie in tin foil for Sam and break another in half for myself. I nibble at it, worried it will give me stomach cramps, but it makes me feel better, so I eat the other half too.

Twenty minutes left. I go upstairs, into our bedroom, and sit at the dressing table. Taking the real bristle hairbrush out of the top drawer, I brush my hair till it shines. The mirror tells me I'm still attractive: no fine lines, no gray hair, and no loose skin under my chin. All is in order externally. It's my heart that feels one hundred years old.

I get up and smooth out the quilt, made by the Amish in Pennsylvania; hundreds of perfect hexagons stitched together by hand. Our first holiday together. Sam had just learned to walk, but was still unsteady on his feet and took a few tumbles. I remember trotting ahead of him, ready to break his fall.

Ten minutes to go now. I go downstairs, wandering through the rooms. Finally, I open the front door. The bright sunlight hits me and I go back inside for my hat. As I walk down the garden path, I wonder, not for the first time, why Americans prefer to leave their gardens open, without hedges or brick walls. Anyone could walk right on in, up to the house, and stare in through the windows. It's so different from French gardens, which are always encircled by high walls or thick bushes, discouraging callers who haven't been invited.

Jean-Luc loves the openness here. He says that what happened in France could never happen here because everyone is frank with each other; no one would have denounced their neighbor, then gone to hide behind closed doors while they were taken away. I don't like it when he talks like this, idealizing his new country. I can't help feeling it's disloyal to France. Years of hunger, fear, deprivation—these things can change a good person into a bad person.

"Charlie!" Marge calls over from the yard opposite, interrupting my thoughts. "Where were you today? We had coffee at Jenny's. We thought you were coming."

"Sorry." My heart skips a beat, and I cover my mouth with the back of my hand to hide the lie. "I needed to do a big shop. I went to Lucky Store."

"What? You went all the way out there? I thought you hated those enormous shopping malls. You should have said. I'd have gone with you."

"I'm sorry I missed the coffee."

"Don't worry. We'll be at Jo's on Friday. Listen, I need to ask you a favor. Could you pick Jimmy up for me, please? I gotta take Noah to the doctor. He's running a temperature and I can't get it down."

"Sure." I attempt a smile, but I feel like a traitor with these neighbors I've known for years.

"Thanks, Charlie." She flashes me a wide smile.

As I walk to school, I remember how the neighbors made us feel so welcome from the day we arrived in Santa Cruz, nine years ago. Within the week we'd been invited over, not just for an aperitif, but for a barbecue. I was touched by the way they all got together for the occasion, their loud, cheery voices declaring how happy they were to meet the new family. A large beer was thrust into Jean-Luc's hand and a glass of white wine put into mine as soon as we stepped into the garden. They fussed over Sam, and a shady place under a tree was found for him to sit on his baby blanket, surrounded by brightly colored toys. There didn't appear to be a formal structure to the proceedings, not as far as I could see anyway. It was a free-for-all, and as soon as a piece of steak was ready, the guests would swarm to the barbecue. I was grateful when a man handed me a plate with food already on it. We sat wherever we liked, pulling wooden chairs around to join groups.

It was all so different from Paris. On the few occasions my parents received guests, they would make seating plans for dinner. The guests would wait patiently and quietly for the host to allocate the places. And no one would ever be served a drink until everyone had arrived. Maman often complained about so-and-so being late and making them all wait an hour for their first drink. Well, the war put an end to those dinners anyway.

Here, there didn't seem to be any rules. Women chatted freely to me, their laughter spilling out; men teased me, telling me how sexy my accent was. I was charmed, Jean-Luc even more so. He fell in love with America from day one. If he ever felt homesick, he never mentioned it. Everything was wonderful and amazing for him: the abundance of food, the friendliness of the people, the ease with which anything could be bought. "This is the American Dream," he kept saying. "We must learn to speak English perfectly. It will be easy for Samuel, it will be his first language; he'll be able to help us."

Samuel soon became Sam, Jean-Luc became John, and my nickname was Charlie. We'd been Americanized. Jean-Luc said it meant we'd been accepted, and that in recognition of this warm welcome we'd received, we should avoid speaking French. He said it would look like we didn't want to integrate. So we only spoke English, even between ourselves. Of course, I could see his point, though it broke my heart a little not to be able to sing the lullabies to Sam that my mother used to sing to me. It distanced me even further from my family, my culture, and it changed our way of communicating, our way of being. I still loved Jean-Luc with all my heart, but it felt different. He no longer whispered *mon coeur, mon ange, mon trésor.* Now it was *darling, honey*, or worse, *baby.*

The bell rings out across the empty playground, interrupting my thoughts. Children come swarming out, buzzing around looking for their mothers. Sam is easily recognizable, with his dark hair shining out from the throng of blonder heads. His olive skin and fine features tell of different origins. A neighbor once said that his long eyelashes were wasted on a boy. As if beauty could be wasted on anyone. What a strange thought.

Sam looks over, smiling his lopsided smile, just like Jean-Luc's. He's too old now, at nine, to come running up like he used to, and finishes talking with his friends before he wanders over, carefully casual.

I kiss him on each cheek, well aware how much it embarrasses him, but I can't help myself. Anyway, a little embarrassment now and again is character-building.

"Go tell Jimmy he's coming home with us," I say.

"Swell." He runs off, but stops suddenly, turning around and taking a step back toward me. "Is Daddy home?"

"Not yet."

Without a word, he walks away to find Jimmy.

When they reappear, I take out the chocolate chip cookie, breaking it in half. Jimmy wolfs his half down.

"There are more at home," I say.

"Yeah!" Jimmy runs on ahead. "Come on, Sam!"

But Sam walks next to me.

Jimmy runs on anyway, disappearing around the next corner. I put my hand on Sam's shoulder. "Don't worry, Daddy will be home soon."

"But what did those men want?"

"We'll talk later, Sam."

"Boo!" Jimmy jumps out at us.

My heart leaps into my throat, and I scream.

Jimmy's laughing hysterically. "Sorry," he manages to say between giggles.

When my heartbeat returns to normal, I pretend to laugh too, releasing the tension of the moment.

Jimmy grabs Sam's arm, and they run on ahead.

When we get home, I set the tin of cookies on the kitchen table in front of the boys. "Have as many as you want."

Jimmy looks at me wide-eyed, grinning from ear to ear. "Gee, thanks."

It brings me a little comfort as I watch them tuck in, enjoying what I've made.

"They're the best ones yet, Mom." Crumbs settle into the corners of Sam's mouth. Jimmy nods in agreement, his mouth too stuffed to utter a word.

"Do you want me to make some for your class?" I offer.

"No thanks. Just for us." Sam looks at me with dark, jealous eyes.

I want to reach out and hold him close, tell him he has nothing to worry about. That my love for him is deeper than the ocean, that it will last forever. Instead, I start preparing the evening meal, grating the zest off the lemons, squeezing them, adding the juice to the zest. I slice the chicken breasts before soaking them in the juice. I'm not following a recipe; it's just how Maman used to prepare lemon chicken for Sunday lunch, before the war.

Chapter Three

Santa Cruz, June 24, 1953

JEAN-LUC

They pull up in front of the City Hall. Jackson switches the engine off and sits there for a minute, staring into the rearview mirror at Jean-Luc. Then the two men get out of the front, waiting for Jean-Luc to let himself out. But he's in no rush, is even tempted to wait until one of them opens his door for him. That would put a different angle on things. Details count. Abruptly Bradley raps on the window with his knuckles. The sound is harsh, twisting the knot of fear in Jean-Luc's stomach. But why is he so afraid? It's totally irrational; he's done nothing wrong. Leaning forward, he pulls on the door handle, stepping out into the morning sun.

They walk up the steps in silence, entering through the grand double doors. It's still early, which is probably why there's no one around. They take him down some stairs, along a dimly lit corridor, then into a room with no windows. Bradley flicks a switch, and a fluorescent light bar buzzes then flickers before flooding the room with bright white light. A Formica table and three plastic chairs on metal legs are the only objects in the room.

"This might take awhile." Jackson removes a crumpled cigarette pack from his breast pocket, tapping it against the table. "Have a seat." He offers the open pack to Jackson. They light up, watching Jean-Luc.

Sitting down, Jean-Luc crosses his arms, then uncrosses them, attempting a smile. He wants them to understand that he's happy to comply, ready to tell them what they want to know.

The men remain standing, their faces rigid. Bradley's greasy skin shines under the fluorescent tube above, shiny red pockmarks catching the light. He takes a deep drag on his cigarette, fills his lungs, then exhales slowly, leaving a thick fog hanging for a second in the middle of the room.

"Mr. Bow-Champ, where did you get that scar on your face? It's quite distinctive."

Jean-Luc reminds himself that in situations like this, it's best not to provoke anything. Passivity is best; he mustn't appear too defensive. *Don't antagonize. Stay calm.* He feels a trickle of sweat slide down his ribs.

"I got it during the war," he murmurs.

Bradley looks over at Jackson, raising an eyebrow.

"Where?" Jackson asks.

Jean-Luc hesitates, wondering if he could tell the story he's used so far, the one where he was hit by shrapnel when a bomb fell on Paris. Instinctively, he knows it won't help him now.

Bradley leans forward, staring intently into his eyes. "What did you do during the war?"

Jean-Luc looks straight back at him. "I was working at Bobigny—the railway station."

Bradley raises a thick eyebrow. "Drancy?"

Jean-Luc nods.

"The concentration camp of Drancy?"

He nods again. He has the feeling he's been cornered, forced to agree with the facts. But the facts don't tell the whole story.

"From where thousands of Jews were sent to their death at Auschwitz?"

"I was just working on the tracks." He holds eye contact; he doesn't want to be the first one to look away.

"To keep the trains running efficiently."

"I was just doing my job."

Bradley's face grows shinier and redder. "Just doing your job? That old line. You were there, weren't you? You aided and abetted."

"No!"

"Drancy was a transit camp, wasn't it? And you were helping them transfer the Jews to Auschwitz."

"No! I wanted to stop them! I even tried to sabotage a track. I ended up in the hospital because of it."

"Really?" Bradley's tone is ironic.

"It's true. I swear."

Chapter Four

Paris, March 6, 1944

JEAN-LUC

After four years, the occupation had become a way of life. Some had adapted better than others, but Jean-Luc still woke every morning with a sinking feeling. This morning he dragged himself out of bed to report for duty at Saint-Lazare station, but his boss didn't hand him his tool sack like he usually did. Instead he stared hard at him. "You have to work at Bobigny today."

"Bobigny?" Jean-Luc repeated.

"Yes." His boss looked him in the eye. They both knew what Bobigny meant.

"But I thought it was closed."

"It is to passenger trains, but it's open for other uses." His boss paused, letting the words sink in.

"Next to the transit camp at Drancy?" Jean-Luc's voice came out as a croak while his pulse raced ahead as he tried to think of a way out.

"Yes. The tracks need maintenance work. We have orders to send six men." He paused. "Don't mess around over there. The Boches are in charge of it now. Try not to let them see your hand."

Jean-Luc had been working for the national railway company, the

SNCF, since he had left school six years ago, at the age of fifteen. But like everything else, the railroads belonged to the Germans now. He looked away, shoving his deformed hand into his pocket. He hardly thought about it; having been born with only a finger and a thumb on his left hand hadn't held him back or prevented him from ever doing anything.

"They don't like things like that." His boss's eyes softened. "You work as well as anyone else, better even, but the Boches like everything... Well, you know. You don't want them sending you to one of their work camps."

Jean-Luc took his hand out from his pocket, clasping it with the good one, suddenly self-conscious.

His father had been a good friend of the foreman, and this contact had helped him get his first job despite his handicap. He'd had to work extra hard to prove himself, but it didn't take long for his colleagues and superiors to realize that his disfigurement had no effect on his dexterity, that he could grip anything between the finger and thumb of his left hand with a firm pincer movement, using his good hand to do the work.

"Do... do I have to go?" He put his hands back in his pockets.

His boss merely raised an eyebrow, then turned around and walked away. Jean-Luc had no choice but to follow him out to the waiting army truck. They shook hands firmly before he got in the back. Five other men were already there; he nodded at them but didn't speak.

As they drove through the deserted streets, the men glanced around, sizing each other up, their expressions grim. Jean-Luc supposed none of them were very enthusiastic about working so near the notorious camp. Thousands of Jews, some communists, and members of the Résistance had been sent there. No one knew what happened to them afterward, though there were rumors. There were always rumors.

As they sped through the empty streets of Paris and then out northeast toward Drancy, they occasionally passed other military vehicles. Jean-Luc watched the French driver salute them as they passed by. *Un collabo!* He could tell. It was a game he liked to play with himself—guessing who was collaborating and who wasn't. Though often the line was blurred. He had friends who got things on the black market. But who was running the black market? Usually it was only the Boches and the collabos who had access to certain goods. It was a gray area, and he himself preferred to only accept items when he knew exactly where they'd come from—a rabbit or a pigeon shot by a friend, or vegetables from a contact with a farm.

A bump in the road jolted him back to the present. Looking up at the other men, he was met with blank stares. Gone were the days of open, easy camaraderie. Gone was the banter of young men out on a new job. A grim silence was all that was left.

Silence. It was a weapon of a kind, and it was the only one Jean-Luc had at his disposal. He refused to talk to the Boches, even when they looked friendly and politely asked him directions. He would simply ignore them. Another thing he did was to take his Métro ticket and fold it into a V shape before dropping it on the ground in one of the tunnels. V for victory. Little acts of defiance were all that were left to him, but they didn't change anything. He felt desperate to do more.

When the Boches had taken over the SNCF, he'd been quite clear with his parents. "I'm not working for the bastards. I'm quitting," he'd told them after just a few weeks of the occupation.

"You can't do that." His father had laid his hand firmly on his son's shoulder, an indication that what he was about to say was not up for discussion. "They'll find some way to punish you. They could send you to fight somewhere. At least you're in Paris now, and we're together. Let's just wait and see how things go."

Papa. Every time he thought of him, Jean-Luc felt a mixture of shame and longing. He'd done as his father had asked, working under the Boches, but it didn't sit well with him, causing him to resent Papa for making him conform like that. And in fact, it had been just as he'd imagined it would be: the initial polite friendliness and professionalism of the Boches gradually turning to disdain and superiority. What else could you expect? He had been shocked by the ignorance and naïveté of some people suggesting that they might not be so bad.

Then, in the summer of 1942, they'd done something that left no doubt in anyone's mind. They'd started to conscript France's men for Service du Travail Obligatoire—forced labor in Germany. Papa had been one of the first. He'd received the papers one week, and the next he was gone. There hadn't been enough time nor the words for Jean-Luc to tell him he was sorry for his sullenness, to tell him he loved and respected him. He hadn't been brought up with the kind of language that spoke of such things.

Glancing out the window, he spotted two enormously tall buildings, at least fifteen floors high. Beyond them was a large U-shaped complex.

"*Voilà le camp!*" The driver looked at them in his rearview mirror. "It's pretty ugly, isn't it? It was built for poor people, but it wasn't finished when the Germans arrived, and they decided to turn it into this." He paused. "Poor people."

Jean-Luc wasn't sure if he was being ironic or not. His tone was flippant, even mocking.

"There are thousands of Jews waiting to be resettled," he continued as he turned the corner, shifting gears. "It's horribly overcrowded."

Jean-Luc stared back at the U-shaped complex, four stories high, surrounded by barbed-wire fences. Guards with rifles stood watch on top of two lookout towers. "Where are they taking them?" he ventured.

"Germany."

"Germany?" He tried to make his tone casual.

"Yes. They have plenty of work out there. You know, rebuilding."

"Rebuilding?" Now he felt like a parrot. But the driver didn't seem to notice.

"Yes. You know, war damage. The English keep bombing it."

"What about the women and children? Are they taking them too?"

"*Bien sûr.* They'll need someone to do the cooking and housework. It will keep the men happier, don't you think?"

"But what about the old people?"

The driver stared hard at Jean-Luc in his rearview mirror. "You ask too many questions."

Jean-Luc looked around at his fellow workmen, wondering what they were thinking, but they were all carefully studying their shoes. For a few more minutes they drove on in awkward silence, then the driver started up again. "The Boches aren't so bad. They treat you okay as long as you work hard and don't show any Jewish sympathies. They'll even drink with you. There's a nice little café over the road; we often go there for a beer. They love their beer!" He paused. "When I started work here, two years ago, there weren't any Germans at all, but I guess they thought we weren't efficient enough, so they sent Brunner and his men over." He paused. "Well, here we are. You'll be lodged here." He turned backward in his seat as he parked in front of one of the high-rises.

The men in the back of the truck glanced at each other, anxiety written across their faces. How long would they be here? Jean-Luc knew that his mother would think he'd been arrested or taken to a work camp. He had to get word to her; she'd be worried sick. There were only the two of them left since his father had been sent to Germany. They had become close, and she relied on him for everything from financial to emotional support. It made him feel protective toward her and had helped him grow into a man.

The guard who met them thrust small backpacks into their hands as they jumped out of the truck, then led the group of men toward one of the blocks. An elevator took them up to their rooms on the fifteenth floor—the top floor. When they looked out the windows, they found themselves facing away from the camp. Jean-Luc gazed up at the gray sky and then down at the tiny roads below, railway tracks weaving their way in and out of the town. But there were no trains to be seen.

He was unpacking the small bag, which contained pajamas and a toothbrush, when a Boche walked in. "*Willkommen.* Welcome to Drancy." Jean-Luc dropped the bag on the bed, turning to face him. The soldier's pale face shone unhealthily, and his thin lips had no color to them. He was young, probably no more than twenty. Jean-Luc wondered what they were doing sending a kid like that to Drancy. Still, he didn't smile at the soldier or even address him. He just followed him out of the room to the waiting elevator.

The same driver was waiting for them outside in the same army truck. "*Salut, les gars!*" He spoke as though they were old friends. Jean-Luc loathed him for it.

When they passed in front of the camp this time, Jean-Luc craned his neck, wondering what it was like inside, remembering the stories he'd heard of the interrogations, the deportations. The driver came to a stop in front of a small station, then turned around, throwing blue overalls into their arms.

"Here—you'll need to wear these. You don't want to get mixed up with the prisoners!"

As they marched through the station, Jean-Luc wondered why it was so quiet and where all the trains were. His eyes roamed up and down the platform. A brown object caught his attention. He took a couple of steps nearer. It was a teddy bear, squashed flat as though a child had used it for a pillow. Farther down the platform, he saw a book lying open, its pages blowing in the morning breeze.

"*Schnell! Schnell!*" A hand pushed him in the back. Jean-Luc stumbled forward, toward the other men who were walking into the stationmaster's house. It was quiet inside, the only sound typewriters clicking away as women in uniform sat with straight backs thumping out words.

"Name?" the Boche behind the front desk barked at him.

"Jean-Luc Beauchamp."

He wrote it down in his ledger, then looked up at Jean-Luc for a moment too long. Jean-Luc turned his eyes away, embarrassed to be standing there in front of a Boche, reporting for work.

"Work hard. No talking." The Boche continued to stare at him.

Jean-Luc nodded his comprehension.

"Now, go check the lines. They are bad—bad work. Tools in hut on platform."

Jean-Luc shrugged a shoulder, turning away without another word.

Chapter Five

Paris, March 24, 1944

JEAN-LUC

Days turned into weeks, and a routine became established. Their day started at eight o'clock, then there was a half-hour break for lunch at twelve, and they finished at six, when night drew in. Jean-Luc's job was to check the tracks, making sure the sleepers weren't too worn, that the fishplates joining the rails together were in place, and that all the bolts were tight. Then another man would quality-control his work. If he had missed anything, his meager pay would be docked and he would have to work an extra hour, by flashlight. He had Sundays off, though, and every Saturday evening he would take the train from Bourget, the passenger station at Drancy, into Paris to visit his mother.

By the evening, he was worn out, too tired to go drinking in the café opposite the camp, even if he had wanted to. But he didn't want to. Who'd want to be socializing with the Boches? So he kept to himself, reading in his room by the light of the small table lamp. The other men kept to themselves too, most of the time. But sometimes the need for human contact drew them together, and they would gather in one of the bedrooms. Inevitably the conversation would turn to the station.

"How come we never see any trains?" Marcel took a drag on his cigarette stub.

"They leave before daybreak." Jean-Luc looked around the sparse bedroom. Blank gray walls stared back at him; the men's eyes were fixed on the cement floor. He understood their wish not to participate in the conversation. Anyone here could be a collabo, put there to spy on the others.

"Yes, but why?" Marcel finally gave up on his cigarette, letting the tiny stub slip between his fingers onto the cold floor.

" 'Cause they don't want us to see them." Jean-Luc took a Gitane out of a crumpled pack, passing it to Marcel. He almost felt sorry for him, trying to understand what was going on right under his nose. "They're deporting the prisoners," he continued. "Hundreds, probably thousands of them."

"*Merci*." Marcel took the cigarette quickly, nodding his thanks.

Jean-Luc felt the other men's eyes boring into him. No one gave precious cigarettes away like that, for nothing. Jean-Luc didn't smoke himself, but he always liked to have a pack on him for moments such as these. It eased the tension. He offered the open pack around to the others.

"But why are they so secret about it?" Marcel continued, staring down at his cigarette as if he couldn't quite believe his luck. "We all know what they're doing."

Jean-Luc stared around at the men's faces. So placid. So gullible. So silent. Taking a deep breath, he decided to throw caution to the wind. "Why do you think they don't want us to see? Huh?"

The silence in the room grew heavier, weighing him down, making him feel powerless, impotent. He took a step toward Marcel, putting his hand on his shoulder, leaning forward so his mouth was next to Marcel's ear. "Because we might start asking questions. If we actually *knew* what was going on, we'd be mad."

"Mad?" Frédéric shouted. "*Putain!* We're already mad. They've taken our damn country! Mad isn't even the word." His eyes darted wildly around the bedroom, from man to man. But no one wanted to meet his gaze. They shuffled their feet. Someone coughed. Someone else blew cigarette smoke out into the middle of the room. The silence grew oppressive.

"Are we really?" Jean-Luc spoke slowly and quietly. "Are we really that mad? Then what have we done to show it?" He stopped, aware that the conversation was getting dangerous, but he couldn't seem to hold back now. "For God's sake, here we are, working for them!" He stopped again, realizing that Philippe was standing against the wall, his eyes blank.

"It's not our fault. We didn't have an army to fight them with." Jacques spoke quietly from the corner of the room. "Not a proper army, and now we have none at all."

"Well, we've got de Gaulle in London." Frédéric's tone was ironic.

"Fat lot of good that is." Jacques took a step forward.

"But where are they taking them?" Marcel looked around the room.

The men gazed down at the floor again.

"Somewhere far away." Jean-Luc's voice took on a surreal tone, as if he were recounting something imaginary. "Somewhere far away from civilization."

"Exactly!" Spit flew from Frédéric's mouth. "Then they switch the French driver for a Boche at the border. They don't want us to know where they're taking them. They don't want us to know 'cause..." He hesitated.

"'Cause what?" Marcel looked at him.

"I don't know." Frédéric glanced away.

"What do you think?" Marcel's eyes turned to Jean-Luc.

"I'm tired, that's what I think. I'm going to bed." Jean-Luc wanted to end the conversation before one of them put into words what they were all thinking. You could be arrested for words.

"But the trains are cattle cars, for God's sake!" Frédéric continued. "And then there's all the personal items we find on the platform after the train's gone. I bet the Boches let them think they can take some things with them to help them resettle. But then..."

An oppressive silence descended as they imagined the fate of the prisoners.

"*Putain!* They're killing them." Frédéric slapped his hand against the wall. "I know it."

Jean-Luc looked over at Philippe, but his face was still blank. He turned back to Frédéric, knowing it was time to stop the conversation. They were all at risk, talking like this. "We don't know that. We don't know anything. Not for sure."

Chapter Six

Paris, March 25, 1944

JEAN-LUC

On Saturdays, he could get away from the camp. As soon as the day was over, he took the train from Bourget into Paris. He liked to get off the Métro at Blanche, looking at Le Moulin Rouge before wandering up Rue Lepic, where he lived with his mother.

But this evening he wasn't ready to face the absence of his father in the apartment. Not yet. So he stopped for a pastis at the café on the corner.

"*Salut*, Jean-Luc." Thierry poured him a glass of the strong aniseed drink, leaving a small jug of water by the side. Jean-Luc added some, watching his pastis turn a cloudy yellow. Thierry put his elbows on the bar, wrapping his hands around the back of his neck, twisting his neck as if it was sore. "*Quoi de neuf?*"

"What's new?"

Jean-Luc drew his eyebrows together. "Nothing that I know of."

Thierry leaned closer. "Any news from your father?"

"Two months ago." Jean-Luc paused. "We had a letter asking us to send him warm socks and food. He says he's fine, just thinner and older."

"Terrible business—taking the men like that. I was lucky I was too old for them, and you . . . well, you were lucky they needed railroad workers. But how are we supposed to keep things going back here? There's no one left to farm the land."

"I know. I know." He'd already had this conversation a hundred times.

"Service du Travail Obligatoire, my arse. It's forced labor for the Boches."

"Of course. But at least we know he's in Germany." Jean-Luc picked his glass up.

He'd done his best to fill his father's shoes, but the little flat he shared with his mother felt more than half empty, as though his father had been replaced by a gaping hole that allowed a bitter wind to blow through the rooms. Every Sunday, he went to Mass at Sacré-Coeur with his mother, and they lit a candle for Papa. Jean-Luc liked to imagine the little flame giving his father courage, wherever he was. He thought of his father often, but it left him feeling morose and melancholic. Papa was such a strong, independent man, the thought of him having to submit to the Boches and their brutality filled Jean-Luc's heart with pity. He didn't deserve that.

Thierry lowered his voice. "Don't worry. He'll come back. Have you heard about the Americans?"

"What?"

He leaned closer still, his voice dropping to a whisper even though the café was empty. "They're going to land in France. Yes! They're getting their troops ready, and then they're going to actually land here and chase the Nazis out."

Jean-Luc stared at him, wondering how he'd heard such a thing. "Well, let's hope it's true." He gulped his drink back.

"Another?" Thierry had already taken the lid off the bottle. "And then all those poor families they sent away will be able to come back—your father too."

"Let's hope so." Jean-Luc swirled the pastis around in the bottom of the glass.

"Maybe the Cohens will be back soon. Their kid, Alexandre, was a cheeky little monster. I'd like to see him again."

Just then two Boches entered the café, and Jean-Luc walked out, leaving his half-finished drink behind. As he left, a wave of loneliness washed over him. Suddenly he missed his ex-girlfriend with a pang. They'd been courting for almost a year and he'd been serious about her; he'd even been planning to ask her to marry him. He liked the way she wanted to enjoy life to the full despite the war; she loved dancing and always seemed to know about the next *bal clandestin*. He liked these secret dances too; they felt like one small victory over the Boches. She'd told him not to worry when his father had left, that it was only Germany and that they needed the labor there, so they'd look after him properly. He'd drunk in her words, letting himself believe them, but as time marched on, he began to doubt them. Began to doubt he'd ever see Papa again. And then he'd grown despondent and withdrawn. How could he enjoy himself knowing his father was probably cold and hungry in a foreign country? He couldn't do it.

When he began to decline her pleas to go dancing, she went anyway with other friends. He should have known it would only be a matter of time before she met someone else, but he'd taken comfort in the fact that there were hardly any eligible men around. He hoped she hadn't got herself a stinking collabo, or worse, a Boche. She wouldn't say who he was, but surely she wouldn't be that stupid. Horizontal collaboration, people called it disdainfully, as if they were morally superior. We're all guilty to a lesser or greater degree, Jean-Luc thought. If he were to name his own kind of collaboration, he would have called it survival collaboration. One had a duty to survive, for all the others who couldn't.

The pastis had awakened his appetite and he began to look forward to his dinner. Maman always saved her rations from the week to cook him a proper meal with vegetables and, if they were lucky, some pigeon. On Sunday, after Mass, they would have a lunch of sorts at one of their neighbors', or at their own home. Everyone would contribute what they could: vegetables from their gardens, pickles they had made the previous year, and sometimes someone would arrive in a cloud of excitement with meat in a paper bag; maybe something a friend had caught, or they had caught themselves. The unveiling of the meat was sacred, and a silence thick with anticipation would fall upon them. Food shared always seemed to go further.

But now these lunches had become something of an ordeal for him. He found he had nothing to say, and the neighbors' gossip alienated him with its pettiness. They appeared to be more concerned about who had managed to get butter on the black market or who had caught a rabbit than who was being murdered. Their chatter was of no value, and when they did broach the subject of the round-ups, it never led anywhere. He felt like he was disappearing inside himself, as though he couldn't remember who he was, or who he was supposed to be.

This Sunday, it was the Franklins' for lunch. Monsieur Franklin's brother had been out hunting in the countryside and had come back with two rabbits. The rabbit stew went down well, and with meat in their bellies for a change, the conversation livened up.

His mother started it off. "When this damn war ends, do you think there'll be any wine left?"

Monsieur Franklin was quick to reply. "Marie-Claire, you know we have some hidden."

"I know no such thing."

"Ha! Very good. Me neither, then. But when this damn war ends, you and I will go down and get it, eh?"

"I'll drink to that." His mother raised her glass of water.

"So, Jean-Luc, how is the new job going?" Monsieur Franklin turned his attention away from the mother to the son.

Jean-Luc felt his pulse rate race ahead, as it did every time his work was mentioned. "Bit too close to the Boches for my liking."

"*Mais oui*, you're right in the heart of it, aren't you?"

"What really goes on there?" Madame Franklin interrupted.

Jean-Luc looked at her a minute, taking in her thin lips and bird-like eyes. She never missed a thing, and he knew anything he said would be repeated the next day when she joined the queues for food.

"I don't know." He looked out the window, avoiding his mother's scrutinizing stare.

"Come on, lad. You must know something. What are they doing with all those prisoners? Where are they taking them?" Monsieur Franklin narrowed his eyes as he stared at Jean-Luc.

"I haven't seen anything. I never see the trains, or the prisoners—"

"I've heard they're cattle trains, not proper passenger trains," Madame Franklin interrupted. "And that the prisoners have to lie on straw, like animals." She always seemed to know more than anyone else.

"I've heard similar," Madame Cavalier added. "And that there are no bathrooms either. They have to pee in a bucket."

"That's disgusting! How do you know that?" His mother spoke for the first time on a new subject. "It must be an exaggeration."

Madame Cavalier shrugged her shoulder. "You've seen what they are capable of. I wouldn't put it past them. They've arrested thousands, haven't they?"

"Therefore they must be shipping them out by the thousand." Monsieur Franklin frowned, turning to look at Jean-Luc. "Maybe you could find out what they're doing with them."

Jean-Luc stared back. "What?"

"Well, you're right there in the thick of it. Can't you discover what's going on?"

"I told you, I never see the trains leaving. I start work after."

"Couldn't you get there earlier?"

"No!" He paused, calming himself, trying to keep his tone neutral. "We are taken to the station by army truck at seven thirty every morning."

"But you're near the station, aren't you? Couldn't you walk there? Have a look?"

Jean-Luc frowned. "I don't know." He paused. "It would be dangerous. They watch us all the time." He looked up and saw the disappointment in their faces. It made him feel like a coward. "Maybe... maybe if I got up very early and sneaked out, I could see one of the trains leave."

His mother gasped, putting her hand over her mouth.

"Good lad!" Monsieur Franklin grinned. "You could get a photo. I have a camera."

A photo? What good would a photo do? He would be risking his life for a damn photo. There must be some other way.

When they returned home, his mother boiled up some disgusting roasted chicory and acorn drink. He took the cup from her, pretending to drink it. "Maman, I've been thinking."

"Oh dear," she laughed. "Not again."

"No, seriously. I need to do more than just take a photo."

"What do you mean, son?"

"I need to do something." He screwed his eyes up. "Something that makes a difference."

She whispered, "What about the Résistance?"

"But I don't know anyone."

"No, neither do I." She put her hand over her forehead. "We must be mixing in the wrong circles."

He raised an eyebrow. "It's not something you can really ask someone, is it? *Are you in the Résistance? Because I'd like to join too.* I think you have to wait to be approached."

"Has no one ever approached you?"

"No, Maman. How about you?"

She shook her head. "But you know, if they had, I wouldn't have hesitated. Then again, what use is an old woman to them?"

She was right. It wasn't up to old women to fight; it was up to young men like himself. He did want to fight; he wanted to stop the trains that were deporting the prisoners to God knows where. But there was that promise, the one he'd made to his father before he left.

Papa had taken him aside while his mother was out queuing for bread. "Son, promise me one thing."

"Of course."

"Promise me you'll look after your mother while I'm gone."

Jean-Luc's gaze didn't waver as he looked at his father. "I promise."

"Now I can leave knowing that the two of you will be safe here. It will help me find my way home." Papa had gripped him around the back of his neck, pulling his face toward his own. Jean-Luc had wrapped his arms around his father and they'd held each other tight for a moment. Then Papa had pulled away, wiping his eyes with the back of his hand.

Papa. He wandered into his bedroom, glancing at the walls and the bookshelves his father had cut, sandpapered, and put up himself. The books were arranged first by subject—adventure stories in one section, fantasy in another—then from the tallest to the shortest, all the spines the right way up. He could order his books in a way he couldn't order his life.

Chapter Seven

Paris, March 30, 1944

JEAN-LUC

"*Eh, les gars.* What's up this morning?" The driver glanced at the men in his rearview mirror.

Jacques shrugged a shoulder, Frédéric grunted. The others remained silent, looking down at their feet as the army truck sped through the dim and empty streets toward Bobigny station.

"Remember, we're the lucky ones," the driver continued. "Better here than at some work camp in Germany."

Jean-Luc stared back at him in the mirror. Why couldn't he just leave them alone? *Putain de collabo!*

"We're just tired," Philippe mumbled, rubbing his eyes.

"Tired? But the day hasn't even begun yet!" The driver shifted the long gearstick, causing a horrible crunching noise of metal against metal. Jean-Luc shuddered, as though in empathy with the gearbox.

The driver sighed. "You might find today even more tiring." He left the remark hanging as though waiting for someone to ask why.

But no one would give him that pleasure.

"The train was late leaving this morning." He caught Jean-Luc's eye. "Yes. Trouble getting the passengers to board. Some of them decided they'd rather not get on." He took his eyes away from the mirror, changing gears again as he turned a corner. It was a smooth change this time, and an expectant silence filled the truck. They wanted to know what had happened, but no one wanted to participate in the conversation.

"So," he started up again, "the platform is still a mess." He pulled into his usual spot. "*Enfin, les gars.* Time to get out."

The six men shuffled out the back of the truck, shoulders slumped like defeated troops being led away by the victors. As they stepped onto the platform, a gust of wind blew something pale along the quay, then upward onto Jean-Luc's face. He heard Marcel's boyish laugh. How could he laugh at a time like this?

Then the laughter stopped. Jean-Luc pulled the item from his face, holding it out at arm's length. It was a nightie. Fragile. Feminine. How had it ended up here, floating down the platform like a ghost? His eyes wandered away from it, to the platform itself. He saw a fancy purple hat. Two black bowlers. A walking stick. A pair of broken spectacles. A porcelain doll, its leg broken. A soft monkey, pink stuffing spilling from its neck.

His stomach contracted into a tight ball, bile rising in his throat. He looked over at the other five men, trying to gauge their reactions. Philippe sighed before walking into the stationmaster's house to report for duty. Frédéric's face turned white and he closed his eyes. The others looked down at the ground, shuffling their feet. He wanted to hear them say something—anything that would help him make sense of the scene in front of him. But there was no sense to be made. It was a world gone mad.

He looked back at the platform, scanning the ground. A larger object toward the end of the platform attracted his attention. Instinctively he knew what it was—too big for a soft toy or a doll, but shaped like one. He told himself it couldn't be. It must be a large teddy bear. Yes, a very large teddy. His mind went blank and he looked at the scene as though it were a movie and the film had frozen. Then the action started up again, and now there was no doubt at all.

"Go into the house!" the guard shouted.

He stumbled into the stationmaster's house. Someone shoved a piece of bread into one hand and a cup of ersatz coffee into the other. He dropped both. As the cup crashed to the ground, hot liquid splashing out, he looked around at the shocked faces, waiting for—dreading—the next scene.

He felt a baton land on his shoulder, but he made no move to protect himself.

"*Achtung!* Outside!" someone shouted in his ear. "Out now! Clear the platform."

Stumbling out onto the platform, he started picking up items: two pairs of broken spectacles, the hat. He was getting nearer to the end of the platform and could feel himself being drawn toward what he had seen earlier. He looked up, scanning the area. He couldn't see it anymore. Could it be that he had imagined it? He must have. Then he saw a group of men dragging something along the ground. He took a couple of steps nearer, wondering if they were dragging a bag full of clothes or rubbish. But in his heart he knew they weren't. He watched as they lifted it up and threw it into a dumpster.

He returned home that Saturday evening in a state of numb despair. He barely acknowledged his mother, going straight to the bedroom that had been his since he was born. Sitting on the bed, he stared at the bookshelves. *Les Trois Mousquetaires* looked down upon him with derision. As a young boy, he'd imagined himself growing up tall and strong, becoming like one of the musketeers, dashing and daring—someone his father could be proud of. Not the weak-hearted man he felt himself to be now.

The door creaked open and his mother stepped quietly into the room. "What's wrong, son?"

He looked at her, at the little lines around her mouth, the dark shadows under her eyes. And he knew he wouldn't be able to tell her.

"I can't do it anymore." He paused. "I can't be a part of it."

"I know it's hard. This damned war is hard on us all."

"You don't know everything, Maman. You don't know."

Sitting down on the bed next to him, she rested her hand on his shoulder. "What don't I know?"

He shook his head as if he could shake the knowledge out.

"I want to know what's upsetting you, son."

He looked into her eyes, which were shining with concern. "No, you don't. Not really."

"Let me be the judge of that. I'm a tough lady, you know."

"No one's that tough, Maman."

"Come on." She squeezed his left hand. "You've always talked to me. Don't stop now. We need each other more than ever, and I can see you're suffering."

"They're killing them." He blurted the words out. "I saw them, I saw them on the platform. Bodies. A baby. There was a dead baby lying on the platform."

He felt his mother go rigid by his side. She took her hand away, clasping her other hand, the knuckles turning white. "A baby? Are you sure? We know they're shooting adults, Résistance people, Jewish immigrants, but—"

"I saw it, Maman, lying on the platform, after the train had left. Then it was gone."

"Maybe you imagined it. You're under a lot of stress, working for the Boches. It's not surprising. You need to rest." She lifted a hand, about to put it on his shoulder, but he hunched forward, burying his head in his hands.

"I knew no one would believe me."

"It's not that. I believe you think you saw a baby, but are you really sure it was there? For God's sake, why would they kill a baby?"

He took his hands away from his face, looking at her. "Why do you think? What do you think this is all about? Arresting every last Jew, taking them away for 'resettlement.' What do you think they're really doing with them?"

"They're sending them to work camps."

"What? Old women? Old men? Babies?" He paused. "They only took Papa to the work camp, didn't they? They didn't take you. They didn't even take me. They wanted me here working on the lines, and they didn't want you because you're not strong enough. So why take all the Jews? Even the old and the weak. They'll be no use to them."

His mother shook her head.

"Think about it, Maman."

"No, son. You're going too far. You have to stop thinking like this. It's not helping."

"Not helping?" He jumped up from the bed, frustration tightening his throat, suffocating him. "Why won't you see what's going on?" He pulled at the books on the shelf, flinging them to the floor, one by one.

He didn't care what happened to him now. He just knew he had to do something.

Chapter Eight

Paris, April 3, 1944

JEAN-LUC

"*Salut, les gars.*" The driver nodded at them as they climbed into the back of the truck.

As usual, the men ignored him. Under normal circumstances, seeing the same man every day, Jean-Luc would have asked his name. But he didn't want to know anything about him. He stared out the window. It was one of those early spring days. The sun was rising, shining out through a cloudless sky—bright, but still too weak to warm the air. His knees twitched up and down with a restless energy. Gripping the back of his neck, he rolled his head around in a pathetic attempt to calm himself. He had to do something. He'd promised himself he would. And now an idea was growing in his mind. It was just an idea, and he didn't know if he could go through with it, but he started to imagine it as if he would.

What if he could manage to derail a train? He would just need to loosen the bolts on the fishplates, then force the tracks out of line with a crowbar, throwing the train off its tracks. It might not even be that hard. But he couldn't do it alone; he needed Frédéric to be his accomplice, to pass his work when he checked it at the end of the day. He knew that if he presented Frédéric with a fait accompli, he would be left with no choice but to go along with it; he wasn't the kind of man to denounce a friend. Was he?

He glanced over at his colleague, wondering. It was obvious that Frédéric couldn't stomach working for the Boches any more than Jean-Luc himself could, but to commit an act of sabotage? That took courage. If caught, they would face the firing squad, but not before they'd been interrogated and tortured first. *Tortured!* He closed his eyes, blocking out the thought before it took root.

Frédéric suddenly looked up at him, their eyes locking in a moment of mutual understanding. What the hell were they doing here?

Jean-Luc's thoughts returned to his idea. Was it worth it? It would probably only delay the train, but that was already something. And it would anger the Boches, that was for sure. His pulse started racing as he imagined the train coming off the tracks—the chaos it would cause. The idea excited him. Could it be his chance to do something? As he imagined putting his plan into action, the impotent anger he'd felt before turned to rage. Rage at them for taking his father away, rage at seeing a dead baby on the platform, as though it had been nothing more than an abandoned suitcase. Then rage at himself and all the others who'd silently stood by, terrified for their own skins.

"Here we are. Bobigny again," the driver announced.

As usual, they went to the stationmaster's house to report for duty and pick up their meager breakfast—a cup of ersatz coffee and a lump of hard bread. He swallowed the brown liquid in one gulp but threw his bread out onto the tracks. His stomach was tied in knots. Could he really do it?

He wandered over to the tool hut, taking out the fishplate bolt spanner and the large crowbar. Glancing over at the other men, who were still chewing their bread, he started to walk along the line, looking out for a gap where a set of tracks met. It didn't take him long to find one. Crouching down, he examined the fishplate more closely. The bolts looked rusted on. If he was really going to go ahead with it, then he would have to do a test first—time himself to see how long it took to undo one bolt, then multiply it by four. He reckoned he had a good fifteen minutes. The guards seemed to pass every thirty minutes on average.

His legs felt weak and he folded them under himself as he sat on the ground staring at the rusty bolts, trying to breathe normally. Sweat trickled down from his armpits and his mouth was suddenly dry. He knew that if he didn't do it now, then he would never do it. And he would have to live with his cowardice for the rest of his life.

Taking a deep breath, trying to slow his rapid pulse, he took the spanner, placing it around the first bolt. He pulled his sleeve back, glancing at his watch—7:41 exactly. He turned the bolt. It was stiff. He pushed down hard, putting all his weight on the spanner. His breath coming fast, he managed to get a turn on it, and then another. After that, it moved quickly. When the bolt came completely loose, he glanced at his watch—7:43 and forty seconds. Nearly three minutes. That meant nine minutes total for the other three bolts. He had time. He could do it.

"Jean-Luc!" Frédéric's voice shot through him like an electric shock. "What are you doing? We're supposed to be working on the other end of the track today."

The spanner fell from his hand, clattering onto the rails. Still on his knees, he looked around, checking who was within earshot. But it was early yet, and only a couple of guards stood nearby, smoking and chatting. They looked at him, catching his eye. He held his breath. But they hardly seemed to notice him as they leaned toward each other, obviously absorbed in their conversation. Jean-Luc let his breath out slowly, then turned back toward Frédéric. He concentrated on keeping his tone low and steady as he said, "This fishplate is loose."

"Well, hurry up!" Frédéric walked away.

Picking the spanner back up, he placed it on the second bolt and turned it, his left hand holding his right to provide more pressure. Around and around it went, steadily and efficiently. In just three minutes, it was loose. He moved on to the third bolt. His hand slipped on the spanner and his overalls clung to him. Three minutes and forty seconds ticked by.

He placed the spanner around the fourth and last bolt. His throat tightened. This one was completely rusted on. It wouldn't budge. He pushed harder and harder, his wrist aching with the effort. He looked at his watch. A minute gone already and he hadn't got anywhere. He needed to undo all four or it wouldn't work. He stopped, taking a deep breath. He'd give it one more go. He knocked at the rust this time before fixing the spanner around the bolt, then pushed down on the metal handle with all his force. It started to loosen. Three and a half more minutes ticked by.

Now he only had two minutes left for the crowbar. He picked it up and pushed it hard into the earth under the track, his heart thumping. He couldn't breathe; he opened his mouth wide, gulping in air. He heard commands shouted out: "*Achtung! Vorwärts marsch!*" But he didn't dare look up. He pushed the crowbar with all his might now. The track began to move. He forced it out of line.

Then a noise behind him made him jump. Heavy footsteps. He turned to look.

It was the chief of the camp, walking toward him. *Merde!* Jean-Luc turned his face back toward the track. Please, God, he prayed. Please, God, make him go away.

The footsteps grew louder. Nearer. Jean-Luc's hand shook as he took the crowbar out, digging it in the other side now as though he were intending to straighten the track.

He twisted his neck, looking at Brunner. He was talking with a guard. Throaty laughter burst out. Then they walked away. Jean-Luc turned back to the tracks, his hands still shaking. He had to do it.

Digging the crowbar back in on the other side, he readied himself to put all his force into pushing the track outward again.

It happened so quickly, he didn't see it coming. The crowbar slipping. Rebounding. Pain seared through his cheek, like a knife slicing it open. He dropped everything, clutching at his broken skin. Blood gushed out over his hands. He couldn't see. Then a blow to his leg sent him reeling. He cried out.

Rough hands pulled him off the track, dragging him away. Then two men picked him up and threw him into a truck.

Chapter Nine

Paris, April 3, 1944

CHARLOTTE

"Late again." Maman pushed a piece of hard bread into my hand as I ran out the door. "You need to get up earlier." She said the same thing every morning, but quite frankly, I considered 6:30 to be plenty early enough. It was a long journey to Hôpital Beaujon at Clichy from our apartment in Rue Montorgueil, but I didn't mind—the commute made me feel quite grown-up at the age of eighteen.

Maman had found the job for me. She wanted me out of the apartment, where I was "reading my life away," as she put it. She also wanted the extra rations it provided us with. Papa didn't want me to go at first—after all, it was a German hospital—but Maman talked him around. She said it wasn't like I was giving away state secrets or even denouncing a neighbor. She added something about "healing the wounded" being a good occupation for young women during wartime. Secretly, I wondered if it might not be a better occupation for young men; it might make them think before waging war. Anyway, the patients weren't all German; there were quite a few French soldiers too, who must have joined up. There were plenty of recruitment offices all around Paris.

I spent my days scrubbing floors, spooning food into the mouths of those who'd lost their sight or the use of their hands, or just sitting and listening to the French patients. The hardest cases were the ones who'd lost a limb but still felt its presence as insufferable pain; "phantom limb syndrome," one of the doctors explained. There was nothing that could comfort them.

It struck me that all men looked the same in a hospital bed. Vulnerable. Harmless. The language they spoke was the only way to work out where they were from. The hospital was run according to strict routines, but comforting the patients was encouraged, and I quite enjoyed this, though I still wished it wasn't a German hospital. The irony of it wasn't lost on me, for there I was, helping the enemy get better, while other, more patriotic French people were risking their lives to do the exact opposite.

When I finally got to the hospital that morning, I went to the locker, taking out my uniform and putting it on, checking in front of the full-length mirror that it was clean and straight. I was almost late, but not quite, and I paused for a minute, turning to the side to study my body. Flat was the word. No bumps or curves to indicate that I was becoming a woman. Four years of occupation had left me with a deep sense of emptiness. It wasn't only the constant physical hunger; there was an emotional hunger too. I was dying to experience life. I knew there was a world out there, a world where people laughed, danced, drank, kissed, made love, and I was missing out on it all.

As I ran my hands over my chest, Maman's words rang in my ears. "No point getting you a bra." I remembered the excitement of having my first period, then the disappointment when they stopped after only three months, as though they couldn't see any reason for having started up in the first place. "You don't know how lucky you are," Maman said. "They're nothing but a curse." But I wanted my body to change, longing to be touched in places I didn't dare name.

I turned back around to see my face. I tried smiling. Yes, that was definitely better. But I didn't feel like smiling, not even when the patients tried to flirt with me. Most of them weren't funny anyway; they just gave me the creeps with their stupid remarks about "cold hands, warm heart" or "love that uniform." I preferred the quiet ones, and I felt sorry for the ones who were in pain but put on a brave face, biting back tears when I helped them sit up.

Smoothing my hair down, I wished I could have washed it. It was greasy, but there was so little soap, and Maman had rationed me to once a week. I wasn't allowed makeup either, but I didn't care so much; my eyelashes were quite long and dark, and if I pinched my cheeks, it looked like I was wearing rouge.

"*Allez! Allez!*" The matron bustled into the locker room. She looked at my reflection in the mirror and I looked back at hers. It put a welcome distance between us. "This is no time to be admiring yourself," she said coldly. "There's work to be done."

"Sorry," I mumbled, taking the mop and bucket out of her hands.

Chapter Ten

Paris, April 3, 1944

JEAN-LUC

"*Ruhig zu halten!*" A piece of leather was pushed into Jean-Luc's mouth. He bit down hard, swallowing the scream. Oh God, what were they doing to him? It felt like they were slicing his face open.

His heart raced as it all came back to him. Brunner striding behind him. The crowbar. The flash of metal in front of his eyes before it smashed into his face, then the blow to his leg. Had someone hit him? Had they realized what he was doing? How could they have? They wouldn't imagine he was trying to sabotage the line. Would they? Oh God, what if they had?

A glint of silver-colored metal caught his eye as he stared up at the fluorescent light. It moved toward his face. He spat the leather out and screamed.

"*Ruhig zu halten!*" someone shouted again. "*Halte ihn fest!*"

His head spun. Blurred faces came into his line of vision then disappeared, replaced by blinding white light. The smell of bleach and disinfectant clawed at the back of his throat, making him want to vomit. German words bounced off his throbbing head. "Please," he begged. "Stop. Stop. I'll tell you—"

"*Es ist aus*. It's finished."

Finished? They were done with him. He wondered what he'd told them. He knew he'd been mumbling, crying, begging. His eyes were wet and his mouth was dry. The pain in the side of his face ripped into him like a jagged knife, and the pulsating ache in his leg vibrated through him. He was suddenly so cold. A violent trembling took over his whole body. If only someone would cover him with a blanket.

Someone gripped his shoulders, pulling him forward as though attempting to make him sit up. He tried to lift his head, but he was convulsing and couldn't control his movements. Then he felt a hand around the back of his head. A glass of water against his lips. He took a sip, and realized that someone had pushed three pills into his hand. He looked down at them as they swam in and out of focus in his trembling hand. They were white, but he had no idea what they were.

"Painkillers." A voice with a German accent spoke.

He swallowed them all at once, gulping more water, then closed his eyes, exhaling heavily with the pain, praying they would kick in soon.

His leg! What had happened to his leg? He tried to sit up, to see it.

"*Nein! Non!*" A hand pushed him back down.

He was on some kind of contraption on wheels. He could feel himself being wheeled away. He laid his head back, staring up at the white ceiling, trying to block out the pain. He could hear a mixture of groaning, talking, and shouting, even the occasional burst of laughter. Sometimes he caught a whole phrase in French, then German interrupted and he was lost again. Where the hell was he?

As they wheeled him along, he turned his head sideways, looking through blurry eyes. He made out rows of white beds. Thank God! It must be a hospital!

He wasn't being interrogated. He was being treated.

The pain began to fade into the background. His head grew light. He only wished for oblivion, and so he let himself drift away.

When he woke, he felt groggy and his cheek and leg still throbbed painfully. He lifted his hand to his face to find it covered in bandages. God, what had he done to himself? His stomach rumbled loudly; he wondered vaguely when he had last eaten. Pulling himself up to a half-sitting position, he looked around. Nurses in white bustled up and down the central aisle, sometimes stepping to the side to see to a patient, thermometer usually in hand.

"*Willkommen.*" A German voice spoke from the bed to his left.

He turned to look at the owner of the voice. "*Bonjour.*"

"You're French. What's your name?"

"Beauchamp."

"What happened to you then?"

"Railroad accident."

"Well, you'll have a lovely scar to show your children now."

"I don't have children."

The Boche laughed. "I mean future children. I'm Soldat Kleinhart, by the way. Nice to meet you. Got shot in the leg—two crazy terrorists shooting off."

"I'm sorry." What else could he say?

"Don't worry. They caught them and they're being dealt with."

Jean-Luc closed his eyes, trying to block out the image of the tortured men that flooded his head. He couldn't take any more pain.

He opened his eyes. Kleinhart was staring at him. He had to say something. This was not the moment to be a hero. "Yes, they need to be taught a lesson."

"Quite." Kleinhart lay back against his pillow. "Fear always works. It's amazing how quickly people learn when taught with fear."

Just the word made Jean-Luc's bowels contract. He tried not to imagine what they might do to him, and couldn't help looking down at his fingernails, checking that they were all there.

A nurse appeared, shaking a thermometer in her hand.

"*Guten Morgen, Krankenschwester.*" The Boche smiled at her.

"Good morning, monsieur." Then she turned to Jean-Luc, looking directly at him with warm chocolate-brown eyes. "Open your mouth, please, monsieur."

Obediently he did as he was told, staring at her as she placed the thermometer under his tongue. He felt the slash on his cheek stretch, as though it might open up again. He closed his lips around the glass tube, calming his breathing as he studied the nurse. She looked very young; her smooth pale skin was completely unblemished, making him think of a blank canvas.

She caught his gaze as she took the thermometer from his mouth. Quickly, she glanced away.

"Where am I?" He tried to make eye contact, but she was looking at the thermometer intently.

Suddenly she turned and looked right at him, her dark eyes shining into his. "Hôpital Beaujon." Her voice felt intimate—a whisper, as if it were only meant for him.

"Hôpital Beaujon?" He stared back into her eyes.

"It's a German hospital."

His heart beat faster, thumping in his ears. Of course! That was why they were all speaking German. But why had they sent him to a German hospital? He glanced around the ward, taking in the bustling efficiency of the Boches, the starched whiteness of the place. He was probably in good hands. But why hadn't they given him any anesthetic before sewing up his wound? Was it because he was French? Or did they suspect him?

Surely if they'd guessed he'd been trying to sabotage the railway, they would have sent him to a public French hospital, or even straight to interrogation. They didn't suspect. They couldn't. But what had happened to his leg?

The nurse was busy tucking in the bottom corners of the sheets. He waited for her to finish, and when she turned back to look at him, he asked, "Do you know what's... what's wrong with my leg?"

Without a word, she picked up the board that must have been hanging at the end of the bed. She looked at it, frowning. "I'm sorry, I don't know. It's all in German—"

"Let me have a look," the Boche in the next bed interrupted loudly.

Without looking at him, she passed him the board.

"Break to the femur." The Boche paused. "Did you get hit by a train?"

"No." Jean-Luc felt dizzy again. "A piece of track came loose and I got hit by it."

"You're working on the lines?"

"Yes, sir."

"Well, you'd better be more careful next time."

Jean-Luc nodded, turning back to look at the nurse. He could tell she was about to leave, but her presence comforted him. At least she was French.

"How long will I be here, Nurse?" He tried to smile, but it hurt too much.

"I don't know. You'll have to ask the doctor."

And then she was gone, leaving him alone with the Boche.

Chapter Eleven

Paris, April 4, 1944

CHARLOTTE

As if the Boche curfew wasn't bad enough, my parents imposed one of their own. I had to be in by eight o'clock, even though, at the age of eighteen, I was dying to go out in the evenings—to cafés, or dancing at one of the *bals clandestins* people talked about in hushed, excited tones. My only entertainment was on Friday nights, when I was allowed to have a few friends around. Maman let us use the library, which was much cozier than the salon, with its stiff upholstered Louis XVI couches. Those in the library had come from our country home, the leather worn and soft. We liked to slouch in them, pretending to smoke and be decadent, when really we just chewed on hard licorice sticks and drank tea that Maman had ordered from England before the war.

"You know Marc has left?" Agnès sucked on her licorice, looking at me out of the corner of her eye.

"But he's Catholic." My heart beat faster. They couldn't have taken him.

"No, silly. He's gone to join the Maquis."

"No!"

"Didn't he come and say goodbye to you?"

I liked Marc, and Agnès knew it. I shook my head. They looked at me, eyes soft with pity.

"Don't worry," Mathilde said. "He didn't say goodbye to anyone. We only know because his mother met my mother when they were queuing for food. She's really upset, of course. The Boches kill them if they find them."

I wondered how she could say such things so casually. "Well, at least he's doing something." I paused, collecting my thoughts. "Don't you want to do something?" I looked from one to the other, but was met only by blank stares.

"It's too dangerous," Agnès finally said. "I'm not running off into the hills to join the Maquis. They're living wild, sleeping outside. Can you imagine?"

"But at least they're trying, aren't they? They're doing what they can." I wanted to defend them.

"I think they're very brave." Mathilde added, "I couldn't do it. I wouldn't be any good to them anyway; I'd give away all their secrets the moment I was arrested." She shuddered. "The Boches do horrible things to them if they catch them."

"Imagine having to carry a hidden message. I'd be a nervous wreck." Agnès spoke quietly.

I let out a breath. "Me too. But if someone asked me, I think I'd want to try."

"Have you heard from Jacques?" Agnès asked abruptly, changing the subject.

Jacques had disappeared one night last month. He'd already been excluded from the Sorbonne because of his Jewish roots, and Mathilde had been passing him notes from other students, but the last time they were supposed to meet, he hadn't turned up. We heard later that he'd been rounded up and taken to Drancy.

"I wish I'd asked him to come and stay with us." Mathilde sounded subdued.

"It would have been too dangerous." Agnès reached out, touching Mathilde's elbow. "If they'd found him at your place, they would have taken you and your family away too."

"I hope we can still be friends when he comes back." Mathilde's voice cracked, and I understood her distress. How many times had we stood by while our neighbors and friends were deported to God knows where? We all felt complicit in some way, though we never voiced it. After all, what could we do?

"Did you hear about the man who shot a Nazi in Printemps?" Agnès changed the tone of the conversation again. She always seemed to hear about things before anyone else. Working in the boulangerie probably helped; people talked while queuing two hours for bread. We looked at her, waiting for more. "Yes, in broad daylight, on the ground floor, where they sell the handbags." She waited a minute for us to take it in. "He knew he'd be arrested and executed for it, but he still did it." She paused. "Isn't that brave?"

"But French prisoners were shot in retaliation," Mathilde said. "Do you think it was worth it?" She stood up from the armchair. "I'm not sure."

I thought for a moment. "I think it just upsets the Boches and makes them behave more badly to the rest of us."

"I agree." Mathilde looked at me. "It's not by killing random Boches that we'll win the war." She slumped back into her chair.

"I've heard de Gaulle is trying to get an army together in England. One day they'll come and help us fight the Boches."

"We should be ready for them when they come." I wished there was something I could do.

"Ready?" Agnès laughed. "I'll be ready all right. More than ready!"

"I'd like one of those handbags in the shape of a gas mask." Agnès changed the topic again.

Mathilde smiled. "Yes, they're just the thing, but they're very expensive."

"And I'd like to get my hair put up in a turban." Agnès touched her loose wavy hair. "They look chic, but my mother won't let me. She says it looks peasant-like."

"Well, you have to do it properly and then set it off with a nice pair of earrings." Mathilde seemed to be enjoying the way the conversation was going, but I wondered how we could be talking about hair and fashion at a time like this. It all seemed so trivial, so pointless. Were we girls really that small-minded? The thought depressed me.

"Did you know that Madame Clermont from the pharmacy is seeing a Nazi?" Agnès changed the subject again.

I nodded. I'd heard the rumors.

"He's SS," she added in a conspiratorial tone.

"That's disgusting." Mathilde spat the words out, her eyes lit up in fury. "That woman deserves to die."

Agnès stood up and moved over to the piano, opening it and hitting a key hard. She started to play "Mon légionnaire." Mathilde stood too and joined in, leaning on the piano, but I wasn't in the mood for singing that evening.

Suddenly Agnès stopped playing. "Charlotte." She turned to look at me. "I hope you don't mind me asking, but why are you working in a hospital for the Boches?"

I felt my cheeks burn. "For your information, they're not all Boches; quite a few of them are French, actually."

"Yes, but they're collabos, so it's the same thing really."

"I think it's worse," Mathilde chipped in. "They didn't have to join up, did they? They chose to."

"Maman got the job for me. She wanted me to work," I said, ignoring the last remark. Mathilde always saw everything as black or white.

"Your mother? But I thought she hated the Boches."

"Of course she does. But she said caring for the sick was a good occupation for young women during wartime." I imitated her bossy voice, and they laughed.

"But you shouldn't!" Mathilde looked at me with cold eyes. "You're an adult. You don't have to do everything she tells you to do."

I stared back at her, thinking that she had a point there; I should start making my own choices.

"I thought you were going to the Sorbonne after your exams. I thought you wanted to study literature. You did so well in your *baccalauréat*." Agnès closed the piano with a thud. It sent a shudder through me; Maman had taught me how to close it gently, without a sound.

"Yes, I really miss studying."

"Well, you can read on your own. You don't need to go to the university for that, do you?"

"It's not the same. There's more to a book than just the words on the page."

Agnès shrugged.

"Anyway, there doesn't seem much point at the moment."

"I know what you mean," Mathilde agreed. "It feels futile to be studying when people are being arrested and killed." She paused. "Maybe your mother's right."

"Yes, Maman said she doesn't see any reason to carry on in education when the future's so uncertain, and anyway, the extra ration tickets are more useful." I paused. "Education is a luxury we can no longer afford."

"Is that what your mother said?" Mathilde frowned.

"No, it's what I said."

"Funny, isn't it, though? When you're so wealthy."

"Morally speaking, I mean."

Mathilde's frown grew deeper. "Morally?"

"Well, we have other priorities right now, don't we?" I hoped I hadn't offended her.

"Yes, but what can we do?"

Agnès stood up and sighed, as though bored with the conversation. "I don't know about you, but I'm always hungry." She patted her flat stomach. "It keeps us slim, though, doesn't it?"

"Too slim." My stomach rumbled as if in agreement.

"We had lamb last Sunday!" Agnès leaned forward, whispering. "Maman pawned her pearl necklace, and she got it on the black market—it was Papa's birthday."

I felt a line draw itself across my forehead. "My mother doesn't like to use the black market."

"But she doesn't mind you working in a Boche hospital? My parents would never let me do that." Agnès's eyes narrowed. "Make sure you stay out of trouble."

I stared back at her, wondering what she meant.

"You know what soldiers are like. They'll do anything for..."

"For what?" Mathilde asked.

"You know." Agnès touched her nose with her finger, looking at me with knowing eyes.

Just then Maman walked in with some fresh tea. "*Bonsoir, les filles.*"

Immediately we stopped slouching and sat to attention, straightening our backs.

"*Bonsoir, Madame de la Ville,*" Agnès and Mathilde chorused.

She poured the tea through a strainer into the porcelain teacups. "Earl Grey."

"*Merci, Madame de la Ville.*"

I sighed, waiting for her to leave the room so we could resume our conversation. But she didn't look ready to go, standing there in her tailored suit, nipped in at the waist. I wished I had a nice suit like that instead of the loose frocks she made for me. I guess she thought I was still a child.

"How is your mother?" She turned to Agnès, a frown of concern creasing her usually smooth forehead.

"Fine, thank you." I felt Agnès tense up. Her mother used to be friends with mine, but then something had happened. Something to do with the war and the black market. "I'm still helping out at the boulangerie, when there's some bread, that is."

"Yes, the queues just seem to be getting longer, don't they?" She turned away from Agnès. "And how are your studies going, Mathilde?"

"Fine, thank you. Well, I mean it's not always easy at the moment; some of the courses have been canceled."

Maman nodded. "You have your books, but it's not the same, is it?"

"No, especially not for science."

"Yes, of course." It looked like Maman had forgotten what Mathilde was studying.

"*Bien*, I'll leave you girls to it then. I'll come back at eight so you'll have plenty of time to get home."

"But Maman, that's only in an hour. They don't live that far away."

"No point in taking extra risks." She turned on her heel and left the room, closing the door behind her.

"Don't worry, Charlotte," Mathilde spoke sympathetically. "My mother likes me to get back well before curfew."

"Charlotte." Agnès looked at me with concerned eyes. "Really, you should be very careful working in a Boche hospital. I'm surprised your parents let you. Some people might get the wrong idea."

"What do you mean?" I felt my heart beat faster.

"Well, you know. They might think you're collaborating."

"No!"

"You know what people are like."

"Stop it, Agnès! Everyone knows Charlotte's not like that." Mathilde's eyes shot daggers at Agnès.

"Of course not! We'll stick up for you." Agnès stood, smoothing out her dress, looking at the painting on the wall. "Is that a Picasso?"

"Yes. Maman got it last week."

She took a step nearer to the painting. "It's very avant-garde. He's not allowed to show his work now, you know. The Nazis say it's degenerate."

"Degenerate?" Mathilde laughed. "Who's degenerate here?"

"It must have cost a fortune." Agnès continued to stare at it.

"It was a gift."

"A gift?" She raised an eyebrow. "Your mother must know some interesting people."

I stared at her, wondering what she was really thinking.

Chapter Twelve

Paris, April 5, 1944

JEAN-LUC

Two days later, Jean-Luc was tucking into his breakfast of toast and butter—they had butter!—when the stationmaster came looming into view. "*Bien, bien.* What have you done to yourself then?"

Automatically, his hand flew up to the bandage on his face.

The stationmaster stood awkwardly, glancing over at the empty bed Kleinhart had just left. He must have gone to the bathroom.

Jean-Luc pushed his toast aside, his appetite suddenly gone.

"No, no. Finish eating. I've just come to see how you're getting on and to ask you a few questions. Do you mind…?" The stationmaster motioned with his hand that he wanted to sit on the bed.

"Of course. Please sit down. There's room." *Merde!* He should have prepared himself for this. How was he going to explain himself?

Step one: don't appear nervous.

He brought his toast back to its place in front of him, forcing himself to take a bite, but it was cold and dry now as he mashed it between his teeth.

"It seems they're looking after you well."

"Yes."

"How's your leg?"

"A fracture to the femur. It should heal soon."

"That's good to hear. It was most... unfortunate."

Jean-Luc frowned. It seemed like something of a deliberate understatement. "I'm... I'm not sure how it happened."

"No. It was after you were struck in the face. One of the Bo... I mean the German soldiers... one of them, well, he thought he needed to correct you."

"Correct me?" His heart thumped hard against his ribs.

"He thought you'd made a mistake." The stationmaster paused. "Well, he was right in a way, wasn't he? That piece of track was perfectly straight. I checked it myself the day before. What were you doing with the crowbar?"

Jean-Luc fumbled around for the right words in his head. Step two: have answers prepared.

"It was... The tracks weren't quite straight. I needed to bring one of them back in."

"Back in? But you dug the crowbar into the other side."

Just then the young nurse appeared. "A visitor? How nice." She smiled at them both. "I just need to take your temperature, and then I'll be on my way."

But Jean-Luc didn't want her to go and leave him alone with the stationmaster. He opened his mouth, lifting his tongue slightly, ready to receive the thermometer. He was relieved to find that he was unable to continue the conversation while he held the glass tube under his tongue.

Lying back on the pillow, he watched the nurse chatting to the stationmaster. He was vaguely aware of them discussing rationing, and he wondered how they'd got on to that.

He tried to concentrate again on his reply to the question about the crowbar.

Step three: stay focused and consistent with answers.

She pulled the thermometer out from under his tongue.

"Thirty-seven and a half," she announced proudly, as if his temperature were solely due to her efforts. "I'll be back for your breakfast tray in a few minutes."

"She's pretty." The stationmaster winked at him as soon as she left. "You're better off here than in Drancy." He paused. "So, was it worth it?"

"What?" A piece of dry toast had wedged itself in Jean-Luc's throat. He coughed, until the stationmaster had to hit him on the back. "What do you mean?" he asked when he got his breath back.

"What do I mean?" the stationmaster repeated. "Well," he leaned closer, so that only Jean-Luc could hear him, "what were you thinking of?"

Jean-Luc stared at him, his eyes growing wide with fear.

The stationmaster came even closer, so close that Jean-Luc caught a whiff of the coffee he must have had earlier. "Listen, a German inspector is coming to see you soon. He'll ask the same question: What were you doing with that damned crowbar? What will you answer?"

He was giving him a chance! He was on his side and he was helping him find a way out. A wave of relief washed over Jean-Luc. The stationmaster was a comrade.

"Listen, tell him what you just told me—that the track needed straightening out to bring it into line with the adjoining one. But don't get nervous or appear hesitant. Lucky for you, it rained later that day, and the hole you dug got messy. By the time he looked at it the next day, it wasn't possible to see where you'd started from. It could work. You have a clean record." The stationmaster paused. "Whatever he says, just stick to your story."

Just then, Kleinhart came back to his bed. He glanced over at them. "What's this? Last rites?"

"No, just checking on our worker here. But he should live to tell the tale."

"Let's hope so. He needs to see that nurse again." Kleinhart laughed.

How Jean-Luc envied his easy privilege. No one was going to come and ask *him* difficult questions.

After the stationmaster's visit, Jean-Luc was left with a feeling of constant anxiety, a knot of fear growing in his stomach. But the days went by without the inspector appearing. Kleinhart sometimes tried to make conversation, the unspoken rule being that it was on his terms, and only when he was in the mood.

"I like France," he declared one morning as bread and ham were laid out before them.

Jean-Luc had learned to wait till he was asked a question before speaking, so he just nodded.

"You know why?"

He guessed this was a rhetorical question, so he continued to wait.

"It's the way everything is so damned good. Delicious wines in excess, gorgeous women, beautiful artwork. We don't have any of that in Germany. Just work, work, work. Everything so hard. We never had time to sit back and enjoy ourselves like you can here. Creating, dreaming. I've always loved France." His blue eyes dug into Jean-Luc, as though hoping to uncover something.

Jean-Luc concentrated on keeping his expression blank.

"You got a girlfriend?"

"No."

"And why not? There's plenty of girls out there with no men. A good-looking lad like you shouldn't have a problem finding one."

"Well, I'm at Drancy all week now."

"Hmm, not the best place to meet girls, is it? But what about here? Some of the nurses are very pretty."

Jean-Luc felt his cheeks redden.

"I knew it! You like her, don't you? I've tried, but she won't talk to me, even though I speak French."

"No." He had to defend her. "She doesn't talk to me either."

"Rubbish! I've seen the way she looks at you."

Four days later, he was moved to another ward. This time he had a chair next to his bed. Gratefully he slumped into it. Hobbling from one ward to the next had been exhausting, even though the nurse had taken his arm—maybe because of that. The close proximity, the light brush of her body against his had set his heart thumping hard, as though he'd just run a race.

She looked at him. "I'm going to remove the bandages from your face now."

He glanced over at her slender hands, imagining them on his skin. "What's your name?"

"Charlotte."

"Charlotte," he couldn't help repeating. "I'm Jean-Luc."

"I know." She grinned, small dimples appearing.

He grinned back, though it tore at his wound. They stared at each other, wide smiles spread across both their faces.

"I'll try to be gentle."

"*Merci*, Charlotte." He wanted to add that he couldn't imagine her being any other way, but he knew that would be pushing it.

Crouching down in front of him, she reached out her hand. Her nails were clean and short, and she wore no jewelry. Her hair protruded from the tiny white cap balanced on her head. It was dark and smooth, cut into a bob, the ends curling forward to meet her chin. He closed his eyes, feeling her nails tapping at the edges of the bandage, easing it off his face. He breathed in deeply; a faint lemony smell reached his nostrils. He took another long breath, savoring the smell of her.

"I'm just going to disinfect it now. It might sting."

He hadn't even realized she'd removed the bandage. He watched as she took a bottle, tipping it up onto a cotton pad. He couldn't help recoiling as the hand holding the pad approached him.

A light laugh escaped her lips. "It won't hurt for long."

The pain shot through him like a fresh cut, and instinctively he brought his hand up to his cheek. But she was quicker than him and grabbed his wrist before he could touch his skin.

"You mustn't touch it! You might infect it." She didn't release her grip on him straightaway, and without thinking, he twisted his hand around, taking hold of hers.

Chapter Thirteen

Paris, April 12, 1944

JEAN-LUC

There was something about Charlotte that drew Jean-Luc in. As he lay in the hospital bed watching her mop the floor in the central aisle, he wondered what it was. Maybe it was her warm, gentle manner; so natural, so unpretentious, totally unaware of how attractive she was. There were no airs or graces about her, no flickering of eyelashes or fake smiles.

Abruptly she looked up from her mopping. He caught her eye and she smiled—a wide, effortless smile. He smiled back, inclining his head slightly, inviting her to come and talk to him.

He saw her glance around, checking to make sure the matron wasn't within sight. The coast was clear, and Jean-Luc's neighbor was under his blankets, facing away, his body rising and falling with his labored but regular breathing. Fast asleep.

"Is everything okay?" Charlotte asked, the smile still playing across her lips.

"Yes, thank you. I just need some company."

"I can ask if anyone wants to play cards with you."

"No. Your company." He saw her cheeks redden and realized what a sheltered upbringing she must have had. "Have you always been a nurse?" He tried to steer the conversation back to where she was comfortable.

"I'm not a nurse," she replied.

"Oh? You look like one."

"It's only because of the war. I was supposed to go to the university to study literature."

"Why didn't you?"

She shrugged her shoulders. "My parents wanted me to work."

He raised an eyebrow.

"It's the war." She paused. "The future isn't clear, and we're hungry now. We get extra rations because I'm working here."

"Yes. That's understandable. So you enjoy reading then?"

"I love reading."

"What's your favorite book?"

"*Le Comte de Monte Cristo.*"

He smiled. "Alexandre Dumas?"

She nodded. "You've read it?"

"Yes, when I was a kid. My dad read it to me. He loved...loves stories. He made bookshelves for me. Every birthday and Christmas he'd give me a book." He went quiet for a moment, remembering his father, his love of reading. Then he continued. "It's a great story, isn't it? Le Comte never gives up." He felt the gap between himself and the heroes of his childhood widening.

"No." She paused. "But is it realistic? The way he keeps coming back after each awful thing that happens to him?"

"I don't know. It makes us dream, though, doesn't it?"

"Dream of being better than we are?"

As he stared into her eyes, he understood her wish to be better, braver, as if it had been written in black and white. "Yes. He stood strong despite all the cruelty that was thrown at him. I loved *Les Trois Mousquetaires* when I was a boy. I wanted to be d'Artagnan when I grew up." He laughed ironically. "And here I am in a German hospital."

"Have you always worked on the railways?"

"Yes, I'd had enough of school by the time I was fifteen. I was happy to get out and learn a trade."

"What about your parents? Didn't they mind?"

He smiled. "No. My father has always worked on the roads, and my mother... well, she looked after us. They were pleased I'd found a job with the SNCF."

"But now the Germans run the SNCF."

"Yes." He saw her glance away and knew she was anxious that the matron would be back, but he didn't want her to leave. "Yes, the Boches are in charge," he whispered. "And I shouldn't have stayed."

"I shouldn't be here either."

He hadn't meant to make her feel bad. "I think it's brave of you."

"What?"

"It takes courage to come in here every day, to see all this pain and suffering. Look around." He paused. "Most of them are young men, just like me. They're not the real enemy. The real enemy are the men at the top—the ones who give the orders. And you can bet they won't end up in the hospital."

She turned back toward him. "But the rest of them are following, aren't they?"

"Do you know how much courage it takes to stand up to a system?" He paused, answering his own question. "More than most have got, and I include myself there."

"And me. I should stop working here."

"No, don't do that... well, not until they let me out. You're the only bright thing in here. You shine out like a—"

"Shh," she interrupted him. Just then his neighbor turned over in his sleep, coughing.

Charlotte took a step backward and, with one last glance at Jean-Luc, walked briskly away.

Chapter Fourteen

Paris, April 14, 1944

CHARLOTTE

"Charlotte!"

I looked over the table at Mathilde, trying to focus on what she'd just said, but her words had washed right over my head. Instead of listening to her, I'd been thinking about Jean-Luc.

"So what do you think? Should I speak to him?"

I dragged my attention back to Mathilde. *Who?* I wanted to ask, but I didn't dare.

"You haven't been listening to a word, have you?"

I looked around the worn-out café, at the old posters of Edith Piaf and Yves Montand hanging off the peeling walls. "I'm sorry. I was miles away."

"Obviously! What's going on? Who are you daydreaming about?"

I felt myself blush. "No one."

"No one who?" She smiled.

I couldn't help smiling back. "Just someone I met at the hospital."

"What? Hôpital Beaujon? A doctor?"

"No."

She lowered her voice. "Please don't tell me you've fallen for a Boche."

"Of course not! He's French."

"A collabo then?"

"No!" I took a gulp of water from my glass. I was sure he wasn't a collaborator; it wasn't his fault he was working on the lines that the Boches now controlled.

"Why was he in a German hospital then?"

"You could ask the same thing of me." I stared down at the wine and coffee stains on the old wooden table.

"I could, but I know you. I don't know him."

I looked up at her. Concern shone through in her eyes. "He works on the railways. He had an accident; he got hit in the face by some track."

"He's a railroad worker?" Her tone betrayed her disappointment.

"Yes." I paused. "I'm not sure he really likes me, though."

"Charlotte, I wouldn't worry about it. I can't see any long-term relationship between you and a railroad worker."

"Don't be such a snob!" I kicked her under the table.

"Okay, okay. What does he look like?"

"You are so shallow!" I grinned. "He's got thick dark hair, parted on the left side."

"The left side? You are one for details, aren't you?"

"And he's got brown eyes...well, not plain brown like mine. There are tiny yellow dots and green darts in them, but from a distance they look brown."

"You must have got close!"

"Well, I have to take his temperature every day."

"Does it go up when you're near him then?" Mathilde giggled.

"Don't be silly. I just wish I knew if he liked me. He's probably bored lying there in bed all day. That's why he talks to me."

"But Charlotte, why wouldn't he like you? You're pretty, intelligent—"

"No, I'm not. I'm skinny and plain."

"For goodness' sake, Charlotte. All you need is a bit of makeup, and maybe you could wash your hair."

"I know. It's flat and disgusting. Maman only lets me wash it on Sunday evenings. There's not enough soap."

"I don't get your mother. You have a Picasso hanging in your apartment, but you have no soap!"

"Picassos aren't rationed. Soap is."

"Your mother won't use the black market, but she has a forbidden artist's painting hanging on her wall. Where's the logic in that?"

"I know, I know. But she has her principles." I paused. "Solidarity. She thinks we should stick together, and if rations are imposed, they should be the same for the rich as for the poor."

Neither of us spoke for a moment. My mother could be harsh, but she was no harder on me than she was on herself.

"I can get you some soap." Mathilde paused. "If you want."

"No, don't worry."

"Anyway." She stretched her legs out under the table. "I'm not sure he's worth it. He doesn't sound right for you."

"He's really interesting and he asks me lots of questions about myself."

"He's just trying to flatter you. Does he talk to the other nurses too?"

"Yes." My excitement faded. It was true—he did talk to all the nurses. I'd seen him.

Mathilde raised an eyebrow. "There you go."

"Yes, you're probably right. I shouldn't think too much of it."

"It's because there are so few men around, Charlotte. It's not normal, and so when one gives you some attention, you just soak it up."

"Yes, you're right. I'll forget about him."

"Good." She leaned over the table, whispering, "The war will be over soon. I can feel it. You'll meet someone better."

The waitress stopped at our table. "More ersatz, girls?"

"*Non, merci*, just some water, please."

Mathilde glanced up at the poster to my side. "Edith Piaf is playing this weekend. We said we'd go."

"I know, but I haven't asked my parents yet. Maman's been in such a bad mood all week."

"We can go to the afternoon show. Don't ask—just tell them you're going."

"Okay, okay. I will."

"And forget about him, all right?"

She didn't understand that I didn't want to forget about him, or meet someone else. I hadn't been able to tell her how easy it was to talk to him, that he was who he was, and I felt I could become more of myself with him. It wasn't even that he said that much, but he left gaps for me to fill. And he watched me so intently when I talked, as though he wanted to soak up every last little detail about me. I loved his questions; they made me feel like I was discovering myself as much as him. No one before had really bothered to find out my views about anything, and my thoughts came out raw, half formed, but he guided me patiently, taking in every word I uttered. I didn't care that he was a railroad worker and hadn't taken any damned exams. I bet he could have passed them if he'd wanted to, but he preferred doing something more practical, more useful.

He felt the same way about the occupation as I did. He didn't want to be working for the Boches either. We were both trapped in a system, and we needed to find a way out. I was dying to do more for my country, and I knew he was too. I tried to think of things I could do in my own way, things that would be little signs of resistance. I could build them up, step by step, until I found the courage to do something more daring, more dangerous. I could start by folding my Métro ticket into a V shape, then dropping it on the ground, as some people did. So far, I hadn't risked even that, not since I'd seen a woman get hit over the head for doing it. They'd made her get down on her hands and knees to pick the ticket up and straighten it out again. I'd cringed in embarrassment for her, but now I wished I'd spoken up instead, told her how brave I thought she was.

Chapter Fifteen

Paris, April 17, 1944

CHARLOTTE

All the way through the Edith Piaf concert I thought of Jean-Luc, especially when she sang "On danse sur ma chanson"—"Dancing to My Song." He made my heart dance, and I couldn't wait for the weekend to pass so I could see him again.

When I arrived at the hospital on Monday morning, I took the mop and bucket, cleaning down the floor in his ward, just like I did every morning. As I neared his bed, I glanced around, hoping the matron wasn't watching me. I knew his neighbors would be taken out for physiotherapy sometime in the morning, and I was wondering if I might be able to snatch a few moments with him. As I mopped side to side, I saw the physiotherapy team coming my way. I held my breath as they swanned straight past me. *Yes!* They were collecting their patients and Jean-Luc wasn't one of them. I concentrated on the mop in my hand, forcing myself not to look over. When the coast was clear, I moved my mopping away from the central aisle, down toward his bed.

He was sitting in the bedside chair, reading a pamphlet. When he saw me, his eyes lit up. "Sit down for a minute, will you? Please?"

"No! I can't do that. I have to make your bed." I put the mop down, moving to the end of the bed, where I concentrated hard on getting all the creases out of the sheet, my hand smoothing out the lines, running backward and forward.

"Charlo-tte." The way he said my name—slowly, deliberately, hanging on to the "tte" as though he were tasting it—made my heart jump.

"Yes?" I tried my best to sound nonchalant.

"There's something I want to tell you."

My hand stopped moving and I looked back at him. The intensity in his eyes burned into me.

"Please, sit down, Charlotte. Just for a minute. There's no one around right now."

I slipped onto the side of his bed, perching on the edge, ready to hop up as soon as anyone looked our way.

"I didn't mean to make you feel bad." He spoke softly. "The other day, when you said you shouldn't be here." He lowered his voice even more, and I had to lean toward him to hear him. "In a German hospital. You haven't done anything wrong. You do what you have to do."

"But it's true. I shouldn't be here."

His eyes turned dark, the specks of light leaving them. "I didn't want to work for *them*. It's myself I'm disappointed in."

I nodded, quickly glancing around to check no one was near. It was okay; the matron and the other nurses were helping with the physiotherapy.

"I made a promise to my father," he continued, looking past me as if he were focusing on some distant point. "When he was taken away for STO..."

"In Germany?"

His eyes looked into mine again as he spoke in a monotone. "Yes. They took him away nearly two years ago. When he left, he made me promise to look after my mother."

I nodded.

"I might not have listened to him, but I felt so bad."

"Why?"

"I'd had an argument with him just before he left." He paused. "It was horrible."

I waited for him to continue.

"I told him we shouldn't be lying down and taking it from the Boches." He stopped, wiping his brow. "I'm sorry. I shouldn't be telling you this."

"No. Go on." I looked around the ward again, but it was still quiet.

"He was just protecting his family. That was his priority."

"It's important to keep your promises. Your father would be proud of you." I touched his shoulder. "You only did what you thought was right."

He shook his head. "What's right has changed, though, hasn't it? My father didn't realize how bad things would get. I think he'd rather see me doing something active now. I want him to be proud of me when he comes back."

I nodded. "I understand. I'm disappointed in myself too."

"Neither of us should be here." He stood up from his chair, putting his weight on his good leg.

I stood too, my face so close to his, I could feel his breath on my cheek. It made my skin tingle.

"Charlotte," he whispered. "We're better than this. I know we are."

My heart stopped. His presence was like a physical force pulling me in, and I felt myself swaying toward him. I closed my eyes for a second. For a lingering moment I felt his lips on my forehead. Anyone looking would have thought it a kind of paternal kiss. Only I knew it was much more than that. It was a lover's kiss.

Chapter Sixteen

Paris, April 18, 1944

CHARLOTTE

"What have you got to be so cheerful about?" Maman snapped at me.

I realized I'd been humming. Immediately I stopped.

"You'd better hurry, Charlotte. You'll be late for work. It's six thirty already."

Now I had a reason to get out of bed in the morning. I leaped out, eager to get to the hospital. And I was no longer hungry; in fact, I'd lost my appetite completely, as though my bursting heart were feeding my hollow stomach. Of course, I told myself to calm down, tried not to let my excitement show, warned myself that he probably talked like this to all the girls he met. But it made no difference. With him I felt like I was stepping out of my skin and into the skin of a more mature, more beautiful woman. The woman I wanted to be. Not only that, he made me feel braver than I'd ever felt before. My heart was stronger—it beat harder. I felt alive. With him I believed I would be ready to stand up for what was right, face dangers I couldn't have dreamed of facing alone. I wanted to be courageous for him. I wanted to be a better person for him.

As the Métro sped through the tunnels toward the hospital, I felt my anticipation growing. I looked around at the weary, expressionless passengers, thinking to myself: I have a secret they'll never know. Though it must have shone out from my eyes. I was on fire with love.

He was due to leave the hospital today. Excitement ran through my bones. I couldn't wait to see him outside, in real life. We'd be able to walk together through Paris, through the Tuileries maybe, hand in hand. The thought thrilled me.

When I came to say goodbye, he was sitting on the bed, still in his pajamas. He hadn't noticed me yet, and I could tell something was wrong. His face was deathly pale. And there was a Boche sitting in the chair next to his bed. What could they possibly be talking about? Jean-Luc was listening while the Boche spoke. I strained my ears to catch the words.

"...sabotage...interrogation..."

Merde! What was going on? The Boche looked very serious.

Suddenly, he turned around, looking right at me. "Is there something you want, Nurse?"

"I need to take the patient's temperature." I took the thermometer from my top pocket with a trembling hand, holding it out as though it were evidence.

Jean-Luc looked up, his eyes wide with surprise. Without saying good morning as he usually did, he opened his mouth, ready for the thermometer. I wished I could have surprised him and kissed him, but instead I stepped closer, placing the thermometer under his waiting tongue. The Boche looked on, sighing, as though bored with the whole hospital routine.

"I thought your patient was leaving today." He turned to address me.

"Yes, he is."

"Then why are you taking his temperature?"

I hated the Boches who spoke French even more than the ones who didn't. "It's procedure," I lied, concentrating on keeping my tone stable and neutral. "Just checking he hasn't developed an infection before we let him go."

I spoke quietly to Jean-Luc. "You look tired. Will you be all right to leave today?"

The Boche looked up at me. "He'll be fine. He just needs to get back to his function now."

His function? It made me want to laugh sometimes, the way they talked. I turned away from him, looking at Jean-Luc instead, but his eyes darted around the room, not landing on anything. I spoke quietly, daring myself to be braver than I felt in front of a Boche. "Your leg is only just starting to repair itself. You should be careful."

This time he looked at me and nodded, but I could tell he just wanted to get out of the place, whether he was better or not.

The Boche leaned forward, staring at Jean-Luc. "Indeed you should. Be careful. We can't afford any more accidents like this. We asked for good workers, not men who can't even keep hold of a crowbar properly. Maybe it's your handicap. Your deformed hand isn't strong enough to be manipulating such heavy tools. We might do better to send you to one of the work camps in Germany, where the work is less skilled."

Jean-Luc coughed, dislodging the thermometer. I took it out, shook it, then put it back under his tongue. When I took my hand away, I let my fingers brush the rough, jagged skin that would become his scar.

The Boche turned his attention to me, narrowing his eyes. "Do you take such good care of all your patients, Nurse?"

I couldn't help it—I felt my cheeks burning up.

He laughed. "Ha, I've embarrassed the poor girl."

I removed the thermometer dangling from Jean-Luc's lips without meeting his eyes. My hands trembled as I looked at the reading.

"So?" The Boche leaned back in his chair. "Is he okay to leave?"

"Thirty-seven degrees." I tried to sound assertive. "A little cold, but he's fine."

"A little cold?" The Boche laughed loudly. "I'm sure you can fix that, Nurse."

He was enjoying himself, that damned Boche. I had to take control of the situation. Turning to Jean-Luc, this time looking him in the eye, I spoke clearly and calmly. "Once you're dressed, I'll bring you the exit papers to sign." Then I glanced at the Boche. "Goodbye, monsieur."

"Don't go rushing off on my account. I'm leaving." He turned back to Jean-Luc. "Any more accidents and we might start to question your capabilities." He paused. "You wouldn't want that." He stood abruptly, saluting us.

We had to salute back; we were in a German hospital. Then we watched as he strode away, his hobnailed boots echoing down the corridor.

As soon as he was out of sight, Jean-Luc laid his head back on his pillow. "Thank God for that. He wanted to know about my accident." He paused, looking at me, as though he wanted to say more. "I think you just saved me, Charlotte."

Chapter Seventeen

Paris, April 22, 1944

CHARLOTTE

We agreed to meet at six o'clock the following Saturday evening. The night before, I couldn't sleep, excitement and trepidation pumping through my veins, keeping me tossing and turning for hours. And on Saturday itself, my stomach was fluttering so badly I could barely eat. Papa put my lack of appetite down to female trouble, even though I didn't have any, and eagerly snapped up my food.

I didn't know what to wear. I needed clothes that didn't make me look like an overgrown schoolgirl, so when Maman was out on Saturday morning queuing for food, I went hunting in her wardrobe. There I found a tweed skirt and an old pair of black leather shoes, the soles of which were now paper-thin, the heels completely worn down on one side. I stuffed odd pieces of cardboard inside, hoping I wasn't going to feel every pebble on the ground through them. Then, using pin nails, I hammered more cardboard onto the lopsided heels and painted them black. The result wasn't exactly comfortable, but they didn't look too bad from the top.

Later in the afternoon, I concentrated on myself. Using a sliver of soap that I had been saving, I washed my hair, adding a teaspoon of vinegar to the bucket of cold water before rinsing it, for extra shine.

Then I used the red paint from my old school paintbox to color my lips, fixing it with a smudge of duck fat I found in the back of the fridge.

At ten to six, I was ready to leave. Thank God Papa was out. Only Maman was there, grating something onto a newspaper at the kitchen table.

"Maman, I'm going to Mathilde's now."

She turned around to look at me. I felt myself blush under her gaze. I knew she'd noticed the care I'd taken over my appearance.

"You know I don't like you out on the streets in the dark. I think I should walk over with you."

"No!" I took a deep breath. "I'm eighteen, Maman, and she only lives two streets away. I can walk there myself."

"Isn't that my skirt?"

I felt my cheeks heat up. "But Maman, my skirts are too short for me now. They're above the knee. It's embarrassing with all those soldiers strolling around."

"Hmm, I've been meaning to adjust that skirt. There's far too much material in it. It looks extravagant, not to mention unfashionable." She tutted, making me wonder which was worse—being unfashionable or being extravagant. "What have you got on your lips? You've painted them! I know what those soldiers will think about that. Go and wash it off."

I felt my cheeks grow redder but couldn't resist defending myself. "I just wanted to look nice for a change."

"Are you sure you're only seeing Mathilde? Who else will be there?"

"No one, just Mathilde and Agnès." I ran out of the kitchen to get my coat before she could ask any more questions.

This was ridiculous, I told myself as I left the apartment. I shouldn't have spent so much time and trouble getting ready. Now I'd just brought unwanted attention to myself.

But I could feel myself tumbling, like Alice in Wonderland, too curious and delighted to reach out and stop myself. All my thoughts were taken up with him. Everything else paled in comparison; the shortages, the soldiers everywhere, it all meant nothing to me. As long as I had Jean-Luc, nothing else mattered. With him I would conquer my fears and anxieties. I would stand up to my parents and tell them that I could no longer work in a hospital for the Boches. Together we would find strength in each other. I couldn't wait to see him again. Every word he'd uttered in the hospital felt etched in my memory, as though he'd been setting down tracks in my mind. Tracks I would never be able to erase.

As I wandered down Rue Montorgueil, I remembered with nostalgia how it used to look, before the Boches arrived. Colorful food markets once lined the street, the smell of warm bread and roasting chickens wafting in the air as men in berets sat outside cafés smoking cigars and discussing politics, while their wives jostled for the best cuts of meat and the freshest fruit and vegetables.

Now, instead of the smell of bread, the vinegary odor of stale sweat swept along the cobbles—the stench of fear. The noises had changed too. Hobnailed boots marked the passing of time, and between the echoing footsteps a hushed silence breathed its way down the street.

I liked to stand outside the patisserie, Stohrer, pretending I was back in a time when the windows were full of row after row of freshly baked pains au chocolat, caramelized pains aux raisins, and croissants as light as air. I would inhale the imaginary smell of warm chocolate and fresh pastry. Window-shopping, Maman called it. But if window-shopping was pretending to shop, then what was pretending to window-shop?

Pretending to pretend. It was what we were all doing. No one knew whom they could really trust. I gazed into the window of the patisserie, trying to breathe more calmly. My stomach rumbled loudly, but I didn't feel the hunger, only the excitement of seeing him again.

Then he was there, saying my name. "Charlotte." He looked so handsome, in a long woolen coat and polished shoes.

"*Bonjour.*" My voice came out dry and stiff and I found I couldn't say his name.

He kissed me on one cheek and then the other. Not one of those typical air kisses people do as a formality. I felt his lips on my skin, and it sent a spark of electricity through me.

"Shall we walk?" He smiled his lopsided smile.

I felt my lips curve with a will of their own until there was a huge grin stretched across my face. I nodded, the words caught in my throat.

I strolled next to him as he walked with his cane. He was doing very well for someone who had broken his leg only three weeks ago. He reached out his left hand, taking mine. His small deformed hand made mine feel enormous and clumsy, and I wrapped my fingers around it, admiring the way he acted as if it were perfectly normal. His lack of self-consciousness gave him strength.

"Shall we walk down to Pont Neuf?"

I nodded. "*Oui.*"

"How have you been?"

"I've been missing you." The words slipped out.

"I've missed you too. I haven't stopped thinking about you."

My heart beat faster and I squeezed his hand in mine.

Abruptly, a couple of soldiers on the other side of the street crossed over to our side. I felt myself tense up.

"Papers," the taller one barked.

Jean-Luc leaned on his cane with one hand while he opened up his long coat with the other, reaching into the inside breast pocket to produce his papers. The soldier snatched them from him.

"Jean-Luc Beauchamp, SNCF." His tone was ironic. Then he held his hand out for mine.

I had them ready and gave them to him without looking at him.

"Charlotte de la Ville. Eighteen years of age. Do your parents know you're out?"

"Yes," I lied.

"With Monsieur Beauchamp here?"

I nodded, my eyes on the ground.

"How romantic, meeting up in secret."

He looked over at the other soldier, and they laughed. Then he handed back the papers.

"Have a lovely evening."

We carried on down Rue Montorgueil, neither of us speaking till we reached the Saint-Eustache church at the end of the street. Jean-Luc broke the silence. "You know, a Boche once stopped me here and asked me if this was Notre-Dame."

"No! What did you say?"

"I said yes, of course." He laughed.

I joined in his laughter and felt my heart lift again.

"Let's go inside." His laughter stopped.

"Okay." I didn't really feel like going into a church, but I could hardly refuse.

Inside, we wandered around the edge, looking at the alcoves and the tiny candles burning. Jean-Luc put a coin in the box, taking a candle and giving it to me. "Let's pray for this war to end quickly."

I made the sign of the cross, whispering a prayer in my head.

When we left the church, we headed across the square toward Rue de Rivoli, then crossed the road in front of the large department store La Samaritaine. Pont Neuf was almost empty, and we sat down on one of the circular stone benches overlooking the Seine. I stared down into the dark water, remembering when there used to be traffic on the river. There was nothing now, only dark crescents of waves chopping and crashing into each other.

"Do you want a drink?"

I watched as he dug into his trouser pocket, producing a silver hip flask.

"What is it?"

"Try it."

I took a small sip. It was rich, and reminded me of family dinners gone by. "Wine! It's delicious. Where did you get it?"

"Don't worry about that. Just enjoy it."

I took another sip and began to feel less nervous. Everything was going to be all right. He was watching me out of the corner of his eye. I took another sip, this one larger—more like a gulp. Then I passed the flask back to him.

"I brought something to eat too." He pulled out a bundle wrapped in paper and handed it to me. I brought it up to my nose, breathing in its smell.

"Cheese."

"Yes, Comté."

It smelled so good and my stomach suddenly felt so hollow. Quickly I pulled the paper off and ran my fingers over the perfectly smooth surface.

"Go on. Eat it." He smiled at me, putting his arm around my shoulder.

I bit into it, and it felt like it was the first time I had ever tasted cheese. So creamy, so rich. I took another bite, then passed it back to him.

He shook his head.

"What's the matter?"

"Nothing. I'm enjoying watching you eat it." He stroked my cheek. "What are we going to do, eh?"

"What, now? This is nice, sitting here with you." I leaned into him, my head on his shoulder.

"Let's dance." He jumped up, pulling me with him.

I dropped the cheese on the bench. "What?" I laughed. "Here?"

"Yes. Here." He put one hand around my waist, taking my hand with the other and kissing it. "May I have the pleasure, mademoiselle?"

"But the pleasure is mine, monsieur." I grinned.

And he spun me around, standing on his good leg, humming a tune I didn't recognize. Gradually we slowed down and I leaned my head on his chest.

"Charlo-tte," he whispered in my ear, sending sparks down the back of my neck.

"Mmm," I murmured.

"These moments are precious to me."

I stroked his back, leaning farther into him.

"When I'm feeling low and wondering when this damned war will be over, I just think of you, and it makes me feel... It gives me hope. It lifts me up again." He kissed the top of my head. Then he put his hand around the back of my neck, pulling me into him. His lips found mine, his tongue flickering over them, pushing them apart. I felt his breath coming harder as our bodies curled into each other.

A tap on my shoulder made me jump. I turned around.

"Papers!" A gendarme glared at me.

As I fumbled in my bag, another gendarme pulled Jean-Luc off to the side.

"Hurry up!" The gendarme tapped his baton in his palm.

I held my papers out with trembling hands.

He snatched them from me, glancing at them. Then he looked up at me, his eyes glinting in the dark. "You shouldn't be out here on the streets, behaving like a whore."

My head spun. I couldn't find any words.

"I could take you in for questioning. What's to stop me?"

I didn't know how to defend myself. I glanced over at Jean-Luc helplessly. He was in deep conversation with the other gendarme.

"Hey, what's to stop me?" the gendarme asked again, his voice louder this time.

"It...it's not curfew yet."

"Ha," he laughed. "Not yet. So hurry home, Cinderella. Hurry home." He handed my papers back to me.

I looked over at Jean-Luc, but I couldn't catch his eye in the dark and he was still busy talking with the other gendarme. I hesitated.

"Go home, Cinderella. Don't wait for your prince." The gendarme's mean smile scared me.

"Go on! Go home. Now!"

I walked away, the blood thudding through my veins. I didn't dare look back. What were they going to do with Jean-Luc? I told myself they were only gendarmes. It wasn't like they were the Gestapo. What could they do if he hadn't done anything wrong? Surely they couldn't arrest him for kissing. I tried to convince myself that he would be fine, that he'd come back for me. But there were no guarantees these days.

On the way home, I went into the church again and lit a candle, praying that they would let him go, that I would see him again.

Chapter Eighteen

Paris, April 22, 1944

JEAN-LUC

Give a weak man a little bit of power, and he'll abuse it. The gendarmes were a typical example. Jean-Luc was relieved to see Charlotte walking away, but now he had to deal with them. Even though they had no grounds for arresting him, he knew that what little authority they had would be wielded against him.

"Indecent exposure!" The one who'd stopped him laughed. "If we'd left them five minutes longer, we could have booked them for that!"

Jean-Luc took a pack of Gitanes out from his trouser pocket and offered it to the one who'd just spoken. "Well, if I'd been lucky, maybe you could have got me for that. But come on, this is France! It's our duty to honor our women."

The atmosphere immediately changed. The gendarme laughed, taking a cigarette, and Jean-Luc offered the packet to the other one, lighting up for both of them with the silver lighter he had inherited from his father. Then, to complete the unspoken pact of brotherhood, he took a cigarette for himself. "You can't arrest a man for having a little fun, can you?" He paused. "I just got out of the hospital. Injury to the leg and to the face." He touched his scar. "She was my nurse."

"Nice!" The gendarme blew a puff of smoke in Jean-Luc's direction. "I bet she took good care of you."

"She did." He laughed.

They joined in his laughter; then, after a little more banter about women, they sent him on his way. He glanced at his watch—almost another hour to go before curfew. That should give him enough time to walk home rather than descend into the Métro's labyrinth of tunnels. He needed to think. Well, actually he wanted to think about Charlotte. *Charlo-tte, Charlo-tte.* He caressed her name in his mind, wondering what it was about her. Maybe it was the contradictions he saw in her: confidence laced with insecurity, naïveté tinged with bravado. He could sense a courage that had yet to surface. He imagined it had been stifled by a strict family upbringing where she'd had little opportunity to express her own thoughts. She was like a butterfly not yet free from its cocoon, its beautiful wings still curled up. She was full of something he felt he'd lost. Hope. The thrill of living. He could hear it in her voice when she talked to him. And she wanted to give it to him, place it in his unworthy palm, somehow expecting him to take it and fulfill it.

Then there was something about the way she held herself, something touching about the way she lifted her chin when she talked to him, trying to look more assertive than he knew she felt. He loved to look at her in profile. She had a perfect profile: an intelligent forehead, not too short and not too high, long, silky eyelashes flickering over eyes of the richest brown, only a shade lighter than the large pupils they encircled. Her nose was fine-boned, maybe just a little too long to be perfect, which only made her all the more perfect in his eyes.

He walked back across the bridge, turning right along the *quai*, glancing over at the closed cafés and bars. What was he doing wandering around like this? Was he tempting fate? Wishing to be arrested? Anything to get out of working at Bobigny. Now he had even less chance of finding a way out. He'd aroused suspicion, so he wouldn't be able to do anything for a long while. He would just have to buckle down and get on with it. But was that possible? Should it be possible? Maybe he should just disappear; that would still be better than working for the Boches. He could escape to the countryside, try to find the Maquis, hiding out in the hills. With his knowledge of railways, he could help them derail trains. But then who would look after his mother? Who would provide her with a little money?

He soon came to Notre-Dame on the Île de la Cité; it gleamed in the dark, its timelessness indifferent to the war. He thought about going in and lighting a candle, but it was getting too close to curfew; anyway, he didn't like those tortured gargoyles hanging on the walls, watching you as you entered. Judging you. So he kept walking. Tonight he felt like being alone in the dark, in this city that used to be his.

Chapter Nineteen

Paris, April 28, 1944

CHARLOTTE

I sighed as I watched our maid, Clothilde, grating a large lump of Swedish turnip on the kitchen table.

"Don't sigh like that, Charlotte." Maman bent down, looking under the kitchen sink and pulling out a bundle covered in newspaper. "We've got pigeon tonight. Pierre killed two this afternoon and I swapped one for that last bit of sugar." She paused, staring at me. "Pigeon is just what you need. Look at you. You're even paler than usual."

I took the newspaper bundle from her and peeped inside. Sure enough, a pigeon lay dead, complete with head and feet. I folded the paper back up, putting the package on the kitchen table, in front of Clothilde. The sight had made me feel sick. I must have sighed again.

"What's the matter, Charlotte?" Maman frowned at me.

"Nothing."

"Yes there is. You've been very distracted all week."

"It's this war. I've had enough of it."

"Don't you think we all have? But you know it can't go on forever."

"But what about all the people who've disappeared? Will they come back? The Jews they've rounded up?"

Clothilde looked up from her grating, giving me a hard stare. Maman's frown grew deeper. "I hope so."

"Hope so? That doesn't sound like you think they will."

"There's not much we can do about it, Charlotte."

"What do you mean?"

"It's out of our hands. It's best not to dwell on it."

"But it's hard not to dwell on it!"

"When you're older, Charlotte, you'll understand that there are some things you cannot change, so you'd better just get on with it and accept them."

"But what if they're wrong?"

"It doesn't make any difference if you can't change them."

"Do you know then? Do you know what they're doing with the Jews?"

"No, I don't! Just be grateful you aren't Jewish."

"What about the Levi family we used to know? Don't you want to know what's happened to them? Will we ever see them again? You were friends with Madame Levi."

"Yes, we were friends, and it makes me sad to know that they have gone, maybe far from here."

"But where, Maman? Where have they gone?"

"Charlotte! Stop it, will you? I don't know where they've gone!"

Clothilde continued to stare at me. I had the feeling she wanted to say something but didn't think it was her place.

That evening, we ate our pigeon soup in silence; only the sound of chewing and swallowing filled the small room. My parents wiped their bowls clean with their fingers, there being no bread left. I looked down at my own bowl of gray broth, tiny bones floating to the surface, and pushed it away.

Papa rolled his eyes at me, slid my bowl over, lifted it to his mouth, and slurped.

Before I went to bed that evening, I looked up the word

"collaboration" in my old school dictionary. It said: "to cooperate with an enemy invader, or to work together on a joint project." That meant the French police were collaborating, but I knew that already. So where did it stop? As far as I could see, everyone was cooperating with the enemy—maybe not willingly, but doing so anyway: serving the Boches meat in the restaurants while going hungry themselves, giving them directions, stepping off the pavement to let them by.

Sometimes people were only too happy to collaborate, like the ones who nodded hello on their way to denounce you, though most denunciations were made by letter. Letters were much safer. Rumors often circulated about who had denounced whom, and what favors they had received in return.

One afternoon, I'd been with a friend when we saw a neighbor whom we vaguely knew shot in the back as he ran away from an identification control. Everyone buried their chins in their collars and hurried home. Wasn't that collaboration? Pretending that nothing had happened?

Then there were the women—but I'd bet they weren't giving away state secrets or even denouncing anyone. They were probably just trying to get extra rations for their families; maybe some of them actually fell in love. I wouldn't dare say it aloud to anyone, not even to my friends, but I thought some of the soldiers looked quite nice and normal. One had smiled at me once and my heart beat quickly as I'd hurried away. I wasn't quite sure if it was fear, or the thrill of a handsome man smiling at me.

Anyway, we'd been ordered by our government to collaborate. They'd told us to cooperate with the Germans, so that together we could build a stronger, more unified Europe.

When the German soldiers had marched down the Champs-Élysées, Papa took me to watch. "It's a historic moment," he'd said, "and we need to see it with our own eyes." Some people were waving flags, welcoming the tall soldiers dressed in their smart dark uniforms; others stood by silently, their lips pursed. Papa didn't have a flag and his face was clouded over. "We're going to have to be very careful," he'd whispered in my ear.

I'd stared at the tanks, trucks, and men, wondering how I was supposed to feel, and what exactly I needed to be careful about. But that was four years ago now; I'd only been fourteen. A lot had happened since then.

Chapter Twenty

Paris, April 29, 1944

JEAN-LUC

Desperate to see Charlotte the next Saturday evening, Jean-Luc had bought himself some time, working another week at Bobigny. He knew she'd be worried about him, and he knew she'd be waiting for him outside Stohrer at six o'clock on Saturday evening. This time he would tell her about his plan to join the Maquis. Maybe she would come with him. He knew she wanted to leave the German hospital, that she wanted to do something more. He knew she had spirit and courage; she just hadn't realized how much yet. It was possible. Anything was possible—you just had to believe. And Charlotte had helped him believe again. She made him remember a time when he'd been alive with the excitement of life, when he had dared to hope.

As he sat on the train into Paris that evening, he leaned his head against the hard, cold window, gazing out into the night. Barren unfarmed fields, left open for the birds to peck at, glinted back at him in the dark. The cattle had all disappeared, eaten by the Boches, who liked their steak medium-rare. Why, he wondered, didn't we protect our country better? Now it was divided, brother against brother. When this war ended, he knew there would be accounts to be settled, families torn apart.

Charlotte was standing there just as he'd imagined, gazing into the empty window of the patisserie. Stopping in his tracks, he lowered his hat over his face as he watched her. Her hands were in her coat pockets, pulling it around, stretching it out over her figure, accentuating her slim waist. Her legs were bare. He felt sorry for the girls, who no longer had stockings. At least the men could wear trousers. She tucked a loose strand of hair behind her ear. How he longed to do that for her. Then she took her other hand out of her pocket, holding it over her stomach. He knew how hungry she always was, and a wave of pity washed through him. If only he could take her out to a restaurant, watch her enjoy a proper meal. He was hungry himself, but he hadn't been able to get anything this time. Taking a step backward, he took out his wallet, counting the thin, overused notes. If he didn't give his mother any money this Sunday, then he could just about afford dinner for two in a brasserie. The thought excited him. Just this once, he thought. The gendarmes wouldn't bother them in a brasserie, and he would be able to talk to her properly.

Putting his wallet back, he strode over to meet her. She turned around, looking straight at him. He put his arm around her, pulling her in and kissing her on the lips. She seemed surprised, and he felt her tense up.

He pulled back. "Charlotte, tonight I'm taking you out for dinner."

"What?"

He stroked her hair, whispering in her ear. "Yes. I'm inviting you." Taking her arm, he pulled her along.

"What happened with the gendarmes?"

"Nothing, I gave them a Gitane each and they let me go."

"Thank goodness. I was so worried." She turned and kissed him on the cheek.

As they continued down the cobbled stones of Rue Montorgueil, they looked out for a brasserie. Soon they came to one on a corner, and he slowed down. "How about this one? Does it please mademoiselle?"

"I...I'm not sure." She leaned into his ear. "I think Papa said collabos eat here."

"Collaborators? Maybe, but that might be better."

"What do you mean?"

"Sometimes it's best to be right in the hornet's nest."

"But what if someone sees us going in?"

He looked around. "There's no one here. Quick." He stepped up to the door, holding it open.

As they walked in, a couple of old men in flat caps hunched over their *ballons de rouge* at the bar turned around to look at them. The smaller one raised his glass and winked at them.

"*Bonsoir, messieurs.*" Jean-Luc managed a fake smile, sensing Charlotte go rigid at his side.

A minute dragged by, but no one came to seat them, and he began to wonder if he'd been a little brash in choosing this brasserie. His eyes were drawn to an ornate gilded mirror hanging behind the bar, reflecting them both in its blotchy glass. Charlotte looked small and scared standing there next to him. He put his arm around her, and when their eyes met in the mirror, he winked. He watched the anxiety lift as she smiled back at him.

The waitress swanned past with a *pichet* of wine and a handful of glasses. "*Asseyez-vous. J'arrive tout de suite.*"

He looked around the narrow restaurant. The large zinc bar took up most of the room, with a couple of tables opposite. Several other small, round tables extended the space toward the back, where it was darker and more private. Taking Charlotte's hand, he walked over to one of these tables, as far away as possible from the only other couple. He pulled out a chair for her, reaching for her coat, then he removed his own and they sat down.

"What do you want to eat, Charlotte?"

"I don't know. I haven't been to a restaurant for ages. What do they have?"

He smiled. "It's just a brasserie. Do you want meat?"

"Yes, okay."

"*Mademoiselle, s'il vous plaît?*" he called to the waitress. He sounded more confident than he felt.

"Monsieur?"

"Two steaks and a small *pichet* of house red."

"There's no steak today."

"What do you have?"

"Croque monsieur, quiche, salade d'endives."

"Charlotte, what do you want?"

"Croque monsieur, please."

"Two croque monsieurs, mademoiselle, and a *demi-pichet* of house red."

The waitress left, giving no indication that she'd heard him. He hoped she wouldn't spit on their food. He himself might have if he thought he was serving collabos.

A couple of minutes later she reappeared, setting down the small carafe and two glasses. She didn't pour the wine, but she did leave a saucer of olives. He offered them to Charlotte, and watched as she placed one delicately between her teeth, biting into its shiny skin, then removing the stone and placing it on the edge of the saucer, next to the stone he had just removed from his own mouth. It felt intimate; what had been in her mouth next to what had been in his. He watched her closely, wondering if she was thinking the same thing.

"I haven't had olives since . . . I must have been fourteen or fifteen, when we still used to go to Provence for August."

"How lovely. I've never really left Paris. What's it like there?" He poured them a glass of wine each.

"It's . . . it's bathed in sunlight, and if you go in June, you can see fields and fields of purple lavender. They grow everything there:

sunflowers that face the rising sun, and fields of olive trees with silver-backed leaves."

"Will you take me there one day?" He held his glass of wine up to the light before breathing in its aroma, then they toasted, their eyes meeting. "To us, in Provence," he whispered.

Charlotte swirled the wine around in her glass as if unsure whether it was a good idea.

"Try it." Jean-Luc took a sip. "It's not bad—for a house wine."

He watched as she brought the glass to her mouth, tentatively taking a sip.

"It's lovely." She licked her lips.

The waitress reappeared and without a word put their plates before them. Jean-Luc's stomach rumbled at the sight of cheese oozing out the sides of toasted bread.

Charlotte's eyes grew wide. "It looks delicious."

"*Bon appétit.*"

He watched as she picked up her knife and fork, cutting off a small square. Then, just before she put it in her mouth, she paused, looking at him. "Thank you, Jean-Luc."

"It's my pleasure. I wish I could do more for you. When this war is over, I'll take you somewhere special."

"This is special." She took another forkful. "It's wonderful to eat proper food."

He watched her eating. Then she took another sip of wine, looking at him out of the corner of her eye. "Aren't you hungry?"

He smiled, glancing down at his untouched food. "I've got my mind on other things right now." He leaned toward her. "I've missed you, Charlotte."

The corners of her mouth turned up and her eyes sparkled. "How much?"

"This much." He spread his hands out over the table, then raised one, holding it against her cheek. "How have you been?"

"Well, I've missed seeing your smile every day."

"And I've missed yours. More than you can imagine." He paused. "Let's eat."

They ate in companionable silence, appreciating the taste of real food.

"How is it at the hospital now?" He hadn't meant to bring the conversation around in that direction; the words had escaped his mouth without him thinking.

He watched the smile fall from her face. "I have to leave. It's wrong to be there." She paused. "I just need to get the courage together to tell my parents." She looked around anxiously as though someone might have overheard.

"Don't worry, no one's listening. But don't let it make you feel so bad. We're all complicit, one way or another."

"What do you mean?" Her eyebrows came together in a frown.

"Well, we've let them have our food, our wine, our land, our houses. It's hard—impossible—for civilians like us to stand up to a military presence like theirs; there's not much we can do alone." He topped off her glass, though she'd only had a couple of sips.

"Yes, but we should try and do something, shouldn't we?"

He nodded. "You know where I work, don't you?"

"On the railroads."

"Yes, but do you know where?"

"Not exactly. I . . . I don't think you told me."

He rubbed his eyes, then looked around the brasserie. No one new had come in, and the two old men had gone, leaving just the other couple several tables away; they seemed more interested in each other than anything else anyway. He leaned forward, lowering his voice. "I work at Bobigny, the station for Drancy—the camp from where they deport all the Jews." He took another swig of wine. Wiping his mouth with the back of his hand, he continued. "Charlotte, they're deporting them by the thousand, and we don't know where they're sending them."

"Aren't they going to work camps in Germany?"

He shook his head. "I think they're taking them somewhere far away and then... they're getting rid of them."

"What? What do you mean?"

"I'm sorry, Charlotte. I didn't mean to talk about it." He put his head in his hands.

She reached out, touching his hand. "Tell me what you mean."

He wondered whether to go on. Maybe he should just keep it light; he could talk about her, flatter her, like he'd done in the hospital. It had been fun, but there were more pressing things on his mind now. Time was running out for such frivolities. He looked into her dark brown eyes, wishing they could have a different conversation.

"They're cramming them into cattle wagons—as many as they can squeeze in. And then they're shipping them off. No water. No food. Someone told me he'd heard one of the Boches boasting that they'd managed to get more than a thousand on the last train."

He watched the color drain from her face.

"I can't do it anymore, Charlotte."

She shook her head as if trying to shake the knowledge out. "But it's not possible. Why would they do that?"

"Shh."

The waitress walked by. "*Tout va bien?*"

"Yes, thank you. Could we just have a carafe of water, please?"

"Of course." She turned on her heel, walking away.

"Don't worry, she didn't hear anything." He paused, lowering his voice and leaning farther toward Charlotte. "Why?" He laughed cynically. "Because this is war, and the Jewish immigrant is their enemy."

"But they're taking French-born Jews too now, aren't they?" She leaned forward, her chin resting on her hand, her eyes darkening. "I wish I could do something."

The waitress came back with their water. She looked pointedly at their half-finished plates.

"*Merci, madame.* Could we have a little more wine, please?" Jean-Luc held out the empty carafe.

She snatched it from him. "*Bien sûr.*"

He watched her as she disappeared behind the bar, then he turned back to Charlotte. "We should finish eating."

"I've lost my appetite."

"We don't want to draw attention to ourselves."

The waitress crept up on them this time, planting the carafe on the table without a word. Jean-Luc poured himself some wine. Charlotte's glass was still full. Abruptly she picked it up and gulped it down as though it were water, then put her empty glass back down and set to work on the cold croque monsieur, cutting it up into little squares, her fingers gripping the knife and fork tightly. He watched her knuckles turn white.

"Charlotte," he whispered. She didn't answer; just carried on cutting the toast up into tinier and tinier squares. He reached out for her pale hand. She snatched it back as if he were about to burn her. Then he heard a small choking sound and saw her shoulders hunch forward. Grabbing the napkin off the table, she buried her face in it.

He stood up, moving over to her side of the table, taking her in his arms. "Let's leave."

Chapter Twenty-One

Paris, April 29, 1944

CHARLOTTE

Once out of the collabos' brasserie, I began to feel better. It must have been the wine making me overemotional like that. I needed to calm down, but my head was spinning, my thoughts all mixed up. Jean-Luc kept his arm tightly around me, using his other for the cane. It made me feel safer. But no one was safe. No one. For a while we walked in silence, my sniffles gradually subsiding. Soon we found ourselves on Rue Saint-Denis.

"Come on. Let's go in here." He took my hand, pulling me into a bar. I didn't want another drink; my senses were out of control. Mixed feelings of loss, guilt, and longing swirled through my head. I didn't know what I might do next.

But he ordered wine for us both.

And I drank it.

We sat on stools at the bar—it was cheaper to drink there, and anyway there were Boches with their women at the three tables behind. I stared at them for a moment, taking in the dark uniforms of the men and the bare legs of the women; they'd drawn thin lines down the backs of them in a sad attempt to make it look like they were wearing stockings. Honestly, who did they think they were kidding? And why did they bother? They thought it looked classy, I guess. Classy! I bet the Boches thought they looked classy too in their smart uniforms. It was all so false. I felt sorry for the women, faking it for the Boches. I hoped they would manage to steal favors in return for giving nothing more away than a superficial smile and a false laugh.

I turned back toward Jean-Luc, my head spinning. I gazed into his warm brown eyes that weren't exactly brown and sensed a stirring inside me, like a magnetic force pulling me toward him. There was nothing false about him. He was good. I felt myself toppling toward him, my hands landing on his knees. Straightening my spine and removing my hands, I looked him in the eye again. But it only made me feel even more unsteady.

"Charlotte."

I closed my eyes, listening to the sound of my name on his tongue.

"I think you've had too much to drink. It's my fault. I'm sorry. I should take you home."

"No!" I laughed, surprised at the sudden determination in my voice. "I like it here. Let's have some more wine." This time I fell right off my stool into his arms. Tilting my face up, I saw his lopsided smile. That was what did it. His smile. I pulled myself up, putting my arms around his shoulders. And I kissed him. It wasn't a soft kiss like his had been. It was a furious kiss. A desperate kiss. I wanted it to transport me. Far away.

Whistling and laughing interrupted us. I felt him pull away. The Boches were clapping. I heard one say, "Now that is a proper French kiss."

Jean-Luc threw some coins on the bar and took my hand. "Let's go." He was mad, I could tell. I'd embarrassed him.

Once outside, he pulled me around the corner. Then he dropped my hand and I heard his cane fall to the ground. He wrapped his arms around me, holding me tight. His lips found mine, and I could feel his breath coming hard. He tasted of salt, like the sea. Like freedom. I don't know how long we stood there breathing into each other as though we were in fear of drowning, our hearts pounding. When his lips finally left mine, I just wanted to sink into him and forget the rest.

"Charlotte," he whispered in my ear. "Let's run away together."

It was all I wanted right there in that moment.

Chapter Twenty-Two

Paris, April 30, 1944

CHARLOTTE

"I'd like you to meet him." I knew it was crazy, but if I was going to run away with him, I'd like them to at least know I was running away with a good man.

Maman stared hard at me. "It's not the right time, Charlotte."

"I can't change the time! I didn't start this war!"

"Charlotte, that's enough. We can't have him for lunch. You know we barely have enough food for the three of us, let alone another."

"That's okay, Maman. He can come for a fake coffee in the afternoon; we can pretend it's *goûter*."

"Maybe he'll bring something." Papa turned around in his chair. "I bet he has contacts, a young lad like that, working at Drancy. He must know how to get hold of stuff." The word "collabo" wasn't mentioned, but it hung there, unspoken.

I'd known they wouldn't want him for lunch and had wisely told Jean-Luc to come at four. No one ever had anything to do at four o'clock on a Sunday afternoon, and Clothilde didn't work on Sundays. My invitation had surprised him, and after he'd accepted, it surprised me too. It was an impulsive idea, and I must admit I was beginning to question my motive. Was I trying to prove something to my parents? Show them that I was no longer their little girl? Or maybe I just wanted to annoy them by bringing home a railroad worker, knowing full well the importance they put on education and class.

"It would only be polite to bring something," Papa continued, interrupting my thoughts. "I expect he'll be wanting to impress us."

All they ever thought about was food. Food. Food. Food. Weren't there more important things at stake here? I turned my back on them both, wandering over to the kitchen sink, looking out the window into the courtyard.

"Why was he sent to a German hospital?" Maman spoke to my back.

"I don't know." I turned around. "Probably because he's working at Drancy."

Papa pursed his lips.

"I'm working at a German hospital, aren't I? What's the difference?"

"Less of that tone, Charlotte." Maman looked at me with narrowed eyes.

Jean-Luc came on the dot at four o'clock, the buzzer making my heart race and my stomach churn. Papa opened the door, shaking hands formally. Maman stood there, her arms folded across her chest.

He held his hand out to her while I held my breath.

Slowly she unfolded her arms, extending a hand toward him. Then he turned to me, and I held my hand out before he could kiss me on the cheek. It felt ridiculously formal, but I didn't want him to kiss me in front of my parents. I caught his smile and felt my cheeks redden as I smiled back.

For a few seconds we stood there as though we weren't sure what we were supposed to do next. Then Jean-Luc opened his bag. "I've brought something." He rummaged through it, finally lifting up a package wrapped in newspaper. "*Saucisson.*"

The atmosphere immediately lightened. The *saucisson* didn't look so great to me—pinky gray and shriveled—but Maman's eyes lit up as she took it from him, putting it away for later.

"Would you like some coffee?" she asked.

Papa laughed loudly. "Coffee! It's ground acorn, like it is for everyone else." He turned toward Jean-Luc. "Let's go and sit in the living room. Bring the *coffee* in, Béatrice."

I followed them into the living room, leaving Maman to prepare the drink. Papa settled down into his armchair, while Jean-Luc and I sat on the couch. I dismissed the urge to take his hand, instead looking at Papa to see how he was going to start the conversation. But he leaned back in his armchair as though distancing himself. Jean-Luc leaned forward.

"Charlotte took great care of me in the hospital," he said.

Papa took a moment to reply. "Yes. She told me you had an accident." He paused. "At Drancy."

"Coffee." Maman walked into the room holding a tray with three cups and some kind of biscuit I didn't know we had. I couldn't help wondering why she wanted to impress him, but I decided to take it as a good sign.

"*Merci, madame.*" Jean-Luc took his cup and saucer and a thin biscuit. "Yes," he continued. "I've been working at Drancy for... for two months now." He looked down at his feet, his cup balanced on his leg. Slowly he took a sip, looking at me over the top of the cup.

"You're a railroad worker." Papa's words sounded like an accusation rather than a question.

"Yes, and I'm a nursing assistant." I blurted the words out before thinking, but I hated the thought of them making him feel inferior.

"We know that, Charlotte." Maman's voice was soft and quiet, as though she were talking to a child. "Everyone has to do what they can in times of war." She turned to Jean-Luc. "How did the accident happen?"

"I was working on one of the lines when a crowbar flew up, hitting me in the face. And when I fell, I broke my leg." He paused. "It was a stupid accident."

Papa raised an eyebrow as if in agreement about that.

"Yes." Maman looked at him. "That's quite a scar you have there."

His hand flew to it, touching its puckered edges. I imagined its roughness under my fingertips.

"How long have you been working for the SNCF?" Papa lifted his cup to his lips. I hoped he was going to be nice.

"Since I was fifteen."

"You left school at fifteen then?"

"*Oui, monsieur.*"

"Before the *baccalauréat*?"

"Yes." Jean-Luc looked away.

I felt embarrassed about Papa's insinuation—leaving school before the *baccalauréat* meant one was condemned to a life of manual labor or menial work. An awkward silence filled the room.

"So." Papa put his cup back down. "What do you do at Drancy?"

I cringed and glanced over at Jean-Luc. His face reddened.

"I help maintain the lines."

Papa coughed and Maman looked down at her drink. More silence followed. I searched in my head for a way to break it.

"Jean-Luc says there are lots of trains leaving from Drancy." I looked at Papa. He raised an eyebrow. "They're deporting the prisoners from there," I continued.

Papa stared at me with stony eyes. Maman froze, her cup midair, and Jean-Luc shunted along the couch toward me. The atmosphere grew thick.

"Charlotte is right." Jean-Luc broke the silence. "Many trains are leaving now. Sometimes with a thousand prisoners on board."

"A thousand?" Papa paused. "On one train?"

"*Oui, monsieur.*"

"How can they possibly get a thousand on one train?"

Jean-Luc shrugged his shoulder. "They must pack them in."

Maman continued to look down at her fake coffee. I knew only too well how she hated this kind of conversation.

"Where are they taking them?"

"Somewhere in the east, I think."

Papa blinked. "Well, they've been arresting thousands, and they must be deporting them somewhere. The east would make sense. Poland, I imagine."

"Yes, most likely." Jean-Luc glanced at me. "But what happens to them?"

"What happens to them?" Papa frowned.

"Yes. I know they are crammed in cattle cars, standing room only." Jean-Luc's voice took on a more assertive tone, and I felt anxious about the direction the conversation was turning so quickly. "And I've seen... I've seen the platform after the trains have left. It's... it's a mess."

"What do you mean?"

"Well, there are things... things that belonged to them—books, hats, suitcases, children's toys. I think they must have to force them onto the trains—"

"Children's toys?" Papa interrupted.

Maman frowned at him. "You know they're taking the children too." She paused, looking at me. "Remember the huge round-up when they took whole families to the Vélodrome d'Hiver, nearly two years ago now?"

Papa put his cup down on the tray and leaned back in his chair again. I looked over at Jean-Luc, hoping to make eye contact, but he was staring down.

"*Bien,*" Maman started. "I hope this winter will be over soon."

Jean-Luc looked up with his cup halfway to his mouth. "It's an awful job." He put the cup back into its saucer. "I don't know if I can keep doing it."

My heart beat hard against my ribs. I hadn't wanted him to be that honest—that direct with them.

Papa whispered, "What do you mean?"

"Well, I'm aiding the Boches in their work, aren't I? I'm helping them deport people to God knows where, just because they're Jewish."

"Why? Why did they make it a crime?" I blurted out, wanting to break the tension.

Papa looked at me as if seeing me for the first time. "They've been taking jobs from French citizens. And they tried to control our economy, just like they did in Germany."

"That's not even true!" Jean-Luc put his cup on the table with a thud, brown liquid sloshing up. "It's all propaganda."

"Who are we to know? Are you a politician? Do you understand economics?" Papa paused, staring coldly at Jean-Luc. "You're just a laborer."

"I know wrong when I see it." Jean-Luc glared back at him.

"Do you? And what are you going to do about it then, young man?"

"I have a few ideas."

Papa sat up straight. "Listen, lad." His tone was firm. "You just have to knuckle down and get on with it. You have no choice. None of us do."

Maman reached out, touching Papa's elbow, a sign that he should calm down.

"Don't we?" Jean-Luc glanced at me. "I think we always have a choice. It's just that it's a difficult one sometimes."

"Don't give me that. Right now, we have no choice. We're trapped. But this war won't last forever. It's not going well for Germany. Just keep doing what you're told to do."

"Is that what I should do?" He stood up. "Do you think I should just stick it out, while they deport and probably murder thousands of our compatriots?" His voice grew louder. "Do you think that's what I should do?"

Papa stood too, his face turning red. "That's enough! I don't like your tone."

My heart froze. He had totally alienated them.

"Well, I don't like what's going on. And I don't like sitting back doing nothing, just grateful that I'm not Jewish." He paused, lowering his voice. "I'm sorry you don't agree with what I have to say."

Papa faced him, drawing his shoulders back. "I think you'd better leave now."

My heart pounded as though it were the only functioning organ in my body. Terrified that this would be it, that I would never see him again, I stood up too, my knees trembling. I threw my arms around his neck, afraid that if I let go, I would tumble down.

"Charlotte!" Maman shouted.

Quickly I whispered in his ear, "Don't go anywhere without me."

Papa's hand landed on my shoulder, pulling me away from him.

I watched in silence as Jean-Luc left. He hadn't answered me.

Chapter Twenty-Three

Paris, April 30, 1944

CHARLOTTE

"You are never to see him again. Never! You hear me?"

Staring down at the parquet, I let Papa's words wash over me, but I could sense Maman's eyes piercing me, willing me to apologize, to be the good daughter. Still my tongue lay frozen in my mouth.

"Look at me when I'm talking to you." He took a step nearer; the smell of rotten acorns on his breath repelled me. I must have backed away, because he took another step forward. "You are an ignorant young girl!" He glared at me. "He can't go around talking like that! Who the hell does he think he is?" He paused, raising his hands. "And right here in our home, too!"

He turned to face Maman. "I told you we were too lax with her." He looked back at me. "She doesn't understand the consequences of talk like that."

"But it's true." My heart was beating hard. "He's not making it up. It's true what he said."

"I don't give a damn if it's true or not." Papa's voice boomed through the living room. I resisted the urge to put my hands over my ears. "That's not the point. You can't go around talking like that." He reached out for my shoulder. "Do you understand?"

I pushed his hand away and ran out of the room into my bedroom, slamming the door behind me.

I would see Jean-Luc again. I would. And no one was going to stop me.

I heard the front door close. Thank God, Papa had gone out. But it was too late now for me to run after Jean-Luc. Panic rose up from my belly as I imagined him escaping to join the Maquis without me. How would I find him now?

God, how I hated Papa. Why couldn't he have listened to Jean-Luc and talked to him as an equal? Why did he always have to assume his superiority over everyone else? Calling him "just a laborer." Jean-Luc knew more than Papa about the war; after all, he was right there at Drancy, in the hornet's nest, as he liked to say. He was best placed to know what was really going on, but no one had wanted to listen to him. Maman always sided with Papa, whatever he said. I didn't know what she thought about anything, not really.

Flopping down onto my bed, I picked up my old flattened teddy bear. My grandmother had made it for me when I was a baby, and whenever I felt lonely or misunderstood, I took comfort in its familiar form. It had soaked up many tears over the years, but now the stuffing had started to come out of its neck; I liked to pick at it, wondering where she'd found all the pieces of brightly colored material that I pulled out. So much had happened over the last few months. Things were changing—I was changing. It was time for me to make my own decisions, to leave my childhood behind me. Decisively, I rolled the bear into a ball and stuffed it under my bed.

The door opened and Maman stood there, looking pale and fraught. I almost felt sorry for her. "Charlotte, have you calmed down now?"

I turned to face her. "What?" I paused, taking in the lines of worry playing around her mouth. "I'm not the one who needs to calm down."

"Charlotte! How dare you talk like that!"

"But it's true, isn't it? Papa was the one who lost his temper, not me." I turned away from her. Honestly, what was the point?

She hovered over me, and I knew she was looking for the words to excuse Papa, though I think she knew I didn't want to hear them. She sat on the bed next to me.

"Why is it impossible to be honest in this family?" I said.

"What are you talking about?"

"No one wants to discuss what is happening." I turned away, lowering my voice. "You just don't want to know, do you?"

"Charlotte, that's not true!"

"Yes it is! You prefer burying your head in the sand." I turned back toward her and saw her swallow, biting her lip, but still I carried on. "We should be more active, more resistant to what is going on right under our noses."

She stared at me, her pupils large pools of black. It was the first time I'd ever confronted her.

"Charlotte, you don't understand." She raised her hand, as though about to touch me, but I flinched and she quickly withdrew it. "You're so young. It's impossible for you to really appreciate the situation."

I sighed loudly. There we were again, beating around the bush.

"Please, Charlotte. You have to make some concessions for your father, and for me too. He's been through more than you know. Maybe we should have talked to you more, but...he didn't want to." She paused. "He was only eighteen years old when he was sent to Verdun during the last war. He saw things one should never see. I only know because of his nightmares." She reached for my hand. "Do you know why he can't enter a butcher's shop? Did you ever wonder about that?"

I shook my head, guessing the answer.

"The smell of blood." She removed her hand, rubbing her

forehead with the back of it. "Like so many of us, he believed Pétain was a war hero, that he was wise to negotiate a kind of peace with Hitler." She paused. "Pétain knew what war was. And he did what he had to, to save us from another."

"But Maman, he didn't, did he? He didn't save us from another. We're sitting here right in the middle of one."

I watched her frown grow deeper, realizing that for her, we were not right in the middle of a war. We were sitting this one out.

"It was very hard for your father," she continued. "We didn't imagine that it would come to this. We both thought it was better to join forces with Germany than fight them."

"Join forces?"

"We had no army to fight them with."

"But...but doesn't that make us collaborators?"

"No, Charlotte. No!" She took my hand again, this time gripping it tightly. "We're just civilians. And we're doing our best to survive—raising families, carrying on—because...because we have to. That's what we do. We're not soldiers."

I wondered if this was the moment I should put my arms around her, but the violence of Papa's outburst still resounded in my head. I wasn't sure how to be now, how to think of my parents. It felt like I was drifting away from them, caught up by another current.

I only wanted Jean-Luc.

Part Two

Chapter Twenty-Four

Santa Cruz, June 24, 1953

JEAN-LUC

"Drancy. So tell us what you did there." Jackson pulls out a chair and flops into it, his long legs stretching out in front of him. Jean-Luc studies him. His protruding forehead and thin nose give him a predatory air. And now it looks like he's homing in on his prey.

"I was a railroad worker. I'd been working for the SNCF since I was fifteen."

"The French national railway?"

"Yes."

"Which was taken over by the Nazis."

"Yes."

"So you were working for the Nazis at Drancy."

"Not exactly." He pauses, scratching his head. Is this what they want from him—a confession that he was another Nazi whore? "I had no choice. I was sent there. None of us wanted to be there."

"I bet!" Jackson leans forward, looking into his eyes. "I bet the Jews especially didn't want to be there. Did you know they were taking them to a death camp?"

"No."

Bradley sighs. "Had you heard the words 'death camp' before?"

"No! Never!" Jean-Luc takes a breath, giving himself a minute to prepare his answer. "Though it was clear to me that many of the prisoners would die on the train or once they arrived at their destination."

"But you're saying you didn't *know* the prisoners were being sent to a death camp?"

He doesn't blink or move a muscle. He's trying to work out the difference between knowing and understanding. He puts his fingers against the space between his eyebrows, trying to ease the pounding in his head.

"Did you know Auschwitz was a death camp?" Jackson insists, his voice growing in volume.

"No! I didn't know."

They look at him coldly. He can tell they don't believe him. They hate him without knowing him.

Jackson stands up abruptly. "Mr. Bow-Champ, is there something else you'd like to tell us?"

Jean-Luc's pulse rate increases. What do they know? Jackson's got his beady eye on him, but Jean-Luc concentrates on keeping his face blank.

"So, nothing to say." Jackson turns to nod at Bradley. "Our investigation is still open. We have to ask you to remain in the state of California in case we need to call you in for further questioning. You are free to go for now."

Jean-Luc's heart beats fast and hard as they accompany him down the corridor, up the stairs, and out the double front doors. When they deposit him outside, he takes a deep breath, savoring the taste of freedom. Everything will be all right.

He wishes he'd asked if he could call Charlotte, get her to pick him up, but he wasn't in the right frame of mind to think of such practicalities. Maybe a bus will come along soon. Impatience runs through his veins, telling him he's done enough waiting. He decides to forget about the money and takes a cab, going straight to work. He's already missed more than half a day.

He phones Charlotte from work in the early evening. She picks up straightaway, anxiety ringing out in her rushed way of talking. "Thank goodness it's you. What happened? What did they want?"

"Don't worry, I'm at work now, but I have to stay late to make up the time. Let's talk when I get home."

"When will you be back?"

"Not till about eight."

"Okay. I'll keep some dinner warm for you."

When the cab drops him off outside his house at 8:30, he suppresses the urge to run up the path. Someone might be watching. Once the front door clicks shut behind him, he breathes a sigh of relief. He stands there for a minute savoring the smell of lemons and rosemary. Home.

Charlotte steps out of the living room. "What happened? What did they want?" The words leap from her mouth. She doesn't even say hello.

"I don't know."

"You don't know!"

He looks at her, eyes aching with fatigue.

"But what did they say?" she goes on.

"Nothing really. They just asked me questions about what I was doing at Bobigny."

"Nothing about..."

"No. Nothing."

"But what will happen if they find out?"

"They won't. It's virtually impossible."

"Virtually!" Putting her hands into her hair, she scrunches it up in tight fists, closing her eyes. Then suddenly they're open again, pupils expanding into pools of black. "Virtually means it's possible. Possible!" Her hushed shouting becomes louder.

He takes a step toward her, reaching out with his open hands, wanting to calm her. "Shh, Charlotte. Is Sam asleep?"

Looking toward the stairs, she nods.

"Come into the living room." He puts an arm out for her.

She avoids his arm, but follows him into the living room.

He sees the tumbler sitting on top of the cupboard. "Did you have a drink?" It comes out like an accusation. He wishes he hadn't said anything, and tries to defuse the tension. "I think I'll have one too. Do you want another?"

"No!"

He reaches into the cupboard and pulls out the Southern Comfort. As he unscrews the lid, she stands behind him.

"We should have told them. We should have told them when we first got here. It's all my fault."

"Charlotte, please."

"But it's true, isn't it? We've had to live a lie. And now someone's going to find out. I just know it."

"Of course they won't. Who's going to be interested after all this time? Nine years later."

The last thing he needs right now is an argument; his nerves are still raw. He sighs, taking a large gulp of his drink. When he looks up again, he sees Sam in the doorway. He looks so small, so vulnerable, standing there in his pajamas.

"Sam." He holds out his hand.

"What's the matter? Where were you?" Sam rubs his eyes.

"Everything's okay. I just needed to help with an investigation. Come here." Jean-Luc opens his arms.

But Sam remains where he is.

Walking over to him, Jean-Luc crouches down to his level, talking in a soft, calm voice. "It's okay, Sam. The men who came this morning wanted to ask me some questions. That's all."

"But what about?"

"Just stuff that happened a long time ago."

"What stuff?" It doesn't look like Sam's ready to drop the subject yet.

"About what happened before you were born, during the war."

Sam frowns. "What happened?" There it was. The question. From his own child's lips.

"You don't need to know, Sam." Jean-Luc pauses. "*On ne voit bien qu'avec le coeur.*"

"What, Daddy?"

"'You only see well with the heart.' It's from *Le Petit Prince*—*The Little Prince*. You remember, that book we gave you last year, for your eighth birthday."

"Can you read it to me? You didn't read to me tonight."

Jean-Luc nods, blinking back tears.

Chapter Twenty-Five

Santa Cruz, July 3, 1953

JEAN-LUC

Jean-Luc watches Sam spinning circles in the sand, his olive skin ripening gently under the California sun. "How about practicing your hundred meters?"

"It's yards, Dad!" Sam leaps up, jiggling up and down with excitement as his father draws a line in the sand.

Jean-Luc raises his arm. "Ready, steady—go!" He drops it in one swift movement.

Sam flies forward, spindly limbs pumping away, forehead screwed up in determination. His new yellow swim shorts flap around his skinny knees, then his legs stretch out one last time to cross the finish line. Panting heavily, he bends over, his head hanging between his knees, gasping for breath—a mini version of a real athlete.

"Twenty-five seconds. Well done, son."

"Wow! Yeah! That's fast, isn't it, Dad?"

"Sure is. Could be a record!" Unable to resist, Jean-Luc wraps his arms around him, soaking up his warmth. But then Sam jumps free, running down toward the ocean, stopping halfway to turn around, cocking his head to one side and putting his hands on his hips as he waits for his father to catch up.

Jean-Luc runs toward him as fast as his good leg will carry him. Standing in the surf, he inhales deeply, savoring the mingling smell of salt and cotton candy wafting over from the boardwalk. He gazes out at the huge expanse of turquoise stretching to meet the horizon. Millions of tiny diamonds twinkle back at him. It's all so bright and beautiful, the lines so clean. This is America, its colors pure and clear—sky blue and gold. In contrast, when he remembers Paris, he sees dull colors running into each other, streaks of gray and black mingling, never mixing, lines vague and untrue. He's in love with his adopted country.

And his son. Every minute he spends with Sam erases another minute of his life before. He opens his mouth and breathes in the taste of happiness. Then he holds his breath as he plunges into the ocean, diving through the waves.

Sam paddles after him, but is pushed back by the tide. Jean-Luc stops swimming, reaching out for his son. Their fingers meet and he pulls him into deeper water. With one hand under the child's stomach, he holds him afloat so he can practice his front stroke.

"Let's play sharks, Daddy."

"What's that?"

"You close your eyes and count to fifty, and I have to swim away, then you come after me and try to catch me."

As instructed by his son, he closes his eyes, counting as Sam slithers off his hands. At fifty, he opens his eyes. *Merde!* Sam is too far out, way out of his depth now. He's waving his arms around. Immediately Jean-Luc cuts through the waves toward him. When he reaches him, he pulls him to his chest, treading water as he holds him tight.

"Daddy, I was scared. It's real deep!"

"You're too far out. Let's go back."

"But now you've caught me, you have to eat me."

"I don't eat little boys. Let's have a proper lunch instead."

"I'm not hungry. Can't we stay longer—please?"

"No. It's lunchtime."

"Please."

"Don't beg, Sam."

When they wander back up the beach, Charlotte has a towel ready for Sam, which she puts around his shoulders, pulling him onto her lap and kissing him on the top of his head. "Was it cold?"

"No. It's real warm. Are you gonna come in?" Sam turns to look up at her.

"After lunch." Charlotte takes out a flask, pouring cups of homemade lemonade, clouds of pulp floating to the surface. She passes Jean-Luc his favorite sandwich—ham and tomato—and Sam his: peanut butter and jelly.

"Can we go camping next weekend?" Sam's face shines with eagerness.

"There's an idea. Where were you thinking of?"

"France."

Jean-Luc nearly chokes on his lemonade. "France? But that's the other side of the world."

"What made you think of that all of a sudden?" Charlotte asks.

"Mrs. Armstrong said we should talk to our gran'parents and ask them what it was like when they were small, then we gotta write about it. Mine are in France. Right?"

Jean-Luc bites into his sandwich, looking out to sea.

"Yes," Charlotte replies. "But it's a long ways away. I could tell you what it was like for your grandparents, growing up in France." She places her hand on Sam's knee. Jean-Luc knows she's trying to placate him.

"Can't I write and ask them?"

"No, Sam. They're too old." She removes her hand, scratching her right shoulder.

Jean-Luc recognizes the gesture; it's what she does when she's feeling awkward or playing for time.

"Too old to write?" Sam insists.

"Yes." She turns around, fumbling in the cooler.

"But why do they never come to see us? All my friends have grandparents, and it's like I don't have any."

"Sam," Jean-Luc says, "remember how we told you the war in France was hard on everyone. We managed to escape with you, but the people who stayed, like your grandparents, they don't like looking back. They want to forget."

"What? Forget us?"

Jean-Luc exchanges a look with Charlotte. "No, not us, but they were sad when we left." He pauses. "Maybe we'll see them again one day. Planes are very expensive, you know."

"Okay." Sam nibbles the crust off his sandwich.

Jean-Luc turns around to look at Charlotte. She's hunched over the cool box, her dark, silky hair loosely tied back with a purple silk scarf. He's worried that the conversation is upsetting her.

"What else have you got in there, honey?" he asks.

She pulls out a brown paper bag and passes it to him, but doesn't meet his eye. The atmosphere lies thick and heavy. So much unsaid.

Then Sam breaks it. "Are they cookies?"

Jean-Luc opens the bag. "Yes, your favorite. Chocolate chip."

"Swell!" Sam reaches out his hand to take one.

Thank God for chocolate chip cookies, Jean-Luc thinks ironically.

Later when Sam has gone off to dig holes in the sand, Charlotte and Jean-Luc stretch out on the picnic rug. Jean-Luc turns onto his side, resting his head on his hand, gazing down at her.

A silence falls on them, and he wonders if she will broach the subject first. He looks at her loosely tied hair falling to the side. He likes the way she always carries scarves with her, draping them around her neck or wrapping her hair in them, sometimes tying one around her waist. She has style. Originality. It's what attracted him to her in the first place. Never one to blend into the background, however hard she might try.

"Jean-Luc."

"Yes?" He can feel it coming.

"Sam is asking questions again. All his friends have family—grandparents, uncles, aunts, all that. But he has none."

"He has us." Jean-Luc runs his finger over her cheek, tracing its curve. "We'll just have to make sure we're enough." He wishes once again that they could have given Sam some siblings. A big happy family would have helped Charlotte cope with her homesickness, would have helped her to feel more settled, but it just didn't happen. They even went to the doctor; he said it was certainly the deprivation Charlotte suffered during the occupation that made her periods stop, but he couldn't say why they never came back. He wanted to run some tests, but Charlotte refused, saying they should just make the most of what they had. Jean-Luc didn't like to insist; the subject felt fraught and fragile, so he dropped it.

When their bodies can't take any more heat and they're too tired to swim, they pack up and leave the beach. They pass a street sweeper in blue overalls leaning on a large broom, the bristles nestling a collection of the day's used fun—ice-cream wrappers, cigarette butts, and broken cardboard boxes. He doesn't appear to be in a hurry to get on with the job.

"Weather's 'bout to change." He points up at the fleecy clouds moving in. "Might be in for a storm."

With their eyes they follow the line of his finger, looking up at the clouds gathering momentum. They hurry away to their car. The prominent hood and smooth lines of the dark blue Nash 600 always bring a sense of pride to Jean-Luc. He never imagined owning such a beautiful car, but here in America, anything is possible. He puts the key in the ignition and immediately the music comes on.

"*How much is that doggie in the window?*"

They join in with the lyrics as they pull out.

That evening, the warm air clings to them. A heavy stillness hangs from the leaves, which have ceased to flutter, and the cat lies stretched out, belly exposed, under the shade of the weeping willow. Jean-Luc and Sam are on the front porch, languidly rocking on the swinging seat, trying to catch a little breeze. Charlotte brings cold lemonade in tall glasses, ice cubes clinking. Jean-Luc takes an ice cube and holds it against the back of his neck. It quickly turns to water, trickling down his back, providing only a moment's respite from the California summer heat.

Sounds of *The Ed Sullivan Show* drift over from the open windows of the neighbor's house.

Jean-Luc looks up at the sky. "I wish this storm would hurry up and break."

Chapter Twenty-Six

Santa Cruz, July 4, 1953

CHARLOTTE

I wake too early, anxiety niggling at my subconscious. Obligations for the day swim into my mind. The Caleys are having a barbecue today to celebrate America winning its independence. I've never enjoyed the Fourth of July. It reminds me that this isn't really my home, that American history isn't my history. I guess I'm just feeling homesick. There are days when I do. Sometimes I think I was torn from my home before I was old enough to know what it really meant. It doesn't mean I'm not happy here. How could I not be? The people are friendly, you can buy anything you need, and the quality of life is good. It's just that there's a yearning in my heart sometimes, for home, for my family, for my country.

There's also something about the institutionalized need to celebrate that disturbs me. Maybe it's the pressure to be so damned happy. Big wide smiles all around, burgers and ice cream, Coca-Cola and beer in abundance from noon till after dark. It's exhausting, but no one is allowed to go home before the grand finale of fireworks. That wouldn't be patriotic.

I suppose it reminds me of Bastille Day on July 14. It makes me remember how far I am from home. I can't help wondering how

Maman and Papa will celebrate. Maybe they'll go to Champ de Mars and watch the fireworks light up the Eiffel Tower, or maybe they'll wander along the banks of the Seine. I'd love to go back and visit them, but Jean-Luc isn't keen. "This is our home now, Charlotte. Our life is here," he says. "We have everything. Forget the past."

Sometimes I think of telling him that my "everything" might not be the same as his, but I know it will only end in a pointless argument, and I hate confrontation. The past isn't as easy to forget as that; you can't just shove it into a corner and pretend it's not there. It's always there, a shadow wherever I go, reminding me of what we did.

I look over at the empty space in the bed next to me. He woke even earlier than me today. When I wander into the kitchen, he's at the table, reading the paper, a large cup of coffee in his hand. I know it will be milky, like a kiddie's version of the real thing—bigger and blander. For some reason, this riles me. Why can't he drink proper black coffee, like a real adult?

"Jean-Luc, I don't want to go to the Caleys' today."

He looks up, eyes widening in surprise "What's the matter?"

"I just don't feel like it."

"But we always go. Sam loves it."

"Well, you take him then. I'm not going. I'm not even sure I like them."

"What do you mean?" His voice takes on a sharp edge. "They've been nothing but friendly to us."

"Josh is creepy."

"What?"

"Nothing."

"Come on, Charlotte. We should go."

I glance out the window. "I'm too tired."

He sighs loudly. "I'll take Sam then. What shall I tell them?"

"That I hate the Fourth of July, all that eating and drinking. Why don't we ever celebrate Bastille Day?"

"Why would we? We're not in France."

"Exactly!"

"Exactly what, Charlotte?"

Maybe I need a coffee. I pick up the coffeepot, then put it back down. Coffee will only aggravate me. In truth, I don't know what I want. Maybe a glass of water will cool me down. I turn on the tap, but I don't stop when the glass is full, letting the water flow over my hand. I stare at it, mesmerized, as I soak up its coolness.

I feel Jean-Luc next to me. He reaches over to turn the tap off, then takes the glass out of my hand. "Charlotte, please, what's the matter?"

"I guess I'm just feeling homesick."

I hear the breath leave his lungs, and I wish I hadn't said anything. He'll never understand. Turning my back on him, I walk out onto the porch, slumping onto the swing seat. Of course, I should be more constructive. There are the prospectuses for various translation courses that I've been meaning to go through. If I got trained and had a job, I might feel more settled, like Jean-Luc with his job at the station. He found it so easy to adapt to American ways: drinking beer with the guys, playing baseball with the kids, eating burgers with ketchup, and all with such damned relish. I would have liked to continue with my studies at one of the universities. I know they have courses on French literature, but the universities here are expensive, and it's true, I can read on my own.

He's come out to the porch now. I wish he'd just leave me alone.

"Charlotte," he starts. My heart sinks even lower. I don't need him to be oh so reasonable, and I don't want his opinion. I already know it. "You know I'd like to go back too," he continues. "One day, when we've saved up enough money and the war is further behind us, we could go for a visit. Go and see your parents. Mine too."

My fingers fidget with the edge of the cushion. I don't want this conversation—it always just goes around in circles. A wave of pity suddenly washes over me. He can't help it. He's just being practical—sensible and practical, like he's always been.

"Doesn't it bother you?" I pause, wondering why I can't help antagonizing him this morning. I must have slept badly. "Doesn't it bother you that Sam doesn't have the same culture as us?"

"What do you mean?"

"Well, we're French, and he's never even seen France. He doesn't speak the language. Don't you worry sometimes that home for him is here?"

"No, I don't. His home is with us, and that's all that matters."

I try to believe him, but I can't help feeling that something's missing; that we've missed something vital.

"I wish we'd spoken French to him when we came here. At least then we could have taken him back one day, and he'd have felt more at home. I wanted to read him the French classics in *French*!"

"Charlotte, we've been through this before. We needed to integrate and we had to learn the language too. If we'd carried on in French, we'd have set ourselves apart, become the little French family who escaped the war. We had to put that behind us, make a fresh start. You know what people are like. They'd have thought we were proud and stuck-up."

"I know, I know, but it just seems like a high price to pay. To lose one's culture. Sometimes it makes me feel so...I don't know—just homesick."

Jean-Luc pulls on his earlobe. "Maybe it was easier for me. I don't think I was so attached to France. In fact, I was happy to throw off my culture, my nationality. It felt liberating."

"But what about your family? Your parents?"

"They're happy for me." He pauses. "You're my family now." Reaching forward, he puts his arm around my neck. "You're all I need. You and Sam."

Chapter Twenty-Seven

Santa Cruz, July 10, 1953

JEAN-LUC

Seagulls screech, and the powerful California sun pierces the curtains. Jean-Luc can feel the real world calling to him as he struggles to pull himself up through layers of sleep. Caught in that space between dreaming and waking, he'd like to slip back into the dream. It's the same dream that's been haunting him recently, the one that always leaves him feeling hollow inside, as though he's in the wrong place, living someone else's life, and he wants to know how it will end. There's a baby crying and a woman holding out her arms, waiting. Then he realizes it's his own mother, her dark hair falling over her shoulders, her smile warm. She looks beautiful. She turns to speak to him, and that's when he wakes. He wishes he could stay in the dream to hear what she's going to say.

The early-morning sun sends slants of light across the room. He'd prefer to have shutters on the windows; he's sure the bright sun here isn't helping his sleep. He always wakes too early, but can never catch up on his tiredness. Still, there's no point lying there worrying. He may as well get up.

It's only six, but he puts the coffee on and starts on last night's dishes. He's running the tap when he hears a car winding its way up their street.

He leans forward, his forehead touching the glass as he follows the car with his eyes. It's getting nearer, slowing down. He can see it clearly now. It's blue and white. Taking a deep breath, he steps back, away from the window, trying to calm his breathing. A police car? At six o'clock in the morning? A shiver starts in the back of his neck, then shoots over his head. He hears the car drawing to a stop and somehow he knows it's parked behind the oak tree. He stands to the side of the window, peeking, waiting to see who's in the car.

Two officers emerge from the front. Then he recognizes Bradley's stocky frame as he unfolds himself from the back seat.

Charlotte and Sam are still sleeping. He would hate them to be woken up like this, so he leaves the kitchen and goes to the hall, unlocking the front door, opening it a fraction. Waiting.

The officers are looking at their watches. One of them shrugs, then they separate to let Bradley take his place in the middle as they walk down the garden path toward him.

His heart thumping in his ears, he opens the door farther, showing them he's there before they have a chance to ring the bell.

The three men look surprised to be facing him so suddenly.

"Good morning, Mr. Bow-Champ." Bradley looks at him from under bushy eyebrows.

"Hello." Jean-Luc holds his breath.

"We'd like you to come into the station for further questioning."

Jean-Luc reaches out for the door, gripping it for support. The breath he's been holding comes back, thudding in his ears. "Why?"

Suddenly they're inside. The shorter officer closes the front door behind them. Jean-Luc steps back. They're in his house now. How could he have let this happen?

"Mr. Bow-Champ, this isn't the right place to talk. You need to come to the station."

Jean-Luc turns away from them, looking at the staircase, thinking of Charlotte and Sam sleeping. He turns around to face the men. "Do you mind waiting outside? I don't want my family to be disturbed."

The taller officer opens the front door and they back out. "Ten minutes."

Turning back to the staircase, Jean-Luc grips the banisters, pulling himself up one stair at a time. What do they know? His heart beats faster as he imagines what they might have discovered.

When he enters the bedroom, he sees that Charlotte is still fast asleep, a soft hiss coming from her mouth. He doesn't want to wake her. There's still a chance he can sort it out. He thinks of leaving her a note, but he doesn't know what he could tell her. Turning away, he pulls on yesterday's pants, throws on yesterday's shirt, but doesn't bother with a tie.

Without a word, he follows the policemen out to their car. He sees the curtains twitch at Marge's kitchen window. Has she been watching?

Fifteen minutes later, they pull up in front of the police station. They take the stairs, then walk down a long corridor, past empty cells and into a small room containing a gray table and four plastic chairs.

"Sit down." The short officer removes a cigarette pack from his breast pocket, takes one out and throws the pack over to his partner. They light up. The tall one sits down, flicking ash into an aluminum ashtray. The other flicks his onto the floor.

"Hey, come on, Jack. Think of the cleaning lady."

"Just keeping her in a job, man."

Jean-Luc watches them exhaling clouds of smoke. They're taking their time, as though they're enjoying it.

"Why am I here?" He's done his best to comply, to stay calm, but now he needs to know.

Bradley finally sits down, his hands on his knees as he leans forward, facing him. "Were you aware that someone has been searching for you for the last nine years?"

Jean-Luc shakes his head. His throat is tight. No words will come. He can't even swallow.

"Her name is Sarah Laffitte. She's Sam's mother."

Part Three

Chapter Twenty-Eight

Paris, May 2, 1944

SARAH

Crouching down, her back against the bed, Sarah mouths to herself, "Breathe." But instead of a calm breath, a frantic moan rises up from her belly. She wants to throw up but doesn't have the strength. Rivulets of sweat drip into her eyes, stinging them. Wiping them away, she quickly returns her hand to her hardened abdomen, hopelessly imagining she can ease the pain that way.

David puts his hand on her damp hair. "You should lie down, Sarah. Please!"

"I... I can't move."

"You have to get onto the bed." He places his hands under her arms, pulling her up toward him. She bites her bottom lip hard, blocking the scream that rises in her throat. When she lands on the bed, she rolls over onto one side, curling her knees up, groaning. "Is the midwife on her way?" she gasps in her next heavy breath.

"No one would come."

"No, David! Please, make someone come!"

"Sarah. It will be okay. We can do this ourselves. I know what to do. I've prepared everything."

Three short, sharp knocks on the front door followed by a pause and then a fourth make her swallow her next protest. She sees the flash of fear in David's eyes. Only one person knocks like that—their trusted friend Jacques. Without a word, David leaves the bedroom.

She forces herself over onto her back, staring at the ceiling, trying to breathe with the pain. Not now, she begs silently. Please, not now.

She hears the front door open, then Jacques' hushed, urgent voice. "You have to leave, tonight."

"Tonight? We can't! Sarah's in labor!" The panic she hears in David's voice sets off the next contraction. It lifts her off the bed with its force, like a terrible energy struggling to be set free.

"Your names are on the list. They're coming for you. Tonight."

She hears David's desperate groan. The pain is still with her, but it is almost secondary to what will happen now.

He returns to the bedroom, closes the door behind him, and leans against it. "Did you hear?"

She nods, unable to speak as the next contraction sears through her, silencing her with its power. Tears mingle with the sweat running down her face. Then David is next to her on the bed, and she feels the coolness of the wet towel he places on her forehead. She reaches out for his hand, ready to grip it tightly as she waits for the next wave.

"Sarah, it's going to be all right. I promise you. I'm going to look after you." His face contorts as she squeezes his hand with all her might.

The contractions are really close now, and she stares up at the ceiling, praying, "Please, God, make it be quick." She releases his hand so he can check on what's happening. Her breath comes in rapid waves now; she can hear herself panting.

"I can see the head! Push now!"

Gritting her teeth, she pushes with all her might. Again and again. She's exhausted, but now she can feel it coming. She gives one last big push.

"Is it all right? David?" She worries that the nightmares she's been having about giving birth to a deformed baby have come true.

"He's perfect." She hears the crack in his voice, and relief washes over her.

"Thank you, God," she whispers.

She hears the snip of scissors and realizes he's cut the cord. Turning to look at him, she sees him holding the tiny new life in his big hands. All her pain has gone.

"Take him. I need to check the afterbirth." David leans forward, putting the baby, still wet, on her chest. She touches his head, stroking the sparse hair, then looks down at his crumpled face. Dark eyes dart around the room, unfocused but learning. They meet hers for a brief second, and she feels a tightening in her womb, an invisible bond being formed. With her fingertips she caresses his little body all over, marveling at the soft, flawless flesh. More than anything, she wants this child to live. She holds him to her breast and prays.

Chapter Twenty-Nine

Paris, May 2, 1944

SARAH

David hands Sarah a glass of water, sitting on the bed next to her. They look down at the baby, sniffling and suckling, searching out her nipple. She feels him grip on for a second, then he loses it again. She knows it will take a day or two for her milk to come in and tries not to worry about it.

David shifts nearer to her. "This moment is precious. The three of us together, here in our home. Whatever happens, we must remember this." He closes his eyes, resting his head back against the wall, and breathes in deeply. She realizes the birth must have been exhausting for him too. All that responsibility resting on his shoulders, and only having seen childbirth from a textbook. Leaning into him, she silently soaks up his smell, musky and slightly sweaty.

He kisses her on the head. "We have to leave when it gets dark, about six."

"What's the time now?" She's lost all sense of time, has no idea whether it's still morning or already the afternoon.

"It's nearly twelve. Jacques said he'd come back about four."

"Four hours. I need to sleep before we go. I'm so tired."

"Of course. I'll make something to eat and pack up a few things."

The baby's eyes are closed now, his mouth slightly ajar. David lifts him off Sarah's chest, holding him against his own, one large hand supporting his tiny back. She understands his need to have him close. Before she lets herself fall asleep, she looks around their bedroom, knowing it might be the last time she sees it. Despite the danger they're in, she feels a sense of peace as she looks at the large oak chest of drawers that used to belong to her parents; at the painting above it of Étretat cliff and beach, the pointed rock jutting out from the sea. They went there for their honeymoon, and David bought the painting from a local artist. It was a perfect day; they swam in the sea, then climbed the cliff up to the church, where they sat on the grass outside, snuggling into each other. "I want to get you something to remember this day by," he murmured in her ear. And then, when they wandered back down into the tiny village, they stumbled across a local artist's studio. The painting was more than they could afford, but they managed to barter the artist down. After all, they were on their honeymoon.

She lets her eyelids close as she drifts off, happy in her memories. Everything will be all right. God will look after them.

The next thing she knows, David is gently stroking her cheek. "Here, I've made you something to eat." Cradling in one hand the sleeping baby, now dressed in a clean white smock, with the other he passes her a plate of small roast potatoes, carrot puree, and a whole leg of confit de canard.

Her eyes grow wide. "Where on earth did you get this?"

He smiles, touching his nose. "Never you mind. I've been saving it for today. You need to get your strength back."

She kisses him quickly on the cheek, then lifts the plate up. As she breathes in the aroma of hot food, she realizes she is starving, and attacks the duck with her knife and fork.

Suddenly she puts her cutlery down. "Where's yours?" How could she not have noticed he wasn't eating?

"I ate earlier in the kitchen."

She knows he's lying, and after another few mouthfuls, she puts her fork down. "I'm quite full," she lies. "I'm not used to eating so much. Will you help me?"

Raising the fork with a piece of duck on the end, she feeds him, and together they share the meal, the baby fast asleep in David's arms. When they've finished, he takes the plate from her, leaning away to put it down on the floor. She kisses him again. "Thank you. That was delicious."

"Yes, now your milk will taste of duck."

"That will be nicer than Swedish turnip, dust, and acorns."

The baby twitches in his sleep, his hands stretching out like starfish. She takes one of them, spreading it out over her own, looking at his tiny fingers, his perfect nails. "Shall we name him after my father?"

"Samuel. Of course." David leans forward, kissing the baby on his head. "He's got long fingers. Maybe he'll grow up to be a violinist, like his mother." He scratches his beard as if thinking something over. "I remember the first time I saw you. You were playing the violin in that orchestra. It was the way you looked so intently absorbed." He pauses. "I wanted you to look at me like that." He grins. "And then one day you did. Though it took awhile."

"Yes." She smiles. "All those Sunday concerts you had to attend!"

"I loved them."

"And I loved seeing you there in the audience, knowing why you were there."

He laughs. "Do you remember when you finally invited me to your home, and your father quizzed me on violin concertos?"

"Yes. You didn't have a clue."

"Do you remember what he said? 'You seem to be more interested in the violinist than the violin.'"

"That was his sense of humor." Tears sting her eyes.

"I know how much you miss him."

Gazing down at her new son, she blinks her tears away. "Do you think Samuel looks like him?"

"Your father?" He strokes the baby's head. "Yes, he has his high forehead, but I think he has the same shape eyes you and your mother have." He pauses. "He's got my father's chin, though; see how it sticks out. He's going to be a stubborn one."

"Wouldn't they love to see him now? They would be so proud." She pauses. "Do you think they will one day? Will we ever find all the people we've lost?" She runs a finger over Samuel's forehead. "Where have they gone?"

"I don't know, Sarah. But we have to keep hoping. Keep praying."

"What if we get caught now? They'd take Samuel from us. I know they would. They'd send us to a work camp and put him in an orphanage." Her eyes fill up at the thought.

"Sarah, we won't get caught. We're survivors."

She looks at him, wondering what makes him think he's more of a survivor than the next Jewish person.

Loud footsteps on the stairs outside make her jump. She grabs David's hand. "What if they come for us now?"

He squeezes her hand. "Jacques is looking out. No one will come now. You know they always come in the night or early morning."

"Not always." They are never safe. It's something she'll never get used to—the constant fear. The knot of anxiety in her stomach has become permanent, but at least it's helped kill her appetite.

"Do you remember our first meal together?" David squeezes her hand again.

She knows he's trying to distract her, and he's right. Her worrying won't help anyone.

She closes her eyes, casting her mind back, doing her best to dismiss thoughts of the present. "I spent all day getting ready."

"Did you?"

"Yes." She opens her eyes, looking into his. "But then just before going out to meet you, I took off the high heels Maman had lent me, rubbed the rouge from my cheeks, and wiped away the lipstick."

"Why?" David looks genuinely confused.

"It just didn't feel like me."

He takes her hand, bringing it to his lips. "I love the way you dress. You always look comfortable. I mean…"

Light laughter bubbles up in her throat. "Comfortable? That doesn't sound very…"

"Sexy?" he finishes for her.

She blushes. He doesn't usually use words like that.

"There's nothing more attractive than someone who's *bien dans leur peau*—happy with who they are. I always felt that with you."

She takes his hand, kissing his fingers. "I never felt I had anything to prove with you. You never judged me or asked me why I had done this or that and not something else. It was as though you accepted me for who I was."

"I didn't want you any other way."

The baby squirms in David's arms, wrinkling his nose. Sarah reaches out, caressing his cheek, and his face becomes smooth and calm again.

"He's just checking that you're still here." David smiles.

"I'll always be here for him. I'll never leave him." Fresh tears spring to her eyes as she realizes she might not be able to keep such a promise. Not now.

As if he can read her mind, David strokes the back of her head, leaning down to whisper in her ear. "We'll keep him safe."

She nods, silent tears slipping down her cheeks.

Jacques arrives at four on the dot. Sarah hears him talking as soon as the front door clicks shut. "We've found somewhere for you to stay, just for a night or two, then we'll get you somewhere better. It's over in Le Marais, Rue du Temple."

"Thank you, Jacques. I don't know how we'll ever be able to repay you. Do you have time to come and see our son?" Sarah hears the pride in David's voice, and it makes her smile. He's going to be such a wonderful father.

"Of course! And how is the mother doing?"

David brings Jacques into the bedroom. First he bends down to kiss Sarah on the cheek, then he lifts back the little woolen blanket.

Sarah watches as Jacques' eyes mist over. He looks at her, then takes a step backward. "Don't worry. I'm not going to let the bastards get him."

Sarah smiles a sad smile. "I know you won't, Jacques."

"I'm sorry I can't stay longer."

"Of course. You must go now." David sees him out of the apartment.

It's a long way for Sarah to walk to Le Marais, so they take the Métro at Passy, planning to change at Étoile. David has insisted on bringing her Amati violin. "Some things are too precious to leave behind. It was your father's before you, and his father's before that. It's not just a violin. It's your history." So she carries Samuel while he carries a briefcase and the instrument, as if they are just on their way to play music at a friend's house. Not running for their lives.

They rarely step out the door these days, and it feels strange to be out. The streets are deserted; only a few soldiers strut up and down, rifles sticking upward. David and Sarah hug the buildings, staying in the shadows, changing their path as soon as they spot a soldier. But Sarah is exhausted. Her lungs ache with every rasping breath; she just can't seem to get enough air. And her abdomen contracts painfully with every step.

When they finally get to the Métro, they are relieved to see there are no soldiers at the gates. They board the last carriage, reserved for Jews. It's empty apart from one old man, a rabbi. His head creaks up as they sit down, like a tortoise peeping out of its shell. "*Bonsoir, madame; bonsoir, monsieur.*" He smiles a toothless smile.

"*Bonsoir, monsieur.*"

He leans forward. "Be careful. They're at Étoile tonight, like a swarm of locusts."

"Thank you." David nods.

"Is that a baby?" The man stretches his head farther forward, toward Sarah.

"Yes, he's ours." David smiles.

The man nods solemnly. "He's very small. How old is he?"

"About six hours."

The man coughs, his eyes brimming over. "Six hours! You had to move." Standing up on trembling legs, he places a heavily wrinkled hand on the baby's head and raises the other hand to cover his eyes. He murmurs a prayer in Hebrew. Then he sits back down again, closing his eyes. When he opens them, they shine brightly under the folds of skin. "God will look after your child. Do not worry. But don't get off at Étoile. It's infested."

They do as he suggests, changing at the next stop, Trocadéro, then again at Marbeuf, finally leaving the Métro at Hotel de Ville. Sarah's head spins as they get off, terrified that they'll be stopped. Her breath comes quickly and it feels damp between her legs; she worries that she's still bleeding, but says nothing.

Finally, they reach the address that Jacques gave them—a tall building next to what used to be a boulangerie. David leans on the heavy wooden door, pushing it open and holding it for Sarah. As soon as they walk into the courtyard, it's obvious that the Boches have been there. Shutters swing open and upturned plants lie strewn across the ground, their roots exposed. Items of clothing blow about in the gentle evening breeze—a solitary beige stocking, a baby's undergarment, and a torn man's shirt. A whisk of wind picks the stocking up, blowing it onto a plant lying horizontally. Bending down, Sarah removes it and stands the plant back up in its pot. It's like the place has been raped.

"David, we can't stay here!"

"We have no choice. They've already been here and the place has been looted. There's nothing of any interest left. We'll be safe." He looks around, and she follows his gaze, wondering if someone is watching. It's eerily quiet.

"Come on." He moves toward the door on the left-hand side of the courtyard. "It's on the third floor."

She just wants to lie down. As she climbs the stairs, she feels a trickle of something slide down her inner thigh. Her head spins with every step. Gripping the solid wooden banister, she pulls herself up, but a sharp pain shoots through her abdomen, making her double over.

David puts the violin down, using his free hand to pull her up, but she doesn't have the strength to move.

"Sarah, I'm going to take Samuel to the apartment. I'll come back for you."

"No! We mustn't leave him alone." Glancing around, she has the feeling she's being watched. Why would the whole block of apartments have been evacuated? They wouldn't all have been Jews living there. The dull walls stare silently back at her. Then she notices bullet holes. They must have put up a fight. That could be why they evacuated the whole building; maybe there were some Résistance fighters involved. She shudders to think where they will be now.

David takes Samuel from her and helps her up, leaving the violin and the briefcase on the stairs as he leads her slowly to the flat two floors up.

"Can I have some water?" She looks around for the kitchen, but the cupboards have been blown to smithereens and the oven door hangs off on one hinge; drawers lie upturned, their contents strewn across the floor, and blood is splattered across the walls. She looks away, swallowing the bile in her throat. "It doesn't matter," she says.

David leads her into a small bedroom. Then, taking a key out of his pocket, he puts it into a tiny lock in the wall that she hadn't even seen. He pushes the camouflaged door open, shining a small flashlight around. She holds her breath, half expecting to find hideaways crouched inside, but it is empty. They creep in. It's just a cupboard really—barely enough room to lie down. But at least it's empty and doesn't smell of anything, except dust.

"I'll get a mattress." He hands Samuel back to her. "Wait here."

She collapses onto the floor with the baby in her arms, too exhausted to answer.

Chapter Thirty

Paris, May 3, 1944

SARAH

Samuel cries softly in his sleep. Sarah would love to roll over and fall back into a deep slumber. The healing power of sleep seems to have soothed her stomach cramps. But she knows her baby must be getting hungry, and she wants to feed him before his soft cries get any louder. It's important that they make as little noise as possible, but it's not only that. She can't bear the thought of him crying. Suffering. It's what scares her the most. She tries not to think about it, but she's seen it happen. Babies, children wrenched from their mothers.

In the pitch black of the tiny room, she picks him up, shuffling herself into a sitting position. It's so warm, she's slept naked. With her finger she parts his lips, helping him find her nipple. He doesn't latch on straightaway, but starts and stops, squirming, as though he's frustrated. She's still worried she doesn't have enough milk.

How lucky she was to have a straightforward birth; only the pain was a shock. *But how long will their luck last*? They should have been safe in their apartment in the affluent residential 16th arrondissement. For goodness' sake, no one even knew they were Jewish till they had to wear that damned yellow star, like a gaping wound, or a target. In retrospect, she wishes she hadn't conformed, wishes she hadn't worn it, but in some perverse way it would have felt like cowardice *not* to wear it. After all, she isn't ashamed to be Jewish; it's her heritage—where she came from. No one will ever be able to make her feel ashamed of that. So she sewed it on as ordered, and went out, her head held high. How naive she was. It immediately changed who she was. People looked at the star, and then at her.

The first time she took the Métro after the star had become obligatory, the controller spoke harshly to her. "Last carriage, mademoiselle." So she got off at the next stop, moving back to the final carriage, swallowing the hard lump of self-pity in her throat.

A week later, her father was arrested for having stapled his star on instead of sewing it. He thought it would be easier to transfer it to other clothes that way. He was spotted by a soldier and sent straight to Drancy—no trial, no inquest, no chance of appeal. They received letters for the next six months, and they lovingly sent packages of food and words of support. Then nothing, and there was no trace of him, as though he'd never existed. She blinks back the tears that spring to her eyes every time she thinks of him.

Next to her, David doesn't stir. He must be exhausted. But she's so thirsty, and hungry too. Maybe that's what's stopping her milk from coming. "David," she whispers. "David, are you awake?"

"No. Why?"

"Can you get me some water, please?"

"How's Samuel?" he mumbles.

"He's hungry, but I don't think I've got enough milk."

"Don't worry. You will." She feels him sit up. "I'll get some water."

"Thank you. I'm so thirsty."

He takes the flashlight and leaves their little room.

Sarah feels like weeping as the baby squirms and moans, latching on one minute, coming off the next. What if she can't feed him properly?

David comes back a few minutes later, handing her a large glass of water. "It's three in the morning, you know. Our little boy has slept five hours. That's pretty good for a newborn. The other good news is that they didn't break all the glasses. Drink this while I go and have a little scavenge."

Gratefully she gulps the water. She was so thirsty. That must have been what was wrong. Surely her milk will start coming in now.

While David is gone, she tries her best to relax, telling herself that they will be safe here, that this madness will be over soon, that one day life will return to normal. They just have to hang on a little longer.

David comes back and she hears the excitement in his voice. "Guess what I found?"

"What?"

"They had food stashed in the toilet tank."

"Is it safe to eat?"

"Yes. It's all conserves. Black currant jam, tuna, olives, pickled peppers." He pauses, then, like a magician, produces a plate covered in food.

Together they share the odd assortment. "I love tuna with black currant jam." Sarah squeezes his hand. "Thank you. I don't know why we never tried it before."

While she tucks into the food, she holds the baby on her nipple with one hand, but she stops worrying about him feeding. After a while, she realizes he's stopped squirming, and she can tell he's swallowing. He's drinking. Leaning back against the wall, she enjoys this new sensation as she feels her milk coming in. Everything is going to be all right.

Later, she dozes off, fully content and with a full stomach for a change.

She must be in a deep sleep, because she dreams someone is tapping at the window, begging to be let in. She's just about to open the window when she wakes up.

There *is* a tapping. But it's not coming from the window. Her pulse jumps. It's coming from the cupboard wall.

"David!" she whispers urgently, shaking him awake.

"What is it?"

"Shh. Listen. Someone's out there."

He goes silent. Sarah can almost see his ears prick up.

She squeezes his arm tight. There it is again. A soft tapping. Three short taps, followed by one longer one.

"It's Jacques." David reaches out to open the door, while Sarah lets out the breath she's been holding.

"It's okay," Jacques whispers. "The coast is clear. You can come out."

Jacques has brought them supplies; mostly food, a few undergarments for the baby, and some diapers. "My wife wanted me to bring more, but I couldn't carry too much in case I was stopped." He pauses. "You'll have to move again tomorrow."

"Why?" David frowns. "It would be good for Sarah to rest for a few days."

"I know, but it's too risky. I'm worried we have a traitor among our group. The Boches are finding our safe houses too quickly, too easily. I can't help thinking someone's giving them tip-offs. Only myself and two other people I trust know that you're here, so you should be all right. But it's safer for you to move." He smiles. "And this time, I have a house for you in the country. It's out in Saint-Germain-en-Laye. Not too far, but you'll have to go by car. I'm getting it organized. You just need to be ready to leave tomorrow afternoon."

David puts his hand on Jacques' shoulder. "Thank you, Jacques. We'll never forget what you've done for us."

Jacques doesn't say a word; he just covers David's hand with his own.

Chapter Thirty-One

Paris, May 4, 1944

SARAH

Something wakes Sarah. Though the cupboard is dark, she knows it's early morning. Her first thought is for her baby. It's like she has been given a gift—the best, most exciting gift ever—and as soon as she wakes, she wants to see him, touch him, check that he's real—that she didn't dream it all.

She can't see him in the dark cupboard, but she can sense him lying next to her, can hear his light, regular breathing. Instinctively, she knows he's fast asleep. A creaking noise makes her jump. It sounds like someone outside on the stairs.

"David," she whispers. "Did you hear something?"

"No." He rolls over in his sleep, reaching a hand out for her. She takes it, intertwining her fingers with his, telling herself it must have been her imagination, that she should just go back to sleep, while the baby's sleeping. She must keep up her strength for what lies ahead. They could be moving every day now. But she doesn't feel safe knowing that *they* are out there looking for them.

A pounding thud shakes the wall. She lets go of David's hand, pulling herself up to a sitting position, sweat breaking out on her forehead. She picks the baby up, holding him tight against her chest.

David is sitting too. She can't see him, but she can feel the rigidity of his body, like a statue next to her, both of them willing themselves to turn to stone.

She hears doors opening and slamming, heavy boots running upstairs, commands shouted in German. "*Schnell!*" "*Bewege dich schneller!*"

She wants to whisper something to David, something about the hidden door, about the key he used to open it. Has he locked it from the inside? Are they locked in? Will they be found? But she hardly dares breathe, let alone whisper. She wishes she could see him. If only she could see him, she would feel safer.

A door slams loudly—more loudly than the others. It sounds like it's the front door to the apartment. She hears David's sharp intake of air. Silently, she prays: Please, God, protect our son. I'll never ask for anything more.

She hears loud German voices. David reaches out for her in the dark, putting his arm around her. He holds her tight, and she holds their baby tighter as they sit there trembling.

"*Hier drin!*" a German voice shouts.

Sarah doesn't understand what it means, but she knows the voice is right outside the cupboard door now. She grips Samuel, praying again in her head: Please, God, keep him safe.

He's still fast asleep, and she wonders that he hasn't woken up with all the commotion. Then he moans softly. She freezes, every sinew and muscle taut. Placing her fingers over his lips, she desperately tries to communicate to him the need to be silent. Frantically she puts him to her breast, but he turns his head away, falling asleep again.

She listens to the loud conversation in German being conducted on the other side of the thin wall. How she wishes she spoke the language now. David's fingers dig painfully into her shoulder, but she doesn't flinch. She almost welcomes the pain as a distraction from the terror mounting within her.

Samuel squirms in her arms, whimpering softly. Maybe she's holding him too tightly, like David's holding her. She relaxes her grip, consciously letting out the breath she's been keeping in. He mustn't feel her tension. It might make him cry.

His whimpering goes up a notch. Her heart freezes. She pushes him up against her breast, trying to get him to latch on, to be quiet. But he pulls his head back, letting out a cry. Loud and sharp.

A huge crash reverberates against the door. Then another, and another. Big black boots come smashing into the cupboard.

Chapter Thirty-Two

Paris, May 29, 1944

SARAH

The mice scurry back and forth, night and day, though goodness knows what they find to eat. Maybe it's the stench of human filth that attracts them, that keeps them there. Sarah smelled it as soon as she entered the women's block. It reminded her of the stables when she used to go riding as a child—the stagnant damp smell of sweat and decay.

She doesn't leave Samuel, not for a minute, terrified that he will be easy prey for such scavengers. The closeness she feels to him comforts her, and she remembers the rabbi's words on the Métro: "God will look after your child." She holds on to this thin thread of hope, telling herself it was a prophecy. It helps cushion her from her fear.

Forty women are crammed into a small rectangular room, squashed onto bunks with only straw to soften them, but they are kind to her when they see she has a tiny baby. They always make sure she has enough water to drink, and some of them even share their food parcels. She has nothing to give them in return, just a small smile. She finds she can't talk. Talking makes her tired, and she needs to save all her energy to feed Samuel. That's all that matters now. Keeping him alive.

There are only two toilets at Drancy, for the thousands of prisoners—one for women and one for men—and they can only go at designated times. Every time she goes, she scans the faces in the long queue, hoping to see David, but she never does. And every day she looks at the list for the next transport, terrified that one day she will see their names there. If only they can hang on, she thinks. This war won't last forever.

But on May 29, their names appear on the list for deportation the very next morning: David Laffitte, Sarah Laffitte, Baby Laffitte. They didn't even ask his name. As though they never imagined he might need one.

Chapter Thirty-Three

Paris, May 30, 1944

JEAN-LUC

Jean-Luc is in a deep sleep when he hears the shouts. "*Raus! Raus!* Time to get up!" First he thinks it's a dream; then, as he comes up through layers of sleep, he realizes the voices are coming from right outside his room.

"Philippe!" he says. "Philippe, wake up!" He feels around the wall, looking for the light switch.

Suddenly their door is kicked open and light from the corridor comes flooding through. "*Achtung!* Get up."

He throws his pajamas off and struggles into his overalls. He's aware of Philippe doing the same. The guard stands by, waiting, then pushes them out to the elevator. The other four men are already squashed into it. "Problem in train," the guard states as he squeezes himself in with them. "Stuck."

When they step outside, it's still pitch-black and cold, no sign yet of the rising sun. The six workers sit in silence as the truck speeds through the dark streets. They're finally going to see a train. Now he'll know if they really are cattle wagons. He guesses they must have loaded the train before they realized it was stuck, so this time he might see the prisoners with his own eyes.

His stomach rumbles loudly and Frédéric looks over at him. "Do you think we'll get any breakfast?"

"Doubt it." Xavier shakes his head. "They'll want that train to get going as soon as possible."

"Yes, before day breaks." Frédéric looks at his watch. "It's only five o'clock."

"*Merde!*" Marcel looks up. "No wonder I'm tired."

The truck draws to an abrupt halt. "*Achtung!*" The guard jumps out and they hurry out after him.

When they reach the platform, they stop dead in their tracks, Frédéric crashing into the back of Jean-Luc. "Oh my God!"

"What the hell?" Marcel puts his hand on Jean-Luc's shoulder as though to steady himself.

They hear screaming, shouting, crying coming from the cattle train sitting on the line, the doors closed.

"Move on! Move on!" The guard behind pushes them forward with his stick. Jean-Luc feels it prodding him in the back. He resists the urge to turn around, to snatch it from him and shove it in his damn face. Instead he moves forward, stepping over items of clothing strewn across the platform: coats, hats, handbags. As he stares at the train, he sees a long, thin hand reaching out from a narrow slit at the top of a car, then another, and another, clutching scraps of paper. The hands open, releasing the papers, which blow away in the breeze. He stops to pick one up, but he can't make out the writing in the semi-darkness. The only light comes from a huge beam focused on the train. He shoves the scrap of paper into his pocket, guessing it's probably a letter for someone—a loved one. He has no doubts left now. These people are heading toward their deaths.

A hand pushes him forward. "*Aussehen!* Look!" A guard stands behind him, shining a flashlight at the tracks. Jean-Luc follows the beam. Immediately he sees the problem: a wheel has fallen into the gap between two tracks. The fishplate that normally holds them together lies open. He doesn't know how they will be able to lift the wheel back onto the tracks. He turns to look behind him. Frédéric's face shines out in the half-light, and Jean-Luc sees a twitch of a smile playing on his lips. Has Frédéric done this? He hopes he has. But what can they do now? He looks around at the soldiers and guards on the platform; there are many, maybe as many as forty. And they all have guns. There are dogs too, snarling and straining at their leashes. It's hopeless.

The hand pushes Jean-Luc again in the back. "See problem?" But Jean-Luc is frozen to the spot. The hand pushes him again. "Look!"

He turns to the angry guard. "What do you want me to do?"

"Fix it. Put train back."

"I can't. The fishplate is broken. We'll need to unload the train and lift it off the tracks to get the lines back together."

"What?" The guard's frown grows deeper.

Another guard approaches, speaking in German; it sounds like a translation of Jean-Luc's words. The first one shakes his head. "No descend train. No unload."

"Impossible! It's too heavy!" Jean-Luc puts his hands up in the air to show the hopelessness of this idea.

"Okay. Okay." The first guard disappears, coming back a minute later with a group of unhealthy-looking men, all bones and hollows of whiteness.

"No!" Jean-Luc looks at the small group of diminished men. It simply won't work; any fool can see that. A larger group of men approaches, and the six workmen step back, leaving them to argue loudly in German.

"*Ja*, unload train!" Someone shouts the command. Immediately, bolts are pushed open, doors slide backward on runners, and prisoners come tumbling out onto the platform. They cry and shout names as they reach their arms out for each other.

Then a shot rings out. "Quiet!"

The noise subsides, crying and shouting turning to whimpering and moaning. But the babies among the prisoners won't listen to the German commands, nor their mothers trying to hush them, and a background noise of wailing continues.

Another shot rings out. The sound of the dogs barking reaches out into the night. "I said quiet!"

A body collapses to the ground. More screaming. Another shot. Then it goes almost quiet, the only sound now the dogs. The soldiers stride up and down the platform, waving their guns, shouting out commands in German, while still more people come tumbling out of the wagon.

"My God, how many of them are there?" Frédéric touches Jean-Luc's elbow.

"There must be about a hundred just in this wagon!"

The soldiers herd the prisoners with guns and sticks toward the back of the platform.

Jean-Luc still can't move. The crowd of prisoners pushes past him, avoiding the hard blows from the soldiers' sticks. Someone shoves a piece of paper into his hand. More pieces of paper are thrust at him. And still he doesn't move. He's never felt so helpless in his whole life. He wants to shout, "Stop!" He wants to turn the soldiers' guns on them. But he is paralyzed, looking on in disbelief. He sees them open another wagon. Hundreds more people come stumbling out. The noise level rises again as they cling to one another, crying and shouting.

Then he feels a hand pulling on the collar of his overalls. He looks down to see a young woman with bright green eyes. Frantically she pulls his head down toward her mouth. "Who are you? You're not a prisoner."

He holds her around the waist so she won't get swept away by the throng. He whispers in her ear. "I'm a railroad worker. Do you want me to take a message to someone?"

"No." She's crying, tears streaming down her face. He wants to hold on to her, not let her go. He turns to the side, protecting her from the surging crowd. It's getting noisier again as more people come stumbling out of the car. He waits for the next shot to be fired.

She puts her arm around his neck, her lips next to his ear. He wants to wipe her tears away, but he knows she's trying to tell him something. "Please," she says. He feels something being pushed up against his chest. Something warm and soft. He looks down.

A stubby nose pokes out from layers of cloth, and dark eyes open, looking straight at him. The background noises seem to fade away as the infant gazes at him solemnly.

"Please, take my baby!"

Chapter Thirty-Four

Paris, May 30, 1944

JEAN-LUC

"His name's Samuel." The tears continue to stream down the woman's face. "Take him!"

Jean-Luc tries to step back, but the crowd is thick behind him too. "No!" He shakes his head. "I can't!"

But she pushes the bundle farther into his chest, her chin set hard and determined. A large man knocks into them, moving her away from him. Jean-Luc feels the distance between them opening up. She's letting go. If he doesn't hold on to the baby, it'll fall, be trampled. He raises one hand, gripping it, and with the other he reaches out for her, but the crowd has already swallowed her up. He searches out her bright green eyes in the sea of people. But he can't see her.

People move around him as he stands there rooted to the spot. The crowd is thinning out now, the soldiers on the periphery getting nearer. He has to hide the baby. With his left hand supporting the bundle, he squeezes his right hand down in front of it, loosening the buttons on his overalls. He shoves the baby inside, then does the buttons up again. He realizes it has made no sound, but he can feel the heat spreading from it, warming his chest. Indecision floods his mind, panic flaring at the base of his spine. What the hell is he supposed to do now?

He looks around. The surge of prisoners is almost clear of the train. He'll soon be exposed. He moves toward them, pushing himself into the throng, trying to lose himself among them.

The stationmaster's house! He should head there. He has to shove an old man out of the way as he pushes through. Two women clinging together block his path. He sidesteps them as he moves quickly back down the platform.

Another shot rings out, and for a moment the crowd seems to stop. Then it surges forward again. Keeping his head down, Jean-Luc keeps on walking. He pushes the door of the stationmaster's house open. It is empty. What now? Think! Time is everything. He goes up the stairs as fast as his injured leg will allow him. He doesn't know what to do, where to go.

The bathrooms are on the second floor. He goes in and closes the door silently behind hm. He could hide here while he decides how to get the hell out. There's a back door to the station through the rear of this house. It's usually guarded, but with all the chaos it might not be right now. He looks out the window; it faces out back, and all he sees is darkness.

He's just about to leave when he hears footsteps coming up the stairs. He glances at the cubicles, wondering if he should hide in one, but he's too late. The door swings open and a soldier walks in.

"*Verdammt noch mal was machst du da?*" The Boche frowns at him. "What are you doing here? This toilet is for Germans only. *Raus!*"

The baby lets out a cry.

"What's that?" The Boche's frown grows deeper.

Jean-Luc is quick. Taking his right hand off the baby, he lunges forward, grabbing the pistol from the man's open holster. It's lighter than he thought it would be. He shakes it to get a better grip. It's the first time he's held a pistol, and he has to look down for a second to check where the trigger is. Once he's got it, he puts his finger on it, careful not to press it. Not yet. He points it at the German, his left hand holding the baby against his chest.

The Boche turns white. "*Dafür könntest du erschossen werden!* You'll be shot for this!"

Jean-Luc doesn't move. "Take your clothes off."

"What?"

He pushes the pistol against the man's forehead. "Take off your clothes! *Schnell!*"

As the soldier fumbles his way out of his uniform, the baby's crying grows louder. Jean-Luc mustn't let it distract him. The next few minutes are vital. With the pistol trained on his prisoner, he moves over to the washing area. He pulls the baby out, placing it in a sink. The baby's cries turn frantic now that he's lost the human contact.

Jean-Luc has to block out the crying as he puts both hands on the pistol. It's time to make a decision. More shots ring out from outside. They'll be looking for him now. He has to be quick. His finger on the trigger trembles and his heart beats faster in anticipation. It's best not to leave any witnesses. But first he needs that uniform, and he doesn't want blood on it.

Soon the uniform lies at the soldier's feet, while the Boche stands there quivering in his underwear. "Don't kill me. I give you time to escape."

Jean-Luc stares at him, taking in his puny white chest and skinny arms. He's no older than himself, younger probably. Not much more than a boy really. More shots ring out. The baby's crying pierces his eardrums. Jean-Luc's nerves feel raw. He can't make a decision with all that noise.

"Baby's hungry," the soldier whispers. "I could get you milk."

"Shut up! How do I get out of here?" Jean-Luc thrusts the gun back to his forehead.

"The door, back of station. No guard now. Show my papers."

With the gun still pointed at his prisoner, Jean-Luc slips out of his overalls. It's going to be harder to get dressed while keeping the gun on him. Or he could shoot him right now, freeing both hands. It would be easier. But then again, someone might hear the shot.

Ignoring the baby's cries, he puts the uniform trousers on with his left hand, followed by the jacket and cap. Then he slips his feet into the boots. He's almost there; he'll have to button up the jacket later. First he has to deal with the Boche. He points the gun at his head.

Suddenly the man is on his knees, begging him. "Don't shoot! Please! I have family."

"I don't give a shit! You think these people don't have families too?"

"I'm sorry! I'm sorry. I didn't—"

"*Ferme ta gueule!* Shut up! Or I'll shoot you now."

The soldier goes quiet. But the baby is still screaming. Something about its crying holds him back from shooting.

He takes the baby from the sink with his left hand, using the other one to aim the gun.

"No! Please!" The soldier is in tears. "I stay here! I no go!"

Jean-Luc counts to three, then pulls the trigger.

Chapter Thirty-Five

Paris, May 30, 1944

CHARLOTTE

"Who's ringing like that?" Maman looks over at me.

"I'll go." Turning away from the sink, I wipe my hands on the towel. The buzzer goes again and I hurry to the front door. The sound of a baby crying reaches my ears. I pause for a second before pulling the door open.

It's Jean-Luc. Standing there in a Boche uniform. Holding a baby. My hand drops from the handle. I feel the blood drain from my face as my stomach lurches in disappointment. A baby! It must be his.

He pushes past me, closing the door behind him. "Charlotte, you have to help me!"

I stand there gaping. I don't know how to ask him all the questions charging through my mind. Whose baby is it?

"It needs feeding!" His eyes dart around.

My tongue feels fat and heavy in my mouth. I will it to move, but no words form. Then I sense Maman bustling behind me.

"What's going on?" She stares at Jean-Luc. "What are you doing here?"

He takes a step farther into our apartment, the baby crying more loudly now. "A woman at Drancy made me take her child. I don't know what to do with it."

Maman raises her voice. "You shouldn't have come here."

"Please! It needs feeding. I had nowhere else to go."

Maman turns to me, her voice brusque and businesslike. "Charlotte, run upstairs to Madame Deschamps on the fifth floor. She's just had another baby. Ask her if she'll feed this one." She grabs my arm before I can move. "Don't tell her about Drancy. Just say we found it on the steps of the old boulangerie."

As I leave, I see her take the baby out of Jean-Luc's arms. "Hide in the bedroom. She mustn't see you."

I hurry out through the door, my mind whirring away. He took a baby!

Breathless, I ring Madame Deschamps' bell. Her small son opens the door.

"Is your mother home?"

He turns around, shouting, "Maman!"

"*Oui*," I hear from the living room. "Who is it?"

He looks at me, a deep frown appearing on his little face.

"Just tell her it's Charlotte from the third floor." I don't wait for him; instead I hurry straight through to the living room.

"Madame..."

"Hello, Charlotte." She smiles at me from where she's sitting in a large armchair, a baby asleep at her breast. "I haven't seen you in a long time, not since you started working at the hospital. How are you?"

"I...I...We need your help. There's a baby...It's starving hungry. Can you feed it? Please?"

"What? What baby?"

"It was abandoned. In front of the old boulangerie."

"I don't know. It's hard enough to feed the one I have."

"We can give you our rations," I say recklessly. "Please!"

"Okay, okay. Give me five minutes."

I watch as she gently eases her own sleeping baby off her nipple and lays it down on the couch. "Laurent," she says to her young son. "Keep an eye on your sister, will you?"

The boy nods solemnly, sitting down next to the infant.

I wait while Madame Deschamps buttons her blouse up. As we hurry down the stairs, we hear the baby wailing.

"Sounds very hungry to me. I hope I have enough milk." She cups her breasts as though measuring their content. They don't look very big to me, and I wonder how she's going to manage it.

Maman comes out from the living room, the baby screaming in her arms. "Micheline. *Merci.* Can you help?"

"I'm not sure. I don't know if I have enough milk. I've just fed mine and I haven't eaten yet today."

"Charlotte, go and get some bread and that *saucisson.* Bring some water, too."

When I come back with the supplies, Madame Deschamps is in Papa's armchair, undoing her buttons. Maman passes her the baby. I stare as Madame Deschamps pushes its head inside her half-open blouse. But the crying continues, amid much squirming and struggling. She takes the baby away from her breast and looks at its shiny red face screwed up in anger. Then she lifts her breast up and pushes her nipple into its mouth. But the baby pulls away, screaming louder. Madame Deschamps sighs, looking at Maman with a raised eyebrow. "A right stubborn one you've got here," she says.

"Please try again." Maman's voice trembles with anxiety.

I'm scared too. What if we can't feed it? Will it die?

Madame Deschamps rocks the baby from side to side and I think she's going to give up. Then humming softly this time, she tries again. Gradually the crying fades away, replaced by tiny sucking sounds. Relief washes over me; I turn to smile at Maman, but her eyes are fixed on the baby, her lips pursed. I can tell she's trying to decide what to do next.

"Maman," I whisper. "I said we'd give her our ration coupons."

Sighing, she walks over to the desk, taking out the envelope we keep in the top drawer. She pulls out our tickets and hands them to Madame Deschamps.

"Poor little thing. I guess its parents were rounded up." Madame Deschamps looks at Maman.

"I don't know. We found it outside, on the doorstep of the old boulangerie."

She tuts. "The things people are forced to do these days. It's terrible."

Maman nods, her eyes locking onto Madame Deschamps'. "Can you take him... her? I don't even know what it is. Can you take the baby?"

"No!" Her tone is harsh. "I can't take the risk, not with four of my own at home." Her voice softens. "What if they're looking for it?"

"A baby?" Maman frowns at her. "Why would they bother with a baby?"

Madame Deschamps lowers her voice. "What if it's Jewish?" Then she pats the baby's bottom. "I don't think it's been changed for a while. It's wet through. And the poor thing has stopped feeding already. It's asleep, but I don't think it's taken much."

Maman looks over at me. "Charlotte, get a tea towel. I'll change the diaper."

"A tea towel?"

"Yes, it should do."

When I come back with the tea towel, I see Maman sitting on the couch, leaning forward, talking in low tones to Madame Deschamps.

I watch as she carefully takes the baby from her, laying it down on the floor. She pulls back the layers of wool that it's wrapped in. It's wearing a gray undergarment underneath. She undoes the buttons, peeling it back. Underneath, the skin appears almost translucent—lines of ribs shining through.

"God, he's filthy. We'll have to bathe him." She pauses, wiping away the gooey yellow mess from around his private parts. "He hasn't been circumcised." She turns back toward Madame Deschamps. "Won't you take him? Please. We could help you out."

"No. I told you I can't." She pauses. "Why don't you take him? Charlotte can help you."

"We can't!" Maman is abrupt.

"But Maman, we could!"

"No, Charlotte. It's out of the question."

"I could express some milk." Madame Deschamps sounds sorry now.

"What about an orphanage?" I hesitate, noticing Maman and Madame Deschamps exchanging glances. "Couldn't we leave him outside an orphanage?"

"He'd be dead within a week." Madame Deschamps' voice is a monotone.

Maman nods. "Orphanages are dangerous places at the moment. He's malnourished already, and quite weak." She turns back to me. "Go and fill the dishpan in the kitchen with warm water."

I do as I'm told. It's only half full when Maman comes into the kitchen, holding the baby. "I've sent Micheline back. She's going to express some milk. It will be easier than trying to get ahold of cow's milk, and probably better for him."

"Please." I try to keep the begging tone out of my voice. "Couldn't we keep him? I'll help you. You can show me what to do."

"Charlotte, we can't." Her eyes glisten, and I hear the note of regret in her voice. "Don't you realize that once they make the connection between you and Jean-Luc, they'll come straight here. They might even send the Gestapo."

"The Gestapo? No!"

"Yes. They'll talk to the neighbors. I hope Micheline won't say anything, but who knows what people might do when put under pressure." She sighs. "We're not safe anymore." She pauses. "Thanks to Jean-Luc."

A shiver runs down the back of my neck. He's put our family in danger. "I'm sorry, Maman." What if they send the Gestapo? What if they arrest us?

"Tell him to come out now. He needs to learn how to look after the baby. He can start by bathing him."

"Jean-Luc," I whisper as I open the bedroom door. "You can come out now."

He shuffles out, his eyes downcast. "God, I'm so sorry, Charlotte. I didn't know where else to go."

I try to smile, but there's a tight knot in my stomach. Thoughts of the Gestapo marching up our stairs fill my mind.

"His name's Samuel." Jean-Luc looks at me.

I nod. "Yes, we've just found out it's a boy."

When we go into the kitchen, Maman turns to Jean-Luc. "He needs washing," she states. "I'll show you how."

She helps us bathe Samuel, then she makes Jean-Luc rub cold cream into the angry red skin on his legs. I watch as he dabs the cream on as though he's scared to touch him. I know why Maman's doing it—she wants to make him responsible. I watch her watching him, and I can see she's furious with him, though she's trying to stay calm. Men don't know how to look after babies. What will he do?

Once the baby is clean and cushioned in the armchair, she turns to Jean-Luc. "Why are you wearing a Boche uniform?"

"It was the only way I could get out of the station."

"How did you get it?" Maman's tone is cold.

"I took the Boche's pistol and made him give it to me. It was the only way."

"Did you shoot him?"

"Only in the leg."

"You should have killed him. Now you've left a witness. They'll be after you." Maman paces the room, looking down at him. "My husband will be back this afternoon. He can't know about this."

Jean-Luc nods. "If they're looking for me, they'll go to my place first. They won't know I'm here."

"How do you know you weren't followed?" Maman frowns at him.

"I checked. There was no one near me."

"But they know you met Charlotte in the hospital. It won't take them long to make that connection. They could be here soon." She frowns. "You have to leave. And you have to take the baby with you. They'll know by now that you took him, and they'll be looking for you. We can't take the risk. We've already involved Micheline." She continues to pace up and down the living room. "She's the loose end that could get us caught. I'll have to make up some story, but you know what people are like. She'll talk." She sighs. "I shouldn't have asked her. I wasn't thinking properly."

"But Maman, we had to feed him. He was screaming. It's not your fault."

"Charlotte, don't you see how we've compromised ourselves?"

"I'm sorry. I should never have come here." Jean-Luc runs his hand through his hair.

Maman dismisses his apology with a shrug. "I don't know how to cover our tracks now." She leans over the armchair, looking at the baby. "What are you going to do?" She pauses, glancing back at Jean-Luc. "You must have a plan."

I know that's her way of saying she knows he doesn't have one.

"Maman, please, we have to help him. Think of a way."

I watch as her eyebrows come together. I peep over at the baby, calmly sleeping, as if the world were a peaceful place.

"Right," Maman says decisively, looking at Jean-Luc. "I may be able to help. But you are never to repeat what I am about to tell you."

Chapter Thirty-Six

Paris, May 30, 1944

CHARLOTTE

"I shouldn't be telling you this." She glares at Jean-Luc, seated next to me on the couch. "If it gets out, many lives could be in danger."

"I understand." Jean-Luc swallows.

Maman looks at him through narrowed eyes. "Yes, but will you be strong enough to keep your mouth shut if they catch you?"

"I'd rather die than put someone else in danger." He leans forward, his hands on his knees.

"Fine, brave words." She pauses. "But no one knows what they'd do till it happens." She turns to look at me. "I'll have to take the risk. I can't see any other way."

Jean-Luc nods.

"I have an uncle, called Albert. He lives in Ciboure, a village next to Saint-Jean-Luc-de-Luz." She stops a minute, rubbing the back of her neck. "He's active down there. He's helped people escape over the Pyrénées; British pilots getting back to England, Jews."

Has Maman been helping people escape? I stare at her, wondering who she really is. My eyes fill with tears of shame. I blink them away, looking at her in a new light.

"He might be able to help you," she continues. "I'll tell you his address and you'll have to remember it. Never write it down anywhere." Her eyes bore into Jean-Luc's. "Are you ready?"

He nods.

Maman picks the baby up from the armchair, hesitating for a second as though she doesn't quite know what to do with it. Then, sighing heavily, she sits down, holding it on her lap. "Twenty-four Avenue de l'Océan—"

"Maman," I interrupt. "Have you helped people before? Have you given them this address?"

She looks at me for a second before answering. "Yes, I have."

"But... but... Why didn't you tell me?"

"Charlotte!" Her voice is harsh. "You should know these aren't things one can discuss."

I'm the ignorant child again, kept in the dark. Half of me is mad at her, while the other half is filled with grudging admiration. I just wish I'd known. It would have changed everything.

"Does... does Papa know?"

"This is not the time to be discussing it, Charlotte. We need to act quickly."

Now I am the selfish child, so caught up in my own world I can't see into anyone else's.

She turns back to Jean-Luc. "It will be dangerous. Very dangerous. You don't speak German, I assume?"

"No."

"You'll have to get out of that uniform then. I can give you a fake ID. We can cut your hair, your eyebrows to fit the photo. I've done it before. And I can give you money." She pauses. "You'll have to take the baby with you. No one else will take him on, and going into hiding with him would be too risky." She looks down at the infant lying peacefully on her lap. "I'm not even sure he'll survive."

I know what she's thinking, but I don't say anything.

"You'll have to take the train to Bayonne," she continues. "And from there go by foot to Ciboure. It's about twenty kilometers. The train will be the hardest part, but as long as you talk to no one—"

"But won't people think it strange for a man to be traveling alone with a baby?" I interrupt again. "He'll be questioned, and how will he get milk?" The terrible thought crosses my mind that she just wants to get rid of him. I don't know her anymore; I don't know what she might be capable of.

"We can give him enough expressed milk for two days, by which time he should be in the safe house." She looks over at Jean-Luc again. "You'll have to have minimal contact with anyone."

"But Maman." I stare at her. "This is crazy! Someone will stop him. I know they will."

"Charlotte," Jean-Luc says softly, touching my hand. "It will be all right. I'll have the fake ID."

"No!" I stand up, an idea rushing through my head. I step toward Maman, then lean down and lift the baby from her lap, holding him up against me. He's so small, so light. I look over the top of his head at Maman and speak calmly, quietly—afraid of waking him. "A couple traveling with a baby will arouse much less suspicion than a man alone with one."

A flash of light crosses her eyes, and I know she knows I'm right.

"No, Charlotte! No!" The light turns to fierce anger.

Jean-Luc stands up too. "You're so brave," he whispers in my ear, putting his arm around my shoulder. Then he turns to Maman. "I'll do everything I can to keep her safe."

"Safe?" Maman hisses. "Are you mad? You can't even keep yourself safe!"

Gently he takes the baby from me, then he looks at Maman. His voice is even and calm, as though he's trying to coax a wild animal. "I know you don't want to lose your daughter. And it will be dangerous. But I swear I'll protect her and this child with my life."

"She's not going anywhere!" Maman's eyes dart from him to me.

I take a step nearer to her. "Maman, please. Think about it. We can pretend to be secret lovers, escaping to get married because we have this illegitimate child—"

"No!" She reaches out, gripping my shoulder. "Anything could happen. We might never see you again!" She swallows. "You can't go!"

I stare at her, realizing that she does love me. Of course she does! My heart fills with regret and shame. Why didn't I see it before?

But I can't stay. An urge burns through me to act now, to do something. "You have to let me do this. Please, Maman."

"You don't understand the dangers. You have no idea..." Her voice trembles, then fades out, as though she knows she's already lost me.

"I understand the risk. And I still want to do it. I *need* to do it."

Chapter Thirty-Seven

Paris, May 30, 1944

CHARLOTTE

Gare Montparnasse is in a state of chaos. Soldiers and gendarmes swarm around, stopping people, checking papers, and shouting orders. Adults look anxiously toward the platforms from which trains are departing, while pale, tired children, past the time for tears, stand numbly by. And all the time people are being turned back from the trains.

"The police are everywhere, Charlotte!"

Only too well aware of this fact, I grip the baby tightly against my chest, glancing around.

"Don't look! Just act natural."

Jean-Luc's so jittery, it's scaring me. If he doesn't calm down, he'll draw unwanted attention to us. I stop for a minute, looking into his wild eyes. My heart thumps hard against my ribs and my palms feel sweaty, but I remind myself who we're pretending to be—lovers eloping with their illegitimate child. What would lovers do?

I stand on my tiptoes, draping an arm around Jean-Luc's neck, the baby between us. I pull him toward me, lifting my face to meet his. "Kiss me," I whisper in his ear.

At first his lips feel rigid and cold, but as mine linger on them, I feel them begin to soften, welcoming me. The noises around us fade into the background. From a distance I hear whistles blowing, children crying, men shouting, while we stand there breathing into each other. My heart lifts. It's going to be all right. I know it is.

Then he draws back. "Let's go. Platform fifteen."

He takes my arm, pulling me after him. Together we make our way to the soldier who's checking tickets and papers before letting people onto the platform. Giving Jean-Luc's fake papers a cursory glance, he tilts his head toward his leg. "How did you get injured?" he asks in a German accent.

"An accident at work." Jean-Luc's face is blank and his tone flat.

People are piling up behind us, but the soldier doesn't seem to be in a hurry. He looks at Jean-Luc's ID, then back up at him, then at the ID again. Does he see something that doesn't fit? Maman did have to hurry, cutting his hair roughly to the same style as the photo.

"Michel Cevanne?"

"Yes." Jean-Luc manages to keep his voice steady.

"Date of birth?"

"Fifth of July 1922."

The soldier turns to me. "What is your relationship with this man?"

"I'm... We're... we're friends."

"Friends? Your papers, mademoiselle."

I pass them to him.

"Is that a baby?" He doesn't look at the papers, but stares at the baby in my arms.

"Yes."

He stretches out a hand, lifting back the blanket with long, slender fingers. "Do you have the birth certificate?"

"I... We... we haven't had time to get one yet."

"All births need to be registered within three days of birth."

My nerves contract until it feels like they'll snap. I don't know what to say.

Then a policeman appears and whispers something in the soldier's ear. They enter into an urgent-sounding, hushed conversation. Jean-Luc glances over at me. I know what he's thinking. Now is our moment.

He grabs my hand, and we run down the platform without looking back. We jump on board at the first door, finding ourselves in an empty carriage for eight. Jean-Luc shuts the door behind us. "Sit down. Act natural."

I sit next to the window, the baby on my lap. Jean-Luc sits next to me. My breath comes fast but my lungs don't seem to fill up. My head starts to spin.

Abruptly the door is pushed open. A guard peers in. "In here!" he shouts behind him.

I grab Jean-Luc's hand. I can't breathe. I watch in terror as the guard holds the door open.

A man carrying a large suitcase squeezes his way in, followed by a woman and three small boys. Jean-Luc pulls his hand out of mine. I let my breath out. Tipping his hat at us, the man sits down opposite, his wife next to him. Their children fight for the two remaining places next to their parents, leaving the last and smallest one standing awkwardly.

"Don't be so silly, Henri. Sit down," the father reprimands the boy.

The boy sits down without a word, on the opposite side to the rest of his family, next to Jean-Luc. Pouting, he starts to pick at the dry scab on his knee.

Nobody speaks. Everybody has secrets. When the train pulls out, the two older boys start wriggling, prodding and poking each other.

"Shh, be quiet. Try and go to sleep." Their mother fixes them with a glare, but the boys continue to pinch each other's knees. "Tell them, Georges."

"Be quiet, boys. Try and rest." Their father looks up, barely focusing on them.

"Papa, I'm hungry. We didn't have any breakfast."

"Be quiet!"

The boy stares out the window. I follow his gaze, out over the gray buildings against a blue sky. Please, God, I whisper in my head. Please, God, let us make it to Bayonne.

Suddenly the carriage door slides open, and a tired-looking gendarme steps in. "Papers," he states, looking at the family, then at us. My heart picks up pace again.

Reaching into his inside pocket, Jean-Luc produces his papers. His hands are steady and his face maintains its cool, amicable regard. I hold mine out with trembling fingers, squirming in my seat but wearing my sweetest smile to compensate.

"Monsieur Cevanne and Mademoiselle de la Ville, traveling with a baby." The gendarme raises an eyebrow.

"We're going to Biarritz to get married," Jean-Luc blurts out.

My fake smile stretches farther across my face.

The guard looks from me to Jean-Luc and back again, his frown growing deeper. "Don't you know there's a war on?"

"It's for the baby's sake," I say. "My father was going to kill me if I'd stayed. And the baby." Now I let the tears fall. I'm aware of the shocked faces of the family. This has added another dimension to their journey.

Silence fills the carriage.

"You're eloping!" The guard lets out a loud dirty laugh. "I think you'd better step outside, monsieur. We need to have a word."

Jean-Luc pats my hand as he reaches for his satchel. "Of course, monsieur."

I watch him leave the compartment, then look across at the father of the family, sitting opposite. He turns away, looking out the window.

Please, God, please, please. I bite on my bottom lip as seconds turn to minutes.

After what feels like an eternity, Jean-Luc comes back in and sits down. Relief washes over me like a welcome wave. I breathe again. He leans toward me, whispering in my ear. "He wanted money. He thinks he knows our secret and he wanted money to keep quiet. One secret to hide another." He touches my knee, looking into my eyes. "A lie that is half the truth is the best lie."

Chapter Thirty-Eight

The South, May 30, 1944

CHARLOTTE

The train finally draws to a halt in Bayonne, and we step out into darkness and silence. Tall apartment buildings face the station, but the shutters are closed as though the residents have left, though they've probably just shut themselves inside.

"Let's head toward the river. The town center must be over the bridge." Jean-Luc takes my hand. When we turn the corner, we see a couple of gendarmes coming toward us. Abruptly, I stop in my tracks. "Just keep going." He nudges me with his elbow.

As we climb the winding street up to the cathedral, the town becomes a little busier, and a few people sitting outside a café turn to stare at us, their faces unreadable. We carry on past the cathedral, coming to a small hotel just around the next corner.

"Let's try in here." Jean-Luc pushes the door open, making it creak loudly and summoning an old lady from her early-evening nap behind the reception desk. She looks at us with rheumy eyes.

"We'd like a room for the night, please." His voice is an octave too high, and he coughs.

"Papers," she demands, holding out bony fingers, waiting.

I take my papers out. She snatches them off me, like a hungry cat, then removes a tiny pair of glasses she keeps in the right-hand pocket of her blouse and scrutinizes them. She gives them back without comment, then puts her hand out for Jean-Luc's. She scrunches up her nose as she studies them, then abruptly looks up, a sly smile playing around her tight mouth. "Not married!" she states in a shrill voice.

"We're on our way to get married." Jean-Luc puts on his most charming smile.

"You'll be wanting separate rooms then, won't you?"

"If you prefer." Jean-Luc sighs loudly, while I look away in embarrassment.

"I do. How long are you staying?"

"Just the night."

"So two rooms, one night—that'll be five francs fifty, breakfast and dinner included."

Digging into his pocket, Jean-Luc pulls out some coins. Her eyes light up as he counts them out.

"Can we buy some milk?" I ask.

"Milk?" The woman's forehead turns to deep creases.

"For the baby."

"What baby?"

I pat the bundle in my arms. She really is a blind old bat.

"A baby! Not married. And a baby!"

I expect her to put the price up again, but instead she asks, "Why aren't you feeding him yourself? You know how hard milk is to come by."

"I've been ill, I can't feed him."

"Ill?"

I feel my cheeks burning. "Yes. Quite ill. I had a nasty infection."

She leans back. "Not tuberculosis?"

"No, nothing like that."

An awkward silence follows.

"Milk is very expensive." Her croaky voice cuts through the silence.

"We know." Jean-Luc smiles at her again. "But it's for the baby, and we can pay."

"I'll see if I can find some for you. Give me another franc and I'll ask my nephew. He's a farmer."

"Thank you. We appreciate your help." Jean-Luc digs out the coin.

"What's the baby's name?" She removes her glasses, putting them back in her pocket.

"S—" I start, but Jean-Luc quickly cuts in.

"Serge," he says.

I close my mouth tightly, holding the name Samuel in my mouth. I must learn to think faster; of course his Jewish name would have given him away.

"Serge," the woman repeats slowly, as if digesting it carefully. "That's a nice name."

She shuffles out from behind the desk and we follow her up the stairs. At the end of a dark corridor on the first floor, she stops, producing a key hanging from a chain around her waist. "*Pour monsieur,*" she declares, opening a door to reveal a small bed rammed up against the window.

"*Merci, madame.*" Jean-Luc walks past her into the room.

Immediately she closes the door behind him, then turns to glance at me before continuing down the corridor till she comes to another door. "*Et pour madame.*" Her pronunciation of *madame* is laden with sarcasm, but I hold my head high as I look around. A single bed dominates the room. "For you and the baby." She stares at me.

I step into the room, a shiver running down the back of my neck. Without another word, she closes the door behind me with a click. Suddenly I feel very alone. I look down at the bed, which is covered in a threadbare dull brown blanket, then lower myself onto it, the baby still in my arms. The creak of old metal springs makes me jump, and I quickly stand up again. A gentle tap on the door makes me jump again.

Jean-Luc walks in. "Has he woken up?"

"No." I pull the bundle of baby away from my chest, looking down at the silky dark hair covering the top of his head. "How long do babies normally sleep?"

"I'm not sure exactly, but it's been twelve hours now." Jean-Luc reaches his arms out and I place the baby in them. What exactly did Maman give him to make him sleep for so long? I hope she knew what she was doing. I watch as he lays the baby down on the bed, peeling back layers of blanket and clothes, exposing his gray woolen undergarment. I look at his stubby legs—like marble, with a network of thin veins running under his almost translucent skin. His tiny feet are covered in knitted shoes; his arms flop to the sides of his head, giving him an air of abandonment. Tentatively I place a finger on his leg. He's so warm, but so still. Bending down over him, I blow softly on his eyelids.

He doesn't twitch.

I turn back to look at Jean-Luc. "He's all right, isn't he?"

"He's breathing. I just wish he'd wake up. It's been a long time." He picks up the tiny body, holding it against his shoulder, patting the baby on the back. Striding around the room, he continues to rub his back, up and down. "Samuel, *réveille-toi.* Wake up, please."

I hold my breath.

Gently he lifts him away from his shoulder, holding him at arm's length. "Get a wet towel."

Grabbing one of the tea towels Maman packed for us, I run out to the toilet in the corridor. As I drench it in cold water, I silently pray: Please, God, I'll never ask for anything again, just make him wake up. Please, God.

When I get back to the room, Jean-Luc is sitting on the bed, deathly pale, the baby lying across his knees. He takes the towel from me, wiping Samuel's face, holding it for longer over his eyelids. All I can hear is Jean-Luc's breathing, deep and heavy.

The baby's nose twitches. Then the minuscule movement turns into a larger one as he wrinkles up his nose, his tiny forehead creasing into a frown. Suddenly an ear-piercing wail breaks the silence.

Jean-Luc grins, relief shining through. "I suppose he might feel a bit grumpy after that long sleep. Let's feed him."

I let my breath out. *Thank you, God. Thank you.*

I prepare the bottle with the rest of the milk we brought with us, then pass it to him, watching him as he sits on the bed, guiding the nipple into the baby's open mouth. "Hush, little one. Dinner's coming, hush."

Crying turns to the regular sound of soft swallowing. Immediately I feel calmed, and sit down on the bed. I wonder to myself why I passed the bottle to Jean-Luc when I could have tried feeding Samuel myself. I suppose I don't feel quite capable yet.

When the bottle is empty, Jean-Luc leans back on the bed, his head resting against the headboard, the baby against him, his cheek squashed up against Jean-Luc's chest. Uncoordinated hands reach upward as Samuel struggles to put both fists into his mouth at the same time.

A knock on the door makes me jump.

"I have a crib for you," a shrill voice trills out from behind the closed door.

I drag my eyes away from the baby and stand to let the old woman in.

She opens the door before I get there, her hand resting on a small wooden cot. "And dinner's ready."

"Thank you. That's very kind of you, madame." I take the crib from her, closing the door before she has a chance to come in properly and ask what Jean-Luc is doing in my room.

"She's just checking up on us." He gets up from the bed. "We'll leave him while we eat. He'll be fine; we won't be long."

"Leave him? Can't we take him down with us? I'm worried."

"We don't want to draw attention to ourselves."

"Can I hold him?"

"Later. We should eat first."

Jean-Luc places him in the crib, but the baby doesn't look in the least bit tired, still bent on trying to cram all his fingers into his mouth.

"He still seems hungry." I look at Jean-Luc. "It doesn't feel right to leave him here alone. Please, let's take him down with us."

"I don't think we should, Charlotte. People will remember us if they see a baby."

"Samuel…Serge," I whisper as I lean over the cot, trying out the names. He pauses for a moment, his movements less frantic as he looks at me. Gently, I rub his tummy. He reaches for my hand as he looks up at me. "Let me pick him up."

"Later. We should go, or we won't get anything to eat. That old bag would be only too happy to take our dinner away. Come on. We won't be gone long."

Dinner is an unidentifiable piece of gray pâté for starters. Dog? Cat? If we're lucky, it might be rabbit. It's followed by a wonderfully hot vegetable stew, and there's plenty of it. Vegetables are obviously easier to cultivate here than in Paris. Three old ladies sit at a round table in the corner and two elderly couples are hunched over their plates in the middle of the room. I eat quickly, swallowing the food in large gulps, anxious to get back to Samuel. Babies can sometimes die in their sleep, and the thought terrifies me now.

"Charlotte, stop worrying. I'll go back and check on him."

But before Jean-Luc can get up, a Boche strides in. "*Bonsoir, mesdames, messieurs.*"

There are low murmurings in reply, and I am vaguely aware of him tucking the napkin under his chin as he sits down. The other guests continue to eat, even more hushed than before.

The old lady, who appears to serve as the waitress as well as the receptionist, shuffles in. When she sees the Boche, she takes a step back, the color draining from her face.

I watch as she recomposes herself.

"*Bonsoir,* Herr Schmidt." She approaches him with her hand outstretched, a fake smile on her lips, contorting her wrinkled face.

"*Bonsoir, madame.* And where is your lovely daughter this evening?"

"She's ill. A touch of gastro, I'm afraid."

I concentrate hard on not looking over, cringing inside.

"That is a shame."

Without looking, I sense the Boche leaning back in his chair, spreading out his paw-like hands on the table. "Send her my warm wishes for a quick recovery, and tell her I hope to see her before I leave." The last words are spoken firmly, making it clear that it is an order rather than a request.

"She's quite green with it. You wouldn't like to catch it."

"I'll take the risk. I'm far more likely to catch something from this rancid pâté you serve here."

"Let's leave," I whisper across the table to Jean-Luc.

"What about the milk? We'll need it soon. You go back to the room. I'll ask in the kitchen."

The Boche clears his throat loudly, then bites into his toast with a loud crunch. Without looking behind me, I leave the dining room, hurrying up the stairs, happy to rediscover the tranquility of our small bedroom.

The baby is murmuring in his cot. I pick him up, rocking him gently, humming a song Maman used to sing to me.

"Dodo, l'enfant do
L'enfant dormira bien vite

Dodo, l'enfant do
L'enfant dormira bientôt."

A sudden pang of homesickness shoots through me. I miss Maman already: her fretting about where our next piece of meat will come from, her perpetual frown, her understated but deep love for her family.

After a few minutes, Jean-Luc walks in. "I've got the milk. It's okay."

"What about the Boche? Did he talk to you?"

"No. He's not concerned with us. It's the girl he's after."

"Poor girl." I can't imagine what it would be like to have to lie down with someone you hated, to have to touch them, kiss them. A shudder runs down my spine, but my real concern lies elsewhere. "I think the baby's hungry again."

"He can't be. He only ate an hour ago. Try putting your finger in his mouth."

Tentatively I place my little finger in his mouth and am shocked at the force of his sucking. I move over to the bed, sitting on it, cradling him on my lap. My stomach lurches, a strong sense of protectiveness surging through me. "Jean-Luc, it's going to be all right, isn't it?"

"Yes, it is. This is the best thing I've ever done." He leans over the baby, kissing the top of his head. Then he looks over at me. "Thank you for everything, Charlotte." He kisses me softly on the lips.

"What about his parents? What do you think will happen to them?" It makes me feel bad, being happy like this while Samuel's real parents are being transported to God knows where.

"It will be terrible for them, but at least they won't have to watch their child go through whatever horrors they are facing. It's our job to look after him now."

Gently he takes the baby from me, placing him in the crib, then he comes back to the bed, squeezing in next to me, leaning back against the headboard. He turns to face me, smiling his lopsided smile. I smile back, a feeling of warmth and peace spreading through my veins. It feels like we're a family. Of course, I know we're not a real family and Samuel isn't our child, but still, I let myself pretend, because it feels so good. I want to look after them both, keep them safe and warm and loved. I turn my gaze to the crib in the corner, where soft noises can be heard.

"I mean it, Charlotte." Jean-Luc twists a strand of my hair around his finger. "This is the best thing I've ever done." He pauses. "And I couldn't have done it without you. Well, maybe I could, but it wouldn't be the same." He kisses my cheek. "I knew you had it in you. I could see it in your eyes."

I put my hand on his leg. It surprises me how natural it feels—my hand on a man's leg. I wouldn't have been able to imagine it just a few weeks ago. "Had what in me?"

"This. This daring. This wild side."

I'm not sure I have a wild side, and I worry for a moment that he thinks I'm more daring than I am. What will happen now? I wonder. Excitement tinged with trepidation runs through my veins, my breath pounding loudly in my ears. I want to say something, but the words stick in my throat.

"I think we should sleep now." He kisses me on the forehead. "We've got a long day ahead of us tomorrow. I'll take the baby in with me; he might need feeding in the night."

I watch as he tucks the feeding bottle into his pocket, lifting the baby with one hand and taking the crib with the other.

Chapter Thirty-Nine

The South, May 31, 1944

CHARLOTTE

The next morning, breakfast is served in the dining room—a basket of stale bread with a bowl of brown liquid to dip it in. Apparently jam and coffee are just as unavailable here as in Paris. We eat quickly, then set off for Saint-Jean-de-Luz. First we need to get to Biarritz, only eight kilometers away. From there we would have been able to take the coastal route, but the Germans put a stop to that when they established the Atlantic Wall. Now we will have to make our way through the fields and farmland that lie behind the coast.

As we cross open land, we keep a lookout for Nazi trucks, but the only person we see is an old lady collecting firewood. Dew hangs in thick drops from the long blades of grass, making our shoes damp as we trek over fields that have been left to grow at will. We are silent, the only noises the sound of our feet, our breathing, and smatterings of birdsong. Jean-Luc carries Samuel in a sling he's made from a long pillowcase wrapped around his body.

After just a couple of hours, we reach the coastline of Biarritz. I look at the ocean stretching out to the horizon, then I see the mountain range to my left.

"Look." Jean-Luc points to the largest mountain. "That's Spain."

"Spain already! It doesn't look so far."

Low clouds hang over some of the peaks, making it difficult to see their true height, while the sun pierces through in rays of bright white, illuminating patches of green, turning them to the color of fresh limes.

I hear a car accelerating quickly, coming closer.

"Get down!" Jean-Luc crouches in the long grass.

My pulse rate races ahead as I lie flat out in the field.

"It's okay, it's gone." The engine sound fades out. "There are some trees ahead; we'll be safer walking there."

I pull myself up, my heart thumping loudly in my ears. We have to cover about fifteen more kilometers before nightfall, but my shoes are rubbing painfully against my heels. I curse myself for taking shoes I'd hardly worn. They're ugly flat things too, but the soles looked solid, and all my other shoes were too worn down, no good for walking long distances. I want to stop and take them off, but I fear what I might find. My heels feel damp.

Jean-Luc walks ahead of me until we are out of sight of the road, then he takes my hand. I attempt a smile, but wince instead. I try to keep going, but after thirty minutes or so, the pain is excruciating. I can't take any more. I pause in my stride. "Can we stop for a minute?"

He turns to look at me with a frown. "We've got a lot of ground to cover. Can you wait another hour?"

I resist the wave of self-pity threatening to overcome me. "No," I whisper. "I think I've got a blister."

"Okay, let's take a short break." He takes his backpack off, then unties the knot in the sling and sits down, leaning against a tree, balancing the baby on his legs.

"Is that him, or just the countryside?" I screw up my nose.

Jean-Luc bends over him, sniffing, and the baby grabs at the tufts of hair on the back of his head. I watch as Jean-Luc peels himself free.

Then he undoes the cotton diaper, using it to wipe away the smeared poo before tossing it to the side. I watch him take out a clean diaper from his backpack. Then, holding my breath, I undo my laces. As I pull the first foot out, I immediately notice the leather at the back of the shoe is stained with dark blood.

Jean-Luc looks over. "Charlotte, your feet! Have you got another pair of shoes?"

I shake my head, my eyes welling up. What an idiot I am!

"Here." He passes me a handkerchief. "Put this around your ankle. Give me your shoes."

Carefully I pull the first sock off, then examine my heel. The skin has been rubbed away, leaving a wide red patch, ripe with blood. Now that the instrument of torture has been removed, I feel no pain and wonder if I wouldn't be better going barefoot.

With the baby balanced on his lap, Jean-Luc kneads the hard leather between his thumb and finger. "We'll make a cushion with the handkerchief. You should have said something; we could have stopped earlier." He passes the shoes back. I decide not to try them until we have to get up again. I know it will be painful, even with the handkerchief.

"I'll feed Samuel." He reaches into the backpack for the flask of milk to fill the feeding bottle.

"Can I do it this time?"

"Sure. Sorry, I didn't mean to take over. It's just that I feel responsible." He places the baby in my open arms, handing me the bottle.

I tip it up, and a few drops fall onto the baby's cheek. He's squirming now from side to side, and it's difficult to get him to take the nipple. More drops fall on his face. "This is cow's milk now, isn't it?"

"Yes, the other milk's all gone."

"Maman said it might be harder to get him to take it. Shall we wait till we stop again?"

"I'm not sure." He pauses. "It might not be a good idea to wait till he's really hungry. And it's been three hours now. Try holding him more upright; I think it might be easier for him to swallow."

I follow his advice, shifting my position, gently coaxing the nipple into Samuel's mouth. He sucks a little, but then turns his head away as if he doesn't like it.

"I think he might take it better if he's hungrier." I stroke his cheek, giving him my finger to suck on. His little mouth grips it tightly. "We could stop again soon."

"Yes. Next stop, we can all have lunch."

Jean-Luc eases the baby back into his sling. This time Samuel's not quite as docile, squirming and moaning while Jean-Luc ties the knot around him. "Come on, little one," Jean-Luc coaxes. "We've got a long way to go."

Tentatively I push my feet back into the stiff leather shoes, while Jean-Luc disposes of the soiled diaper behind a rock.

As we continue to stride through the trees, Samuel's moans turn to cries. I feel like crying myself, every step making me wince in agony. A wave of panic rises from my belly as I reflect on the enormity of what I've undertaken. "Impulsive" is the word Papa often used to describe me, and he's right. I am. But I'm brave, too. In my heart, I know I've done the right thing. Together Jean-Luc and I are going to save this baby, and that's what matters most.

If only I hadn't worn these damned shoes. "Jean-Luc, let's stop and get ourselves sorted out. Please."

His eyes grow wide in surprise as he looks at me. "We've only been walking for a few minutes; Samuel will quiet down once we get going."

I nod, swallowing the tears forming in my throat, pausing in my stride to bend down and take my shoes off.

"Charlotte, what are you doing?" He stops in his tracks, making the baby cry louder.

"I'll walk in my socks. Keep going."

The earth is soft and spongy underfoot, and it's a relief not to have the shoes cutting into me. Only the occasional stick or stone jars into the soft sole of my foot. The crying gradually dies away as the baby drifts off to sleep. We walk in companionable silence for a while, and my spirits begin to lift again. It will be all right, I think, though there are still a couple of things I'm unsure about.

"Jean-Luc, should we call him Samuel or Serge?"

"What?"

"Samuel does sound Jewish." Just saying the word "Jewish" out loud feels like a crime, and I look up guiltily.

He pauses in his stride, looking at me. "But it's the name his mother gave him. We can't use it now, but as soon as we get out of France, we can."

"I like it, actually."

"Me too. It's a good solid name. How are your feet?"

"Better without the shoes."

"We'll get you something to wear when we cross the Pyrénées." He takes my hand, raising it to his lips, kissing it softly. "I'm so happy you came with me, Charlotte. I'll never forget these few days with you. You're so brave, and you don't even know it."

"Well, that's not really bravery then, is it? I'm just no good at estimating risk." I grin as if I'm joking, though deep down I wonder if it might be true.

"Yes, you're a little nervous, aren't you? I can see it every time a tree groans. You jump."

"I do not!"

"You do!" He laughs. "So, that makes you brave. You're scared, but you're doing it anyway."

I smile, happy to let him have his way.

After another couple of hours, we find a secluded spot under a large oak tree. Samuel is groaning now, obviously hungry. I take him, angling the bottle into his mouth. He sucks it, then pulls away, crying loudly, his mouth full of milk.

"He doesn't like it."

"Here, let me try." Jean-Luc holds his arms out, and reluctantly I pass the baby over. The crying increases in volume, but before he offers the bottle, he sways Samuel in his arms, kissing his face. It appears to calm him down. I watch, fascinated, as Jean-Luc squirts out drops of milk onto his finger before giving it to Samuel to suck on. Only then does he give him the bottle, gently guiding the nipple into his waiting mouth. How does he know what to do?

"Have you got brothers and sisters? It looks like you know how to feed a baby."

"No." He smiles. "It must be instinct."

A tiny wave of jealousy and unease washes over me. I've never even held a baby before. It's not that I'm not interested; I just don't know anyone who's got one. There's only Micheline Deschamps from upstairs, but I've really only seen hers from a distance.

After Samuel has drunk the whole bottle, Jean-Luc puts him up against his shoulder, rubbing his back. Suddenly an enormous belch makes me jump. We both laugh.

"How do you know about that then?" I ask. "I wouldn't know to do that."

"My mother used to look after the neighbor's baby, and I remember her patiently waiting for the belch after feeding her. But usually it would take longer." He lays Samuel down on the grass, leaving him to kick up his little legs. Then he pulls out the bread we bought that morning, and the dry *saucisson* we've carried all the way from Paris, slicing it with his penknife. It's tough and chewy, but I eat it hungrily, and there is a large chunk of creamy Brie to help it down.

Feeling a little sleepy, I lie back on the grass, closing my eyes. Jean-Luc lays his head gently on my stomach. "This is perfect," he whispers. "Time out of time. We're running for our lives, but here we are lying in the grass like we're on a picnic."

I know what he means. I feel safe here with him and Samuel, as if the world with all its troubles has agreed to leave us alone. It's a false sense of security, I tell myself, and we shouldn't stay for long, just a few more minutes. Running my fingers through his hair, I wonder how this much happiness became possible. I'm thrilled and amazed at how you can get what you wish for; you just have to want it more than anything else—be ready to sacrifice everything else for it. And I have, I realize. I've left my family and friends behind. My father will probably never speak to me again, and my mother—it's difficult to say. She knew she couldn't do anything to stop me, so she helped me, but I knew she was angry with me for having put her in such a difficult position. There were no kisses goodbye, just practicalities, though that has always been the way with her.

"Charlotte." Jean-Luc speaks my name softly, interrupting my thoughts, turning his head toward me. "There are no rules, are there?"

My hand slowly traces the outline of his nose. "What do you mean?"

"I mean, we make our own rules. We're not following the path that was set out for us. We decided our future for ourselves."

"Our own rules? Yes, but I think we still need the principles we were brought up with."

"Principles? What are they? My only principle is not to let principles get in the way of living."

My finger comes to rest on his forehead. I'm not entirely sure I understand what he's getting at. "But we still need something, something stronger than ourselves; values that are handed down from generation to generation. Don't we?"

He takes my finger, bringing it to his mouth, kissing it. "Are you talking about religion?" He pauses. "Do you really believe in God? After...after everything?"

"I do now." A small laugh escapes my lips. "Actually, I do." I lift my finger away from his mouth. "I prayed for something once, and God heard."

"He answered your prayer?"

"Yes."

"What did you ask for?"

"I can't tell you that. It's between me and God."

"You're making me jealous."

"Don't say that. It sounds blasphemous."

"Sorry. I wonder what you asked for, though. Was it for a handsome man to steal you away?"

I pinch his cheek softly. "Well, I'd still be waiting if it was that, wouldn't I?"

He laughs, a light, bubbly laugh that eats its way into my heart.

"I wish we could stay like this forever." I kiss his cheek.

Chapter Forty

The South, May 31, 1944

JEAN-LUC

By the time they get to Saint-Jean-de-Luz, the sun is beginning to sink between streaks of low cloud in a pink glow, the waves crashing onto the shore in a timeless rhythm. Tall, ornate houses stand on the street opposite the beach, little bridges stretching across the road connecting the front doors to the seafront promenade. It all looks so picturesque, Jean-Luc's mind begins to wander, imagining beach holidays—playing in the sand, soaking up the sun in peace and safety. He shakes his head, closing his eyes tight, wondering if one day this kind of dream will become normality.

They need to head to the small village just over the river—Ciboure. The bridge is easy to find, but Ciboure itself is a maze of narrow, twisting streets. They wander around in what feels like circles. But there's not a soldier to be seen, it's eerily quiet, and Jean-Luc can't help wondering if they're being watched through cracks in the walls.

"The curfew starts soon." Charlotte's voice is an octave too high. She puts her shoes back on, and he sees how much they hurt her with every step she takes, but he says nothing.

When they turn the next corner, he recognizes the street name straightaway—Avenue de l'Océan. Samuel is moaning and squirming against his chest. He knocks softly on the door, but no sound comes from the other side. This time he raps his knuckles hard against the wood, leaning forward to listen for any hint of movement.

"*Oui?*" The door opens a crack, but remains locked by a chain.

Jean-Luc steps back, letting Charlotte put her mouth to the crack. "We've come about the hens. One of them is sick," she whispers. It's the secret code her mother gave her.

Jean-Luc holds his breath as he listens to the chain sliding along its track, then the door opens. They quickly step over the threshold while the woman looks up and down the street before closing the door behind them.

The smell of boiled cabbage wafts down the long, dark corridor. Samuel wriggles against Jean-Luc's chest, whimpering softly.

A large man appears from a door leading out onto the corridor. "Who is it, woman?" he shouts as he shuffles toward them.

The woman looks them up and down, then stands back, shrugging her shoulders and letting him through.

"What have we got here?" The man glares at them through dark blue eyes set in a square and heavily lined face.

"I'm Charlotte de la Ville; you must be my great-uncle Albert." She leans forward, about to kiss him on the cheek, but he pulls back.

"*Quoi?*" He's about to say something else, but his words are swallowed up by a coughing fit. The woman pats him hard on the back. "*Ça va! Ça va!*" He pushes her hand away.

When he's regained control, his eyes move from Charlotte to Jean-Luc and back again, but he doesn't say a word and the atmosphere lies thick around them.

"*Alors?*" he finally says.

"My grandmother is your sister. My mother told us to come here."

Suddenly he reaches for Charlotte's chin, twisting it around, his thumb under it. Jean-Luc sees her tense up, and his heart beats harder, worried they've got the wrong man, the wrong address.

Then abruptly he lets go. "Yes, I'd recognize those eyes anywhere. You look a lot like her. Do you have something personal from her?"

"From whom?"

"Your grandmother. My sister."

"No." Charlotte frowns.

For a moment they stand there waiting, the smell of cabbage growing stronger. Then Charlotte coughs. "She gave me a brooch... for my eighteenth birthday."

"Show me." He scratches at his beard, his eyes narrowing as he studies her.

With trembling fingers, she unfastens the buttons on her coat, removing the brooch that is pinned to her blouse.

He takes it in his rough, calloused hands, running his fingers over the smooth surface of the green gem. "I remember this. Who gave it to her?"

"It was her father, for her twenty-first."

For a quiet moment they stand there while he turns the brooch over in his hands. Then, reaching forward, he lays it in her open palm, gently closing her fingers around it. "You'd better not lose it." He pauses, a smile almost reaching his lips. Then abruptly he grips her by the shoulders, pulling her to him, kissing her loudly, twice on each cheek. When he releases her, he turns to look at Jean-Luc. "Who's this, then?"

Jean-Luc offers his hand. "Jean-Luc Beauchamp, very pleased to meet you, monsieur."

Albert's eyes narrow again as he looks him up and down. "I like to know a man before I shake his hand," he states gruffly.

Jean-Luc's hand falls to his side. As if sensing his rejection, Samuel's soft whimpering turns back to crying. Leaning forward,

Jean-Luc undoes the folds of cloth, pulling him out, holding him up. "And this is Samuel."

"Your son?"

"No," Charlotte answers quickly.

Albert's face changes as his wary eyes grow warmer. "We'd best go and sit down."

They shuffle along the dark corridor to the kitchen. Albert sits at the end of the long dining table, like a king looking upon his court. Jean-Luc notices the scorch marks of hot dishes and forgotten cigarettes. Passing the baby to Charlotte, he digs into the backpack for the flask. When he shakes it, the sound of a tiny amount of liquid slopping around seems to echo through the room.

"Do you have any milk?"

"We can get some." Albert turns to the woman. "Marie, go and ask Pierre."

She shuffles away without a word.

Jean-Luc fills the feeding bottle with the remaining milk and passes it to Charlotte. She fumbles around with it for a minute before managing to get Samuel to take it, and he finds himself holding his breath as he waits for the baby to start drinking.

"How old is he?" Albert frowns. "He looks very small."

Jean-Luc shrugs. "We're not exactly sure. Probably only a few weeks."

"You traveled from Paris with a young baby that's not even your own?"

No one says anything for a minute, then Charlotte looks up. "He's very good. And we were lucky we didn't get stopped." Jean-Luc hears the pride in her voice.

"So?" Albert raises a hairy eyebrow. "Why come here? What do you want from me?"

"We're hoping you can help us." Charlotte looks at him. "Maman said you've helped people escape to Spain."

Albert scratches his beard, looking from Charlotte to Jean-Luc and back again. "But why do you need to escape? What have you done? Is Jean-Luc Jewish?"

"No," Charlotte says.

Jean-Luc takes over. "I'm a railroad worker. I was working at the station at Bobigny—Drancy."

"I see." Albert's thick eyebrows come together, making deep lines on his forehead.

"I knew I had to get out. I was waiting for the right opportunity. First I tried tampering with the rails, but that only landed me in the hospital. Then, one morning as a train was leaving, a woman begged me to take her baby... to save him."

"This baby?"

"Yes."

"So it's true. They're transporting the Jews from Drancy."

"Yes, by the thousands."

"That's what I heard. But where are they taking them?"

"I don't know for sure, but I think it must be somewhere far out east. They change drivers at the border. Only the Boches know where they're really going."

The lines on Albert's forehead grow deeper. "Only the Boches. The bastards!"

Charlotte stands up. Jean-Luc can see she's trying to pacify Samuel, who's crying loudly now. They all look up as Marie comes bustling back in with a metal jug. "Two packs of Gitanes, this cost me."

"We have cigarettes." Jean-Luc digs into his breast pocket, pulling out a couple of crumpled packs. He pushes them along the table.

"So." Albert lights up. "This woman asked you to take her baby?" He holds the pack out to Jean-Luc.

"Yes." Jean-Luc shakes his head, dismissing the offered cigarette. "She begged me. She knew what would happen if she took him on that train."

"So why not pass him on to someone else for safekeeping?"

"We didn't have anyone. And...well...we were in a hurry to get out of Paris. I needed a Boche's uniform, you know, to get out of the station."

Albert nods, an inkling of a smile playing on his lips.

"I had to shoot a Boche in the leg to get one. Then I knew they'd be after me, and I had nowhere safe to leave the baby." He pauses. "I went to Charlotte's. I didn't know where else to go, and her mother helped us. She told us about you and gave us money."

"Did she now?" Albert coughs, and it sounds like years of phlegm are being dislodged.

Marie gets up and whacks him on the back. "I told you it was time to stop smoking."

"You'd deny me all my pleasures if you could, wouldn't you, woman?"

She tuts loudly, but continues to rub his back.

"I'm surprised your mother let her only daughter go like that. She knows how dangerous it is."

"She couldn't stop me." Charlotte holds her head high.

"Thank God I don't have daughters." He laughs a throaty laugh. "I always said they were nothing but trouble. Have you thought about where you'll go after you get into Spain?"

"America." Jean-Luc looks at Charlotte. "Land of the free."

"Not a bad idea. France is going to be hell for a few more years yet. Once this damned war is over, there will be retributions to be faced. I can only imagine how ugly that will get." Albert looks at the young couple as if making a calculation. Finally he speaks. "It's difficult with a baby. The *passeurs* don't like taking babies."

Charlotte glances over at Jean-Luc.

"Babies are unpredictable. They cry. It can cost lives." Albert flicks ash into the large metal ashtray. "It's a risk. If he cries, you could be discovered. And they don't want to have to kill a baby." He pauses. "Sometimes it's the only option. One life sacrificed to save the others." He stares at Charlotte with rheumy eyes. "No one wants to kill a baby."

"Except for the Nazis." Marie speaks up, her voice thick with disgust.

"But... but we can't just leave him." Charlotte swallows, her eyes darting from Marie back to Albert.

"There must be a way," Jean-Luc says. "We could give him something to make him sleep. It worked on the train."

"Maybe." Albert scratches his beard again. "Maybe. But you have a better chance of making it over the Pyrénées alone. We might be able to find a family to take him in—"

"Is he circumcised?" Marie interrupts.

"No." Jean-Luc answers quickly.

"That'll make it easier," Albert says.

"We're not leaving him." Charlotte's voice is loud and clear.

Jean-Luc is surprised by her assertiveness, but he waits, weighing their options.

"Well." Albert takes a long puff on his Gitane, exhaling slowly, savoring it. "I have warned you. And it will be difficult to find a *passeur.* Only Florentino might do it."

"He's a good baby. He hardly cries. He sleeps most of the time," Charlotte says hurriedly.

Jean-Luc looks at Albert. "Do you have someone in mind that we could leave him with?"

"Not right now. We'd have to see. But I can tell you one thing. Those bastard Boches are damned tenacious. I've seen them take children away before, children without their parents, crying and screaming. They're hunting down every last Jew in France, whatever their age."

"No!"

They all turn to look at Charlotte.

"I said no," she repeats. "We're not leaving him behind."

The lines on Albert's forehead grow deeper. "It's a hell of a tough climb over the Pyrénées. Not everyone makes it. Especially not with a baby."

"We're not leaving him!" Charlotte raises her voice.

Jean-Luc sees tears form in her eyes. He watches as she swallows the lump in her throat. He understands how she feels, has noticed her growing closer to the baby with every day that's passed, but he's more pragmatic than she is. He'll consider the risks carefully before making a decision.

Or will he? He took the baby without making any conscious decision at all. He wonders for a minute if the best decisions are made with the heart. In his heart, he feels a surge of love for Samuel, a need to protect him, to see it through, whatever the risk.

"We're taking him. We'll make it. I know we will." His heart pumping hard, he stares at Charlotte.

Chapter Forty-One

The South, May 31, 1944

CHARLOTTE

"I've put you in here," Marie announces when we follow her upstairs, Samuel still asleep in my arms. I look around the room, taking in the lumpy double bed, wondering if it's for Samuel and me, or Jean-Luc and me, or all three of us.

"We only have this room available." She seems to have read my mind. "So the three of you will have to make yourselves comfortable here."

"It's fine. Thank you. Samuel can sleep between us." Jean-Luc smiles at her.

She grunts. "As you like."

I'm not quite sure what else she expects us to do.

"Well then," she continues, "I'll leave you alone so you can get settled. Good night."

"Good night. Thank you for everything. You've been very kind."

Without another word, she leaves us standing there.

My arms are beginning to ache with the weight of Samuel, so I put him down on the bed. He's drifting off and doesn't make a murmur.

Jean-Luc picks up a pillow, putting it on the floor. "Maybe it will be better if he sleeps here. I don't want to roll over in the night and squash him." Lifting Samuel, he places him gently on the pillow, covering him with his coat, tucking the arms in under the pillow. I watch as he tenderly kisses him on the forehead. Then, turning back to me, he whispers, "We should try and get some sleep. He'll probably wake in a few hours."

I nod, sitting down on the bed, wondering what will happen now. My heart is beating hard, though I'm not sure if it's from excitement or anxiety.

With his back to me, he unbuckles his belt, letting his trousers drop, then bends down and pulls them off along with his socks. His shirt hangs down, and I watch as he unbuttons it, lifting it off. His shoulders are broad and square, his back forming a perfect triangle, coming to a point as it disappears into his underpants. I suppress an urge to stand up and run my fingers all the way down his spine.

Suddenly he turns around. "Do you want me to put the light out?"

"If you like."

He flicks the switch on the wall, and all is dark. He slips into the bed, and I too get undressed, leaving my underwear on as he has done. I realize I've been holding my breath, and I try to breathe out silently, but the sound is horribly loud and heavy in the silent room.

"Are you all right?" he asks.

"Yes, I'm fine." I hope he can't hear the tremor in my voice.

Turning toward me, he kisses me on the forehead. At first I think it's because he can't see properly in the dark, and really he was hoping for my mouth, but then he says, "Good night, Charlotte. Tomorrow might be a long day."

Tomorrow! How many tomorrows do we have left? What if we get caught? We'll be sent to one of the camps from where people never return. I close my eyes, trying to dismiss the thought, trying to calm myself, but my mind whirs away. I'm confused. Why didn't he kiss me properly?

"Jean-Luc," I murmur in the dark.

But my whisper is met with silence. Is he asleep? Already? I turn onto my side, facing him, wondering how he is lying. Tentatively I slip my hand over toward him, feeling the small hump of a shoulder. He's on his side, his head turned away from me. My fingers touch him softly, searching out his spine, alighting on each vertebra as I move down. When I come to the small of his back, I let my hand rest there, in the dip, feeling the rhythm of his breathing, soaking up the warmth of his skin. Then I continue down, wondering, wondering what it will be like to touch him. Gently I slip my hand under the elastic of his underpants. The thought crosses my mind that I don't want to die without knowing him completely.

He murmurs. My hand freezes.

"Charlotte," he whispers, turning over, reaching out to find my face with his hand. "I want it to be perfect. I want us to get married in a church with God as our witness. Then I want to bring you champagne while you lie down on a bed of rose petals..."

I smile in the dark. "It doesn't have to be like that. I mean, I don't mind not getting married in a church. I don't care if we don't get married at all."

"But I thought..."

"I don't believe God only lives in churches, and I think we might have his blessing anyway."

He strokes my face. "You sound very sure of yourself."

"I am. I've given it some thought."

"I'm glad to hear it." He kisses me gently on the mouth, then kisses around all the way to my ear. "What about rose petals and champagne?" His breath is hot.

"Mmm," I murmur. "Another time. Now I just want you."

Chapter Forty-Two

The South, June 1, 1944

CHARLOTTE

The next evening when we sit down to eat, three rapid knocks on the door shoot through the room like a pistol. I pull Samuel closer to me. Jean-Luc jumps up.

"Stay calm." Albert leaves the room. "It's our signal."

He soon returns with a large, stocky man. "Our *passeur*, Florentino."

I watch as the bear of a man removes a flat beret from his head. When I stand to greet him, I can't take my eyes off the deep lines etched in his face. His eyes, in contrast, are bright, like those of a younger man. Holding Samuel with one hand against my chest, I offer him the other. He takes it in a firm grip, his enormous hand enveloping mine. He makes me feel small and fragile, almost insignificant.

I withdraw my hand, and Marie passes him a glass of red wine. He nods his thanks before guzzling it down as though it were water, then he turns to Albert. "No baby."

I grip Samuel tighter.

"I know, I know." Albert shakes his head. "But it's necessary. They can pay more."

"No baby." Florentino holds out his glass for a refill.

I glance over at Jean-Luc. What will we do now? He catches my eye and takes out a wad of notes he's prepared from his back pocket. As he flicks through them, he looks at the *passeur.* "How much more?"

"No! No baby!" Florentino puts his empty glass down with a thud.

Albert slaps his hand on the *passeur*'s shoulder, leaning over to whisper something in his ear.

I watch as the lines on Florentino's forehead grow deeper. Then, abruptly, he turns back toward me, holding out his arms. "Baby."

"What?" Instinctively I pull Samuel back.

"Charlotte, he wants to see." Jean-Luc touches my elbow.

With trepidation pumping through my veins, I place the sleeping infant in the man's enormous hands. He glances at Samuel, then lifts him in one hand, laying him against his shoulder.

Please don't wake now.

With a sudden and swift movement, he changes him over to the other shoulder. Samuel squirms in his sleep but doesn't cry. I can't help feeling a rush of pride. Then Florentino grunts, fixing Albert with his bright blue eyes. "You know what happens if the baby cries."

Albert nods, looking at me. I turn away from the intensity in his gaze. It won't happen. It can't happen.

Jean-Luc coughs. "We won't let him cry." He takes a step toward me, putting his arm around my shoulder. "We know how to keep him quiet."

Florentino stares at him, a thick eyebrow slightly raised, as though he's working out exactly how he might know how to keep a baby quiet. Then abruptly he passes Samuel to Jean-Luc, reaching his large hand out to the table to pick up his refilled glass.

After taking a couple of gulps, he barks out a list of instructions. "Tomorrow, twenty-two o'clock, farmhouse, Urrugne. Hard work. One thousand five hundred pesetas now, one thousand five hundred next time."

Jean-Luc counts out the notes my mother gave us. "Thank you."

Florentino grunts, turning back to Albert. "Give cognac for baby."

Albert nods, and my stomach lurches, but I hold my tongue. We just need to get Samuel out of France.

Florentino sits down, and Marie brings him a plate of pâté and pickled vegetables. I watch as he shovels pieces of slimy red pepper into his mouth. We are putting our lives into this man's hands, but he doesn't even seem to like us very much. The danger of crossing the Pyrénées is too close now. I close my eyes, blocking out my fear. "Confidence," I whisper to myself. Everything will be all right.

Chapter Forty-Three

The South, June 2, 1944

CHARLOTTE

The next evening, under cover of darkness, we set off alone. Marie has given us both a pair of cord-soled espadrilles; apparently they're the best things for climbing the Pyrénées. I'm just relieved they're not big hard leather boots, and I am able to squash the backs down—the skin on my heels is still tender. Jean-Luc carries a small bag containing a change of clothes, milk, cognac, and water, while I carry Samuel, the long pillowcase tied around me, holding him close against my chest.

In silence we follow the trail that was described to us, but the brisk pace soon makes me hot and clammy. I lift Samuel away from my body, letting some air circulate, but the movement wakes him, and I feel his fingers reaching out, clinging onto my light coat. "Shh," I whisper, pulling him back closer to me, covering his head with my hand. He settles back into me, and I decide I can put up with the extra heat his little body is giving out. In a few days' time, if all goes well, we will be safe and ready to start our new life. Reaching out for Jean-Luc's hand, I pause in my stride.

"It's okay, Charlotte. We're going to make it."

"I know." I squeeze his hand, but we don't speak again, the only sound the soft impression of our feet on the rough ground, and the hooting of owls.

We haven't been walking for long when Florentino steps out soundlessly from the darkness. Without a word, we follow him through a small pine forest; the numerous trees and the ground covered in small soft twigs absorb any sound we make. I feel safer here with Florentino than I did on the trail, but he walks so quickly, darting in and out among the tall, thin trees. I feel my breath rasping in my chest and a ring of sweat gathers around my hairline. Briskly I wipe it away, blowing air up onto my hot face. I worry for Jean-Luc with his cane, but he doesn't slow down, not once.

After a few hours, we come to a farmhouse. Florentino pushes hard on the heavy wooden door and lets us in. It's dark inside except for the light of a couple of dim candles. I heave a sigh of relief, impatient to sit down and unstrap Samuel. My neck aches with the weight of him and I feel a rivulet of sweat dripping down my chest. An old woman comes to greet us, helping me out of my light coat and unknotting the pillowcase tied around my back. I lift Samuel out, watching as he screws up his eyes, probably sensing the change in environment. His face is red and I realize he must have been just as overheated as I was. He brings a tiny fist up to his mouth and lets out a cry.

Jean-Luc is soon by my side with a bottle ready. Taking Samuel from me, he makes soothing noises as he cradles him in his arms. I look at the ragged couch and gratefully flop onto it, watching Florentino and the old woman whispering together as she heats something up on the stove. It smells of nutmeg and garlic, and my stomach rumbles loudly.

The woman turns around, passing me a bowl of the broth. It's delicious, and I slurp it up greedily, watching Jean-Luc out of the corner of my eye as he whispers to Samuel while he feeds him. I know Samuel will be looking up at him with his innocent brown eyes. Jean-Luc is falling in love with the baby, and I'm falling in love with him. I've never seen such tenderness in a man before, but what surprises me the most is his ease and total lack of self-consciousness. He doesn't seem to care what anyone thinks. How refreshing.

I close my eyes, happy but exhausted.

It feels like I've only just dozed off when Florentino shakes me awake, handing me a bowl of hot milk and a piece of baguette. Someone must have taken my espadrilles off last night and covered me with a blanket. I sit up, sipping the milk, noticing that Jean-Luc uses his milk to prepare a bottle for Samuel. Florentino stands against the stove, his exasperation evident in his deep, regulated breaths, as though he's counting them out, waiting. As soon as the baby is fed, he passes us old blue workman's clothes, like the ones he's wearing. We put them on quickly, then Jean-Luc helps me tie the long pillowcase around my back so I can carry Samuel.

Once outside the hut, Florentino hands me a thick branch to be used as a walking stick. He looks at Jean-Luc's cane. "Good, you have a stick, but if you are slow..."

"I can run with this stick." Jean-Luc laughs nervously.

Florentino ignores him, pointing a finger ahead and starting to walk, his strides long and silent.

I support Samuel with my hand under his bottom, taking the strain off my neck and back. All I can see ahead of me is the dark shape of Florentino. The earth smells of fresh wood, evoking memories of Christmases past. I wonder what my Christmases will be like now. Will the three of us form a happy family? Will we have children of our own one day? But these thoughts for the future seem surreal, almost like a fantasy. All that matters right now is getting Samuel to safety. The rest will come later.

It feels like the whole world is sleeping, except for the birds, chirping out to each other. A sudden cracking noise makes me jump. I freeze, my left knee in midair. I can only just make out Florentino now, marching away from us.

"Come on!" Jean-Luc whispers.

We run to catch up again. Florentino turns around when we are just behind him. "Branch broke," he grunts. "I'll tell you when to be afraid." His tone is dry.

There is no time to look at the beauty of the new day dawning; our eyes need to be constantly on our feet, looking out for twisted roots, loose stones, or muddy patches. Soon the terrain becomes steeper, and I pant heavily, trying to keep up. Then soft ground begins to give way to slated rocks. I slip. Instinctively one hand flies to Samuel at my chest, while the other reaches out to break my fall. He lets out a cry. I lean down, murmuring softly in his ear. "It's all right. Everything's going to be okay." I'm talking more to myself than him, but my words seem to soothe him, and he goes quiet again.

Florentino looks back at me, and in the half-light I catch a glint in his eye. He really doesn't trust us to make this journey, and I am pretty sure he would feel justified in abandoning us if he thought it necessary. I'll show him, I whisper to myself.

Suddenly he stops, pointing to a mass of trees. But before we can tell which way he's going, he's vanished. My heart pounding hard against my ribs, I follow Jean-Luc into the trees, guessing which way he took. Thank God, we soon see his bulky form threading its way through the spindly pines, out to a clearing, where we suddenly come face-to-face with a steep cliff. A gap the width and depth of a large human body runs vertically down from the top of it. Florentino is there at the bottom, his legs spread across it, his hands spanning it as he grips the sides. There is no time to think. No time to feel the fear. Jean-Luc pushes me in front of him. "Go."

Quickly, I pull the espadrilles up around the backs of my feet, or surely I will slip backward out of them. Using all the strength in my legs, I push myself up into the gap, reaching a hand out, groping for the first rock ledge, the other hand still gripping Samuel.

"You'll have to use your other hand too," Jean-Luc shouts up. He gives my bottom a shove, egging me on. But I'm too afraid to take my hand off Samuel. What if the pillowcase isn't strong enough to hold him? What if he falls forward? Tentatively I move my hand away from the baby, stretching it out to the next ledge. But immediately I return it. I can't let him go. I'll have to put the other hand out to grab hold of the ledge instead. But it's too far away. I'm stuck. Frozen with indecision, I make the fatal mistake of looking up. I'll never make it.

Florentino's red face swims into view. I sense his anger. It freezes me farther into the rock. His large feet start to slide back down the gap in the cliff. Soon he's just above me. "Give me the baby," he rasps, holding out a hand. But I can't move a muscle. He lands next to me and reaches forward, slipping his hand into the pillowcase, pulling Samuel out. Then, like an agile bear, he scales the cliff again using only one hand.

Don't look up or down, I silently tell myself. Concentrating only on the next handhold above me, I move up through the gap slowly, gaining confidence with every step I take. I hear Jean-Luc's labored breathing as he comes up behind me. For a moment I wonder how he's managing to hold on with his injured leg, but I dismiss the thought. All that matters is that he *is* doing it.

"*Allez*," Florentino whispers urgently from above.

I glance up to see him lying down, leaning over the cliff, his hand reaching out for me. Suddenly I realize how far up we've come. How far down I could fall.

"*Allez*," he whispers, more loudly this time.

Closing my eyes, I reach up toward him. He wraps his strong hand around my fragile one and pulls. I push up with my legs, hoisting myself toward him. Rolling onto my side, I land next to him. *Thank you, God.* I dare not look down as he helps Jean-Luc up.

Unceremoniously he hands Samuel back to me, making me feel like a bad mother. But I'm not his real mother! How could it be then that fear for him paralyzed me?

I'm hoping for a little rest after the exertion of that climb, but no, Florentino is straight up again. And Samuel is restless now, moaning and squirming against me. Maybe he can sense my fear and fatigue. But just when I think I can go no farther, Florentino signals for us to stop. We flop down around a large tree, my legs giving way before they hit the ground. Samuel whimpers. "Shh," I murmur, stroking his head.

"I'll feed him," Jean-Luc whispers in my ear.

I wonder if he'll add the cognac as we were told to do, but he doesn't, and Florentino doesn't appear to notice. Instead he closes his eyes as he leans against the tree. My muscles heavy and aching, I do the same. As my eyelids drop, I'm vaguely aware of Jean-Luc taking a clean cloth from the bag, folding a new diaper. Then, just as I'm abandoning myself to sleep, Florentino pushes me with his hand. "*Allez.*"

"*Non!* Please, can we rest?"

"Rest when you're dead." He holds his hand out to help me up.

"I can do it. I can," I whisper to myself, forcing myself up onto heavy legs.

"Are you all right to take Samuel?" Jean-Luc looks at me with concern.

I nod.

We trudge along, no longer under cover of the trees, and then the climb is up, up, and up, loose sheets of slate slipping beneath our feet. I reach out my hand, grabbing tufts of hard, prickly grass to balance myself.

We've been climbing like this for what seems like hours when Florentino stops, diving behind some rocks. He quickly reappears, snorting as he produces a bottle of clear liquid. He takes a large gulp, passing it to Jean-Luc.

Jean-Luc sniffs it. "Eau de vie." He takes a swig, bringing tears to his eyes. He coughs before drinking again, then passes it to me.

It burns my throat but calms my jittery nerves. I look up to see

Florentino grinning at me as I suppress a cough. He holds out his hands, pretending they're trembling uncontrollably. "Eh, eh?"

"Yes," I admit. Of course I'm petrified. But we are alive, and the alcohol has taken the raw edge off my fear.

He digs in his pockets, coming up with a small paper bag, which he passes to me. Dried apricots. Gratefully, I stuff a couple into my mouth, then pass the bag to Jean-Luc.

Florentino taps his wrist, holding up five fingers. Five minutes. "*Allez! Allez!*" he urges.

Surely it must be lunchtime. I'm still hungry and so thirsty. We've been walking for hours, and I need something to keep me going. My reserves of energy have been used up. My thoughts turn to Maman and how she tried everything to stop me from leaving. Now I understand that I could die up here in the mountains, but I didn't stop to think twice about it. Was that bravery or idiocy?

The bundle of Samuel is making me hot and sticky, the pillowcase pulling down on my aching neck with his weight. Florentino watches me as I adjust it, trying to make it more comfortable. He holds out his large hand, but I shake my head. Partly due to my pride, and partly because I like the feeling of the baby's little body lying right next to my beating heart.

After an entire day of walking, with only momentary breaks, the darkness begins to settle in. Florentino finds us a sheltered spot behind a large rock, and we collapse on the ground. Jean-Luc and I huddle together for warmth; no question of lighting a fire to warm our stiff, tired joints. Florentino passes us some dried ham and a handful of raisins. Then, by some miracle, he produces a whole Camembert, which he proceeds to tear into three parts, spilling out its thick, creamy insides. He hands it out quickly before it runs onto his fingers. I bite straight into the middle of mine, savoring the smooth, rich softness of a pleasure almost forgotten. Florentino makes a lot of noise licking the gooey cheese off his fingers, too much noise for a man who's insisted on silence. He passes the eau de vie around again, and we knock it back like hardened drinkers.

Exhausted and forbidden to talk, we quickly fall asleep. When I wake, suddenly, I can only see a few inches in front of me, but I sense something is terribly wrong. Leaning over, I touch Samuel's cheek. It's surprisingly warm. I lean toward Jean-Luc; he's breathing heavily, his mouth slightly open. Then I turn to look at Florentino. My heart jumps up into my throat. The space where he was lying is empty.

A sudden cracking sound shatters the silence. I suppress a scream. A gunshot rings out. Shouting. More shots.

Jean-Luc jumps up, grabbing Samuel. Together we huddle behind the rock. A small cry escapes from the baby. Jean-Luc leans over him, stifling the noise.

Then we see Florentino running toward us. "*Allez! Allez!* Now!"

Grabbing our bags, we run, stumbling over rocks, slipping on slate. Thank God Florentino told us to keep our shoes on to sleep. I feel Jean-Luc at my side, breathing heavily. My head is swimming, the ground swirling beneath me. It takes all my strength to keep going.

"Stop!" Florentino whispers under his breath, pointing to a thick tree. Bending over, he points to his back. He wants us to climb on him to clamber up the tree.

I take Samuel back from Jean-Luc. "You go first. I'll pass him to you." Don't think, I tell myself. Just do it.

Jean-Luc climbs onto Florentino's broad back, hoisting himself up onto the lowest branch. I do the same, Florentino raising himself to half standing so I can pass the baby up to Jean-Luc. Then I grab the same branch, pulling myself up into the tree. In a moment, Florentino is beside us. I can't work out how he did it with his great bulk.

Samuel lets out a whimper, and Jean-Luc immediately gives him his finger to suck on. Thank God, he goes quiet. I don't doubt for a minute what Florentino might do if he felt he had to.

In the distance I hear footsteps crunching on the ground. Holding my breath, I freeze myself into the tree, pretending I am part of it.

The footsteps grow quieter. Can we dare to believe they are retreating?

We wait a further thirty minutes, my joints growing stiff and numb, but I will not let myself move till Florentino gives the order.

"Down! *Allez!*" he whispers across the branches. "They're going after another party."

I scramble down the tree. My ankle catches on a stub, and I tumble backward. The air is knocked out of me as I hit the hard earth. I roll over and vomit. The ground spins before my eyes. Lying facedown in the dirt, I wish for oblivion.

I feel Jean-Luc's arms around me, pulling me up, but my legs are like jelly. I slip and slide against him. "Charlotte." I hear him whisper my name, but his voice sounds miles away. "Charlotte, you have to get up."

"You go on," I hear myself answer as my knees buckle beneath me. "Take Samuel. Leave me here."

But his arms hold me tight. "I'm not leaving you anywhere." He buries his head in my hair. "I'm not going without you."

His words make me want to cry. My exhausted body just wants to surrender, but I have to go on. I must. I can't give up. On trembling legs, I force myself upright, and with Jean-Luc's arm around me, we stumble through the darkness. I soon realize that neither of us is carrying Samuel. Florentino, five steps in front of us, has him. The *passeur* belongs to these mountains. They are tough, unforgiving, and enduring, just as he is. But the mountains do not know us. We are intruders.

Eventually we come to a stream, where we take a few minutes to stop and drink. The sun is just rising behind the trees. Samuel, maybe sensing the dawning of a new day, lets out a cry. Yes, it is breakfast time.

"Can we feed him?" I ask Florentino.

He nods. "Don't forget the cognac."

I watch Jean-Luc add a glug of cognac to the milk before taking Samuel back from Florentino. I'd quite like some myself. My nerves are still raw.

As we march on, Florentino carrying Samuel again, I hear the river before I see it. Then, through the trees, I glimpse swirls of blue. It's flowing fast. I swallow the fear growing in my throat. Maybe we will be able to take the bridge, but we were told it is usually guarded; only to be used as a last resort, if the water is in full flood.

We clamber along the riverbank looking for a good place to cross, my feet slipping and sliding in the soggy earth as I try to keep up.

After about twenty minutes, Florentino stops. "No," he whispers.

We look at him, confused.

"It's too dangerous. No crossing today."

"What?" The word jumps from my mouth like an accusation.

"Too dangerous," he repeats.

What are we supposed to do now? Go back? We hired him because he could cope with the danger, and now he's scared! We have to go on. The thought of turning back is more frightening to me than the river.

"Please." I put my hand on his arm, begging him with my eyes.

"Not today." He pauses. "In the dark. Tonight. We'll wait for night."

Chapter Forty-Four

The South, June 3, 1944

CHARLOTTE

Maybe Florentino is right after all, and it's better to wait before crossing the river. It's the most dangerous part, and now we'll have time to recuperate before taking it on.

We walk on for about another hour, then he points to a large boulder a little farther back from the bank, and we settle down behind it. I heave a sigh of relief, grateful to be able to rest for a while, though one of us always needs to be awake, keeping a lookout. I'm terrified I'll fall asleep when it comes to my watch; I'm so exhausted, I almost drop off when we're walking. So when it's my turn, I make sure it's time to feed Samuel. I've got the hang of it now, and enjoy watching him drink from the bottle, his eyes becoming drowsy as his little fingers open and close as though searching out something to grip hold of. I give him my first finger, and he immediately grabs it, clinging to me as though he's scared I'll disappear. His need for me pulls at my heart, urging me to fulfill it. "Don't worry," I whisper. "I'm not going to leave you." His legs kick up and down as he drinks. I take hold of a foot, bringing it to my lips.

In the afternoon, we move on down the river, careful to keep watch for patrolling soldiers. I dare not watch the water as it gushes past, shooting sparks of fear through me, making my pulse race, then slow, then race again. We can no longer even whisper to each other, the river drowning out any other sound.

After a light supper of nuts and cheese, we wait for dusk. Slipping off our espadrilles, we push them into Jean-Luc's backpack. I take Samuel, who is awake again and peeking out with unfocused eyes, as if he can sense the danger.

"Get a good foothold. The current is strong." Florentino stares at me.

I almost roll my eyes at him, but stop myself and turn to Jean-Luc. "Can you make sure the pillowcase is tied properly behind?"

For the third time, Jean-Luc checks that the long pillowcase is wound tightly around me, holding Samuel firmly in against my chest. "Yes, he can't fall out."

Florentino bends down to roll up his trouser legs, then steps into the water. When he's found a foothold, he holds his hand out for me, but I can only just see it in the fading light. Taking a deep breath, I put a foot in, holding Samuel to my chest with one hand, reaching out for Florentino with the other. The icy water makes me gasp, while the current tugs viciously at my legs. I squeeze Samuel up against my chest, my stomach shriveling with fear, terrified now that the pillowcase will come undone. But my arm's not long enough. I can't reach Florentino.

"*Allez!*"

Wedging one foot behind a small rock, I pull the other into the river, my legs trembling with the effort. I stretch my arm farther. It's still too far.

"Give Samuel to me." Suddenly Jean-Luc is next to me, his hand on my shoulder. But we agreed I'd take Samuel because of Jean-Luc's leg. Anyway, I wouldn't risk passing him over while standing in the gushing river.

"I can do it!" I reach again for Florentino, but he's too far. It's hopeless. I'm stuck. If I lift my foot to move nearer to him, the force of the river will suck me down. Yet I have no choice.

I pull my foot up. Suddenly I'm lunging forward, wildly off balance. I grab for the nearest stone. Samuel lets out a sharp cry. Then another.

"Get up!" I hear Florentino yell.

One hand tight against Samuel, ignoring his cries, I raise myself up, digging my feet into the riverbed, my legs shaking wildly. Again I reach for Florentino. This time I touch his fingers. Instantly he wraps his large hand around my wrist, pulling me toward him. "Shut the baby up! Get Jean-Luc's hand."

Samuel screams louder and louder, but the river carries his cries away. The realization of what I have to do hits me like a fist in the stomach—I have to lift my hand away from Samuel so I can pull Jean-Luc toward me. I know the pillowcase was tightly tied, but what if it's come loose with the effort of that one step? Why, oh why, did Florentino put me in the middle with the baby? He should have taken Samuel himself. Hatred for our guide pulsates through me. I close my eyes.

"Now! Do it!" Florentino shouts above the gushing of the river.

"Charlotte," Jean-Luc calls out. "Samuel is safe! Give me your hand!"

But my hand refuses to leave the baby.

Jean-Luc digs his cane into the riverbed, pulling himself across. Helpless, I watch his arms and legs trembling with the strain. He takes one large step, thrusting his hand out to reach mine. For a second my hand leaves Samuel as I reach out to grab Jean-Luc's, gripping it tightly.

Violently, without warning, Florentino tugs my other arm. Stumbling on the slippery rocks, I lunge forward again. Samuel jolts upward. I scream.

"Give the baby to me!" Florentino shouts. "Now!"

I can't do it. His anger terrifies me. It sounds like he wants to throw Samuel into the river. But his enormous hand is already reaching for him. "Now!"

While I'm still fumbling with the pillowcase, he snatches the baby away from me, pulling him out by his arm, as though he were pulling a rabbit by its ears.

I scream. Then, gulping back my tears, I continue to sidestep across the river, Florentino pulling me on one side, while I pull Jean-Luc on the other. When we eventually reach the other bank, I collapse on the ground, shivering and shaking uncontrollably.

Florentino thrusts the crying baby into my arms. "We were very lucky. I said no baby."

I bury my head into Samuel, trying to smother his cries. He's wet through and screaming with terror. I hold him tight, rocking backward and forward on my knees. Surely we will all die by this damned river! Then I feel a hand on my shoulder.

"We're in Spain, Charlotte!" I hear the crack in Jean-Luc's voice as he starts to cry. "We're in Spain!" He falls down next to me, his arm coming up, wrapping its way around Samuel and me. Together in a tight knot, we sob. Then we laugh—hysterical mad laughter.

I feel Florentino tugging at me, pulling me up. He takes Samuel from me, not roughly like before, but gently, holding him around the body. As I watch him, I'm vaguely aware of Jean-Luc scrabbling in the rucksack, looking for dry clothes. Already Florentino is peeling off the baby's wet rags, then he undoes his own jacket, and by the light of the moon, I see his large hairy chest as he lays Samuel against it, doing the jacket up again. Samuel's crying is muffled, but I can hear already that the sound is fading.

"Make the bottle!" I turn to Jean-Luc, who is already adding a dose of cognac to the milk.

Florentino snatches it from him, pushing it down under his jacket, into Samuel's mouth. Then we're up again, running through the trees. Florentino, still holding Samuel, pulls me along through the darkness, and I pull Jean-Luc along.

I lose track of time as we move blindly through the night. Every crack of a branch, every scuttling animal makes my heart jump. Then we're heading downhill, and it's easier. At last Florentino draws to a stop. "There now. See the light?"

I stare out into the blackness, seeing nothing. Then I spot a glimmer of a light; it seems to grow brighter the longer I look at it.

Laughter spills out of my mouth. I can't control it.

"Charlotte, shh." Jean-Luc squeezes my hand, but I'm still laughing as we half run, half hobble toward the house.

I fall into the arms of the woman who opens the farmhouse door. Then it's all a blur. I am only vaguely aware of a blanket being placed over me. Then nothing. Blissful nothing.

Part Four

Chapter Forty-Five

Santa Cruz, July 10, 1953

JEAN-LUC

"Mr. Bow-Champ, we have reason to believe that Samuel isn't your real son."

Jean-Luc can't move, can't breathe. "She's alive?" he whispers, more to himself than anyone else. It can't be true. No one survived.

They stare at him. Bradley nods, but no one speaks.

"How did she... How is it possible? Are you sure it's her?"

"You admit it, then: Samuel isn't really your son?"

"What? Yes. No."

"You're under arrest for kidnapping. Anything you..."

He must have misheard. His head is spinning. "Kidnapping?"

"Yes." The tall officer looks at him with cold eyes. "You have the right to remain silent, but anything you say can be used in court."

"Kidnapping?" He grips the sides of his chair.

No one replies. They continue to stare at him.

"But I didn't kidnap him! You've got it all wrong. He would have died if I hadn't taken him." *Kidnapping?* The word spins in his head. He has to make them understand it wasn't like that.

"I want a lawyer," he blurts out.

"Do you?" The officer smirks. "What else have you got to hide from us, Mr. Bow-Champ?"

"Nothing." He realizes that for the first time, it's true. He has nothing left to hide. For a moment, it feels refreshing. "I have nothing to hide." He sits up straighter in the chair. "I was only trying to protect Sam."

"Really?" The officer has that ironic look in his eye again. Spirals of cigarette smoke wind their way upward. "Trying to protect the boy from his own mother? All she had to go on was that scar on your face and your deformed hand. But she never gave up. She's been searching for him for the last nine years."

How is it possible? When he saw the horrific pictures that came back from the camps, he immediately dismissed any thoughts of her having survived. Of the tens of thousands who were sent there, only two and a half thousand made it back. No, it's impossible. Auschwitz was an extermination camp, and no one survived more than a few months. If they weren't murdered on arrival, they were worked and starved till they collapsed. That frail-looking woman who thrust her baby into his arms, how could she have survived?

"Did you search for Samuel's mother after the war?" Bradley breathes out a cloud of smoke.

Almost imperceptibly, Jean-Luc shakes his head. He stares at the gray walls, the fluorescent light buzzing in his ears.

"Thought not. And why was that?"

"I never imagined she was still alive." His voice is flat. The air has been knocked out of him.

"Still, you could have looked. After all she'd gone through, you should have."

Jean-Luc looks away, still unable to understand how she could have survived.

As if he can read his mind, Bradley continues, "They were on one of the last trains to Auschwitz, in May, just a week before the D-Day landings."

For a moment, silence hangs between them. Jean-Luc knows that anything he says will sound horribly superficial now.

"They survived, both his parents, seven whole months of hell at Auschwitz. Then they had to walk through eighteen days of ice and snow till they were halfway safe. Eighteen days with nothing to eat except snow. Of course, many died, but not Mr. and Mrs. Laffitte. You know what kept them alive?"

Jean-Luc looks at him with wide eyes. He knows.

"Yes, the thought of being reunited with their son." Bradley stubs his cigarette out, grinding it down into the aluminum ashtray.

"You've spoken with them?"

"Yes. I've spoken with them."

He wants to ask in what language. How can he be sure it's really them?

As if reading his thoughts, Bradley continues. "I spoke with Mrs. Laffitte on the phone, in French."

A line crosses Jean-Luc's forehead.

"You're not the only one who can speak French, Mr. Bow-Champ. I'm French Jewish, through my mother. We left in '39, started again."

The officers standing behind Bradley glance at each other.

"How are they?" Jean-Luc asks. It sounds trivial, but it's not. He wants to know.

"Samuel's parents? Much better now." Bradley taps his pen against the table. Then, taking another cigarette from his breast pocket, he lights up, inhaling deeply. To Jean-Luc's surprise, he holds the open pack out toward him.

Jean-Luc shakes his head, wondering why he's offering him a cigarette now. It unnerves him.

"Yes," Bradley continues. "Mrs. Laffitte wept with joy when I told her the good news. She said she had always known her child was alive, said she'd felt it in her blood."

Jean-Luc wishes he'd taken the cigarette. He doesn't smoke, but it would give him something to do with his hands. His breathing is coming fast, and he can feel sweat collecting under his hairline. He knows what's coming next. He can feel it.

"She said she knew that one day she would be reunited with her child. I guess she just didn't realize how long it would take." Bradley blows out smoke, watching it circle upward. "But now that day has come."

Please, no! The pit of fear in Jean-Luc's belly grows.

"They want their son back."

He swallows the mounting bile in his throat. He has to stay in control. He can't let them do this.

"But... Sam lives here now. This is his home."

"You entered America illegally with a baby you had taken from his parents in France."

"But it wasn't like that. I didn't snatch him from her. She gave him to me."

"Gave?" Bradley raises an eyebrow. "Or entrusted you with his safekeeping until the war was over?"

"What's going to happen to Sam?" This is all that matters.

"The French want us to send you back there. They will decide what to do with you and with the boy. Against our advice, Mrs. Laffitte has asked that Samuel remain with your wife until the outcome has been decided upon. She doesn't want him to be more traumatized than necessary. She's consulting with some psychologist or psychiatrist. She really does have his best interests at heart."

Chapter Forty-Six

Santa Cruz, July 10, 1953

CHARLOTTE

The doorbell cuts through my dream, slicing it apart, visions of my parents evaporating as I remember I'm in America. It's funny how my dreams take me back now, as if I were a child again. They leave me feeling disorientated, and it takes awhile to readjust to reality. I reach out a hand, patting the place next to me. Jean-Luc's not there. He must have gotten up early again.

"Mom," Sam shouts. "It's the doorbell."

"Can you go? I'm not dressed yet." Maybe it's later than I thought. Turning to look at the clock, I see it's 7:30. It might be the mailman.

Marge's voice echoes through the house. "Hi there, Sam. Is your mom in?"

What can she want at this time of the morning? I pull the sheets off, put on my dressing gown, and go downstairs.

"Hi, Marge." I greet her from the last stair.

She looks flushed, as if she's been running. She's wearing her bright orange sundress, and it clashes with her red cheeks. I can see her waiting for Sam to go back upstairs.

"Charlie." She sounds concerned. "Is everything all right? We saw the police car."

"What?" My heart freezes.

"The police car, this morning."

I grip the banister. I feel like I'm falling from a great height. I pull my dressing gown belt tight, forcing myself to stay upright.

"Charlie, is everything okay?" She takes a step toward me.

"I just got up too quickly. I'm fine." I hold my hand up. *Don't come any closer.* My legs feel like they're turning to dust. I collapse onto the stair.

Marge's face looms large. She sits down next to me, but the stair is narrow, and I feel her flesh through my dressing gown. Her sweet perfume hits the back of my nostrils. It makes me feel sick.

"What's going on, Charlie?"

I can't form any words. There's a dam in my head, about to burst. "I...I don't know what the car was doing there, Marge. I don't know. I should get dressed."

But Marge doesn't move. "You know you can talk to me. We're friends."

"I'm okay," I whisper through gritted teeth. "I'll call you later."

She puts her hand on my shoulder. "Charlie, you've been distant these last few weeks. I can see something's troubling you."

I shake my head, trying to make my voice lighter. "Everything's okay."

"Come on. I can see it's not. You know a problem shared is a problem halved."

I just need her to go. I need to think. Standing up, I move toward the front door and open it.

She looks at me with wide, disbelieving eyes. "Well, you know where I am if you need me." She gives me one last meaningful look before leaving.

Through the smoked glass I watch her distorted shape walking away. Then I turn back to the stairs, leaning on the banister. The police have taken him away. They know.

The phone explodes in my ears. *Oh, God, please make it be Jean-Luc, telling me he's on his way home, that there was some mistake.* I pick it up. "Hello."

"Charlotte."

"Jean-Luc. Where are you?"

I can hear him trying to form words, mumbling.

"Jean-Luc?"

"Sam's parents are alive."

"What? What are you saying?" I clasp the phone to my ear, unable to make sense of what I've heard.

"Charlotte, they both survived."

"What? But... but how? It can't be true." I drop the receiver. My hands are shaking, my whole body overtaken by a fierce trembling. I hear his voice on the other end of the phone, but I can't pick it up.

Chapter Forty-Seven

Paris, May 30, 1944

SARAH

"Please, God, no! Please, no!" Sarah covered her ears and closed her eyes, rocking her head from side to side, crying the words. What had she done? It wasn't possible. What kind of a mother would do that? Had she lost her mind? She hadn't stopped to think about it properly. She'd seen the man looking in horror at them, and knew he wasn't part of it, but neither was he a prisoner. He was a railroad worker. A decent man, she could tell. Otherwise she would never have given her baby up. No, she would never have given him to just anyone. She'd looked into his eyes and she'd known he was a kind man. David would understand. She'd had no choice. Now she had to look for David. They'd been separated in Drancy, and she hadn't been able to find him when they'd crowded onto the buses, nor at the station. She had to tell him. He would be grateful that his son wasn't in this cattle truck.

The train shunted forward. Someone elbowed her in the ribs. The screaming went up a notch. "*Fermez vos gueules!* Shut up!" someone shouted. "It's too late now!"

Too late now. She'd done it. He was gone. Her arms empty, she was nothing more than a hollow body. Numb. She would make herself numb. Her numbness would shield her. The shell of her body was on the cattle wagon, but her heart and soul would always be with Samuel. And she would find her way back to him, she promised herself.

"Sarah, is it you?" A hand tugged at her sleeve.

Reluctantly she turned around to see a familiar face she couldn't quite place.

"It's me, Madeleine. From school."

"Madeleine Goldman." As she spoke the woman's name, she was dragged out of her daze, back into the present.

Madeleine grabbed her hand, tears in her eyes. "Where are they taking us?"

"I don't know."

"They already took my husband." Madeleine reached out for Sarah's other hand, gripping her tightly. "I hope they take us to the same place." She looked into Sarah's eyes. "Thank God we don't have children."

Sarah's heart stopped beating, unspoken words forming hard clusters in her throat. How could she say such a thing? How would she know?

She pulled her hand away from Madeleine's grip, her heart shrinking into a tight ball. She couldn't breathe. Her throat seized up. Then the breath came back in a gust. She let out a sob, then another, painfully, as if they were being wrenched from her womb. Madeleine wrapped her arms around her and held her.

For hours they stood clasped together as the train shunted along the tracks. Madeleine talked on and on, about the war, the disappearances of family and friends, where they might be heading. But all Sarah could think about was Samuel. Where was he now? Had he been fed? Was he crying for her? Her own fear, her hunger, her burning thirst meant nothing to her. She could and would endure. But Samuel—so small, so innocent. The thought of him suffering cut into her heart.

A woman near them moaned softly while her young son clung to her skirt. One man prayed, some cried, and some were silent. People had begun to relieve themselves in the bucket in the corner of the wagon, and it was already slopping over, barely soaked up by the straw. The smell of urine, shit, and stale sweat clung to the back of Sarah's throat. She buried her head in Madeleine's shoulder, desperate to go to the toilet herself but unable to in front of everyone.

"When will they let us out?" Madeleine whispered in her ear.

There was only enough room for a few people to sit, and after many long hours Sarah's head was spinning and her knees felt like they were seizing up. Then someone nudged her. "Your turn to sit down." Realizing there was a rotation—ten people could sit at a time—she lowered herself slowly to the floor, carefully folding her stiff limbs. Her breasts were hard and painful, and she took the opportunity to massage them, making milk ooze out. Samuel's milk. She scrunched her eyes shut, refusing to let the tears spill, silently begging God for someone else to be feeding her son now.

When she opened her eyes again, she noticed Madeleine staring at the damp patches on her linen blouse. They were just about visible in the dim light of the windowless cattle truck.

"I'm so sorry." Madeleine's voice trembled. "You have a baby?"

Sarah was grateful that she'd used the present tense. It gave her hope. She spoke slowly, deliberately, each word painful. "Samuel. He's one month old."

Madeleine squeezed her hand.

"I gave him to someone. To keep him safe."

"You did the right thing. Can you imagine trying to feed a baby here? We're dehydrated ourselves."

"I have to get word to my husband, David. He's somewhere here."

"We'll write him a message and give it to one of the men to pass on." Madeleine paused. "They won't let men and women be together, will they?"

Sarah shook her head, knowing that they would be separated.

"They'll give men different work," Madeleine continued. "It will be harder for them." She paused. "We'll probably be in the kitchens. It will likely be a huge work camp, maybe a mine."

Sarah nodded.

Out of her breast pocket, Madeleine produced a pad of paper and a pen. "Write small, so it can be hidden easily. You never know."

But they did know. They knew they were heading somewhere terrible, that they would be treated cruelly, that they might even die there. They knew, but still they hung on to that thin thread of hope.

Sarah wrote in tiny, careful letters: *Our son is safe. I gave him to a French railroad worker. I know he will look after him. Stay alive so we can find him again. Your loving wife.* No names. It was safer that way. Folding the paper into a small square, she put it in her trouser pocket until she'd worked out which man she could entrust it to.

The truck had grown quiet, the moaning and crying and unanswered questions having all died away. Their mouths dry and their stomachs empty, the prisoners had shut down. Madeleine and Sarah huddled together. A young girl, her teeth chattering, drew closer to them, and without a word Madeleine reached out an arm, taking her into their fold. "What's your name?"

"Cecile," the girl whispered.

"Where's your mother?"

"She was taken last year."

Sarah's heart lurched, seeing this motherless child. She clutched Cecile's hand. "We'll look after you."

Whenever the train stopped, they shouted out, begging for water, but nothing was given to them. Finally, on the second day, they were given tepid water to drink and they heard Polish voices. As the train pulled out again, they gazed out through the holes in the planks at a flat, bleak landscape.

On the third night, the train stopped and did not move again.

The prisoners waited in silence, terrified, starving, and exhausted. Then the doors were yanked back.

"*Schnell! Schnell!* You filthy animals! Get out!"

They scrambled out of the wagon, clutching one another for support. Floodlights came on, blinding them. Dogs snarled, baring teeth like daggers, straining on their leashes to get at the prisoners. The SS held truncheons and whips, and among them were some women, in long black capes with hoods, and tall black leather boots.

"Men to the left! Women to the right!"

Sarah gripped her message tightly, looking for someone to pass it to. She picked the nearest man, shoving it into his fist. "Please, give this to David Laffitte."

"Ranks of five! Now!" A truncheon landed on the head of a woman next to Sarah. Instinctively, Sarah reached for her, holding her up before she could slip to the ground.

Exhausted, rigid with fear, and stiff from three days cramped in a cattle truck, they moved into lines of five, one behind the other. Sarah scanned the group of men, searching for David, but she couldn't see him.

"*Schnell! Schnell!*" A shot rang out and the thud of a body landing on the ground resonated through Sarah's head. She couldn't look. She clung to Madeleine and Cecile, the three of them bonded now by this madness.

"Hey, how old are you?" The man pointing a stick at Cecile was an inmate, wearing striped trousers and jacket.

"Thirteen," she answered.

"No you're not! You're eighteen."

"But I'm thirteen!"

"You'll die if you're thirteen." In a quieter voice he added, "Just say you're eighteen." He moved on down the line.

Another inmate took his place, screaming at them, "Didn't you know? In 1944, you didn't know! Why have you come here? You should have killed yourselves rather than come here." He pointed to clouds of black smoke against a sky only a shade lighter. "That's where you'll end up. The crematorium."

Madeleine turned around and vomited. Sarah suddenly understood where the terrible smell was coming from. Now she had no doubt in her mind. She had done the right thing when she gave her son up.

They had arrived in hell itself.

Chapter Forty-Eight

Auschwitz, November 1944

SARAH

Only the hope that she would find her son again kept Sarah alive at Auschwitz, though without her close-knit group of friends, it would probably have been impossible to survive.

In the third week, when they were queuing for the midday watery soup, a woman she didn't know pushed into her. "Take this," she whispered, shoving a hard piece of bread into Sarah's hand. "There's something inside."

Terrified of being caught, Sarah slipped out of the queue, glancing around to check that no one was looking. Only Madeleine, a few places behind her in the queue, had noticed, and Sarah felt her friend's eyes piercing her back as she sneaked off. Any secrets here were best kept locked away in your heart. They had ways to extract information. Terrifying screams often pierced the dark, empty nights.

A shiver ran down her back as she bent over the lump of bread. The edge of a piece of paper was just visible. Not wanting to waste precious food, she carefully sucked off the stale bread till she could pull the paper out easily. She squinted as she read the writing: *Love of my life, you did the right thing. You are brave and true. Stay alive. We will find our son again.*

Tears fell onto the note, making the words run. She wondered what he'd had to do for such a dangerous favor. Pushing the damp paper back into the bread, she ate it slowly. Now David was with her. She would carry him around and he would nourish her more than food ever could. "I will survive. I will get through this," she whispered to herself.

Madeleine was suddenly next to her. "What are you doing?" She frowned at Sarah. "Don't you want the soup?" She raised her spoon, letting the pale, watery liquid fall back into the bowl. "It's crème de cabbage again." Her ironic smile didn't reach her eyes. "You haven't lost your spoon, have you?"

"No." Sarah lifted her top, showing her spoon, which was attached with a piece of old string. She'd had to save her bread for two days to get the flimsy metal implement, but it had been worth it. You couldn't eat the soup without a spoon.

"Are you ill?" Madeleine reached out, feeling Sarah's forehead.

"No. I'll get some now." Sarah walked away quickly before she was tempted to tell her about the message. It wasn't that she didn't trust her friend. She did. But she knew they could do things to you that could make you betray even those closest to you.

The sun shone bright, as if mocking them in their misery. Their thirst was intolerable. Sarah's jaws felt locked together and her teeth like they were glued to her cheeks. Thirst could drive you mad, and it became an obsession for her. She dreamed of water, she longed for it night and day, would have paid any price for it. One especially hot day, she managed to trade some bread she had saved for a bucket of water. She plunged her head into the bucket and drank it all down. After that, she felt better and the obsession lifted.

It wasn't possible to survive alone, not when something as commonplace as losing your shoes meant being sent straight to the gas chambers; after all, it was easier to replace women than shoes. Sarah had a close group of friends, Madeleine, Simone—someone Madeleine knew from her neighborhood—and the young girl from the train, Cecile. They supported one another, and the older women looked out for Cecile, especially during the interminable roll calls. Often they were woken at three in the morning and marched outside, but they wouldn't be counted till dawn broke. When one of them felt too weak to stand, the other women would gather around to hold her up. When they were finally marched away, there were always bodies strewn across the ground. They would be shot if they weren't already dead. Sarah scrunched up her eyes when she heard the guns, but never looked back at the fallen women.

After roll call, they were marched through swampy fields for two hours, then given shovels and hods—wheelbarrows without wheels, which had to be loaded and carried to a ditch to be emptied. All day, except for a break for the watery soup at midday, they dug and lifted and carried. It was backbreaking, but if they paused for a minute, the guards would send the dogs over to snap and bite at their heels, or come themselves to deliver blows. As they worked, they had to listen to shouts and cries of pain, while the guards stood around chatting in groups, even laughing. By the end of the day, they were feverish, and some had dropped, never to get up again. But Sarah and her group of friends always tried to find one another, supporting each other as they began the long march back, the strongest singing "La Marseillaise," the others joining in if they could. Some days, they didn't sing at all.

One evening on their way back, the male prisoners passed in front of them. Sarah desperately scanned them, searching for David. But he wasn't there. A deep fear gripped her intestines. What if he'd died? How could she survive then?

As one of the prisoners walked by her, he dropped something at her feet. A pair of woolen socks. She picked them up, stuffing them under her striped dress. Back at the barracks, she took them out and a piece of paper fell from them. Just three words were written on it:

Don't give up. It looked like David's writing, but she couldn't be sure. Please, God, she prayed, keep him alive.

It was clear from the outset that many of the women would die. It was too degrading, too shocking for lots of them to bear. Even going to the latrine was taking a risk with your life, as it meant wading through excrement and crouching over a long open sewer, trying not to fall in. Some had neither the strength nor the desire to adapt to this hell, but Sarah had both. Though her body was shrinking as if feeding on itself, and her breasts had disappeared, her determination to find Samuel gave her the strength to carry on when others dropped.

While they toiled and fought for their lives on a daily basis, winter drew in. If they fell at roll call now, even if they were picked up afterward, it still meant death. There was no way to change the wet, muddy clothes that froze to their backs. The fate of each one of them depended on those around them, and individualism disappeared. It was this that kept them going. On the raw edge of survival, they rose to do things they never would have believed themselves capable of. Life wasn't so much about friendship. It was about solidarity.

Sarah was growing weak. Open sores on her back had become infected. Simone was a dentist for the SS guards and so was able to get extra items of clothing and even medicine from the place they nicknamed "Canada"—so called because they imagined Canada to be a land of unimaginable plenty. She bathed Sarah's sores in disinfectant when she could get some, but they just wouldn't heal. Then one day she came with good news. She had managed to get Sarah a job at the infirmary, scaring the rats away from the living and carrying the dead outside. Rats thrived at Auschwitz, and some had reached the size of cats. They even dared to bare their teeth at Sarah as she raised the spade to chase them away. At first, she couldn't stand to look at them and just waved the spade wildly in an attempt to disperse them, but she soon grew braver, and after two weeks she even killed one, smashing it on the head as it stood on its back legs, staring at her defiantly. It gave her a rush of pride, making her feel powerful in this world where she had no more value than the rats. It was the rat or her, and she had won.

When she carried the dead outside, she held her breath and closed her eyes, but still it made her retch. If only she could have covered them in sheets or something, it would have helped, but their starved bodies were naked as she took them to the dumpster. How could she do such a thing? Shouldn't she have refused? Let herself be sent to the gas chambers rather than treat the dead with such disrespect? If it hadn't been for the thought of Samuel, she might have, but now she had a duty to survive.

The job saved her from working outside through the harsh winter months, and also gave her the opportunity to steal medical supplies. If she were caught, it would mean instant death, but when Cecile fell ill, she had no choice. The poor child's fever was burning her up, and she could no longer stand during roll call. They had to cluster around her, propping her up. It was probably typhoid, and only antibiotics could save her. Sarah knew that they were kept in the glass cabinet in the room where operations were carried out. It was normally empty at lunchtime; all she had to do was sneak in there and grab a couple of pills. But the day she planned to do it, the guards didn't leave the room. There was always someone in there.

When she got back to the barracks that evening, Cecile was delirious with fever, imagining that she was back home with her family. She held on to Simone. "Maman!" she cried. "I thought you'd left me."

"You have to get them tomorrow." Simone looked at Sarah over the top of the child's head.

Sarah nodded, determined to find a way.

But the next day came and went and still the room was never empty. She couldn't get the drugs. How could she?

Distraught, she returned to her block that evening. Simone saw her coming and held her arms out to her. "It's too late," she whispered. "She's gone."

Cecile's death affected them deeply. They hadn't managed to protect the child. Their guilt at having outlived her ate into them all. They stopped singing, and instead of telling one another stories like they used to in the evenings, they hung around other groups, always on the outside looking in.

They couldn't go on like this. Sarah understood that they mustn't give in to apathy; they couldn't let themselves become like the "musulmen"—those poor creatures with the blank look in their eyes, more dead than alive.

It was all part of the Nazis' plan to rid them of their humanity. She wondered if it helped them to no longer see their prisoners as human. How else could they treat them as they did? And on this scale? Beating them, torturing them, murdering them. How had it become possible? These questions spun around and around in her head. No one in the normal world would be capable of imagining how far human beings could sink. She wondered if people would even believe them if by some miracle they ever got out alive.

Chapter Forty-Nine

Auschwitz, January 1945

SARAH

Sarah had been at Auschwitz for seven and a half months. She felt like she had aged seventy years. She was no longer the same person. She walked like a long-term prisoner, her head and shoulders stooped forward, pulling the weight of her diminished body, her legs shapeless and swollen, her lips red from bleeding gums. There were no mirrors, of course, but she knew this was how she looked, because they all looked the same.

The snow had been falling for weeks now, maybe months. It seemed like forever. She was terrified David would catch pneumonia and be sent to the ovens, but he seemed to have good contacts. He managed to send messages to her every few weeks, and she sent her own whenever she could get something from Canada to pay the messenger.

Rumors were rife all through the winter—the Allies were coming, the Red Cross was negotiating for their freedom, the Russians were on their way—but they never came to anything. Then one night in January they heard artillery in the distance. Sarah and her friends sat up in their bunks, hugging one another tightly. Could they dare let themselves hope? They didn't sleep the rest of that night, excitement running through their tired veins.

The next day, Sarah went to the infirmary as usual. The doctor was talking to the patients when she arrived. "Tomorrow night the camp will be evacuated. The sick will remain here."

Her heart sank; they were to be sent somewhere else before they could be freed. She watched as some of the sick tried to scramble out of bed, desperate not to be left behind for the Nazis to shoot. Others too ill or too numb to care didn't move or speak. Sarah collected as many blankets as she could and ran back to her block to warn the other women.

"They'll shoot anyone left behind." Madeleine held on to Sarah's shoulders. "They won't want any witnesses. And where will they take us? Do you know?"

"No. But I brought blankets. We still need clothes, or we'll die of cold. And shoes! We must have shoes!"

The guards spent the day burning documents, then they made the prisoners clean out the blocks. "We don't want them to think you lived like pigs," they screamed.

Early the next morning, long before sunrise, thousands of them were marched to the gates. Little more than skeletons, they'd covered themselves in layer upon layer of clothing or blankets, slumping under the weight like exhausted old donkeys. The searchlights came on. Hundreds of SS guards and their dogs surrounded them. The snow continued to fall. "*Schnell!* Hurry! Hurry! Fall into ranks!"

The gates to the camp opened.

Block by block they marched out. Sarah's group had to wait for the forty or so blocks in front of them to leave before they could get going. She fingered the bread in her pocket. No. Later, she told herself. You'll need it later. She knew there would be no food or water for the prisoners. What would the guards care if they died in the snow? It would probably suit them—save them the job of killing them.

"Faster! Faster! You filthy flea-ridden dogs."

They all began to run. The blood pumped through Sarah's veins, warming her up, energizing her tired organs. Her heart beat hard. She was alive! They were leaving Auschwitz and she had survived!

Like a machine, they marched on and on. They had to keep up or they'd be killed. Many shots rang out on the long march; anyone who tried to run off into the woods was instantly shot, as were those who got left behind, or those who fell, though they were usually just trampled over in the stampede. One foot in front of the other—it was all she had to do. Keep going. But she was so thirsty, so hungry, so tired. A girl near her scooped a handful of snow off the coat of the woman in front, shoving it into her mouth without pausing in her stride. Sarah copied her, holding it in her mouth as it melted. Then she fingered the bread in her pocket again, but she might need it later, tomorrow even. They had no idea how long they would have to go without food.

More people began to collapse into the snow, giving in to the release of death. The rest marched over or around them. There was no choice—it was a matter of survival. Sarah wondered what kind of a person she would be if she survived now. "Don't think. Just keep going," she whispered into the dark. "You have to live." But the thought of death lingered on. To no longer exist. To cease to be. No more pain. No cold. No exhaustion. Nothing. She was near to giving in, but she knew David was out there somewhere. She could hear his voice whispering in her head. *Sarah, Sarah. Love of my life. Come and find me. Find me.*

Without thinking, she tried to break ranks to run ahead. She had to get to him.

A blow to her head sent her reeling. She closed her eyes as she collapsed into the snow. The soft whiteness felt like a blanket welcoming her. At last, she could sleep. She buried her face in its coolness, knowing she would find David again in her dreams.

Then hands were pulling her up. "Sarah! Get up!" Simone's face swam into view.

"Let me sleep." Her head was too heavy for her body. She just wanted to slip into oblivion. But where was David? Had she found him? "David. Where is David?"

"He's here somewhere. Get up! You need to find him."

Sarah felt another pair of hands reach under her arms, pulling her up. A shot rang out, then another. The sound reverberated through her shivering body. She hadn't died. She had to stay in this world. Whatever happened, she had to keep going—had to forget her feeble body and let her spirit take her. God, carry me through this, she prayed. With the aid of the women on each side of her, she mustered all her strength, ignoring the throbbing in her head, and pulled herself up out of the snow. Kissing her friends on their cold lips, she murmured, "You will live. Promise me you will live!"

They dragged her forward, and that was their answer. Together they stumbled, they tried to run. At last the sun came up, but it brought no warmth. An icy wind cut through their layers of clothes, slicing through their skin, into their weak and tired bones. Many more women dropped.

"You've done twenty kilometers!" the Kommandant shouted. They had reached an abandoned village, not a soul in sight. "Time for a rest."

They crowded into a large building, the roof fallen in. Inside, the snow was thick, but they were sheltered from the cruel wind. Prisoners dropped down into piles, asleep before they hit the ground. But Sarah had to keep going. She had to find David. If she slept, she would die. So she left her group, clambering over bodies, through rooms with broken walls. "David! David!" she called out. If she didn't find him now, she wouldn't be able to go on. She had no force left. "David!" Her voice grew weaker as she searched for him in the blanket of faces.

"Sarah!"

It was him! Blood pumped through her veins again. She had found him! The voice was coming from a pile of bodies propped against a wall. She ran toward them.

It was his eyes she saw first. His dark brown eyes shining out from a sea of snow. She threw herself at him, covering him with her body, her hands reaching for his face. She gripped it in her bony fingers, looking into his eyes. "Is it you? Is it really you?"

"Sarah, you found me."

Chapter Fifty

Santa Cruz, July 10, 1953

JEAN-LUC

After they let him telephone Charlotte, Bradley and the two officers left the interview room, locking it on their way out. Jean-Luc has been sitting there for what feels like hours, but when he looks at his watch, he sees it's only been fifty minutes. He's desperate to get to Charlotte. He should never have broken the news to her like that, on the phone. What was he thinking of? It must have been the shock. The guilt.

An officer he hasn't seen before enters the room. "You're on a flight tomorrow morning. You can go home, pack a bag, then you have to come straight back here."

"But I haven't seen a lawyer. I want to see a lawyer."

"A lawyer can't help you. We're sending you back to France. You can have one when you get to France."

"But... but what about my rights?"

A smile stretches across the officer's face. "Mr. Bow-Champ, I don't think you understand the seriousness of your crime. And we have no reason nor wish not to comply with the French. It will be up to them now to decide if it was kidnapping or... something else.

The matter is out of our hands. We'll take you home now; you can have ten minutes to pack."

"Ten minutes! But I need to talk with Charlotte and Sam. I can't just leave like that."

"I said ten minutes. Now quit your whining, or it'll be down to five."

"Please..."

Folding his arms, the officer looks down at his wristwatch.

Without another word, Jean-Luc gets up and follows him out to the waiting car. Thank God, there are no handcuffs. He gets in the back with the officer. They drive to his home.

"We'll wait here," the officer says when they pull up behind the oak tree.

Jean-Luc gets out of the car, vaguely aware of Marge's kitchen curtains twitching. He walks up the garden path and pushes the front door open. Cautiously he breathes in, wondering where Charlotte and Sam are. An eerie silence seeps from the walls.

He hears shuffling noises coming from the kitchen. He goes on through, the blood racing through his veins.

Charlotte, a small suitcase in her hand, stands in the middle of the room. Her mouth drops open when she sees him, the color draining from her face.

He knows what she's doing. His heart sinks, heavy with the weight of her pain. "Charlotte." He reaches his arms out to her.

"We have to go. Now!" she screams at him.

He touches her shoulder, bringing her gently toward him. He can feel all her hot energy dissipating.

She falls into him.

"Shh, shh... *mon ange.*" He feels her body give way as she sinks down to the floor, as though she's crumbling away under his fingers. Sinking with her, he crouches down, stroking her, murmuring, "Charlotte, Charlotte."

Someone coughs. He looks up to see Sam standing in the doorway, his little face ashen.

With one arm still around Charlotte, Jean-Luc opens up the other. Wordlessly Sam walks into the fold. He wraps his little arms around Jean-Luc's neck and whispers in his ear, "Daddy, please don't go away again. I'm scared."

Chapter Fifty-One

Santa Cruz, July 13, 1953

CHARLOTTE

"Why can't we go to France with Daddy?" Sam runs into the bedroom, jumping onto the bed next to me. I want to wrap him in my arms and hold him safe forever. It feels like the world in all its ugliness is crashing into our lives, and I won't be able to protect him from it.

"Sam, your father had to go to help with a police investigation." I stroke his silky hair. "It's not a holiday."

He sticks out his lower lip. "But I wanted to go camping in France."

"I know. Maybe one day."

He gets up, pulls the curtains back, and looks out the window. "Mom, why is the cop out there?"

"He's looking after us."

"Why?" He turns around, scrunching up his forehead. "Why do we need looking after?"

A shiver runs down the back of my neck. What can I say? "Just in case."

"In case of what?"

"In case the bogeyman comes. Come on, time for bed now."

"But who is the bogeyman?"

"He doesn't exist. It's just a saying."

"Why did you say it then?"

"Come on, Sam. Time for bed. Bogeyman or not."

He looks at me with round, alert eyes. "I can't go to sleep."

I lean over him, kissing him on the forehead. "Course you can."

"I can't, I'm scared. Can I sleep in your bed? Daddy's not here."

It's tempting to have him near me. I'm scared too. "Okay, just this once."

After I put him in our bed, I go down to the kitchen, pulling back the net curtains to stare out at the police car. They think I might try to escape with Sam; not that they've said anything, but it's there in the way they look at me, suspicion edged with something verging on pity. I don't know what to do with myself. Time is slipping away while other people are deciding what will happen to our lives. Marge hasn't been back. In fact, no one has even called. I imagine it didn't take long for the news to get out. That'll give them something to talk about during their coffee mornings.

Without intending to, I find myself wandering into the living room, pouring myself a glass of Southern Comfort. I drink it quickly, feeling it taking the edge off my raw nerves. I'm tired and confused. Maybe I should get an early night; things might be clearer in the morning. I creep back upstairs, glad that Sam is in my bed. I need him near me. Without putting the light on, I get undressed and pull on my nightie. When I slip into bed, I hear his breathing, light but regular. He must be asleep already. I lie on my back, concentrating on breathing down into my abdomen, trying to relax.

Sam lets out a long, heavy breath, turning over. Then he turns back, facing me. I lie there rigid as a piece of metal. I feel him move closer to me, his silky hair caressing my arm. I roll onto my side and stroke his head.

"Mom," he whispers. "What investigation is Daddy helping the police with?"

"It's complicated, Sam." Maybe it will be easier to explain in the dark. I've been putting the moment off, aware that everything will change once he knows. "Sam..."

"Yeah."

"There's something I should tell you."

"What, Mom?"

"About you. It's your story."

"What story?"

I kiss the top of his head in the dark. "You remember how we told you about the war, when you were born in Paris, and how we escaped across the mountains and the ocean to come to America?"

"Yeah."

"We had to leave. There was so much fighting, bombs dropping. We were scared the Nazis were going to blow up Paris."

"Yeah, I know."

"When you were born, it was so different. It's hard to imagine. Every day people were being arrested and killed." I continue to stroke his head. "What I'm going to tell you now is hard to understand, so please listen carefully and let me get to the end. Okay?" I reach for his hand.

"Okay, Mom."

"You were born into the war, and even though you were only a tiny baby, you were arrested and taken away to a horrible prison."

"Why would they put a baby in prison?"

"You were born in the wrong place, Sam. They were arresting all the Jews in Paris and taking them to an awful prison. Many died. But somebody rescued you."

"What's a Jew?"

I wonder how to explain it. I'm not really sure myself whether it's a race or a religion. "It's...it's someone whose parents were Jewish. It's passed on from one generation to the next."

"What? Like being color-blind? That's passed on, and so is eye color, isn't it?"

"Yes, it is, but it's nothing like that. It's more to do with your history—where you're from, your religion."

"Are we Jewish?"

"No." We've never talked much about religion, though Sam knows many of the Bible stories. We married in a Catholic church after we arrived in America, but Jean-Luc and I both feel a little uneasy with the indoctrination and the rules of religion. Maybe it's because we've disobeyed so many of them.

"So why were we in the prison?"

I'm not sure how to go on now. How do I tell him he's not our son? I don't think I can do it.

I take a deep breath, putting my arms around him, pulling him into me. I breathe in his smell—lemon shampoo and a slight musky odor. The lump in my throat grows hard. I kiss the top of his head and stroke his soft cheek. Then I pinch his nose gently, like I used to when he was small.

He lies there, warm and soft, and I feel him soaking up all my love for him. For a minute we lie there. Safe. Together.

Then he begins to fidget. I can't put it off any longer. I have to tell him.

"Sam, you were in prison because you were Jewish."

"But you said we weren't Jewish."

"We're not, but you are." I take his cheeks in my hands. "Listen carefully, and let me get to the end. Okay?

"The person who saved you from this prison was your father."

"Daddy?"

"Yes. He smuggled you out when no one was looking. You were tiny—only about a month old."

"Where were you?"

"I wasn't there. Just listen, Sam. Your father was working on the railroads at the prison."

"Yeah?"

"When he took you, he had to hide you, but you were so small, it wasn't hard. He hid you under his coat." I pause, gathering my thoughts, aware of the awful impact they'll have once they're released. "Sam, he couldn't bring your mother and father with him too. He couldn't hide them like he hid you."

"What...I don't understand. You mean you?"

"No. Your real parents are Jewish. They were prisoners too, but Daddy couldn't save them. He could only save you."

"But I don't understand. You're my parents!" He sits bolt upright and reaches behind him, flicking the switch. Light floods the room.

I squint. But I'm desperate to see Sam, so I open my eyes to the blinding light.

"Why are you saying this?" He puts his hands over his ears, as though he can block out the truth.

I reach out for him, putting my hands over his. "Sam, *mon coeur.* I'm so sorry. We're...we're not your real parents. Your real parents were taken away during the war."

"No!" He jumps up. "No!"

"Sam, please. Listen."

"No!" He shoots out of the room.

I hear his bedroom door slam. I have to go to him. He can't be left alone to make sense of this nightmare. I pull my dressing gown on, giving him a few minutes to calm down. When I open his door, he's lying on his bed, his head buried in the pillow.

"Sam," I whisper.

He pretends not to hear me. I walk farther into the room and sit on the bed. "Sam, we love you so much."

"Why did you say all those things then?" His voice comes out muffled. He turns over, staring at me with angry eyes. His fury wrenches at my core. He wants us to be his real parents as much as we do.

"Sam, I know how hard this is for you." I take his hand out from where it's hiding in his pajama sleeve and hold on to it tightly.

"You don't want me, do you? You don't like me anymore."

"No! No! That's not true!" How could he think such a thing? "We love you so much. We brought you here because we wanted you, and we'll never stop loving you." He has to understand that my love for him is pure and unconditional; that nobody could love him more than I do.

I see tears spring into his eyes, slide down his cheeks, and I watch as he sticks his tongue out to catch them. I imagine their salty taste—comforting, like the sea.

He's staring up at the ceiling, his big brown eyes still watering up.

"There's a spiderweb," he announces abruptly.

Startled at his change of topic, I follow his gaze upward.

"I hate spiders!" He wipes his face with his sleeve. "They climb up your nose and out through your mouth while you're asleep. Not many people know that. I read it and then I knew it, and it was too late to unknow it. I hate it—all those things happening without you even knowing."

"Sam, I'm so sorry. We didn't want to have to tell you like this. You're still so young. It's difficult for a boy to—"

He jumps up from the bed, wild eyes darting around the room, coming to fall on the fort Jean-Luc made for him. I know what he's going to do. I can feel it as though I were in his head. He picks it up, lifting it out in front of him. Then he throws it down. It splits at the sides, breaking open. He bends his knee, then brings his foot crashing forward, smashing it into smithereens.

I gasp, remembering Jean-Luc building the fort out of odd bits of wood and old popsicle sticks, putting the pieces together in exactly the right places. All that time and love, gone.

Sam collapses onto the floor, lying in front of the broken fort, curling his legs up to his chest, sobs racking his body.

I lie down next to him, but I don't touch him. The moment is too fragile. "Sam, we love you so much. We wanted to save you. In our hearts we are your real mom and dad. We always will be."

Chapter Fifty-Two

Santa Cruz, July 15, 1953

CHARLOTTE

They're watching me all the time. They call it surveillance, but it feels more like house arrest. They're not the only ones. I sometimes see Marge at her kitchen window, twitching the curtains. A young officer sits outside the house in his blue-and-white car for the whole neighborhood to see. No wonder no one calls anymore. He's a few years younger than me, recently married, with a new baby; hence the gray bags under his eyes. Polite and unimposing, he keeps a respectful distance between us, as if he's embarrassed to be checking up on me like this. He's just doing his job.

I decide to invite him in for a coffee. I want him to know I'm just a normal mother, and not some anonymous face. Also, I might learn something from him about the trial. I walk out to his car with a straight back and my head held high.

He steps out when he sees me coming, smoothing down his crumpled pants and straightening his cap. "Mornin', ma'am."

"Good morning..."

"John," he fills in for me.

"Good morning, John. I was wondering if you'd like to come in for a coffee."

"I'm not sure that would be appropriate."

"I see." I look at him, noticing the slight tremor in his hands as he straightens his cap again. "What do you think I'm going to do? Lock you up in my house and run away?"

He laughs. It's a high-pitched, nervous laugh and he covers it up by coughing, rolling his hand into a manly fist as he brings it up in front of his mouth.

"I've got some homemade cookies too," I say, turning back toward the house.

As I guessed, he doesn't want to appear rude, so he follows me in. When he enters the house, he removes his cap and moves his hands to the edge of it, letting it glide through his fingers, around and around, again and again.

"Come through to the kitchen."

He watches as I put the coffee beans in the grinder, turning the handle.

"Wow." He smiles. "Real coffee."

"Yes, we like our coffee."

There's a minute's silence, then he coughs again.

"Don't worry about checking up on me like this." I want to put him at ease. "You're just doing your job."

"Yeah, it's not the most interesting bit. I prefer to be out and about." He pats his stomach as though he's already put on pounds sitting out in the car for all of three days now.

"Any news on the trial?" I try to sound casual.

"No, but don't worry. It will be quick, as it concerns the welfare of a minor."

"A minor?" I frown. Sam's the major person in this whole trial.

"Yes, since a child's welfare is concerned, it will have top priority."

"But once they understand that Jean-Luc didn't kidnap him, that he saved him, they'll stop the trial, won't they? They can't really charge him with kidnapping, surely?"

"Mrs. Beauchamp, I can't tell you anything. I don't know anything."

I've made him uncomfortable. He's sipping his coffee, though it's still too hot to drink. I bet he can't wait to get back to his car.

"I'm sorry, of course you don't." I take a deep breath. "How's your baby?" I ask.

"Swell. He's a great little guy. Don't seem to like to sleep much, though."

"Oh dear. We never had any trouble with Sam. He always slept well."

"Guess you were lucky."

"Yeah," I continue. "He loved his sleep and his food. What we call a *bon vivant* in France. He was such an easy, happy baby. We really were lucky."

"Thanks for the coffee, Mrs. Beauchamp." He puts his cup down decisively and stands up.

When I accompany him to his car, I see the mailman cycling away. Silently I pray there'll be a letter in the mailbox from Jean-Luc. This waiting is killing me. I can't sleep, can't eat. I'm barely functioning. I look across the street at Marge's house. I've thought about going over there, telling her the truth, but somehow I don't think she'll be ready to listen now. It's funny how all the friendly faces of the neighborhood have evaporated into thin air. I had hoped that one of my so-called friends would come over to ask for my side of the story. The chance to explain, even if they didn't understand, would have helped. But the curtains are closed at the kitchen windows, and no one's in their yards these days.

When I open the latch at the back of the mailbox, I see one thin letter. Quickly I pull it out, staring at the postmark. France. I rip it open.

My dearest Sam, my darling Charlotte,

The two of you are everything to me—my home, my love, my life. Every day I thank the stars above that you came into

my life. The past nine years have been more than I ever dared hope for, and they have brought me more happiness than I ever deserved.

Sam, through your eyes I have seen the world in its brightest, most beautiful colors. You have taught me so much: that we are born good, that life is worth living, worth fighting for. That we always have a choice. The best choice I ever made was you. Taking you was the best thing I ever did.

Your mother will have told you your story by now. It's a special story, for a very special boy. You are brave and courageous, and even though difficult times lie ahead, I have faith in you. You are stronger than you realize.

Once we escaped to America, both your mother and I fell in love with you, and we didn't look for your real parents. Please forgive us for this.

Charlotte, you gave me faith in myself, I became a better man because of you. Now, you must be clear that this is all my doing, my fault. You had no part in it. Remember how I didn't let you talk, how I wouldn't let you speak of the past. I said it was all behind us, that I would build a new life for us here in America. You wanted to tell the truth about our story, but I wouldn't let you. Remember that through all this, you are innocent.

Stay safe, for Sam.
All my love, forever,
Jean-Luc

The idiot! He wants to take all the blame, when it was my fault. When it was I who refused to go to the authorities. I'd fallen in love with Sam and was worried that one of those Jewish organizations would take him away from us to "repatriate" him. I had terrifying visions of him being adopted by a Jewish family in Israel. I knew it had happened to children who were hidden in the war and whose parents had been killed. I convinced Jean-Luc that we couldn't take the risk—that Sam was better off with us, believing he belonged to us, because I couldn't have lived without him.

Chapter Fifty-Three

Santa Cruz, July 16, 1953

SAM

I miss my friends. It's all gone creepy quiet. No one calls anymore, and I haven't seen Jimmy out in his yard. I get it now—my story. I just want Daddy to come home and for things to go back to normal. Mom told me to stay inside and lie low for a while. But it's so boring. Deadly boring. I could go to Jimmy's, I suppose; she'd never know if I'm quick, unless the cop tells her, but I could duck around the back of his car. I've seen him snoozing loads of times.

I jump up, run out the front door, up the yard, behind the cop car, and across the street. I hold my finger on Jimmy's bell.

There's no answer. I ring again, this time holding the bell down for longer. The curtains at the kitchen window move, and I see Marge looking out at me. I wave, then feel stupid when she doesn't wave back. It gives me a heavy feeling inside. She moves away from the window and I stand back from the door, waiting for her to let me in.

Slowly the door half opens. "Oh, Sam. Hello."

I don't know why she pretends to be surprised it's me.

"Hi," I say. "Can Jimmy play?"

Before she can answer, I hear feet running down the stairs and Jimmy's there. I feel better already.

But then he stops on the bottom stair. "Hey, Sam."

"Hey, Jimmy."

"You should hear all the things everyone's saying about you."

"Shh, Jimmy," Marge says.

"Can he come upstairs, Mom?"

Jimmy never used to have to ask for permission.

"Come on, Sam." At least he doesn't wait for her answer, but shoots straight back upstairs.

Without looking at Marge, I run after him.

"You have to set the table soon, Jimmy," Marge calls after us. "Sam can't stay long."

We both ignore her and make a space among the pieces of Meccano in his bedroom to put our butts. "What you making?" I ask.

He looks at me. "Nothin' much."

There's a silence, and it makes me feel bad.

"Everyone's saying your dad's a Nazi." He looks at me through narrowed eyes.

"What?"

"Yeah. And then he kidnapped you. Because you were a baby."

"What's a Nazi?" I remember Daddy's letter and try to be brave.

"Well, it's real bad. They were Germans who tortured and shot people, in the war. They all wore long black coats and high black boots, and they marched through towns killing everyone." He takes a breath. "Was your dad really a Nazi?"

"No!" I can't help it. Tears spring to my eyes. I wipe them away with the back of my hand, swallowing the rest. Then I look at Jimmy long and hard. "He was never a Nazi. He was fighting the Nazis, secretly. He saved me from them. They were gonna kill me, so he took me. He never kidnapped me. Then he escaped here to America with my mom."

"Wow! That's real bad." Jimmy stares back at me, and I can tell he's working out whether to believe me. "Is your mom your real mom?"

I shake my head, remembering how we always laughed so much, till our sides hurt, and when we stopped we couldn't remember what made us laugh in the first place, and that would just start us off again. Jimmy has always been my best friend.

"But why were they gonna kill you?"

"'Cause I was born in the wrong place, and in war they do bad things to children, even babies."

"Yeah." Jimmy looks down, and I can see he's thinking about this. Then he looks up again, his eyes warmer than before. "Who are your real parents, then?"

"I dunno. They were prisoners too, and they nearly died. But they didn't."

"Are you gonna meet them?"

"Maybe, dunno."

"Why is there a cop outside your house every day? Where's your dad now?"

"He's in France, helping them with the investigation. The cop looks after us now instead."

"Cool." Jimmy frowns. I can see he's not sure about the whole story. Me neither. I don't get why we need the cop. Some kids don't have dads, but they don't get cops looking after them either.

He pokes me in the ribs. "Wanna help me make a car now?"

Chapter Fifty-Four

Santa Cruz, July 16, 1953

CHARLOTTE

The TV is off and the house is quiet. "Sam!" I call.

He must be up in his bedroom. I'm just about to go check on him when the doorbell rings. It's the young officer, John. He takes off his cap, wiping his feet on the doormat as he comes in. "Mrs. Beauchamp. I have some news." He pauses, looking down at his feet.

The way he says it, fading out, almost muttering the last word, scares me. It's not going to be good. I just know it.

"Come in." I stand aside.

"Thank you, ma'am." He clutches his cap in front of his groin.

"Can I get you a drink?" I put on my pleasant hostess voice, going through the formalities, putting off the moment of knowing.

"Yeah, please. Thank you." Please and thank you in the same breath. He must be very uncomfortable.

"Coffee? Juice?"

He follows me into the kitchen. "Juice would be great. Thanks."

He watches as I pour orange juice into a glass. "Sam knows about his parents and all?" he asks abruptly.

"Yes."

"How is he?"

"It's confusing for him. He's missing his father terribly. We both are."

John nods, as though he understands, and we sit down at the kitchen table. I watch him as he drinks his juice. He has an open face and bright blue eyes. His hair is dark blond, brushed to one side, his nose is small—delicate, even, and his chin is round. He looks so young. Studying him, I take a sip of water from my own glass. Distracted, I miss my mouth and water drips onto the table. Before I have time to get a cloth, he's up on his feet, pulling the tea towel off the metal bar in front of the oven door. I let him wipe up the water.

"Did you sew it?" He holds up the tea towel, looking at the embroidered picture of Pont Neuf. "It's pretty."

"My grandmother did." Why does he want to talk about the damned tea towel?

"You carried it with you when you escaped? All this way?"

"Yes, I have three. Sam slept wrapped up in them." I feel the years slipping away, the clocks turning backward. It feels like I'm back there now, slipping, sliding, desperate to escape.

"Have you been in touch with your family in France since you got here?"

"Not really. They found it difficult to forgive me for what I put them through." I pause, thinking about the selfishness of my decision. "I just ran away without a thought for them."

He nods.

"I was very young."

"Yes, we all make mistakes when we're young."

"Mistakes? Is that what you think it was? A stupid mistake?"

He goes red. Poor guy. It's not his fault.

"What news do you have?" I ask. I'm ready to hear it now. "Is it about the trial?"

"Yes, it was very quick—for a trial. They were talking about it at the station just before I left for my shift. They'll send someone soon to tell you officially."

I stare at him. It must be bad.

"You're here now, John. Just tell me." I'll shake it out of him if I have to.

I watch him swallow. I bet he wishes he'd just stayed outside.

"The jury was unanimous, Mrs. Beauchamp."

"Unanimous?"

"Yes. I'm sorry. I don't know how to tell you."

My heart lurches. I take the tea towel from him to wipe my eyes, praying: Please, God, don't let it be too bad. "Just tell me. Please."

"They found your husband guilty on the charge of kidnapping, but due to extenuating circumstances, he's only getting two years. It's just a token sentence really."

"But he's not a kidnapper! He's not!" I jump up, knocking my glass over. Everything's swimming out of focus.

"Mrs. Beauchamp, they had to give him some kind of a sentence or people might have made a fuss."

"People? What people? He's not a kidnapper. He saved Sam!"

"Sit down, Mrs. Beauchamp, please. There's more."

A sharp pain cuts through my chest. I gasp. No words come. The room starts to spin, around and around. There's no air. Everything goes black.

He's holding my head up, supporting it on his bent knee. Water's dripping down my face, and my wet shirt is clinging to me.

"I'm sorry," he's saying. "I threw some water over your face. You weren't coming around." He puts his hands under my arms and attempts to pull me up, but I have no muscle tone. I flop back down to the floor. He stands there looking at me. "I'm sorry you're so wet. Would you like some water?"

I look at him and laugh. More water? Awful hysterical laughter spills from my mouth. I can't stop it. I try to push words out, but the laughter takes over again.

"Please, Mrs. Beauchamp. Let me help you up." He tries again. I force the laughter back down, and this time I manage to get up. I let him place me back on the chair.

"Maybe you should have something sweet. You're very pale." He brings over the tin of cookies, holding it out to me. The smell fills me with nausea. I shake my head.

He puts the lid back on, then looks up at me, his bright blue eyes staring into mine. "You know, my father died in France."

I don't want to know. I just want him to leave. Two years! How is that possible?

"He was in the navy. He was there on D-Day. An officer. We went to a service in Normandy after the war. Where they buried them, the cemetery, y'know—it's American territory now."

I wonder why he's telling me this. I don't care. "Two years? Are you sure?"

"Yes. Normally it's much longer for kidnapping."

"But how can they accuse him of kidnapping? He's not a kidnapper, is he?"

He pauses. "I'm sorry, Mrs. Beauchamp. It's not for me to say."

"But they've got it all wrong, haven't they?"

"I can't say. It wouldn't be professional of me."

"Professional?"

"Yeah. It's not up to me anyway, is it?"

"But what do you think?"

"You should have given the boy back, after the war." He holds my gaze. There's sympathy in his eyes, but a hard stubbornness too.

"What else is there? You said there was more... Where's Sam?" Dread fills me.

"He's gone to his friend's house."

"What? He didn't ask."

"Don't worry, he's still there." He touches my shoulder. "Mrs. Beauchamp, for what it's worth, I think you've been a great mother to Sam. I can see he's happy and well loved. I understand you wanted to keep him and forget the war, but you know, at the end of the day, he's not your child, is he? Look, you've got some time now to talk with him, make him understand."

I stare at him, terrified about what's coming next.

"They came to a decision. About Sam."

I screw my eyes up tight, as if I can block it out. I don't want to know.

"Sam is to be returned to his natural parents, in France."

"No! No!" The room begins to spin again. I feel his hands on my shoulders. I collapse into him, silent sobs convulsing through my body.

"Mrs. Beauchamp, please. You have to hold yourself together. For Sam's sake."

Calm down...I have to calm down. I must stay in control. Closing my eyes, I take a deep breath, holding on while the air reaches every muscle in my body. He's right. Sam is all that matters now. I have to be strong so I can save him.

I open my eyes, pulling back, standing up. "Thank you for telling me, John. I appreciate it." I wipe my face and look at him. I need to think properly. "I'm going to the bathroom," I say. "Will you wait here? Please. I don't want to be on my own."

His forehead creases in concern. "Of course. I'll be right here."

Quietly, I go upstairs, into Sam's room. I take his backpack, which is lying in the middle of the floor, and hold it upside down, tipping his school books out onto the bed. I throw in his pajamas, a sweater, a pair of pants, some clean underwear, his toothbrush, and his cuddly penguin. I'm being practical, calm even. All my energies are focused on saving Sam. It's all that matters now.

I creep back out into the hall and along to the bathroom. I flush the toilet. Then, leaving the tap running, I go to my own room and put a couple of things in an overnight bag. I remember to go back to the bathroom to turn the tap off, then I go back downstairs and hide our small bags next to the hat stand.

"John," I say as I walk into the kitchen. "Thank you for being here."

"Really. It's nothing. How are you feeling now?"

"I'm trying to hold myself together, for Sam."

He nods, the look of concern still there in the crease across his forehead. I need to get him out of the kitchen, where he has a view across the street.

"John, do you mind if we sit in the living room, just for a few minutes, while I work out what to say to Sam? I don't know how to tell him."

He looks at his watch. "Sure," he says. "My shift ends in a couple of hours."

I stare at him. "Does that mean someone else will be here?"

"Yes."

"What will they do?" Oh my God, they'll want to take him away. I know they will.

"I don't know. I'm sorry. I don't know if they'll take him straightaway or wait."

They could take him away in two hours! I have to get him out. Immediately. I'll need to be far enough away in two hours. A wave of panic rises up from my stomach. I want to throw up. But instead I go to the sink and fill a glass with water, forcing my breath down into my abdomen. I have to keep it together. For Sam.

I glance over at Marge's house. No sign of the boys. They must be playing inside. Our car is in the driveway. Thank goodness I didn't put it away in the garage this morning when I came back from shopping.

I turn back to John, putting on my false hostess voice. "Shall we go through to the living room?"

He follows me out. I sit on the couch, folding my legs up under me while he takes the armchair. I start to cry. "I'm sorry, John," I say between snivels. "I'm making this hard for you."

"It's okay." He coughs in his manly way, his fist rolled up.

"I'm going to wash my face." I put on a trying-to-be-brave voice. "Give me ten minutes to get myself together. Do you think you might be able to help me work out what to say to Sam?"

"Yes. Of course." He's flattered that I'm asking for his help. I can tell by the way he purses his lips, as if he's already giving it some consideration.

"Thank you, John. I'm so glad it's you they asked to watch over us."

Now he can't help smiling. It makes me feel manipulative. I realize I would do anything for Sam. Anything to keep him safe.

I leave the room, closing the door behind me. I pick up the bags next to the hat stand, then noiselessly I open the front door and lock it behind me.

Chapter Fifty-Five

Santa Cruz, July 16, 1953

SAM

"Sam, Sam." I hear Mom calling my name.

Jimmy looks at me. "Sounds like your mom's looking for you."

"Yeah." I try to sound like it's no big deal, but I'm wondering if I'm going to be in trouble. Or maybe Daddy's home. That would be swell. Taking the stairs two at a time, I charge downstairs.

Mom's there, standing by the front door.

"You can't come in," I hear Marge say. "It's okay for Sam, but you can't come in."

Mom doesn't answer her; just grabs my hand and pulls me away.

"I went to Jimmy's, Mom. I'm sorry I didn't tell you."

She stops and looks into my eyes. I wait for her lecture, but instead she says, "We have to go away, Sam. Now. There's no time to pack. Get in the car."

"What? Where are we going?"

"I'll tell you on the way. Just get in the car."

I do as I'm told. I can tell this is important.

We pull out of the drive, tires screeching. I look around and catch Marge staring at us, her mouth wide open. Mom's driving like we're in a car chase. It makes me scared. She's acting kind of crazy.

"Where's the cop, Mom? What's happening? Where are we going?"

She doesn't look at me. "Let me concentrate on my driving, Sam."

I want to cry, and I wipe my eyes with my sleeve, trying to be brave. I stare out the window.

When we get onto the highway, she puts her hand on my knee. "It will be okay, Sam."

"But where are we goin', Mom?"

"We have to run away."

"What?"

"You remember what I told you about your birth parents, Mr. and Mrs. Laffitte?"

"Yeah."

"Well, something has happened."

"Daddy is coming back, isn't he?"

"It's not about Daddy right now. It's about you, Sam. Mr. and Mrs. Laffitte want you back. They want you to go and live with them in France."

"But I can't."

"I know you can't. But they want you to go anyway. They want you to learn French and be their son."

"Don't worry, Mom. I won't go. I don't wanna go."

"I don't want you to go either, but they can make you."

"They can't. I just won't go."

"I'm afraid they can. That's why we have to get away. So they won't find us."

"Just tell them I don't wanna go."

"They won't listen to me, Sam. They're still very cross that we didn't track them down after the war. They were looking for you."

"But I wanna stay here. I want Daddy to come back."

Suddenly she swerves into another lane, overtaking three cars. One of them honks at her. "Shut up!" she yells.

I jump in my seat, my heart beating hard. I'm not sure if she's talking to the driver of the honking car or me. I look at the speedometer. We're driving so fast now, the needle has gone past all the numbers.

"Mom," I say. "You've pinned the speedometer."

"Yeah, I have." She laughs, but it's a crazy, high-pitched noise, and I don't like it.

"What about Daddy?" I wish he was here.

"He'll be able to join us later, once we get settled."

I lean back in my seat, trying not to cry. I don't want to run away. "But where are we goin'? Where will we live?"

"Mexico, Sam. We're going to Mexico."

"Mexico? But that's not even in America!"

"Don't worry. It's not far. Why don't you put some music on?"

I turn the radio knob and recognize the tune straightaway.

Oh, my pa-pa, to me he was so wonderful...

"It's Eddie Fisher," Mom says.

The words of the song make me want to cry. Daddy would know what to do now. He'd be able to tell them I can't go and live in France. I wish he was here so bad. "When's Daddy coming?"

"I'm not sure yet. We'll have to see. But I know he's thinking about you every minute of every day."

That makes me feel a bit better. I close my eyes. They feel dry and sore, and my eyelids are heavy. My head flops to the side, and I lean against the window.

When I wake, it's dark and we're still driving. I'm dying for a pee. "Can we stop, Mom? I need the bathroom."

"Okay, but you'll have to be quick."

We pull into a gas station, and she gives me a quarter to get some snacks while she fills the tank. The sign for the bathroom points around the back of the shop, but there are no lights, and it's so dark.

Trying to be brave, I follow the wall with my hands, waiting to feel a door. A bird screeches, making me jump.

"Mom!" I scream.

There's no answer.

"Mom!" I call louder. "Mom!"

"You should put the light on." A lady's voice comes through the dark.

Suddenly I'm drowned by bright light. I screw my eyes up.

"I think your ma's getting gas."

"Okay," I say, opening the bathroom door, in front of me now. I shut myself in the cubicle, feeling like an idiot. The sound of my pee hitting the pool of water at the bottom of the toilet echoes in the empty room. I wonder if the lady outside can hear it.

When I come out, the lady's gone. I see Mom walking into the shop, so I follow her as if nothing happened. I hear the lady telling her, "He was scared on his own, out the back. It's pretty black out there when you don't put the lights on." She laughs.

"Sam," Mom says. "Get yourself something to eat, quickly now."

I grab a Hershey's bar from the nearest stand and hold out a quarter to the lady.

"It's late to be traveling." She takes the money and smiles at me with warm eyes. I smile back.

"Well, we have a long way to go," Mom answers.

"We're going to Mexico," I add.

Mom flashes me an angry look. I wish I'd just kept my mouth shut.

"Mexico?" the lady repeats. "What's in Mexico?"

"Family," Mom replies.

I know she's lying, again.

The lady rings the Hershey's bar up on the cash register, then counts the change into my open palm. "Five cents, fifteen cents, twenty cents, twenty-five cents." I look at her instead of the money. Her forehead is creased in the middle, her eyebrows pointing down toward her nose. "All right, darlin'?"

I nod and turn around to leave through the door Mom is holding open for me.

When we get back to the car, we drive off quickly, speeding out of the gas station. I open my chocolate bar, wishing I'd chosen something bigger. I'm suddenly starving.

Chapter Fifty-Six

California, July 16, 1953

CHARLOTTE

It's nearly midnight when we reach the border. Sam's slept most of the way, his head lolling over at what looks like a painful angle. Reaching over to straighten it, I hear him murmur in his sleep. He looks beautiful, and I absorb every little detail: his black silky eyelashes curling up, his straight dark hair, his smooth olive skin. His eyes are the same almond shape as mine. People often comment on how much he looks like me. It feels like he has come to resemble me physically, as though his growing body watched mine and took its form from me. He doesn't look much like Jean-Luc, but he has his way of laughing and his lopsided smile.

He's been so easy to love. As we trekked across the Pyrénées, I grew to love him as if he were my own. A warm baby, wrapped around my body, occasionally lifting his eyes to look at me and take me in. Sometimes I deliberately leaned forward, making him feel as though he were about to fall, so that he'd stretch out his little fingers, gripping on to me more tightly. He needed me, and I responded to that need so naturally and effortlessly.

Why can't they leave us alone? How can they expect to build a peaceful future when they keep dragging up the past? The thought of Sam suffering brings a tightness to my throat. How much more painful to watch one's child suffer than to do the suffering oneself. I'll do anything to protect him. Anything.

There's a line of traffic. As we get nearer, I see officers checking passports. I suppress an urge to reverse and drive back the other way. Please, God, I whisper in my head. Make everything be all right.

A harsh knocking on the window makes me jump. There's an officer standing there. I roll down the window, my hand trembling.

"Passports, please, ma'am." He peers over at Sam, who's opened his eyes now.

I hand them over.

"Wait here, ma'am."

My pulse is beating hard in my ears. *Please, please, God.*

He comes back with another officer. "Step out of the car, ma'am."

No! They can't! But they're opening my door, pulling me out by my elbow.

"Turn around." An officer pushes me in the back. I'm up against the car, and he's running his hands up and down my body. I bite my lower lip, willing myself to stay calm. For Sam's sake.

Then I feel the cold metal of handcuffs on my wrists. I hear the click of the lock. I swallow my scream, and look over at Sam. An officer has his arm around him and is whispering in his ear. Sam turns his head to find me.

"I'm sorry," I mouth. Biting down harder on my lip, I stifle the animal cry starting in my belly.

Chapter Fifty-Seven

California, July 17, 1953

CHARLOTTE

The pain inside me grows like a balloon being inflated, stretched beyond its limits, near to the point of bursting. I try to hold it in as it squeezes my intestines up into my throat, pushing hard against my heart. It's too much for me to contain, and when the police car pulls up at the station, when they tell me to get out, I can hardly move. Doubled over, handcuffed, I climb the steps. Along the corridor, bright fluorescent lights glare at me. We stop in front of a cell. Despite my crippling pain, I look up and see there's someone already in the barred room, a woman with smudged streaks of mascara running down from her eyes to her mouth, long naked legs sticking out from under a short denim skirt.

The officer unlocks the handcuffs, freeing my stiff arms. Immediately I bring my hands around, gripping myself, holding the pain in. The metal clank of the key turning in the lock rings in my ears. I stumble into the cell, collapsing on the concrete bench. There's nowhere for the pain to go now. The balloon explodes. My body convulses, heaving sobs wrenched from deep within me.

"Shut the fuck up, would ya?" the woman shouts.

But the pain racking my body is unstoppable now, my sobs

increasing in volume. I hope the woman will hit me. Physical pain would be better than this. Then I feel her next to me. She puts her head right up next to mine; the smell of whiskey breath hits me. I wait for her fist to make contact with my face.

"They'll put you in the fuckin' loony bin if you carry on like that," she whispers in my ear. "And then you'll never get out."

I wish she'd hit me instead. Her words scare me. I take a deep breath, forcing it down into my abdomen. Holding it there, I make myself go quiet.

She goes back to her place opposite. I bring my legs up onto the bench, curling them under me, and lie there in the fetal position, trying to make my mind go blank. Thoughts will start me off again.

"So, what's so bad? What'd you do? Kill your husband?" She cackles as if she's said something amusing.

I have no words to tell her what I did.

"You wanna know why I'm here?"

I curl up tighter, not letting out a sound.

" 'Cause I been sellin' something that belongs to me. How fuckin' crazy is that? Bet you did something much worse. God didn't give me much in the way of brains, but he gave me tits, legs, and a nice ass. Gotta use what you got, ain't ya? There ain't nobody to look after me, so what am I s'posed to do? Lie down and die?"

I hear her stand up, footsteps coming toward me again. Then I feel her hand on my head. "You're in a bad way, ain't ya?"

It feels like a lead blanket has been placed over me. Everything is so heavy. I close my eyes, and let myself fall into oblivion.

The next thing I know, someone is turning the key in the lock. The officer walks in with a woman in a white lab coat.

"Get up, Mrs. Bow-Champ." The officer's voice is harsh.

I look at the woman and back to him again. They are both expressionless. Terror seizes me. Are they going to put me away?

I know I have to stay calm, have to appear compos mentis. Slowly

I unfold my legs, putting my feet onto the floor. I stumble as I try to stand, so I lift myself gradually from the bench. I see the hooker sleeping in a sitting position, her head bent over at an awkward angle. I would like to move her, make her more comfortable, but I don't dare touch her. Instead I follow the officer and the woman out of the cell.

We walk down the corridor, stopping at a small office near the end, on the left.

"Where's Sam?" I promised myself I would wait to ask; that I would do everything to appear calm and in control, but I need to know.

"We'll explain everything in the interview room, Mrs. Bow-Champ."

When we enter the room, they sit down on one side of the table, motioning for me to sit opposite. I fidget on the plastic chair, suddenly desperate for the bathroom. I don't allow myself to say anything, aware that my desperation will only make them crueler.

"Mrs. Bow-Champ," the officer starts.

I stare at him. Waiting.

"What you did was very irresponsible and foolish—"

"Where's Sam? Is he okay?"

He nods. "He's fine. He'll be on a flight to Paris shortly."

"What?" My voice comes out as a croak from my tight throat.

"Yes. Today."

Daggers of pain shoot through my stomach. I hug myself, trying to block them out. "Please, please don't send him away like that. Please let me see him."

The woman hands me a plastic cup of water. I want to push her hand away, but instead I take a tiny sip.

"As I was saying," the officer continues, ignoring my pleas. "Your actions yesterday could get you into a lot of trouble."

I look into his eyes. "I'm sorry...I was distraught. I wasn't thinking straight." The hooker's words about the loony bin ring in my head.

"Quite." He takes out a cigarette packet, offering it to the woman in the lab coat. She shakes her head. "I'll let you proceed with the questions now." He leans back in his chair, smoking, watching us as if we're some damn TV show.

"Mrs. Bow-Champ." The woman raises her eyebrows. "Why did you try to cross the border with Samuel? You were told not to leave your house, unless you informed the officer outside."

"I'm sorry. When I heard the news that Sam's parents wanted him back, I panicked. I don't want to lose him." My throat constricts painfully. I stop myself from thinking about him, taking a deep breath in. One breath at a time, I tell myself.

"We are concerned about your mental state, Mrs. Bow-Champ. We know that your husband put undue pressure on you, preventing you from going to the authorities about Samuel when you should have. To live under that kind of pressure over a prolonged period of time can be quite detrimental to mental health. We want to make sure you are stable enough to return home."

"Home?" Suddenly I'm confused. "You mean Paris?" The thought of Paris, of being near Sam and Jean-Luc, makes my pulse beat faster.

"No." She coughs, then looks at the officer. "I don't mean Paris, Mrs. Bow-Champ. I mean your home here."

My heart sinks.

The officer flicks his cigarette onto the side of a metal ashtray, looking up at me from under bushy eyebrows. "You need to stay in the state of California and agree to have weekly sessions with the psychiatrist."

"You mean I can't leave this country—"

"This country," he interrupts, leaning forward, glaring at me, "that has welcomed you and been your home for the last nine years. No."

"Maybe one day you'll be able to return to France," the woman says more kindly. "This is not a permanent ban on travel. It's just till we can verify that you have accepted the fact that Samuel is not your son."

Chapter Fifty-Eight

California, July 17, 1953

SAM

The big lady with hairy arms is talking to me in her annoying voice. "Samuel, you should eat something. You can come to the cafeteria with us and choose whatever you like."

I want to slap her wobbly cheeks. "When can I see my mom?" I ask again.

She breathes out heavily. "We've already told you. It's best that you don't see her before you go."

I clench and unclench my fists under the table, trying to stop myself from crying. "I'm not goin' anywhere. I wanna see my mom!"

"Samuel, please. Be reasonable."

That's it. I can't contain it any longer. I jump out of my chair, my fist flying forward, smashing right into her flabby mouth. I feel my breath coming fast, like I've just run a race. I hit a marshal. Will I go to prison now too?

I stand there. Waiting.

The man steps forward and grabs my arm. I'm too scared to pull it away. He marches me down the corridor. My heart is beating hard. What are they going to do with me?

He takes me into a small room. There's a white table and two gray chairs.

"You can wait here till you calm down." He releases my arm from his tight grip and closes the door behind him on the way out. Then locks it.

I ignore the chairs and sit on the floor in the corner of the room, my knees bent up under my chin. I won't cry. I won't. Not anymore. I cried and screamed when they took Mom away. I remember shouting at them, "But she hasn't done anything!" They said I'd understand later, but I never will.

My stomach twists and growls. The last thing I had to eat was the Hershey's bar last night. I didn't want the bowl of cornflakes they gave me this morning, but I was thirsty, so I drank the glass of milk. I wish we'd made it to Mexico. I'm so tired now; my head feels dizzy. I close my eyes, leaning my face onto my knees, feeling my eyelashes flickering against my skin. I like the feeling, and open and close my eyes again and again.

A noise wakes me. It's the key turning in the door. The marshals walk in. The man still looks cross, the lady looks sad.

"Samuel, we understand how angry you must feel." Her voice is sickly sweet. "I forgive you for hitting me. I know it was just your anger and confusion coming out."

"Still," the man interrupts. "If you do anything like that again, there will be consequences."

"Let's have some lunch." The lady puts on a fake bright voice.

"Come on, kid," the man adds when I don't budge.

"When can I see my mom?" I ask again.

They look at each other, and the man raises an eyebrow. Then he reaches down, pulling me up by my elbow.

They take me to a cafeteria where people queue up to choose their food. "Have whatever you like," the lady says.

When I get to the cash register, my tray is still empty. I won't eat, though my stomach feels hollow. They find a free table and we sit down. I can feel people staring at us, I look around at them and they look away.

"Babysitting," the man whispers to the lady. "And I'm working on a case. I don't have time for this shit."

"Shh." The lady looks at him out of the corner of her eye.

But I bet he wanted me to hear. He hates me. I can feel it.

The lady puts a plate of fries in front of me and opens a can of Coke, poking a straw in the top as she slides it over to me. I take a fry. The lady smiles and I put it back. I don't touch the Coke. She picks up her hot dog and bites into it, ketchup squirting out the sides. "Samuel, let's start again." She swallows a mouthful of hot dog and looks at me. "We got off on the wrong foot. I know this is hard for you. We can call the psychologist who talked with you earlier and see if she could see you again. Would you like that?" She smiles at me like she's just offered me a present.

I wonder how she can be so dumb.

But she doesn't shut her big mouth. "Your mom here, she and your father too, for sure they did the right thing when they brought you to America. But they should have informed the authorities when they arrived. Then we could have traced your real parents and saved everyone a lot of pain."

"I don't care! I'm glad they didn't. I want my mom." I run my hands through my hair, afraid that I might use them to hit her again. "I wanna go home."

"Samuel, you have to understand, home isn't where you thought it was."

I put my hands over my ears, trying not to hear.

It's impossible, though. The man speaks loudly. "Samuel, your real parents have a right to see you. You're their son, and your mother only gave you up because she had to. Don't you want to meet her?"

"No! She's not my real mom. I hate her." I look up, glaring at him.

"Sam-uel." The lady's eyes get larger. "You mustn't say that. She's suffered so much."

"Good. I hate her. I wish she was dead." I can feel people turning in their chairs to look at us.

"You don't know what you're saying." The lady's cheeks have gone bright red. "You're upset."

I can't help it. Tears fall down my cheeks. My chest hurts as I try to hold them back. I can't get any air.

"We should go." The man stands up, putting his arm around my shoulder. It makes me feel trapped. I can't move away, and my chest is going up and down so quick, like I'm drowning.

Chapter Fifty-Nine

Paris, July 17, 1953

SARAH

In her soul, she's always known her child was alive somewhere. A mother can feel these things.

The moment she pushed her baby into the arms of the railroad worker has remained etched on her mind. Time and time again she's replayed it in her imagination, locking away in her memory the exact form of the scar cutting into the side of his face. And when he wrapped his arms around Samuel, she saw he only had one finger and a thumb on his left hand. She knew then that he would take care of her son, just as the rabbi on the Métro said—he would keep him safe. She knew she would find him again. She just hadn't realized how long it would take.

She rolls over, trying to find a comfortable position on her pillow, but really she's too excited to sleep. Tomorrow is the day she hardly dared believe would ever come. Pure joy races through her veins, an emotion she barely recognizes. It makes her realize just how numb she's been, how she's only been going through the motions of living during the last nine years. For the first time since she gave him up, she feels alive. Grateful to be alive. "Thank you, God," she whispers into the pillow.

Of course, he's not a baby anymore. He's already nine years old, and a fine-looking boy, judging from the photos they've been shown. She peered at the pictures, looking deep into his eyes, and recognized her family. Her father's gaze shone out from Samuel's dark, intelligent eyes, sparkling with curiosity, and he had her mother's fine nose. David was present too, in the way he held himself, proudly sticking out his chin. The only likeness she couldn't see was the one to her.

She knows it won't be easy. He doesn't speak French, and they'll have to find a way to communicate, but their connection will be deeper than language. This makes her wonder, once again, about the Beauchamps' bond with her son. She doesn't like to dwell on this thought, as it leaves her with a feeling of disquiet to contemplate the relationship her child has established with the people he believed to be his parents. Worst of all is the thought of Samuel loving another woman as his mother. The strength of that bond terrifies her.

She likes to imagine that he's closer to the man than to the woman. This makes sense in her mind, as it was he who took Samuel. Maybe the woman didn't even want to take on someone else's child. That would help explain why she never spoke French to Samuel, her own mother tongue. How could she not have sung him the songs she learned herself in her own mother's arms?

Enough. She must stop churning up the past. It's over now. She needs to plan for the next stage. The psychologist told them that Samuel should be fluent in French in about six months, as long as they stuck to the immersion method, meaning total exposure to French with no interference or translation from his first language; she can't bring herself to call it his mother tongue. So they are never to revert to English—not that they could if they wanted to—and he is to have no contact with the parents who brought him up, not even by letter.

She's been fretting all day, getting his bedroom ready, buying food that she imagines nine-year-old boys like. First she made her own challah bread, adding raisins for a special treat. Then she bought a large bag of potatoes, because a friend told her that they ate potatoes all the time in America, with everything, even breakfast. Imagine that! She could make potato latkes for a starter, then gratin dauphinois to go with the lamb kibbeh. Or would that be overdoing it? For dessert, she'll make apple cake with honey. She usually saves this recipe for New Year's, but she wants to make it now to mark a new beginning, repentance and forgiveness going hand in hand. She can't wait for mother, father, and son to sit down to a meal together, to break bread together. It's all she wants, and the thought of it makes her heart beat faster in anticipation.

David turns away from her in his sleep. She puts her arms around him, burying her head into his neck. "Are you awake?" she whispers.

"No," he mumbles.

She lies there feeling restless. David turns back around, reaching for her hand under the covers.

"Everything will be all right, won't it, David?"

"Our son is coming home, Sarah. We will be able to live again."

"I wish…I just wish Beauchamp hadn't got that two-year sentence, though. It seems too harsh. He did save Samuel's life."

"I know. I know. But the decision was out of our hands. And we mustn't forget, he did keep him hidden from us all these years."

She squeezes his hand. "Yes, I know. Remember when he was born?"

"How could I forget?"

"You were so brave, delivering him on your own."

"I think you were the brave one."

She smiles in the dark. "I trusted you, and I knew you knew what you were doing."

"Yes, being a research biologist has its uses, doesn't it?"

"I was glad I had him at home, but it was hard having to leave so soon after the birth." She snuggles into him, remembering how they had run to the safe house.

They stop there. Neither of them can talk about the following night, though they both think about it. Sarah knows David blames himself for what happened. He couldn't protect her and their son as he'd promised to. He held on to her as she held on to their baby, the army truck they'd been shoved into speeding through the dark, empty streets of Paris.

"I'm sorry, Sarah. I'm sorry." He put his jacket around her, and she knew he wanted to give her everything. He would have given her the shirt off his back and sat there naked if he thought it would help her.

When they got to Drancy and the men were separated from the women, he clung to her, taking blows from the guards. In the end, she had to beg him to let go. "Live," she told him. "Stay alive for me and Samuel."

And she knew he would.

Chapter Sixty

California, July 17, 1953

SAM

"I can't go to France. I'm American, and I don't speak French," I tell the lady again when we get back to the little room after lunch.

"A clever boy like you will learn quickly. At least it's the same alphabet."

I stare at her.

"Chinese would be much harder," she adds. "Sit down, I'll get you some comics to read."

I do as I'm told because the man is watching me. I'm scared to be left in the room alone with him, and I look down at the table when she leaves so I don't have to see his cold eyes. But I hear him step toward me. I bury my head in my hands, wishing the lady would come back.

"Listen, lad." He puts a hand on my shoulder. "You're gonna have to toughen up. No more of this cryin'. We have work to do here and you're makin' it difficult." He squeezes my shoulder hard. It hurts. I hold my breath so I don't make a sound.

The door clicks open. I let out my breath and look up. It's kind of a relief to see the lady again, beaming away, with a stack of comics in her arms. She spreads out a collection of *Captain America* and *Batman and Robin*. I want to say thank you, but the words won't come.

"I'll stay with him." She turns to the man. "You can get on with your work."

I pretend to read *Captain America*, waiting for him to go.

"Remember what I said, lad," he says as he closes the door.

The lady sits next to me and takes out some papers. "What did he say to you?" she asks without looking up.

"I dunno." I pretend to read my comic again.

"I'm not a psychologist, Samuel, but you can talk about it. It might help."

I shake my head, watching as a fat tear falls onto the comic, smudging the print.

"I just wanna see my mom."

"Samuel." She exhales a long breath. "You'll be okay. You have your real mom and real dad now. You must be excited to be meeting them soon."

"I don't wanna meet them. I wanna see my mom. Is she comin' back soon?"

"Please, Samuel, stop saying that."

"My name's not Samuel! It's Sam!"

"It's Sam here in America, but I think you'll find they call you Samuel in France."

I stare at her. What does she mean?

"Samuel's your real name, and they don't shorten names in France. The psychologist told me. She's been looking into it. It seems there are a few differences you'll have to get used to."

"But I'm not going! I told you I'm not goin'."

"Okay, okay." I wonder if she's finally understood. But then she says, "They have great schools in France, you'll soon make friends."

"I don't want new friends. I want my old friends."

She puts her hand on my shoulder. "Samuel, you'll stay here tonight, then Mr. Jackson will take you to France tomorrow."

"No! Please, no! I'll be good. I promise." I jump up. "Please don't send me away. Please."

"Shh, shh." She stands up, putting her arms around me.

I can't help it. I fall against her big soft chest, hiding my head in it. Tears come quickly. This time I don't try to stop them. It hurts too much inside. I feel snot running from my nose onto her clothes.

"Shh, honey," she whispers, her hand on the back of my head. "Let it out. Better out than in."

I hear the door click open again and someone's footsteps as they come into the room. This person touches my arm lightly, then squeezes it. "This won't hurt. Just a little prick."

Chapter Sixty-One

Paris, July 18, 1953

SAM

I missed the take-off. I can't remember the landing either. The doctor gave me a shot, maybe two. One in the room, and one before getting on the plane. I can't remember the night between the two days, but I know there must have been one, because now it's another morning.

My head is leaning into a soft cushion, and I realize I'm sitting in a blue room in a big white chair. My head feels fuzzy. When I look around, I see a man with brown hair, wearing a pink shirt. He's staring at me. I want to drift off into another world again. I let my eyes close.

I hear him talking like I'm in a dream. He has a strange accent. It reminds me a little of Mom's; sometimes the words go up when they should go down.

"We know this is very hard for you. Samuel. Samuel." I open my eyes and he passes me a glass of orange juice. "Drink this."

I take a sip of the drink. I'm so thirsty, I drink it all. He gives me a pastry. I sink my teeth into it. It's buttery and delicious, and it makes me realize how hungry I am.

"You want another?" he says.

I nod, and he takes another pastry out of the paper bag he's holding.

I sink my teeth into it, swallowing it in three bites. It feels good to have something in my tummy. I don't want to think about what will happen to me now. It will only make me feel sick and dizzy again. I look at the man, wondering why he's wearing a pink shirt. It's a girl's color.

He starts talking again. "Your real parents went through so much, and now they are very excited to meet you." Not only does he have a pink shirt, he's also wearing a purple tie.

"Am I in Paris?"

"*Mais oui.* It's been a long journey, but we are happy you are here now." He smiles at me.

"When can I see my mom?"

"Samuel—"

"My name's Sam."

"Sorry, Sam." He pulls up a chair next to me. "We are going to do our best to help you. Can I tell you a story?"

I shrug my shoulders.

He starts this story about some tiger that gets lost in the jungle and is adopted by a gorilla family, but when he gets to the bit about the tiger having to be carried up the trees by the gorillas I start to lose concentration. His voice is soft and gentle, and I know what he's trying to do. It's pathetic. Now there's a good word. Pathetic. That's what he is. The marshals were just dumb. This man in his girl's pink shirt is pathetic.

"Sam." He touches me on my shoulder.

"I wanna go back to sleep." I turn my head back into the cushion and close my eyes.

"Sam, your parents are here to see you now."

"Mom, Dad? They're here?"

"I mean your French parents, your real parents."

"They're not my real parents. I told you!" I jump out of the chair, but my legs feel like jelly. I fall back down. My head hurts so bad. I clutch at it, trying to stop the hammering.

He puts his hands on my shoulders. I try to push them off, but I can't. I feel so weak.

"Sam, please. You need to calm yourself."

"Leave me alone."

"We all need to make this work, including you, Sam. Please stop this."

"Will you let me go home?"

"We—" A knock on the door interrupts his answer.

Two people walk in.

Chapter Sixty-Two

Paris, July 18, 1953

SARAH

"Samuel... Samuel." Her eyes water as she looks at him. She can see he's been crying, but he's beautiful, just like she's pictured him in her imagination, his silky dark hair, his smooth olive skin, his fine nose, and his dark brown eyes. She wants to drink him in, like a lost traveler in the desert, gone for days without water.

She feels David grip her hand, almost painfully. "It's Samuel, isn't it? It's really him." His voice cracks, and she drags her eyes away from her son to see a silent tear sliding down her husband's cheek.

"Yes, David. It's Samuel."

She turns back to face her son. She can hardly believe he's real. "Samuel," she murmurs. "We've found you."

David puts his arms out, stepping toward him, reaching out to him. Sarah sees Samuel go rigid, backing up against the wall behind him.

Putting her hand out, she stops her husband. "Wait."

The psychologist who followed them into the room coughs. "He'll need some time to adjust. Let me introduce the interpreter. This is Madame Demur."

For a moment, their eyes are drawn away from Samuel to a slight woman in a pale blue suit, standing next to the psychologist. They shake her hand.

"I'll translate for you into French and for your son into English."

Your son. Yes. It's true, they have a son now. But he's standing as far away as he can get from them in the small room, his hands flat against the wall, his eyes wide with terror, like a cornered animal.

"Good morning." A man wearing a pink shirt and a charcoal-gray suit holds out his hand. "Mr. and Mrs. Laffitte, it's a pleasure to meet you."

Sarah realizes he must be the deputy mayor.

"Please sit down." He pulls out chairs. Obediently they sit down, forming a small semicircle. The man pats an empty chair next to him. "Come and sit down, Samuel." His voice is gentle and kind, but Samuel stares at him with contempt, not moving from his place against the wall.

David grips his beard, as though holding on for dear life. Sarah's throat feels raw, so many words she wants to say trapped there.

Samuel says something in English. They wait for the interpreter. "He says he doesn't feel well."

"Tell him we can go home now." David pulls on his beard. Sarah knows he just wants to leave the room and take his son home.

The interpreter turns back to Samuel, translating into English.

He shakes his head vigorously backward and forward, his silky dark hair swishing from side to side.

Sarah can see she'll have to distract him somehow. Opening her handbag, she fumbles around with trembling hands, looking for the photos she brought with her. She holds them out. "Samuel, do you want to see some pictures of your family?"

The interpreter translates, and Samuel shakes his head again. "I wanna go home. I feel sick."

She doesn't need a translation for this, she gets the gist, but the lady translates anyway.

"Tell him his home is here now." David lets go of his beard.

As the woman translates, Sarah watches her son's face turn even paler. Quickly she holds out a photo. "Look, Samuel." She stands up, taking a step toward him. Relief washes over her as he looks down at the picture of her mother and father. "This is your grandfather and your grandmother. Your grandfather was very handsome, just like you." She places a shaking finger next to her father's image. Her voice cracks as she remembers the last time she saw her parents.

Samuel looks away.

David takes over, his long fingers dancing around his beard as he talks. "Tell Samuel that he needs to go to his new home now." He waits for the lady in blue to translate, then continues, "We know this will be hard for him. He is only a child, but we must not pity him because he is a child. It's our job as adults and parents to help him build his character, to help him find out who he is and where he truly belongs." He stops again, waiting for the translation. "We recognize what Jean-Luc Beauchamp did in saving our son from certain death at Auschwitz, and we also understand how he could have assumed that we perished there. But now we need to focus on Samuel and make this transition as smooth as we can. We are his parents and we love him."

Sarah's not sure whom this speech was meant for. She wonders if it's David's way of letting Samuel know what he thinks. Of course she knew this first meeting would be difficult, that Samuel would most likely reject them. They prepared themselves for this, agreed they would have to be patient, that they would have to give him time.

Suddenly Samuel makes a strange noise, clutching his stomach, bending over double.

Both Sarah and David reach for him. But it's the deputy mayor who takes Samuel by the arm, leading him out of the room. Unfortunately, they don't make it in time, and Samuel vomits everywhere, lumps of orange flying out of his mouth onto the dark blue carpet. Then he collapses against the man in the pink shirt.

Chapter Sixty-Three

Paris, July 18, 1953

SARAH

The doctor said that Samuel's fainting fit was due to long-distance travel and his body losing its natural rhythms; that he would be fine in twenty-four hours once his internal clock reset itself. Sarah doesn't believe a word of it. She knows it's the trauma of leaving the people he's known as his parents, the people he loves. She couldn't look as the doctor slapped his face, bringing him around. She hung her head low as he gave him some pills with a glass of water, looking up just in time to see his head go limp again. Guilt filled her heart, taking away all the joy she'd felt before.

David carries him out to the car now, laying him on the back seat. Sarah gets in the other side, lifting Samuel's head, holding it on her lap. She strokes his hair, amazed at the lightness and smoothness of it. Love for him fills her aching heart, and she wants to, needs to absorb every little detail of him, to hold on to him and never let him go.

As the driver maneuvers the car through the narrow streets toward their home in Le Marais, David turns around in the front seat to look at her. She doesn't know what to say to him. This isn't how they were supposed to bring their son home, drugged and unconscious.

"David, he'll be all right, won't he?"

He just carries on looking at her, his pupils dark pools of sorrow, his face pale like the moon.

"Maybe we should have gone to America to meet him first. This is too traumatic for him."

David twists himself right around, so he can talk to her. "Sarah, we knew it wouldn't be easy. We're going to have to be very strong. Remember what the psychologist said about children being highly adaptable. He just needs time. We will be a family again."

Family. What does it really mean? She's missed the most important years of Samuel's life: his first smile, his first steps, his first day at school, learning to read, making friends, his curiosity. She wasn't there to answer his questions as he tried to make sense of the world. These are the things that make a parent. She's a stranger to him, and he to her. Not only a stranger, but a foreigner too.

She can't dismiss the sinking feeling that they've made a terrible mistake, bringing him back to Paris like this. No one stopped to question whether they were doing the right thing. It was all so clear in their minds: that the child should be returned to his true parents. There's that word again. Parents. She's not sure she really feels like one. A terrible feeling clenches at her heart, telling her that she doesn't even know this boy.

When they get to the apartment, David carries Samuel up the stairs, all the way to the fourth floor where they live, into the bedroom. He lays him down on the bed, takes off his shoes and jacket, and covers him with a blanket. Sarah watches from the doorway as he kneels on the floor next to the bed, leaning over their son, stroking his hair back from his forehead to kiss him. Then he reaches into his jacket pocket, pulling out a small wooden box. She steps farther into the room, standing behind him now, watching as he kisses the box, then places it on the pillow next to Samuel's head. She can feel the tears behind his eyes as if they were her own. Then she sees them slide silently down his face.

David, who's been her anchor through all these years. David, who understands her pain but refuses to let it drown her. David, who's always held her up, keeping her head above water, when all she wanted to do was close her eyes and let her body sink. She's only seen him cry once, when she found him after they were evacuated from Auschwitz. He collapsed in the snow, hanging on to her, saying her name over and over again, like a prayer, tears streaming down his face.

He is a resilient man and his faith is as solid as a rock. But she's not sure that resilience is what is needed right now. Resilience is too rigid, too hard. Instead of holding steadfast to their principles and their rights, maybe they should keep more of an open mind. The trouble is, she doesn't know what is needed. She's lost, and nothing is what it seemed.

Chapter Sixty-Four

Paris, July 25, 1953

SAM

Last week, on my first day here, I woke up in a strange bed and found a little wooden box on my pillow. It looked like a mini treasure chest. Parts of it were carved out and it had a small hook to open it. I pulled the hook back; the inside was covered in red velvet, and it was actually filled with mini treasure. There were some coins, a chocolate wrapped in gold paper, shiny colored stones, and a piece of paper rolled up and sealed with real red wax, like a scroll. I opened the paper and read the message. It was in English: *Samuel, our son, you are the treasure we never stopped looking for.* I crumpled it up and pushed it back in the box.

A whole horrible week has gone by now. I sleep most of the time, and sometimes, when I'm lucky, I have nice dreams about home.

But this morning, noises from the kitchen pull me out of my dream. I try to block them out and slip back into sleep. It was sunny, and I was just about to bite into a ball of chocolate ice cream. I don't always have good dreams, so I want to hang on to this one. I'm almost there when I hear my name. I bet they're talking about me, saying how terrible I am.

It's all so different here. So horribly different. Everything is old.

It's not a place for children. Even the smells are old, like polished furniture, cigar smoke, and smelly cheese. I miss the smells of home: warm doughnuts, cotton candy, the oily fumes from the Funland rides.

The people are different here too. They're pointier, pricklier. They kiss you on the cheek, but it's not a real kiss. It just floats by. I always stand there like a stick, pretending I'm somewhere else. I miss the hugs in America—warm and soft. The people here don't smile either when they meet you. They say *bonjour* with straight lips, not like home, where people smile all the time. Everything is bigger and better in America.

The only thing I kind of like is *goûter,* the snack they have in the afternoon—baguette still warm from the boulangerie, stuffed with squares of dark chocolate. The rest of the food is a bit weird, and at mealtimes it all comes separately. First there are vegetables, like grated carrots, then a piece of meat or fish, and then after that, sometimes salad. Usually there's dessert, but often it's just fruit cut up. And you're never allowed to help yourself to something from the cupboard or the refrigerator. It's always got to be served properly. They don't even know what a hot dog is! They don't have soda pop, just some purply-red syrup they mix with water, called grenadine. It doesn't taste like anything.

Maybe the strangest thing, though, is the bathrooms. The actual toilet is a hole in the ground, and you have to stand on ridges on the side, then crouch over the hole to pee or poo. My feet usually get splashed. It's not even in the apartment; it's out in the hall.

At least I've stopped crying; well, in the daytime anyway. At night I sometimes wake crying when I have the nightmare that keeps coming back. The one where I'm running through forests in the dark, jumping over wide creeks, falling down hidden craters, running, running till my legs stop working. Then I give up and lie there terrified, waiting for the monster to eat me. Just as it's about to bite into my foot, I scream. The scream wakes me up. In my nightmare, I scream loud, but when I wake, the real sound is tiny. I want to put the light on, but I'm worried the monster is hiding somewhere in the room, waiting to snap my hand off. I want to cry out for someone, but I'm too scared of my own voice to shout. Anyway, there's no one here who can help me. So I lie there trying to find happier thoughts. I make pictures in my mind of the beach, the ocean, the schoolyard filled with playing and shouting. Sometimes it helps me go back to sleep.

There's an empty place inside me. Every morning when I wake, it's there. It never goes away. The memory of Mom being taken away by the cops makes it open up larger, so I try not to remember that. She screamed my name again and again, and I think she even hit an officer, or was that me? My memories are getting jumbled.

Everyone keeps telling me, "This isn't your fault." I don't understand what they mean. Why would it be my fault? It's because I was born in the wrong place, like Mom said. But I didn't get to choose where I was born. If I had, I never would have chosen France, that's for sure. I hate this place.

It hurts in my tummy, and my legs are itching like mad again.

"*Sam-uel, le petit déjeuner est prêt.*" Beard Man's voice comes through the door.

I roll over to face the wall. "Go away, go away. My name's Sam," I whisper into my pillow.

Suddenly he's in my room, opening the windows to pull back the metal shutters. Light comes flooding in.

"*Qu'est-ce qu'il fait beau.*" His voice is falsely bright and cheerful. He leans down and ruffles my hair. "*As-tu bien dormi?*"

I drag myself out of bed, putting on my slippers and dressing gown, and then sit on the edge of the bed. I'm in no hurry. I look around the room, at the wooden airplane hanging from the ceiling on a wire coil, hovering over the desk. At the framed photo on the wall of some people dressed in black—or is it just that the photo is black and white? Maybe they're really wearing bright purple, or green. Anyway, no one's smiling in it. On the same wall, there's a clay bust of a sailor, with bright yellow hair and dressed in a stripy blue-and-white shirt. It gives me the spooks.

"*Allez, Samuel.*" Beard Man moves toward the door.

I have no choice but to follow.

Breakfast is a basket of cut-up baguette and a bowl of hot chocolate. It's spread out on a plastic yellow tablecloth. They don't use plates; instead they collect the crumbs up afterward in their hands and throw them out the window. They dip their bread into their bowls of coffee, but I don't dip mine into my hot chocolate. I spread plenty of butter and apricot jam on my bread. How disgusting to have all those crumbs floating in your drink! And who ever heard of drinking out of bowls? They don't have any proper cups in the house, just tiny coffee cups, like a little girl's tea set.

They talk, but I don't understand a word. I've only learned to say *oui* for yes and *non* for no.

After breakfast, I go to my room to get dressed. My clothes are all folded up in a shiny wooden wardrobe that smells like it's a hundred years old. There's a large metal key in the door—I've tried it, and it actually works. You could really lock someone in there. Most of my clothes are my own from home. Somehow they arrived here, just like I did.

I pull some jeans out from the shelf, and my yellow T-shirt. As I get dressed, I wonder where they'll take me today. I've already seen the Eiffel Tower. I looked at all of Paris as though I were on a plane.

Beard Man opens the door and walks right in. "*Allez, Samuel. Nous allons sortir, toi et moi.*"

Somehow I understand that he means we're going out. Don't ask me how I know, I just do. I get up and follow him out of my room, then out the front door, down the staircase, and onto the street.

The pavement's so narrow we can't walk next to each other. This is good, 'cause I have a horrible feeling he would take my hand if he could. Instead he walks behind me, his hand resting on my shoulder like a lead weight. Sometimes he squeezes it to make me slow down, then he points at something, gabbling away in French.

There are no houses in Paris, no yards either. It's all apartments and funny little shops. There are patisseries, which are really cake shops, except the cakes are different from home. There's shiny bread in the shape of braids and moon-shaped cookies covered in icing sugar. I'd much rather have a jam doughnut. As we walk along, I look up at the small windows sticking out from the rooftops. I try to imagine Nazis running up the narrow staircases, shouting and shooting.

Beard Man directs me into a shop. A bell rings as we enter, and a man comes out from behind a curtain at the side. He shakes Beard Man's hand, then kisses him on each cheek. I'll be next. I get ready for the prickly beard, but the man just shakes my hand, holding on to it firmly, looking at me with dark brown eyes. I look away. I notice watches and gold chains shining out from glass cabinets. The man goes back behind the counter and lifts out a tray of gold rings on a red velvet cloth.

Beard Man studies them. Then he points at one, and the man takes it out, turning it around in his long fingers. He replaces the tray under the counter and brings up a set of metal rings held together by a circle of wire.

Beard Man takes my hand, placing it on the counter. I try to pull it back, but he holds on to it tightly. "*Allez, Samuel. C'est un cadeau pour toi.*"

I think *cadeau* means present. I let my hand go limp.

The man puts metal rings over my middle finger until one of them fits. "*Bien, très bien. Je fais ça toute de suite.*"

"*Merci, mettez 'S. L. 1944' à l'intérieur, s'il vous plaît.*"

We go to Maison de la Presse next. I look at the sheets of paper piled up on the shelves and can't help feeling impressed at all the different colors with their matching envelopes. I imagine myself writing a letter to Mom on purple paper, because that's her favorite color. She has purple soap at home, called lavender. "Just for me," she said when I once picked it up. "Boys don't want to smell of lavender." This unexpected memory kicks me painfully in the tummy.

Beard Man's busy talking to the man behind the counter. I see him take out a glass case full of pens. "*Voilà, les stylos plumes,*" he says in a proud voice.

"*Viens, Samuel.*" Beard Man holds out an arm.

I take a small step forward, deliberately missing his arm.

"*C'est pour l'école. Tous les enfants doivent utilizer un stylo plume à partir de six ans. Tu peux en choisir un.*" Beard Man looks at me.

I guess he's saying I can choose a pen. Even though I understand, I stand there like I don't.

"*Samuel, s'il te plaît.*" He swings his open hand over the pens, making it clear that I have to choose one.

I look at them. I like the light blue one best. I take my hand out of my pocket and lift the pen from the tray. When I take the lid off, I see a pointed nib. I push my thumb onto it, testing out its sharpness.

"*Faîtes attention!*" the man behind the counter shouts.

He makes me jump. I drop the pen.

Beard Man picks it up and gives it back to him. "*Oui, celui-ci. Merci.*"

The man nods, but I can tell he's cross by the way he rolls his lips as he places the pen in a wooden box. Slowly he hands the box to me.

"*Merci, monsieur,*" Beard Man whispers in my ear.

I don't say a word. I can't speak French. The words refuse to make themselves. But I want the lavender paper, and an envelope too. I try to work out what to say; then, like a baby, I just point at the paper.

"*Mais oui, bien sûr, du papier aussi.*" Beard Man is smiling. "*De quelle couleur?*"

This question is easy to understand. "Lavender," I say.

"*Lavande?*"

"*Oui*, lavender."

With a small frown, Beard Man picks out a sheet of the purple paper. Now I point to the envelopes. I can see he's confused. He's wondering why a boy would want purple paper. Maybe he's guessed what I want it for, and now he won't get it for me, but then he reaches for an envelope too.

After he pays, we leave the shop, his hand on my shoulder again, steering me along. We go back to the jeweler's, and the man there produces a small box. I look the other way, but out of the corner of my eye I see him take out a gold ring. Beard Man turns around to show it to me, pointing at the engraving on the inside, *S. L. 1944.* He holds it out, and I know he's waiting for me to give him my hand so he can put it on my finger.

But I don't want it. Rings are for girls. I scratch my leg instead.

He leans down, pulling my hand away from my leg. "*S'il te plaît, Samuel.*"

I go numb as the ring is fed onto my finger. It makes me feel like a dog with a shiny new collar. Then Beard Man kisses me, holding on to my shoulders as he looks into my eyes. "*Je t'aime, mon fils.*"

I can't wait to get home so I can scratch my legs in peace. They're burning up.

When we get back to the apartment, Pretend Mom isn't there. I go into my bedroom, sit on my bed, and pull up my jeans leg. The patches of red-raw skin are getting larger. I scratch them, digging my nails in. It feels good. Now they're hot and numb. I know the pain will come later.

I sit at the desk, staring down at my hand, at my finger, at the ring. I wonder how much it's worth. I bet it's real gold.

Beard Man walks into the room, smiling at me as if everything is okay. I look away, my eyes blank. He puts his hand on my shoulder, reaching up for a book on the shelf above the desk.

"*Est-ce que tu connais Tintin?*"

I know it's a question about the book, but I don't know what, so I just sit there looking at the wall, ignoring him.

"*Samuel, Tintin est un garçon qui vie des grandes aventures. Je vais te lire une histoire.*"

Something about adventures, I guess. I just keep looking at the wall.

Then he starts reading, and his voice changes. I can't help looking at him as he puts on the evil voice of the baddy, then growls just like a little dog. He turns toward me, pointing to the pictures. I see the white dog and the baddy whose face is covered in hair. "Milou," he says, pointing to the dog.

I point at the beard in the picture, then at his beard.

He laughs. "*Oui, oui, barbe. J'ai une barbe aussi.*"

Hah, so beard is *barbe*. Now I can call him Barbe Man.

He points to the dog. "*Chien.*"

But I don't want to learn any more words. I look away from the book.

He carries on, walking around the room, doing funny voices, trying to show me the pictures. But I just look at the wall again. I wish he'd leave so I can write to Mom.

At last he closes the book and puts it back on the shelf. The room feels suddenly very quiet, and I can feel him looking at me. I pretend I'm a statue and sit there not moving a muscle. If I make myself invisible, he might just give up and go away.

But instead he says a string of words in French. I bury my head in my hands, then I feel his hand on the back of my head, just resting there. I wait for him to go.

Finally he leaves the room. Now I can write to Mom. I'm not allowed to, so I'll have to keep it secret, and then I'll have to find a way to mail it. I put the pen on the paper and push down, pulling the pen forward to make the letter M, but nothing comes out. I push harder. Now it just leaves a scratchy mark. What's wrong with this dumb pen? I lift it off the paper, squeezing the nib between my fingers. Suddenly ink shoots out everywhere. Stupid pen! I throw it to the side of the desk. I won't cry. I won't.

I hear someone come into the room, but I don't look up. Then I feel a hand rubbing my back, hear someone picking up the pen and sighing. The flowery smell tells me it's Pretend Mom. I peek out and see her shaking the pen, then putting the nib to a small piece of white paper. Out of the corner of my eye I see her writing flowing smoothly out of the pen. I lift my head an inch higher to see what she's writing.

Cher Sam
We love you—nous t'aimons
Please—s'il te plaît
Give—donnes
Us—nous
A chance—une chance

She puts the pen down in front of me.

I draw a circle to test it. It works for me too now.

I write: *I wanna go home.* Then the pen blocks up again, and the ink comes out in blobs. The lump in my throat gets bigger. But I won't cry. Instead I ram the fine nib into the paper, again and again.

She reaches out for my hand, holding it tight. I can't move it now. She kneels down next to me, taking my other hand. She tries to pull me toward her.

I freeze, my whole body going stiff. She pulls me harder. I pull back. It's like a fight. I feel my breath coming quickly.

Then I see Beard Man in the doorway.

"Sarah!" His face is red. "Mais qu'est-ce que tu fais?"

Chapter Sixty-Five

Paris, August 20, 1953

SARAH

She doesn't know how to be a mother to him. She hasn't had the time to learn. It's too hard to be suddenly given a child, a child with a character already formed. With an awful sinking feeling, she wonders if it's too late. She's lost her baby forever and this unknown child has replaced him. They try to go through the routines of a normal life, but nothing's normal. Though exhausted, both physically and mentally, she finds it impossible to slip off into sleep these nights.

"Stay still, please, Sarah, you keep waking me up."

"I don't know how you can sleep!"

"We have to. We need our strength to deal with Samuel."

"But can't you hear him crying?"

"He'll stop soon. He just needs time to adapt to his new life. I know it's hard for him, but he will survive, and he'll be stronger for it."

"Stronger? But at what cost?"

"Sarah, what do you want me to do?" She can hear the frustration mounting in his tired voice.

"I just don't know how you can lie there and go to sleep while he's crying. I can't."

"That's why children need fathers as well as mothers. Naturally, you're softer than me, but we have to stay firm and not give in to pity. It won't help him grow and learn who he really is."

"Who he really is? He's a nine-year-old boy in a foreign country who's just been wrenched from the only family he's ever known."

"Sarah, please. We'll talk about it in the morning. We need to sleep now."

She turns away from him, tears sliding down her cheeks, but she doesn't make a sound. David's right, of course: they need to gather their resources to deal with the angry displaced boy they've been given. David has always been the strong one, but she knows he's suffering too; he just refuses to allow himself to face his doubts. He pretends they're simply not there, pretends that everything will be fine once Samuel has adjusted to his new life, that if they are consistent and patient, he will come back to them. Sighing quietly, she pulls the blankets aside, slips her legs out of the bed, and sits up.

"I'm going to get some water," she whispers, her voice cracking.

"Don't go and see him," David whispers. "You'll only make things worse."

Worse? she thinks. How can things be worse?

She feels her way around the bed and opens the door into the corridor. She has to walk past his bedroom on the way to the kitchen, and she presses her ear up against his door. It's gone quiet. Did he hear her coming? He probably doesn't want her to come in. He hates her. She can feel his hatred like a force field surrounding him.

But she has this need to see him, to touch him, to know he's real. She still can't quite believe her son is back. Gently she pushes the handle down, silently opening the door. Tiptoeing toward his bed, she listens out for the sound of his breathing, but she hears nothing. She crouches down, wanting to check that he's really there. Laying her hand on the blanket, she runs it over the surface till she feels the solid shape of him. She knows he's lying there awake, holding his breath, willing her to leave the room. "Sam," she whispers. "*Je t'aime de tout mon coeur.*"

Still nothing. Then he lets out a long breath and she feels him shudder. She strokes his body through the blanket, humming quietly. Then she begins to sing.

"Dodo, l'enfant do
L'enfant dormira bientôt."

He turns his head, and she feels his warm breath on her face.

"Can you go now?" He rolls over to face the wall. "Leave me alone."

Chapter Sixty-Six

Paris, September 2, 1953

SARAH

Today is a big day for children all over France—*la rentrée.* Life finally goes back to normal after the two months of summer vacation. Those who can afford it, and even those who can't, usually leave Paris in August, and those who stay behind benefit from the emptier streets. Sarah and David love Paris in August, and never go away; instead they take advantage of the lack of cars to bicycle through the city, through the Jardin du Luxembourg, then along the Seine to Canal Saint-Martin, where they leave their bikes to have a glass of wine in one of the cafés along the canal.

Sarah remembers both the thrill and the terror of *la rentrée* when she was a child. The class lists attached to the wall in the playground, parents and children crowding round, anxious to discover their teacher and classmates for the year. She's grateful to be able to do this with her own child at last. David is coming too, and she knows he's looking forward to it as much as she is. It will help things settle down into some form of normality. Routine is what they need now. It's been hard to keep Sam entertained; he has no interest in anything, not even the Eiffel Tower. He just looked over the edge, expressionless, refusing to be impressed.

"Shall I wake Samuel up?" David comes into the kitchen, where she's setting the table for breakfast.

She turns to look at him. "I'm not sure he's understood what's happening today."

"I know. I talked to him last night and read that story about the child starting school. I pointed to the pictures and then to him, but I never know what he's thinking."

"No. He's not sharing anything with us yet."

"Give him time. I can tell he's picked up a few words of French, against his will, of course." He pulls on his beard. "It will do him a world of good to start school. He'll have no option but to learn the language. He'll have to, to survive."

"I hope it's not going to be too hard for him. Children can be cruel, you know, to outsiders. He's not one of them, is he?"

"Don't worry. I've spoken to the director, and he's promised to look out for him." He puts his hand on her shoulder. "Once Samuel gets into a routine, once he starts mixing with children his own age, everything will gradually fall into place. One day he'll understand that we're doing this because we love him."

Sarah nods. "Yes, let's go and wake him now. Breakfast is ready."

David knocks on Sam's door, pushing it open at the same time. "Samuel, *c'est l'heure.*"

The shape in the bed doesn't move. Sarah watches from the doorway as David goes over, putting his hand on the blankets. "Samuel. *C'est l'heure aujourd'hui.* School."

"What?" Sam turns around to look at him, and Sarah can tell from the look of horror on his face that he understands.

She comes into the room, opening the wardrobe. She pulls out his ironed dark trousers and a gray shirt, then puts them on the bed next to him.

He sits up and shakes his head. "No! No school. I don't wanna go! I can't speak French."

Sarah looks at him, understanding what he's said, but finding no reply. She points at the clothes on the bed and leaves the room. David follows her out.

They drink their coffee in the kitchen, waiting for their son to appear. Ten minutes go by, then fifteen. He's not going to come.

"I'm going to get him." Sarah leaves David sitting at the table, buttering his bread.

When she goes into his room, her heart stops. She closes her eyes at the scene, wishing, just wishing, she hadn't had to see it. He's under the bed, and the stench of urine claws its way up her nostrils. Without a word, she walks toward the bed. She puts her hand on the neatly ironed pile of school clothes. They're wet through.

She wants to scream at him, call him a disgusting little boy. Instead she holds her breath, swallowing her anger, then reaches under the bed and pulls him out by his elbow.

He's not got his pajama bottoms on. She stares at his legs in horror. They're covered in patches of raw skin. He looks at them as if he's forgotten all about them, then back up at her, eyes wide with fear. He's obviously been trying to keep them hidden from her.

She reaches down to touch them. They feel damp at the same time as dry. "Oh no, Sam." She'll have to call the doctor; he can't possibly go to school like that.

When she goes back into the kitchen, David is still sitting at the table, waiting patiently for his little family to join him. "David, there's a problem." She waits for him to turn and look at her. "Samuel's legs are covered in an awful rash. I'll have to call the doctor."

"What? Wait. Let me see him first."

She follows him out of the kitchen, down the corridor and into Sam's room. Sam is sitting on his bed now, a blanket over his legs. David wrinkles his nose, turning to Sarah. "What's that awful smell?"

"Don't worry about that now. Just look at his legs."

David stretches out his hand, about to remove the blanket, but

Sam holds it down. David stands back, a frown deepening. "Has he wet the bed? What's wrong with his legs?"

"His skin is raw. You have to see it."

David turns back to Sam, kneeling down now in front of him. "Let me have a look." Gently he pulls the blanket aside.

Sarah's heart feels like it's breaking as she looks at the poor child, sitting there, exposed.

Suddenly Sam leaps up and runs out of the room. The front door slams. He must have gone to lock himself in the bathroom.

David's sitting on the floor now, his face deathly pale, his eyes staring blankly ahead. "What are we going to do, Sarah? What are we going to do?"

"I don't know. I'm going to call the doctor. We need help."

"Call that Polish one. He speaks English. Samuel needs to talk to someone. I'm going to talk to him through the door and wait for him to come out."

But he doesn't come out, and an hour later, the doctor arrives. They explain the situation to him, then leave him to talk to Sam through the locked door.

After fifteen long minutes, Sam comes out. Sarah and David leave the doctor to examine him in private, aware that their presence will only make things worse. They wait in the kitchen. Sam's hot chocolate has gone cold, and a feeling of utter rejection spreads through Sarah.

David looks as dejected and hopeless as she feels. "I love him so much," he says. "Whatever he does, I'll never stop loving him."

Sarah looks at him, at the gray lines around his eyes, at the sadness in the downward slant of his lips. "I know. That's how parents are supposed to feel."

"Is it? It hurts so much."

"Yes, it does." She sits down heavily.

"I don't know what more we can do for him. Truly, I don't."

"I know. All he wants is to go back home." Silent tears fall down her cheeks.

David sits next to her, putting his arm around her. "His home is here. We're his parents."

"In his eyes we're not, are we?"

"Not yet. But one day he'll accept the truth. We have to show him that we won't give up on him." He pauses, frowning. "We've been through worse than this, and we made it. When I was weak, you were strong. And now I'm going to be strong for you." He reaches for her hand.

Sarah doesn't know what he can do to help her.

"Eczema," the doctor tells them when he comes out. "Probably aggravated by stress." He gives them a prescription for various pills and creams. When they show him out, he turns back to them. "This is a very difficult situation. You will have to be extremely patient and gentle."

Chapter Sixty-Seven

Paris, September 3, 1953

SARAH

The next day, Sarah decides to teach Sam at home. School can wait. The psychologist said that with total immersion he would learn French in six months; that it would come naturally, like a baby learning to talk. But Sarah feels his resistance like a wall surrounding him. Babies don't have this kind of opposition blocking their language acquisition. It's not the same thing at all.

She needs to get Sam more involved instead of leaving him to mope.

There's the memory game she bought before he came. They can play it together in French. You have to pair up the baby animal with the adult animal. She can teach him animal names like this.

She takes his hand and brings him into the living room. He lets himself be led. She sits him on the soft green armchair that used to belong to her grandmother. Then she turns to the dark wooden cupboard where they keep photos, cards they've received, and the new games. Setting the cards out on the glass coffee table, she mixes them up facedown. Then she turns over the first one. It's a baby kangaroo. "*Kangourou.*" She reaches for the next one; it's a baby lion. "*Lion.*"

Sam stares at her like she's crazy, but she just smiles back. "À toi."

For a moment he sits there, staring blankly ahead. Then slowly he reaches out for a card, turning it over. It's a kitten. He turns another. It's a cat.

"Tu as gagné!" With a surge of pleasure, she sees him reach for another card. He's participating! She mustn't get too excited, it's only the beginning, but for the first time she can see a tiny light glimmering at the end of the long, dark tunnel. Then without a word, he disappears back to his room.

They eat croque monsieur for lunch. This is one dish he appears to enjoy. After lunch, she decides to take him to the Jardin du Luxembourg. It's quite a long way, and they take the Métro. She knows he likes the trains. His little face lights up each time one comes hurtling through the tunnels.

In the gardens, she leaves him to take it all in, sometimes pointing at something, saying the word slowly in French. He looks at her but doesn't repeat the word. She doesn't push it. One step at a time. They walk past the lake, stopping to look at the miniature wooden sailing boats blowing about on the water. Sam turns away. Children stand around holding long wooden sticks, ready to poke their boats back into the water if they come near the edge.

Sarah gestures toward the boats. "Veux-tu essayer?"

He shakes his head, and she knows he's understood.

An ice-cream truck draws up next to the lake. She decides not to ask him what he wants, but pokes her head through the window. "Vanilla, please." She looks over at Sam.

"And for the young man?" the ice-cream seller asks, following her eyes. "Chocolate? Strawberry?"

She watches Sam closely, wondering for a moment if he'll refuse to answer.

"Chocolate," he finally says.

The man grins. "English or American?" he asks.

"American," Sam replies, the pride in his voice ringing out.

"*Oh là là*, 'ot dog!"

"Do you have hot dogs?" Sam sounds excited for the first time since he arrived.

"*Mais non!* No! This is France! Never the hot dog." The man laughs, turning around to dig into the boxes of ice cream. He turns back with a perfectly round ball of dark ice cream sitting on top of a cone, gleaming in the late summer sun.

Sam takes a step forward, reaching for it. "Thanks."

"*Merci*." The man winks at him.

Sam ignores him, and Sarah feels the heat of embarrassment rising to her cheeks.

Licking their ice creams, they wander over to the play area. It's full of toddlers rolling in the sand, sliding down the slides. Mothers sit on benches nearby, chatting away to each other. Sarah can't stop the pang of regret at the years she missed with Sam. Beside her, he's so still, she can feel his sadness seeping through his skin. She's acutely aware of how his heart aches for his home. It's too much for one small boy to hold in. She feels cruel, cruel to want her own son back.

That evening, David comes home from work with a large rectangular package covered in brown paper. Instantly, Sarah knows what it is. She stares at him, defiance in her eyes. She told him she would never play again, and there he is standing with a violin under his arm.

"No, David." She wants to cry, to scream, to run from him. How could he? He knows how she feels.

"Sarah, please." He stares back at her, his eyes unwavering. "Don't you think they've taken enough from us?" He walks past her into the living room.

She waits outside, hovering by the door, listening to him removing the paper, opening the case. Then he plucks a string, and her heart stops. She can't breathe. It's all coming back: tuning up before a concert, the thrill of playing before an audience, the pure beauty of the music. She thought it all belonged to the other world—the one she left behind. She takes a step into the living room, and sees David hunched over the violin, gently plucking at the strings. Then she sees silent tears slipping down his cheeks onto the shiny polished wood.

She sits next to him, taking the instrument from his hands. She plucks the strings herself now, closing her eyes as she adjusts the pegs to get the right note. The heat of his stare burns through her skin. He wants her back. She can feel it. His yearning for the woman he used to know is tangible.

When she's finished tuning, she stands up, placing the violin under her chin. With her other hand she takes the bow, drawing it far back as though she's about to shoot an arrow. This is how it feels—like she's going to battle. It's time to fight again for the life they once had. Summoning all her courage, she plays the first notes of Mozart's *Eine kleine Nachtmusik*, David's favorite piece.

She watches him as she plays. This is for you, she's telling him without words. For you.

They are so lost in each other, they don't notice the little boy standing in the doorway, watching, listening, an expression of wonder on his face. When Sarah finally senses his presence and glances over at him, he doesn't turn away like he usually does, but looks her straight in the eye. She's taken back to the baby who gazed up at her while she fed him. At long last she's seen a glimpse of the child she left behind. Holding eye contact with him, she continues to play without missing a note, her heart soaring with the music.

Chapter Sixty-Eight

Paris, September 14, 1953

SAM

They're sending me to school. However much I hate it, I won't cry. I remember Daddy's letter. I'm braver than I know. Pretend Mom and I walk almost next to each other, but she's half on the pavement and half off, 'cause the pavements are so narrow. My heart is beating hard, like I've just run a hundred yards, but I haven't. I'm only walking.

When we get to the school, I see lots of children going through the gates. I stop and look at the sign: *L'École des Hospitalières-Saint-Gervais*. It sounds more like a hospital than a school. Maybe it's a school for sick children. I think I might be a sick child now.

All the other children go in on their own, but *she* comes in with me and we walk down a corridor with gray carpet that makes everything feel hushed and especially quiet. I can tell we're on the way to the principal's office. I guess he wants to meet me first 'cause I'm new and I'm probably a special case. People say that when they're talking about children who are bad.

We stop outside a door with a name on it: *Monsieur Leplane*. Pretend Mom looks at me, and I can tell she's almost as scared as me. I just stare back at her as if I couldn't care less, but really my tummy hurts and my legs itch like mad.

She knocks, and a small man with fuzzy black hair opens the door. "*Entrez, entrez,*" he says, as if he's in a hurry. When we're in his room, he stands behind his desk, books poking out on either side, like they're about to slide onto the floor. He lowers his glasses and looks over them at me. "*Bonjour, Samuel.*"

I know he's waiting for me to say something, to see if I speak French, but French words still won't come. Even when I want them to. Like now.

"Hello," I mumble.

He frowns, then looks at Pretend Mom and says something in French.

She bends down so her eyes are just in front of mine, and whispers softly, "*Au revoir, Sam.*"

I ignore her. But then she's walking out the door, and suddenly I don't want to be standing there all on my own.

Monsieur Leplane walks around to his side of the busy desk and sits down. "*Samuel, assieds-toi.*" He points to a chair.

I do as I'm told, sitting on my hands. If my hands are free, I know I'll start scratching. Photos of row upon row of serious-looking schoolchildren stare down at me from the wall behind his desk.

"Your father told me your story."

He speaks English!

He takes his glasses off to look at me better. "Samuel, we know this is hard for you, but this is where you belong. This is your real home." He puts his glasses back on. "And we're going to do everything we can to help you adapt to your new life here. It won't be easy, not in the beginning, but when you start mixing with other children, things will start to . . . to fall into place."

I can't help it; I scratch my leg through my trousers. He looks kind, and his English is real good, but I can see he's on *their* side. Not mine. No one is on my side. This thought makes my throat go hard. I blink the water out of my eyes. I will not cry. I will not.

"Let me tell you something about the history of this school," he says quietly. "It's connected to your story, but your story ends better."

It's a stupid story, I want to scream. But I don't. I just keep scratching my legs.

"On the morning of the sixteenth of July 1942, just two years before you were born, nearly all the children from this school were arrested. Only four were left in September. Can you imagine that? Arresting children? Do you know what their crime was?"

I think I know the answer, but I don't say anything.

He looks at me, waiting.

"Were they born in the wrong place?" I mumble.

"Yes, you could say that. They were Jewish when it was a crime to be Jewish."

I'm still not sure what Jewish means exactly—something to do with religion. I know Hitler hated the Jewish people. He wanted to kill them all, even the babies.

"The Nazis made it a crime to be Jewish."

"My dad was *not* a Nazi! You don't even know him!"

"I know he wasn't, Samuel. That's not what I said." He comes around to my side of the desk and puts his hand on my shoulder. "Your father, Jean-Luc, did a very brave thing. He saved you from the Nazis. I wasn't talking about him. It was the French gendarmes who arrested the children and handed them over to the Nazis. I think many people did things they wish they hadn't. War does that to people."

"I love my dad, he's the best dad in the whole world." I gulp back the big lump in my throat.

"You're right to love him, Samuel. No one's asking you to stop loving him. But you know, your mother here did a very brave thing too, something that most mothers wouldn't be strong enough to do. Even though you were only a month old, she gave you up because she knew it was your only chance of survival. She missed out on all those years with you, and now she wants you back. Can you understand that?"

I shrug my shoulders. I don't want to think about her.

He stares at me, waiting for me to say something.

"She doesn't own me," I whisper.

"Of course not. No one owns anyone, but children belong with their parents."

"My parents are in America."

"You believed they were. But now we know they're here in France."

"No! My real mom and dad are in America."

"And one day you'll be old enough to go and visit them all on your own, but for now, you have to give this new life a chance. It's an opportunity for you; you can learn French, discover your history, learn about another culture—"

"I don't want to. I hate it here."

He scratches his head, looking at me like he's trying to work something out. Maybe he's thinking over my problem. I have a feeling that he might understand more than the marshals and the psychology person I spoke to. None of them really understood that I'm American, not French.

"Enough history for today." He looks at his watch. "Let's think of the future now. For a better future we need to educate the young, don't we? So let's get on with that."

He's just like all the others. He won't help me. I wipe my face, telling myself that I will get back home, to America. One day I will, I swear.

"Let's go and meet your class," he says.

I want to go to the bathroom so bad, but I'm scared to ask.

When we get to class, the children are sitting at separate wooden desks. They all stand up. "*Bonjour, Monsieur Leplane,*" they say together, then they sit down again.

The class teacher is a lady with long dark curly hair and tanned skin. She smiles at me with warm brown eyes, reminding me of Mom. She puts her hand on my shoulder, leading me to the front of the class. I'm not sure exactly what she says as she introduces me, but I hear "*Les États-Unis*," which means America. The children look at me, sizing me up. They don't smile and neither do I.

I'm placed next to a boy called Zack. To my relief, he grins at me as I sit down. He looks like fun, with his wide smile, a gap showing between his front teeth. "I'm half American," he whispers. "Stick by me."

At last, someone to talk to.

The teacher finds the *stylo plume* in my pencil case and puts it in my hand. Zack lets me copy from him, but there's a lot to write and my hand begins to ache. I feel a blister growing on the inside of my middle finger.

When the bell rings for recess, I follow Zack out to the playground. "My father is American," he says as we walk outside. "He met my mother when the American soldiers came to free Paris. He jumped off the truck when he saw her in the crowd and kissed her. All the American soldiers were kissing the French girls." He laughs. "Maman said they were so happy to be free from the Nazis, they kissed them back."

I don't know what to say, so I just smile at him.

"That was 1944, and I was born in 1945," he says proudly.

This makes him a whole year younger than me. I guess they put me down a year because of my bad French.

I'm desperate for a pee and my legs are itching again. "I need the bathroom."

He looks at me for a moment before answering. "They're over there." He points to a small concrete building.

I run off. When I get there, there's a group of boys hanging around. They're going to test me, I know it. I hold my head up, avoiding their cold eyes as I pass by. The doors are open, and I can see that the toilets are those holes in the ground. It's okay, I tell myself. I need to go so bad; I've been holding it in all morning. I want to scratch my legs too. I step inside one, but there are no locks on the doors, and it stinks of poo. My tummy shrivels up and suddenly I don't need to go anymore. I just wanna get out, but I have to go past the group of boys again. I make the mistake of looking at them.

They start making whistling noises under their breath. I don't know what to do.

One of them pushes me into a stall, hard. My feet slither and slide. I put my hands out, reaching for the wall. It feels slimy. Vomit rises up into my throat.

Laughter rings out behind me.

Then the bell rings and I hear them run off. Quickly I pull my trousers down just as the pee starts to run down my legs.

When I find the class again, everyone is writing in silence. The teacher smiles at me, pointing to my seat.

"Did you get lost?" Zack whispers as I sit down.

I nod. I will not cry. I will not.

There are more words to copy, and I lose myself in the boredom of it. After a while, the bell rings again.

"See you after lunch," Zack says as we leave the room.

"What?"

"After lunch," he repeats.

We go home for lunch?

Pretend Mom is there with the real mothers at the gate. I see her looking around for me, the veins sticking out on her long neck. I lower my head, losing myself in the group. I could duck down and run away! I save this important piece of information for later, letting myself be dragged along with the other kids.

We stop at the boulangerie on the way home to get a baguette.

I grab it from the lady, and as we walk home, I tear bits off, stuffing them into my mouth.

I wait for Pretend Mom to get angry, but she just touches me on the shoulder. "*Tu as faim après l'école, n'est-ce pas?*"

She thinks I'm hungry, but I'm not. I just want to annoy her. When we get to the apartment, I run straight to the bathroom in the corridor, crouching down over the hole in the ground. I wash my hands after, turning the rectangle of soap around and around till all I can see is lather. I feel the soap getting smaller and smaller.

"Sam," Pretend Mom calls out. "*Ça va?*"

I push my hands together so the soap squirts out onto the floor, then I put my shoe on it, squashing it down, rubbing it around, making the whole floor slippery. I walk out with soap on the bottom of my shoe, squishing it into the floor as I go into the kitchen. I do these bad things 'cause they make me feel a bit better. I never used to do things like that; I never even thought about it.

I see her look down at the floor, and I know she's seen the mess I've made. I hope she's going to shout at me. I don't know why, but I want to make her angry.

"*Enlève tes chaussures, Sam.*" She crouches down, undoing my laces. I stare at the back of her head and wonder how old she thinks I am. Four, maybe?

I let her pull my shoes off my feet. She's pretending she hasn't even seen the sticky soap. Then she looks up at me, and I see that her green eyes are shiny with tears. She blinks and tries to smile, but I know she wants to cry really. It makes me feel bad inside. Real bad. Without a word, I follow her into the kitchen. I watch as she cuts up what's left of the bread and puts it in a basket. Then she gets out a bowl of grated carrots and puts that on the table too.

"*Assis-toi.*"

I do as I'm told and sit down. She sits next to me and we eat the bread and carrots. I wipe my plate clean with the bread, like she does.

I don't feel like being naughty anymore. Then she puts some meat and potatoes on the empty plates. There's apple pie for dessert, the apple slices so fine and regular.

"*Viens,*" she says after lunch.

I follow her to the living room, the worst room in the apartment, with its gold-colored couch for two sitting in the middle of the room and large wooden chairs on either side. There's no TV, just books in a glass cupboard.

She takes one out and sits on the couch, patting the place next to her.

I sit next to her, but only 'cause I feel sorry for her. Not too sorry, though—she could let me go back to America if she really wanted to. She holds the book out and starts reading aloud. I don't understand a word, and I start imagining giving a letter to Zack to mail, for Mom.

Chapter Sixty-Nine

Paris, September 14, 1953

SARAH

How is it possible for a child of nine to fall asleep at one o'clock in the afternoon? Sarah watches Sam's eyes grow heavy as she reads to him. She has to shake him awake to take him back to school.

It's because he's not been sleeping properly at night. She hears him cry, and sometimes he shouts out in his sleep; sharp, angry American words she doesn't understand. In the daytime he's often lethargic; she finds him curled up on his bed, asleep in the middle of the day. Other times he's quietly aggressive, devising plans to annoy them. Then there are his legs. All the words he cannot say are coming out in his raw, weeping skin.

How long can she let it go on like this? David tells her to be strong, to hold on, but it feels like they're being cruel, not strong.

When they walk back to school after lunch, Sam dragging his feet a couple of paces behind her, she can't help cursing Charlotte Beauchamp. Why on earth couldn't she have spoken French to the poor child? Why would she deprive him of his mother tongue? It doesn't make any sense to Sarah; she can only imagine Charlotte must be a woman of few principles, only too happy to escape France and forget her history, even her own family.

"Hi, Sam!" A boy with a mass of curly hair comes running up to them, grinning from ear to ear.

"Hey, Zack."

Sarah turns to look at her son, surprised at the intonation in his voice. He sounds happy, normal, just like any other kid.

Zack stops and kisses Sarah on each cheek in greeting. She smiles at him. What a nice, polite boy.

"*J'aide Sam en français*," he announces proudly. "*Mon père est Américain*."

So much for the immersion method! Quite frankly, she doesn't give a damn about it; she's just glad to see that Sam's made a friend.

Together the two boys trot off to class without so much as a backward glance. For the first time, Sarah feels like something normal is happening for her son. She can't help the feeling of hope that rises through her. She walks home with a lighter step, thinking about how important friends are at this age, and how with Zack's help, Sam will soon feel much more at home.

When she gets back, she lets herself in with her key, but is surprised to hear voices coming from the living room. Puzzled as to why David would be home in the afternoon, she walks on through to the living room.

"*Bonjour*." She looks at the stranger drinking tea from their best china.

"Sarah, this is Jacob Levi. I met him at the synagogue." David rises from the couch.

"It's a pleasure to meet you." The stranger stands, stepping forward to kiss her on each cheek. "David has told me so much about you and your incredible story."

Incredible isn't the word she would use. Tragic, maybe, shocking, terrible, unimaginable, but not incredible. She doesn't know what to say, so she moves to the couch, sitting down. The men follow suit. An awkward silence hangs in the room, making Sarah wonder what they were talking about before she arrived.

David coughs. "There's some coffee left if you want it, Sarah."

"No thank you."

"We were just talking about Paris during the war, how frightening it was." Jacob looks at her with dark, serious eyes. "I got out in 1939, before it became...impossible. We had family in New York. They took us in." She wonders why he feels the need to explain himself.

"If we'd known, we would have left too." David stares down at his cup.

"Of course. But no one back then imagined...could imagine what would happen..." Jacob trails off.

"No." David picks up the conversation. "It was one thing deporting immigrants, but French-born citizens too. That wasn't expected. By the time we knew we had to get out, it was too late."

"Quite." Jacob puts the cup he's holding back onto the saucer. He looks pensive, and Sarah wonders what's really brought him into their home. "But I'd seen it before." He pauses. "It always starts with almost insignificant measures, you know, things you can live with, like not being allowed to own a bike or a radio. It makes you feel uneasy—alienated, but life goes on. Then further restrictions make it much more awkward: limiting the places you can go, where you're allowed to shop. You can no longer mix with non-Jews." He picks the cup up again. "And finally they take away your livelihood. Then it becomes almost impossible to support your family; your children go hungry, and you begin to think to yourself: they're trying to kill us. But by then, it's too late. You no longer have the money or the connections to get out. You're basically a sitting duck."

Sarah's heard it before, and every time she feels embarrassed about their naïveté during the occupation of Paris, imagining that because they were French citizens with a French name, going back two generations and living in the chic 16th arrondissement, they would be safe. They'd witnessed the huge round-up in '42, but still they hadn't made any plans to escape. They hadn't wanted to run away. Was it pride, courage, or denial?

She knows David will try to defend their lack of initiative.

"A sitting duck? Yes. First, we had to wear that yellow star, then we could only travel in the last carriage of the Métro. The Boches were in the front, so that was fine! Then we were not permitted to cross the Champs-Élysées, enter theaters or restaurants. And then they stopped us from shopping in certain places." He coughs, pulling on his beard. "But life went on. Shows continued, people dressed up, went out, fell in love." He pauses. "Sarah and I met in the summer of 1940. We had a quiet wedding a few months later and moved into a small apartment my parents owned in the sixteenth."

"Were you working?"

"Yes, I was one of the few Jewish people who still had a job, and I managed to keep it till '43."

"You did well."

"The research I was doing at the time into cancer was important; they needed me. I thought we were safe. We didn't really understand the danger of our situation, not until it was staring us right in the face."

"Indeed. It was beyond imagination. Beyond anyone's imagination. But you two must have had your wits about you to survive for so long in Paris."

"Survive is indeed the word." David releases his beard. "Once I lost my job, we understood it was all we could hope for—to survive."

"You must have had good friends to help you."

"We did, but we didn't go into hiding, we just tried not to leave the apartment. Friends brought us food when they could, and when Sarah had to go out, she wore her coat without the yellow star." He pauses. "It was always a dilemma, whether to wear the star or not. If you did, you invited random arrest, but if you didn't, well, you know: if they asked for your papers, that was it. But you couldn't wear it one day and then not the next. People got to know who was Jewish and who wasn't. And there was always someone ready to denounce you."

"That's what I find hardest to understand... all those denunciations."

"Do you know that before the war, hardly anyone even knew we were Jewish? Our name gave nothing away—my father wasn't Jewish; it was my mother." He pauses, pulling on his beard again. "They were taken away a year before us. They wouldn't move to a safe house one night when we gave them the warning."

"I'm sorry." Jacob bows his head.

Silence fills the room.

After a few minutes, David picks up the conversation again. "Sarah is technically more Jewish than me; both her parents were Jewish."

They both look at Sarah. But she doesn't want to think about her parents. She swallows the hard lump in her throat and forces herself to speak.

"It was safer for me to go out. It was more likely that they would stop David. They'd taken most of the men from Paris, so a man stood out. But a scrawny woman like me barely attracted attention. There were many of us, queuing for food for hours. They ignored us more often than not."

"When you came back after the war..." Jacob hesitates. "Why didn't you go back to your home in the sixteenth?"

"Too many memories," Sarah says quickly.

"We wanted to be among our people." David nods. "We couldn't go back to the life we'd had; besides, someone else was living in our apartment."

Jacob shakes his head. "It happened. Many people are still fighting to get their places back." He coughs and sets his cup back into its saucer. "It's a miracle you survived Auschwitz." He turns to look at Sarah. "Both of you."

"One hundred and ninety days," Sarah whispers.

"We were young," David says. "And we were stronger than a lot of the prisoners who'd been there longer. Remember? We were on one of the last trains. When did it leave, Sarah?"

This date is etched on her mind: May 30, 1944. The day she gave their son away. She knows David knows it too; he's just trying to keep her included in the conversation.

"One week before the D-Day landings," she says. "One week exactly." She's never been able to say the date itself.

"We knew the war couldn't last much longer," David continues. "We just had to hang on. Knowing that Samuel was alive kept us going. He was our hidden strength, our guiding light."

"David managed to get messages through to me." Sarah speaks quietly, her voice dream-like as the memories come seeping back into her mind.

"We were young, and our hearts were strong." David rises, moving over to where Sarah is sitting. He puts his hand on her shoulder. "We had every reason to fight for our lives. And we did."

Silence fills the room as they think about the ones who never returned. Sarah would like Jacob to leave so she can go and lie down. Her heart is heavy, and all the energy has seeped from her body, leaving her feeling listless.

He seems to sense her thoughts and stands up. "Well, I've taken up enough of your time. I look forward to meeting Samuel, but there's no hurry. God will always be ready to welcome him into the fold. Whenever you feel it's right."

Sarah nods, leaving David to see him out. Then, without a word, she goes into the bedroom and lies down in the dark, the shutters still closed from the night before.

Chapter Seventy

Paris, September 17, 1953

SAM

"Want to play marbles?" Zack asks at recess time. We join a group of boys kneeling on the ground, and Zack pulls out a small green bag. "You can share mine today." He gives me three. They're the see-through kind with colors spreading out like feathers in the middle. I look closely at the blue one; it's not plain blue, but has two shades, just like my favorite one at home. I hold it tight in my fist, my tummy aching for home so bad.

I watch the other boys make triangles with their fingers, screwing up their eyes as they get ready to flick their marbles. I sit on the ground with them. The smell of hot tarmac makes me think of the boardwalk, burning my feet in the hot summers. The memory hits me hard in the gut, and my eyes sting with tears. But I blink them away and make myself think of the game instead. I've always been pretty good at marbles. I'll show them what I can do. I lie down, taking my time to line my marble up. With one eye screwed up tight, I flick it with just the right amount of force. Too much and it will fly past the target. Too little, and it won't make it far enough.

Yes!

"*Pas mal*," one of the bigger boys says. He means not bad, which means really good actually. It feels like when a teacher says your work is excellent, but it's an even better feeling.

I look at the boy. "*Merci.*"

He nods at me. A nod like that is a sure sign of respect.

Another boy pushes me out of the way. "*Mais dépêche-toi. La cloche va sonner.*"

I understand what he said—the bell is going to ring. French words are creeping into my head like ghosts walking through walls. I don't mind so much, but there's no way I'll ever speak the language.

After recess, we have music. Zack tells me that they call the teacher Tonton Marius, because he's from the south. I must look blank, because he adds, "You know, from Marcel Pagnol."

"Who's he?"

"*Mon Dieu!* You really don't know anything, do you? He's a famous writer and he makes films, and the main character from his best books is called Marius and is from the south. Haven't you seen *Manon des Sources*? It came out last year."

I shake my head, feeling the heat rise to my cheeks. I'm not used to being the one who doesn't get stuff.

"I went to America once," Zack says in a softer voice. "But I can't remember it—I was only one. My dad said he'd take me back when I was older. Is it true everyone has a TV there?"

"I guess so." Everyone I know has one, but I'm not sure that means every single person in America does.

"Wow! Is everyone rich?"

"I don't think so." I remember the street sweeper. He didn't look rich. I've never really thought about it.

After music with Tonton Marius, it's math. I've always been pretty good at math, and there are no words involved, just a long list of sums. I get on with them quickly.

The teacher walks up and down the lines between the desks, tapping now and again on a desk with a ruler when she finds a mistake.

She comes and stands over my desk. "*Bien, Samuel, ça se voit que tu as déjà fait des mathématiques.*" Her voice is soft, like a song. I look up and smile. I guess she just told me how well I'm doing. "*Maintenant, il faut travailler ton français.*"

Later, Zack says, "Do you want to come to my place after school?"

"You bet!" Anything's better than going back to the dreary apartment. "Can you get your mom to ask Sarah?"

"Who's Sarah?"

"The lady who picks me up."

"What? I thought she was your mom."

"No, my mom's in America."

"But Monsieur Leplane said you were coming to Paris to live with your parents. He said you'd been moved—displaced, he said, 'cause of the war."

"Did he? Well, he doesn't know the whole story. It's secret."

"Secret? What do you mean?"

"I'm not really supposed to talk about it."

"But I'm real good at keeping secrets. Swear on my life." He puts his hand over his heart and looks so serious it makes me want to laugh.

"I'll tell you as soon as I can, Zack, promise. Just not yet."

"Okay." Zack shakes my hand. It makes me feel real grown up.

"But I'm sure Sarah will let me come."

So, as planned between us, after school, Zack gets his mother to ask Pretend Mom if I can come for a play date. She looks pleased with the idea, smiling over at me as if it's the best news she's ever heard.

"Come on, she said yes." Zack pulls me along. I glance back and see Pretend Mom following us, chatting away to Zack's mom.

"Is *she* coming too?" I ask.

He looks back at them. "Yeah, guess so. Why?"

"Nothing, just wondered." Damn! She's probably telling Zack's mom the whole story. Now Zack will find out. And then he'll know I lied to him and that will be the end of our friendship. What can I do?

"Zack," I say, "I have to tell you a secret. When we're on our own."

Chapter Seventy-One

Paris, September 17, 1953

SARAH

Sam has a friend. It's the glimmer of light she's been praying for. She's spent a lovely afternoon chatting to Zack's mother, and in her new friend she's found a sympathetic audience, eager to listen and help if she can. A wave of optimism sweeps through her as she envisions a future where Sam plays with his new friends while she and David talk with the parents; outings together over the weekends, picnics in the summer, visits to the zoo, the parks, museums.

"More tea?" Zack's mother offers.

"Thank you, but no. It must be late; we should probably be going. It's been lovely." She glances at her watch: 6:30! David will be back from work any minute now. He'll be worried to find them gone. "I'm so sorry." She stands up. "I had no idea it was so late. Thank you so much for your hospitality."

Sam drags his feet as they walk back. He's doing it deliberately because he can see she's in a hurry. When he stops to look in a shop window, she grabs his hand, pulling him along. "Come on, Sam. It's late."

The force of the resistance in his thin arm makes her gasp. She lets go. There's no point fighting him, it will only make matters worse, so she pretends instead to look at the window display too. She knows it won't take long for him to get bored and move on.

Two minutes later, he walks on, and this time she pretends they're in no hurry at all.

When they enter the apartment, David is standing behind the door. "Where have you been?"

She feels Sam freeze by her side.

"Samuel made a friend at school. I met his mother and we had *goûter* together."

She sees David let out his breath. "I was worried."

Sarah touches his arm. "I'm sorry, I didn't notice the time fly by."

"No, I'm glad you had a nice time. What did you do?"

"We just drank tea and chatted."

Sam slips away to his room.

"I'll go and say hello to him properly," David says.

Sarah follows him down the corridor to Sam's room. When they knock and walk in, Sam looks up from his desk, quickly shoving a piece of purple paper into his drawer.

"*Bonsoir, Samuel.*" It looks like David's pretending he hasn't seen anything, but she can't help wondering what was on that piece of paper. "*Alors, c'était comment, l'école?*" He strolls farther into the room.

Sam looks from David to Sarah and back again. "Okay," he finally says.

"*Bien, bien.*" David is smiling. "*C'est une bonne nouvelle. Je suis content.*"

She leaves to prepare dinner. David follows her into the kitchen a few minutes later. "He seems happier now that he's started school. I knew that being with children his own age would help." He takes out two wineglasses, putting a dash of cassis in each before adding white wine. "So what's this friend of his like?"

"Zack? He's lovely, very polite and well brought up. His mother is charming too."

"How do the boys communicate?"

"You know children. They always find a way." She coughs to hide her unease at the white lie. She doesn't want to see the disappointment on his face when she tells him Sam's new friend is anglophone.

"Yes, of course." He pauses. "It's going to be all right, isn't it, Sarah?"

She takes her glass, waiting for him to take his. They clink them together, looking each other in the eye, but she can't answer his question. She's still not sure that everything will be all right.

She takes a sip of her kir. "He's hard to reach. Very hard. It feels like we have a high mountain to climb, and we're not even sure what the view will be like from the top."

"What do you mean?"

"Well, he will adapt. He'll have no choice. But I don't know if he'll ever be able to love us."

Chapter Seventy-Two

Paris, September 17, 1953

SAM

I only just managed to shove the letter into the drawer when they came into my room. Not that they would understand it, but they'd see it was in English and they'd guess who I was writing to.

I take it out again. This time I put a book nearby in case I need to cover it up suddenly. I read it back to myself.

> ***Dear Mom,***
>
> ***I love you. I miss you so much, it hurts me inside. Your the best mom in the world and Daddys the best dad. I dont care what anyone else says. They dont understand. Pretend Mom and Dad are weirrd. I call him Beard Man cause he's got this real bad wirry beard. You and Daddy are my real parents and I'm gonna find a way to come home. So dont worry. I wish wed gotten to Mexico. I hate it here. I love you.***

I concentrate hard on my writing, careful not to lift the pen off the paper except between words. I wonder what else to tell her. I don't have a plan yet, but I want her to know I'm going to try.

The door clicks open. My heart jumps up into my throat. Quickly I hide the letter under the book and open it, pretending to read.

Beard Man comes right up to the desk. "*Ça va, Samuel?*" He leans right over my shoulder. "*Qu'est-ce que tu lis?*"

I know he wants to know what I'm reading. "*Tintin.*"

"*Laisse-moi le lire pour toi.*" He reaches out to take the book. But I'm quicker than him and push my elbows on it, keeping the letter safe.

I point up at the shelf above the desk. "That one," I say.

He takes down a book. "*Les Trois Mousquetaires, bien, très bien!*"

It's *The Three Musketeers*! Daddy's favorite book.

Beard Man opens it and begins to read.

I leave *Tintin* open on the desk, the letter hiding underneath, and pretend to listen, but really I'm thinking about what else I can put in my letter, imagining Mom's face when I turn up at home.

I realize Beard Man has stopped reading and is staring at me. There's a frown deepening on his forehead, as though he's trying to work something out. Then he says, "*Samuel, je sais que c'est difficile pour toi, même très difficile. Mais on t'aime et on va faire tout pour que ça marche.*"

He means it's difficult for me, but that we have to walk forward. I'm pretty sure that's what he said, anyway.

Oh no! He's coming back to the desk. I can tell he's going to pick *Tintin* up, and then he'll see the letter. Quickly I slip it out from under the book, letting it fall on the floor. I cover it with my foot.

"*Essayons Tintin maintenant. C'est plus amusant.*"

I knew it! Thank goodness I got rid of the letter.

Taking the book from the desk, he begins to read again, putting on special voices for the different characters. He's loud and boyish for Tintin, then mean and sneaky for the bad guys. But he does the dog best of all. It almost makes me laugh. As his voice booms out, he moves around the room, throwing his arms around, acting out some of the parts. I stare at him. He's really good at the voices. I know he does it to make me smile, and I nearly do. He's trying to be funny and nice, but it doesn't change anything. I don't want him to be my dad. I never will.

Chapter Seventy-Three

Paris, September 18, 1953

SARAH

Last night, Sarah poked her head into Sam's room and saw a sight that made her throat tighten. David was reading to him, and it looked like Sam was truly listening, his eyes focusing on his father and not on some unseen point as they often were. Creeping back to the kitchen, she offered up a silent prayer of thanks.

Today is Friday, and Shabbat begins at sunset. After Sarah drops Sam at school, she goes home to prepare the challah, the sweet bread they break before they start the meal. As she's not permitted to do any work between sunset tonight and sunset on Saturday, she needs to make sure everything's ready. This means getting all the shopping done, as well as the food ready for the next day too. She enjoys the preparation for Shabbat almost more than Shabbat itself. There's a comfort in the ritual. Counting out the candles, she places them in the candelabra.

She decides to do the housework before the shopping and cooking. First she tidies the kitchen, then she moves on to the sitting room and finally the bedrooms. As she makes their bed, she remembers all the sleepless nights spent praying that they would find Samuel, trying to work out how to track down the railroad worker at Drancy, the one with a long scar running down the side of his face, almost touching his eye. The Nazis were efficient with their record-keeping, so it wasn't hard to get his name. The International Tracing Service was put on the case, but they were told it might take years. And it did.

The waiting and false hope was hard to bear, and after five long years, David told her that they had to stop, that they had to accept their loss. Sarah couldn't seem to move forward. Sometimes when she closed her eyes she could still feel the silky softness of her baby's head beneath her lips, could still smell his milky innocence. She didn't feel that she could be complete again till she found him, and in her heart she knew he was alive. She could feel it, just like she could feel his heart beating when he was in her womb. David thought they should try for another child, but Sarah didn't know how to tell him that her body felt alien to her, that it disgusted her. When she looked at herself in the mirror for the first time after Auschwitz, she thought she was looking at a ghost of the Sarah who had died there. She was unrecognizable. Bones protruded at odd angles, tufts of gray hair sprouted from her head, her eyes like hollows in a skull. This image of herself remained with her for a long time, and it was at least a year before she could look in a mirror again. She had to get to know herself again. And David. They were changed.

But time ticked by. Relentless and indifferent, weeks turning to months, months turning to years. Years as her child learned to love someone else as his mother, someone else as his father. She would sell her soul to have the last nine years of Samuel back.

She tries not to wallow in the sense of loss that she feels, tries to remember how lucky they've been compared to many others. They are alive, and their child is alive too. It's so much more than they could have expected after they were taken to Drancy on that dark morning only two days after she'd given birth.

She wanders into Sam's room, rearranging the books on his desk, folding his clothes, which are strewn across the floor, putting them away in the drawers and cupboards. She picks up his pillow, intending to smooth it out, but instead she breathes in its smell—the boyish odor of sweet sweat.

Quickly she puts the pillow back, telling herself to stop procrastinating. There is a lot to be accomplished today, but she's so tired. She'll rest for just five minutes; it will give her the energy to carry on. She lies on his bed, closing her eyes, breathing in the scent of him. A sense of peace comes over her, making her feel closer to her son, lying here on his empty bed, than she has since he arrived.

Opening her eyes, she feels ready to tackle the day's chores. She gets up and lifts the sheets and blankets, tucking them in properly. A piece of purple paper catches her eye. Without thinking, she pulls it out and looks at it. It's a letter.

She drops it as though it's scalded her. Though she doesn't understand it all, she understands enough. Crouching on the floor, she grips her stomach, cramps shooting out from deep inside her. It feels like when her water broke, before she gave birth to Samuel.

Chapter Seventy-Four

Paris, September 18, 1953

SAM

It's Friday, but I wish it was Monday. I didn't manage to get the letter out from the side of the bed before school. Now I'll have to wait till after the weekend. School is better than being with Pretend Mom and Beard Man. I hope we'll go to Zack's for *goûter* again. Maybe I could ask to see him on the weekend.

I'm real disappointed when everyone goes straight home after school. No play dates. And when I go into my room, there are fancy clothes laid out on the bed, black trousers and a white shirt, just like last Friday.

I hear the click of the front door, and Beard Man soon appears in my room, "*C'est Shabbat, Samuel.*" He bends down to kiss me on the forehead.

I suddenly feel a pain in my tummy, remembering Daddy coming home from work, pulling me into his chest, the smell of lemon soap. "How's my little guy doing today?" he'd ask. The empty place inside me opens up again.

"Go away, go away," I whisper. But I can feel him standing there, can hear him breathing, scratching his beard. Then I hear his footsteps moving away and the click of the door again. He's gone. Now I can get my letter out and finish it.

I lie on the bed, pushing my hand down the side. But it's not there. I untuck the sheets. Phew, it comes flying out. It's all crumpled, so I smooth it out, then take my pen out of my satchel and sit at the desk to finish it: *I'll come back soon, Mom. I can't stay here mutch longer. I hate it so bad. I'll find a way to get back*. I'll give it to Zack on Monday morning.

I'm pushing it back down the side of the bed when Pretend Mom comes into my room. For a moment she just stands there, looking so white, her green eyes shining like a cat's. Then she points at the clothes on the bed. "*Ce soir on fête Shabbat. Il faut que tu t'habilles avec ces vêtements.*"

She wants me to put those fancy clothes on again. She leaves the room 'cause she knows I won't get dressed in front of her. I bet she's worried I might pee on them, but I don't want to do the same bad thing twice. That would be boring. Anyway, her shiny eyes made me feel bad inside, a bit like the homesick feeling.

When I leave my room in the dressy clothes, I see she's lit the candles, just like last Friday. It makes the dreary apartment feel a bit cozier, but a bit spooky too. She's wearing a long black dress and has put her hair up. Gold loops hang from her ears and her green eyes look so sad in the flickering light. I stare at her; she's quite pretty actually. For a second I wonder what it would have been like if she'd been my real mom. Maybe I might have liked her. I guess I would have, and even Beard Man too. Kids always like their parents. It's a strange thought.

She smiles, holding out her arms to me. But I walk right past her.

She drops her hands. Beard Man kisses her on the cheek and takes his place at the table. He pats the seat next to him. My legs feel like they're being licked by flames, and my stomach twists in pain.

"I'm going to the bathroom." I leave quickly before he can say, "*Toilettes, Samuel.*"

I go out into the dark corridor. Luckily no one is in the bathroom. I lock the door and pull down my pants to look at the bandages. I scratch the surface of them, but it's not enough. So I slide my hand down under them and dig my nails in. It feels good. The white cloth loosens up, beginning to unravel. At least now I can have a real good scratch.

"*Sam-uel?*" I hear Beard Man's voice behind the door. "*Tout va bien?*"

It makes me jump. "*Oui,*" I shout back, trying to wind the bandages back around my legs. I only just remember to flush the chain in time.

They smile at me when I walk back into the dining room. I'd like to ask them what all this is about; why they make a special dinner on Fridays but don't invite anyone. Beard Man says a prayer, then cuts a large loaf of shiny bread. He puts the slices in a basket and passes it to me. I put a piece straight in my mouth. I'm starving. It's nice, like the brioche we sometimes have for *goûter.* Afterward, there's a kind of meat stew, with many different dishes on the side. Pretend Mom and Beard Man talk to each other. I hear my name now and again, and sometimes they look at me as if waiting for me to say something, but I just look down at my plate.

After dinner, we clear the table, but no one washes the dishes. The kitchen's a mess, dirty plates piled up in the sink. I'm surprised they don't tidy up. Instead they move into the living room. Beard Man's hand is resting firmly on my shoulder so I can't sneak off to my room to be left in peace. Well, I could, I suppose, but I can't be bothered.

Pretend Mom passes a large book to him, and he takes it carefully as though it might break. I guess it's the Bible. He sits in one of the wooden chairs, flicking through the pages. I sit on the golden couch with Pretend Mom. There's a hush in the air as he chooses a story to read. I recognize it straightaway from the list of pairs of animals that goes on and on. Some of the animal names are the same in French as in English, like *lion*, *tigre*, *léopard*. I work out that *serpent* means snake from the way he hisses after saying it. I wonder what flood is in French. But I'm feeling sleepy, and the words run into each other, like a song I don't know the words to. I lay my head on the arm of the sofa.

Chapter Seventy-Five

Paris, September 19, 1953

SARAH

Sarah wakes early, as she often does these days, David snoring softly next to her. Leaning over him, she tries to read the time on the clock, but can't make out the hands in the semi-darkness. Never mind, she'll get up anyway; it will be nice to have a coffee on her own, get her thoughts together before the day starts. Silently she slips out of bed, sliding her feet into her slippers.

In the kitchen, she puts the beans in the grinder and turns the handle. Making coffee takes time, but she finds the smell comforting and the process soothing. Since their return from Auschwitz, she's found a pleasure in mundane tasks that she never felt before. She takes her time over the dishes, meticulously cleaning every piece, then wiping them dry till they shine. Before, she would have left them to drain. But now these rituals help settle her nerves.

"You up already?" David walks into the kitchen. "What's the time?"

"I don't know. It must be about seven."

"What do you want to do today?"

"I don't know." Their Saturdays used to have a routine to them—synagogue in the morning, followed by a simple lunch at home and a stroll around Le Marais in the late afternoon. But now they have to find things to do—things a nine-year-old boy might like. Sarah misses going to the service, and she knows David does too.

"David, why don't you go to the synagogue and I'll take Samuel out for a walk? Maybe the Tuileries."

"I'd like us all to go to the service together, as a family. I don't want to go on my own."

"I know." She turns back to the coffee, pouring the ground beans into the filter. "But it will be awhile before he can go. It would just upset him now and might put him off forever." She glances at David. He's frowning.

"He understands more French than he's leading us to believe."

"I know." Sarah smiles, thinking how stubborn Sam has been about not learning French, though still she can see his child's mind soaking it up like a sponge. "But he didn't even go to church in America—well, only at Christmas and Easter."

"It must be strange to raise a child with no faith. How can you teach values and principles with no reference?"

Sarah looks at him, wondering for a moment if he's right, wondering if this means Sam has no values and principles. But she can't believe that. Despite his anger and his need to show them he doesn't want to be with them, she can see he has good manners and a sensitivity to others that he tries to hide. He doesn't really want to hurt them; he just wants to go home.

"At least he's had some exposure to religion," David continues. "He knows who God is. He has been in a church before." He frowns, and Sarah can see he's working it out. Then he continues. "I think it's important that we emphasize it's the same God. We need to find common ground where we can."

"What about Christmas?"

David smiles at her. "Christmas? You're thinking too far ahead."

"Yes, but you know in America it's a huge event. The whole country celebrates."

"I suppose we could always give him presents and pretend they're from some benevolent fat man with a red coat and a white beard." He grins. "There's not too much harm in that, is there?"

Sarah knows he's being ironic, and she's not in the mood for it. He's always been adamant about not celebrating Christmas. Distractedly she pours boiling water over the coffee in the filter.

"Is everything ready for today?" David puts his hand on her shoulder.

"Yes. All the food is prepared, and I did the cleaning yesterday."

"Good." He takes the coffeepot from her. "Now sit down. Today is a day of rest and worship. I know how you like to keep busy, but let's remember God on this special day."

How can she tell him that this is what disturbs her the most? How can she tell him that she doesn't know how to pray anymore? Her mind swarms with confusion and doubts; she can no longer tell the difference between right and wrong. Is it wrong to want her son back? Wrong to punish the man who saved him? She didn't want him punished. Every time she thinks about it, her heart contracts with guilt. Apparently it was out of their hands, but prison! It seems so unfair. They've all been punished, too much and for too long. She just wants the suffering to end. Sometimes it feels like she's a recipient of everyone's pain, soaking it up till her heart wants to burst open. She feels it all too much. She's asked God for guidance, for strength, but it feels like he's no longer listening.

He answered her prayers when she begged him to keep her son safe. That should have been enough. But no. She wanted more, didn't she? In her greed and selfishness, she wanted her son back, not only to love, but to possess.

Chapter Seventy-Six

Paris, September 21, 1953

SAM

Monday at last. Phew! I'm so glad to get away from *them.*

I take the finished letter for Mom out from under my mattress and put it in my school satchel. I'm so excited about giving it to Zack to mail. I even have fifty centimes to give him for the stamp. I stole it from Pretend Mom's purse.

As soon as I get to school and sit down, I hand it to him. "Zack, I need you to do me a favor, please. Can you send a letter for me?" I give him the fifty centimes.

Zack turns the letter over in his hand. "Why can't you do it yourself?"

"I'm not allowed."

"Oh, yeah, okay then." He stuffs the letter and money into his pocket.

"Will you be able to do it tonight?"

"Sure. I'll tell my mum I need to mail a letter to my pen pal in America. I never write to him, but sometimes he writes to me."

"Thanks, Zack. You're a true friend."

Zack pats me on the back. I feel real grown up, like we're men hatching a secret plan. "Make sure you get airmail," I add.

"Of course."

The rest of the day follows the same kind of pattern as last week. Writing in the morning, reciting poetry, gym, then home for lunch, and back again for math and maybe music or art. In a way, it's not so bad going home for lunch. It gives me a break from all the kids, and I get a lovely warm baguette every day, straight from the boulangerie.

Marbles is our usual game, but now I've taught Zack backgammon, and we play after school sometimes. He's pretty good, but not as good as me. The empty feeling inside me is still there, but when I'm with Zack, I pretend I'm back home playing with Jimmy, and then it leaves me for a while. It's when I'm alone in the apartment with Pretend Mom and Beard Man that it's worst. My legs always itch more in the evenings. Maybe I'm allergic to something in the apartment. Daddy's allergic to bananas; he gets a rash if he eats them. Maybe my rash is like that. My legs always itch like mad as soon as I get in from school, and I usually go straight to the bathroom to have a good scratch.

On Thursday, I realize I forgot to put a return address on my letter. How will she be able to write to me now? I'm so stupid!

Chapter Seventy-Seven

Paris, September 28, 1953

SARAH

Sam is still maintaining the barrier he's built around himself, trying hard *not* to learn French. But despite his best intentions, she can see he's coming to understand more and more. Without realizing it himself, he's following instructions instead of looking blank like he did when he first arrived. Every day she reads to him after lunch, and every evening David reads to him at bedtime. Sometimes he won't even look at her, and she can feel him a hundred miles away, but other times, she sees recognition in his eyes when the story or a character is familiar. His eyes are easy to read, just like David's. Neither of them can help but show their emotions through them. She's seen the hatred and defiance in Sam's, the confusion and disappointment in David's. They're both so proud, so stubborn.

As she wanders into Sam's room, she feels small and powerless. Sam is sitting at the desk, doodling on a piece of paper. She looks over his shoulder, but he quickly covers the paper with his arm.

"*Sam, est-ce que tu veux jouer au backgammon?*"

"*Non, merci,*" he immediately replies.

"*On pourrait lire une histoire ensemble?*"

"*Non.*"

She is at a loss. His desire for her to leave is tangible. "*Viens, m'aider dans la cuisine.*" One last attempt.

He scrapes his chair back loudly, making her wince at the sound of the legs scratching the old oak parquet. Standing, he turns to face her. His brown eyes are dim and cold. "I wanna go back to America."

Sarah's heart feels too heavy for her body. She reaches out a hand to touch him, and for the first time, he doesn't flinch at her touch, but holds her gaze.

"Oh Sam." She attempts to bring him toward her. He yields slightly, and now their eyes are just a hand's span away. She knows it's the closest she'll ever get to him. "*Sam, chéri, est-ce que tu peux me donner une petite chance?*"

His eyes fill with water. "I just wanna go home."

Chapter Seventy-Eight

Paris, October 24, 1953

SAM

I think Pretend Mom's beginning to give up. Sometimes I see her looking at me with those green cat eyes. They look so sad, and I can't help feeling sorry for her. But she made me come here, so it's her own fault. Why couldn't they have just left me alone?

Sometimes with Zack I laugh, but I'm careful when *she*'s around. She must never catch me laughing or even smiling. There's no risk with Beard Man, except maybe when he reads *Tintin* and puts on a girlie voice for a bad guy.

But time is running out, and maybe soon everyone will think it's normal for me to be here in Paris. The French words are beginning to make meanings; words have crept into my head, even though I've tried to block them out. But I will never, ever let myself become French. Not if I have to stay here a hundred years.

I have to escape. Maybe I could go to the prison where Daddy is. It's called La Santé, and it's right here in Paris. They think I don't know where he is, but I'm not as dumb as I let them believe. I've heard them talking about it, and even though it was in French, I understood some of it, and I heard the name. I remember it 'cause *santé* means health, and I thought it sounded more like a hospital than a prison, just like my school sounds more like a hospital than a school.

But that's a stupid idea. Daddy can't help me; he's a prisoner too, like me. Anyway, they wouldn't let me in. I bet they'd just bring me straight back here. I don't think kids are even allowed to go into prisons.

On Saturday, they go out together in the morning without me. I think they said they're going shopping, or maybe to the synagogue. I'm not sure. Anyway, I know they'll be out for a while because they've left me a plate of meatballs, bread, and apple on the kitchen table.

I'm so excited my heart's thumping like I'm about to run a race. This is my chance! But I make myself wait ten minutes to make sure they've really gone before I grab my school bag and stuff the food into the front pocket. It will probably only be enough for one day, so I open the cupboard and pull out a box of cookies and add it to my bag. I need to hurry now. I can always buy more food if I need it. I'm ready. No. Wait. Money!

I go to the hall and see that Pretend Mom has left her purse on the table. There's a fifty-franc note in the front. It's a lot of money, and together with the money I might be able to get for the ring, I could have enough. Quickly I go back to my bedroom and grab a sweater, but just as I'm leaving, the mini treasure chest on my desk catches my eye. I grab it, shoving it into my bag.

Now for my passport. I go back into the hall and open the drawer in the bureau, pulling out all the papers and documents, spreading them across the desktop. I run my hands over them, feeling for the thin book with the photo in the front. But there's nothing like that. Just papers.

I could go without it. If I sneak onto the boat, I won't need it anyway. But if I *can* buy a ticket, I'll have to show my passport. I go to the living room, but there are no cupboards or drawers there, just one bookshelf packed full of books. I run my fingers over their spines, checking to see if it's been squashed between them. But there's nothing. Where could it be?

Their bedroom? I've never been in there, and I don't really want to go now, but I need that passport. Slowly I open their door, peeping around, even though I know they're gone. It smells dusty and old, and the shutters are closed. When I put the light on, I see a polished chest of drawers under the window, but I don't think it will be in there 'cause the drawers are too big, like they're for clothes. I look at the bed; it doesn't even look big enough for two people. There are bedside tables on each side. I reckon Beard Man sleeps on the left, 'cause there's a newspaper on the table, and he's always reading papers.

I open the top drawer on the other side. It's full of photos; the one on the top is of me back home on the beach. I shove it into my pocket and continue to feel around. My fingers hit the edge of a thin book. I pull it out. It's a passport! I open it up, but the photo isn't me. It's *her.* I throw it down and look again. There's another passport. This time it's me. I stuff it in my pocket and run out of the room.

Chapter Seventy-Nine

Paris, October 24, 1953

SAM

A drop of rain splashes onto my cheek. When I look up, I see thick gray clouds crossing the sky. But it's too late to go back and get a coat; I have to get to the Saint-Lazare station. I found out from the teacher at school that trains from Saint-Lazare go to Le Havre, and Le Havre is the huge port where all the boats leave from.

But first I have to sell the ring. I don't want to do it here, though. It would be better to find somewhere farther away from the apartment, where no one will recognize me. Rue de Rivoli is full of shops, and I can walk there. Drops of rain splash around me, and I get wet as I hurry through the crowds. When I reach the main street, it feels like legs are swallowing me up, while elbows and bags with sharp corners jut into my shoulders. I'm small and invisible as I slide between people, letting myself be carried along by the crowd.

Soon I realize I'm in front of the big department store, La Samaritaine. I don't want to go in there, so now I have to push against the flow of people. I'm glad to break free from them, even though the rain falls straight onto me now in big drops.

I look at the windows as I pass by, but I can't see any jewelry shops. Then I see a man and woman come out of a shop holding an umbrella over themselves, looking down at something in his hand. I just know it must be a ring.

Taking a deep breath, I walk into the shop, straight up to the counter. "*Bonjour, monsieur.*" I stand on tiptoe, slipping the ring off my finger, holding it out toward the man. "*Je veux vendre.*"

The man stares back at me. His cold dark eyes make me shiver. He gabbles away in loud, angry French. The only words I understand are "*Non! Non! Et non!*"

I shove the ring into my pocket and run out of the shop.

Bang! I run straight into someone. I look up and see a tall man in uniform. A cop! He shouts at me in French, but I have no idea what he's saying. My legs feel like they're turning to jelly and my heart beats hard. What if he arrests me? Will he take me to jail? I stand there frozen to the spot.

"*Allez! Allez!*" He pushes me in the chest.

Phew! He just wants me out of his way. I turn and run. I have to get away from this street. There are too many people. Maybe I should forget about selling the ring and just find the train to Le Havre.

I wonder when Beard Man and Pretend Mom will get home. How much time do I have? They'll go crazy when they see I've gone. They'll call the cops for sure. But Paris is a huge city and they'll never be able to find me with all these people.

Just in front of me, I see the big "M" for Métro. *Hôtel de Ville* is written in curly letters above the staircase. I run down the steps and see turnstiles. I need to get a ticket.

There are people behind little windows selling tickets, so I go to one and look at the lady sitting there. She looks very strict. I feel scared and try to talk in my best French. "*Une ticket, s'il vous plaît, madame. Pour Saint-Layzare.*"

She looks down at me. "*Pardon?*"

"*Une ticket pour Saint-Layzare.*"

"*Quoi?*" Now she looks real cross, but I'm sure I said it right.

"*Il veut dire un ticket pour Saint-Lazare.*" A lady behind me speaks over my shoulder.

"*Ah, bon. J'ai rien compris avec son accent. Trente centimes alors.*"

That's thirty centimes. As I take the coins out of my pocket, I turn to thank the lady behind me. Her smile sends sparks through my heart. It's just like Mom's, and her eyes are the same chocolate brown.

"*Comment tu t'appelles?*" she asks.

"Sam."

"*Sam? Pas Samuel?*"

"*Non, je suis Américain.*"

"*Américain? Dites donc. Quel âge as-tu?*"

"*Douze ans,*" I lie, standing up straighter.

"*Douze ans?*"

I can tell she doesn't believe me. She looks just like Mom does when I tell a lie; her knowing smile seeing right through me.

The nice lady buys her ticket, and I follow her down to the Métro. On the train, zooming through the tunnels, I look around at the other passengers. A man with a cap pulled low over his forehead stares back at me with dark eyes. Quickly I look away. He takes his cap off, and I can't help staring at his shiny hairless head.

"*Es-tu tout seul?*" He leans forward, touching my knee with his cap.

I shrink into my seat, looking away.

He's still staring at me when the train screeches to a stop, so I jump off, even though I've only gone one stop. Strangely, the nice lady gets off too, and I follow her. I know I'm supposed to be going to Saint-Lazare, but I feel like staying close to her. And I reckon I could try to sell the ring again and then get back on the Métro. We come out to a square, with cafés around the edge. When she crosses the square, I do too. She walks past a big church that looks a bit like Notre-Dame, then on up another street. The street sign says *Rue*

Montorgueil. We pass a shop selling chocolates, another selling cheese, then one selling slimy stinky fish.

She walks into a cake shop with the word *Stohrer* written above in blue. In the window there are neat lines of chocolate eclairs, smooth lemon tarts with labels of dark chocolate, and buns with juicy raisins poking out. My stomach rumbles, and I check on the food in my bag. Quickly I stuff a meatball in my mouth. Yuck—it tastes like my school bag, all tough and leathery. I'd much rather have a chocolate eclair.

But I don't have time. I want to sell my ring. I run past the shops with food on display, people shouting out, "*Poisson frais de ce matin!*" "*Huitres d'Arcachon!*" "*Pommes de la ferme!*" Then I hear footsteps behind me, like metal hitting the cobbles—the kind of footsteps a cop or a soldier would have. Regular. Solid. The sound scares me. I want to turn around to check who it is, but if they see my face... well... What if they're looking for me already? I start to run, and I don't slow down till the footsteps have gone away.

The shops look dirtier, grayer now. I stare at a woman standing in a doorway. Her stockings are like black spiderwebs, stretching across her white skin, and her skirt looks like it's made of red plastic. She scowls at me with horrible purple lips. "*Qu'est-ce que tu veux?*"

I don't like this street—it's spooky. And I'm tired, wet, and hungry. I see a tailor's shop with naked dummies in the window. Then there's a shop with the words *Prêteurs sur gages* on a piece of card stuck in the window. I have a feeling it means a place where you can sell secondhand stuff. I've seen it in a shop before, near the apartment.

I'm real scared, but I push open the door anyway, stretching my back, standing taller, pretending to be braver and older than I am. I walk up to the counter. A thin man with a shiny face appears from a door behind it. Leaning his elbows on the counter, he stares down at me. "*Oui?*"

I take the ring out of my pocket and hold it out.

He takes it from me without a word, turning it over in his bony fingers. His nails are real dirty. I'm trying to look calm, but shivers run down my back.

He looks up at me. He's noticed the engraving. "*S. L. 1944... C'est toi?*"

I nod.

"*Cinq francs.*"

I'm not sure that's the right price for a gold ring. "*Dix francs*," I say bravely.

He smiles, showing crooked yellow teeth. Then he shakes his head, laying a five-franc note on the counter.

I take it and run.

Chapter Eighty

Paris, October 24, 1953

SARAH

David carries the shopping bags into the kitchen.

"You go and see Samuel," Sarah says. "I'll put the shopping away." She takes the raspberry tart out from the top of the bag, putting it carefully on the table. It was expensive, but they bought it because it's Sam's favorite. Food, she thinks. How she used to fantasize about it, how it used to invade her dreams. And now they have it, whatever they want really. But she still feels empty.

"Sarah." David stands in the doorway, his face deathly white.

"What is it?"

"He's not in his room."

"Look in the living room. He's probably fallen asleep on the couch."

"I looked. He's not there."

"He must have gone to the bathroom then."

David shakes his head, staring at his feet.

"Go and look. He must be there." She runs out into the corridor. The room's not locked. She pushes the door open. It's empty.

"Sam! Sam!" She runs back through the apartment, in and out of each room. Hoping against hope. "He's not here!" She reaches out for David, her knees losing their muscle, turning to pulp, the ground slipping away beneath her.

He takes her by the shoulders, leading her to a chair in the kitchen.

"What are we going to do?" She gulps down air. It feels like she's drowning. "We must call the police. Quick! Call them!" Her heart pounds in her ears, her veins pumping hard. "David! Please!"

"Sarah, we need to think this through. Do you have any idea where he might have gone? Friends?"

"What? Yes. There's Zack. Let's try him." She jumps up, already halfway to the front door.

David runs after her, grabs her elbow, and pulls her back. "Sarah, wait. Please."

"We have to hurry. He could be far away by now. Oh God! Where has he gone?"

"Calm down for a minute. Please."

She brings her hand to her throat as if holding herself back. Then she's dashing toward the door again. They're wasting precious moments. She knows they have to find him before he gets too far. He's so small, so naive, he doesn't understand how cruel people can be, he doesn't know about all the sick people out there.

"I'll wait here in case he comes back," David shouts after her.

She doesn't stop as she runs to Zack's. Zack himself answers the door.

"Have you seen Sam?" She doesn't even say hello.

He frowns, shaking his head.

"Please, Zack. He could be in danger. Do you have any idea where he might have gone?"

Zack just shakes his head again. She searches his eyes for some kind of clue. Then his mother appears.

"What's happened?" She frowns just like her son.

"Sam's disappeared. Have you seen him?"

"No."

"Are you sure, Zack? Think carefully. Please. Do you know where he might have gone?"

She waits for a reply, precious seconds ticking away.

Eventually he whispers, "He might have gone back to America."

Of course! Where else would he go? It makes her want to laugh hysterically. America! How can he possibly imagine he could get that far? She'll have to go to the police right now. She hesitates for a second, wondering whether to go home first. She decides against it. Time is vital.

She runs to the police station. Arriving there, she is breathless, gasping for air. It's as though everything is in fast motion, everything except the officer sitting behind the wooden desk. He's in slow motion. He stands, scratching his belly.

"My son has...has gone missing! Help me!" Her breath is raw, scratching at her throat.

Too slowly, he reaches a stubby finger out to a buzzer on his desk. Its shrill ring fetches another officer—a taller, leaner man. "Come this way, madame."

She follows him into a small room. "Sit down." He pulls out a plastic chair.

But she doesn't want to sit down. She wants him to jump up and start looking for her son.

"Name?" he asks, his pen hovering over a pad of paper.

"Samuel Laffitte. Please, he's only nine. We need to find him quickly."

"Mrs. Laffitte, we can't start looking for him till we have some details. I'm sure you understand."

She nods, tears of frustration welling up. She swallows them and tries to answer his questions calmly and quietly.

He takes notes, looking up sometimes, creases growing between his eyes. "I think I should come to the apartment," he says. "See if we can find some clues, and speak with the boy's father."

They drive to the apartment in a police car. He puts the siren on, which she takes as a good sign. He understands the urgency now.

David throws the door open before they have time to knock. "He's taken his passport!"

"No! Please, no!" Sarah leans into the wall, clutching her stomach.

"Please stay calm. We'll find him, Mrs. Laffitte." The police officer turns to David. "What else has he taken? Money?"

"Maybe. I don't know."

"Do you have any idea about where he might be heading, given that he's taken his passport?"

"California," Sarah whispers.

"California?"

"His adoptive family is there. He's only been living with us since the end of July." David's voice is flat, a monotone.

"Yes, Mrs. Laffitte explained the situation. Most unfortunate indeed." The officer coughs. "We are lucky in that we know where he's likely to be going, and in that way his options are limited. He won't be able to take a plane, but that doesn't mean he won't try; kids don't think that far ahead. So he could be heading for the airport, in which case it should be quite straightforward to find him. Or he could be going to a port. Or he could be on his way to visit Monsieur Beauchamp in prison—that option would be the easiest for us. We'll phone through to La Santé to check."

"But he doesn't know which prison he's in!"

"We need to explore all the options. Most kids come back within twenty-four hours, when they get hungry." He pauses. "We'll send a couple of men to the airport."

Sarah wishes he'd just do it. Quickly. Crucial minutes are ticking away.

He continues, "We'll phone through to Le Havre. They'll be able to check the trains arriving and the boats leaving."

"But Le Havre's not the only port. What if he's gone to Calais or Dunkirk?"

"True. We'll phone there too, and alert police at the railway stations."

"But what if he's already arrived there and got off the train? We went out at midday and now it's three o'clock. He's had time to get there by now." Sarah throws herself into a chair, her head spinning with all the possibilities.

"We'll have our men check the boats leaving port. Don't worry. We'll get him back. Now, do you have a recent photo?"

Sarah gets up to fetch the photos Charlotte Beauchamp sent before they met Sam. There's also his extra passport photo. She hands them over without a word.

The officer looks at the photos, then slides them into a leather wallet. "I'll be in touch. Do you have a phone?"

"Yes," David replies quickly.

"You need to stay here, in case he comes back. Don't worry, we'll find him."

David sees him out.

Another sharp pain clutches Sarah's abdomen, like a snake twisting itself around her intestines. She bends over, holding her stomach. In her head she whispers: Please, God, please. Forgive me. You saved him before. Save him again. I'll never ask for anything else. Keep him safe. I will give him up. Please just bring him back, I beg you.

Chapter Eighty-One

Paris, October 24, 1953

SAM

I can't stop shivering as the engine starts up and the train moves forward. I look out the window. *Au revoir, Paris.*

My stomach rumbles. I guess I should eat something; it might help warm me up. I open my bag and take out the bread. I put the rest of the meatballs inside and take a bite. It tastes stale and leathery, and it makes me feel bad inside—eating food *she* made for me. They'll know by now for sure that I've gone. I bet she'll be crying. I swallow the lump of food in my mouth and put the rest of it back in the satchel. Maybe I'm not that hungry after all.

I hunt around in the bag, checking what else I brought with me. My hand comes across the small wooden chest. I take it out and open it, looking at the colored stones. I hold them up to the light one by one, wondering if they're precious. They're not shiny, but the colors are nice. I put them back and close the box, thinking instead about how happy Mom will be to see me. I bring my legs up to my chest, hugging them, trying to get warm, as I stare out at the gray buildings against the gray sky.

I must have dozed off, because a man is shaking me by the

shoulder. At first I think I'm dreaming, and it takes me a few minutes to remember where I am.

"*Billet.*"

He wants my ticket. Quickly I pull it out of my pocket and show it to him.

He looks at it, then gives it back without saying a word. I'd like to ask him what the time is and how much longer the train will take. It's real dark now outside.

The train screeches. It must be stopping. I look out the window. I can just make out the sign in the half-darkness—*Le Havre.* I grab my bag and jump off the train. There's a guard at the end of the platform, checking tickets, so I get mine ready. I wonder how far it is to the port. Maybe there will be a bus. The crowd moves forward slowly. There's a family of five in front of me, and it takes them ages to find their tickets. I wish they'd hurry up; I want to get on that boat. Finally they go through. I hold my own ticket out for inspection.

"*Comment tu t'appelles?*" The guard doesn't look interested in my ticket.

"Samuel."

"*Passeport.*"

"*Mais j'ai mon billet.*"

"*Oui, et maintenant je demande ton passeport!*"

I take my passport out of the bag. My heart is thudding hard. But it *is* my passport, and I am allowed to take a train. Everything will be okay.

I hold it out to the man.

A hand lands on my shoulder. "Samuel Laffitte."

Chapter Eighty-Two

Paris, October 29, 1953

SARAH

The boy they bring back to them on that black night is a diminished version of himself, even more withdrawn and morose than before.

He's fighting them with silence, using it like a sharp knife. It's ripping into Sarah's soul, tearing it to pieces. Once again, David puts him to bed with a story he refuses to listen to, his head turned toward the wall. They go straight to bed after they've tucked him in. They're both exhausted through to their bones. But sleep doesn't come easily.

"David," Sarah whispers in the dark.

"Please, Sarah. We need to sleep."

"But I can't. I feel terrible."

"Sarah, you have to stop this. We have done nothing wrong. It's not wrong to love your child, to want to raise him. You mustn't feel guilty like this."

The words she really wants to say are stuck in her throat, like a cancer growing. So instead she skirts around it. "I'm not strong enough, David. I can't do it."

"Give him more time."

"We've given him time. Time is not helping. His resentment for us grows stronger with every day that passes."

"He won't be able to keep fighting us like this. He'll run out of steam, and we'll be ready to catch him when he falls. He will come back to us. We just need to be patient and keep our faith."

"Faith," she murmurs.

He turns to face her. Sighing, he reaches for her hand. "We all have our moments of doubt, Sarah. This has been very hard for us, but you've been so brave. You've always been brave."

"I didn't want to have to be that brave."

"I know you didn't." He strokes her hand under the sheet.

"Sometimes I feel so angry inside, then sometimes I feel guilty. I just don't know how... how..." Tears slip down her cheeks.

"It will be all right, Sarah. It will. I promise you."

"How could it have happened? Auschwitz—how was it possible?"

David continues to stroke her hand. "Sometimes man is evil."

"But was he not created in God's image? David, it's—"

"Shh, shh. It's going to be all right."

But she can't sleep, can't eat, and can't keep still. Her nerves are raw, as though they're about to split open any minute. Her body aches from her shoulders down to her toes. It feels like the last two months have aged her well beyond her years. She can't take any more, can't see the point in having their son back if it's only to witness his pain. She turns away from David, trying to calm herself, but the panic is rising up from her belly, threatening to overcome her. She pulls the sheets aside and slips out of bed.

She goes to the kitchen and opens the window, breathing in the cool night air. She would like to pray, to ask for guidance, but she no longer feels worthy. When she tries to find the words, she encounters only a void. She looks out into the dark night. "God," she whispers. "If you have something to say to me, say it."

A cold silence answers her. And she understands why. Twice she begged God to keep her son safe, and twice he answered her prayers. But the last time she promised something in return. You can't break a promise to God, can you?

Putting her hands on the windowsill, she leans out, dark thoughts playing in her mind. What if they had died at Auschwitz? Sam would have continued to live in ignorance of his true history. He would have grown up happy and free from it all. No religion. No history. Free.

She wants to be free too. Free from all this guilt, pain, and anguish. Gazing out into the night, she realizes there is only one path to freedom and peace.

For the first time in months, she sleeps calmly and wakes feeling ready for the day.

As she and David set the table for breakfast, she broaches the subject. "I've been thinking. I've got an idea. It might help."

"Yes?"

"I could visit Beauchamp in prison. I could ask him questions about Samuel, find out more about how he was brought up, what he was like as a small child. It might help us understand him better."

David pauses as he fills the coffee grinder with beans. "Let me think about it."

This is as much as she could have hoped for. Patience.

He looks at her. "It's seven thirty, time to wake Samuel."

She can't help resenting the way this task is always left to her. She dreads getting him up in the mornings. He's so lethargic, as though he's crawled deep within himself, putting himself into a state of dormancy or hibernation. As she pulls back the covers and strokes his shoulder, coaxing him to sit up, his little body resists her touch. The eczema on his legs and elbows needs taking care of before he can get dressed. She rubs the cream in softly, then passes him clothes for the day, leaving him to dress while she prepares his hot chocolate. She brings his drink into the bedroom; an excuse to check that he's not climbed back under the sheets.

Today, she talks softly to him. "Sam, don't fret so much. We'll work out a way to make you happy again. I would give my soul to see you smile; my heart too, to hear you laugh." She looks into his eyes, but they are blank, no glimmer of understanding peeking through.

When they get to the kitchen, David is gulping back his coffee. He puts the bowl down on the table with a small thud. "I need to leave now. Samuel should get up earlier." Bending down, he grips the boy's arms and kisses him, once on each cheek.

Sarah sees Sam go rigid, as though he wishes he were made of stone.

After breakfast, she takes him to school. She no longer tries to hold his hand or even walk next to him. The pavement is too narrow anyway. Instead she walks ahead, and he drags his feet behind her. The school's only around the corner and it should just take five minutes, but she has to allow fifteen to get there.

Chapter Eighty-Three

Paris, October 29, 1953

SARAH

The front door shutting makes Sarah jump. David must be back from work. She leaves the living room just as he's removing his coat and hat. Taking the hat from him, she dusts it off with the back of her hand, placing it on top of the hat stand. When she turns back to face him, she's shocked by the paleness of him.

"I'll go and say hello to Samuel."

"Of course. Would you like me to get you a drink?"

"Yes, a pastis, please. I'm feeling a little sick." He always drinks pastis when he's feeling ill. He says it kills off bacteria more quickly than any medicine.

She watches as he turns his back on her, walking down the hallway to Sam's room.

"He's not in there," she calls after him. "He's in the living room."

She's only just finished pouring his drink when he comes into the kitchen.

"Samuel's asleep." He scratches his beard. "He's asleep on the couch. Sometimes I think it's his way of escaping."

"Do you ever wonder what he dreams about?" She hands him the glass.

"Well, we don't choose what we dream about, but if he could, I expect he'd be dreaming about America. His heart is still there."

Sarah nods, leaning back against the sink. "I wish…I wish he could think of his home as here, but it's too late, isn't it? Home is set in your mind from a young age, and then it's fixed."

"I don't know, Sarah. I don't know anything anymore." David pulls a chair out from under the table, slumping into it. "I'm just so tired. I don't feel well."

She sits down next to him. "So am I. I feel like I've been beaten from the inside. The fight is going out of me."

He turns to look at her. "Do you remember, Sarah? Do you remember how hard it was to keep believing, to keep fighting? Sometimes I just wanted to close my eyes and wait for the sweet release of death to take me."

"I know." She strokes his arm gently, understanding his need to go back over it. She feels the same need to relive it sometimes. Maybe it's her mind trying to make sense of it all. But there was no sense. Maybe it's because each time she plays it back, she hopes the sharpness will be slightly less killing. That a memory replayed a thousand times will lose some of its potency.

"I think I would have died if I hadn't known Samuel was alive somewhere," David says. "I clung on because I wanted to find him again."

"So you knew too? You knew he was alive?"

"I didn't know, but I held on to that thread of hope. I made myself strong for him; I wanted him to be proud of his father wherever he was."

"He gave me strength too." She pauses. "It was our love for Samuel that kept us going, wasn't it?"

She sees a solitary tear slide down David's cheek, losing itself in his beard. She knows how hard it is for him to talk like this. It upsets him too much. He needs to stay in control, and these overpowering emotions make him feel like he's losing his grip. She knows this, though he has never explained it to her. Now that he's started talking, she wants to keep the conversation going. It will help them both.

"I remember one day when I was digging that trench outside the camp," she continues, still stroking his arm. "It was so hot, and we had no water. I remember wiping the sweat from my brow, then licking it from my hand. Then I noticed a guard standing next to me, watching me. I flinched, expecting a beating. But instead he asked if I was thirsty." She pauses. "I didn't dare reply. Then he pulled out his canteen and offered it to me. I didn't want to take it. My fear was worse than my thirst. But he pushed it into my hand. I took one gulp and tried to give it back. I thought it might be a trap—that I'd be shot for drinking from a guard's canteen. But he told me to finish it. So I drank it all." She stops stroking David's arm. "I didn't even say thank you."

David sits up straight. "It wasn't the water that saved you that day, was it? It was seeing an act of kindness in hell itself. It gave you hope."

"Yes, and it made me believe someone would be taking care of Samuel. And then when I saw you through the snow in that broken building, I knew we would all be together again."

He takes her hand. "I don't know how you recognized me. We all looked the same; like skeletons. I was ready to give up even though I knew the war was over. I just wanted to lie down and die. Then I heard you call my name, like a dream, and suddenly you were there, holding me, saying my name over and over."

She squeezes his hand. "I was looking for you. I knew you'd be there."

"And I knew it couldn't be a dream because I was so damned cold. Then I heard God telling me to keep my faith and stay strong, that soon our ordeal would be over."

"But it wasn't, was it?"

He takes a gulp of pastis and shakes his head.

They sit in silence, each lost in their memories. Sarah remembers the stories David told her afterward. They're his memories, but she likes to visit them, imagining the ingenious ways he managed to get messages to her, helping her keep her faith. With his research skills, he was taken on in the medical laboratory under the supervision of the notorious Dr. Mengele. He spent his days in the relative warmth of the lab, staring at cells under the microscope. Often he was left on his own, and he managed to get ahold of medical supplies for other prisoners. He was taking an enormous risk, but he was clever and hid them in unlikely places. He put small antibiotic tablets into his ears and penicillin under the soles of his feet. These were highly valued items and could be easily traded for a message carrier. They knew about the experiments now, but David knew back then. He told Sarah that knowing what they were doing had made him feel complicit in some way. It was impossible to remain unscathed. And he still carried the guilt.

"How does everyone else who survived manage?" Sarah wonders how others have coped. Maybe the only solution is to block it out. "Sometimes I wonder if it really even happened."

"It's hard for everyone, but no one really wants to hear about it. They don't want to have to imagine what we went through. But nothing's ever the same once you've seen hell, is it?"

She leans into him. "No, nothing's the same." She pauses. "Sometimes I feel so alone."

"I'm here, Sarah." He takes her hand. "I know I'm no good at saying things, saying how I feel. But I'm here for you." Unshed tears shine in his eyes.

"I know you are." She squeezes his hand. "David, what we lived through—it's not of this world, is it? Not this world now. It can't be."

"It's not." He wipes away the silent tears running down her face.

"We came back from hell. Somehow we have to learn to forget what we saw there."

"Learn to forget. Yes. If only we could."

"Maybe we can't forget, but we can forgive."

His words take her by surprise. She realizes it's not something she's ever considered, and she'd always assumed he hadn't either. Forgiveness.

"I don't think I can. I don't even think I want to."

He looks down at the table. "I want to. I won't make excuses for them, but...but I think I would...I would be able to forgive if I were a better man."

"No! You are a good man. It's too much to ask. You always ask too much!"

"What do you mean?"

She didn't mean to say it, but now the words are out. "You expect so much from everyone: Samuel, me, yourself. But we're only human. Sometimes it's just too hard." Her tears start afresh, and she pulls a handkerchief from her pocket to wipe her nose.

He takes his hand away, scratching his beard. "I'm sorry if I've been hard on you both. I didn't mean to be."

She looks sideways at him, watching his Adam's apple going up and down as though it were a heavy weight. She can feel his pain, can almost hear the words blocked in his throat. She wishes she could ease it. "David, we should be grateful for what we have. It's a miracle Samuel survived. And he saved us too."

"Yes, he did."

"Isn't that enough?"

"What do you mean?"

"I don't know. Maybe we've been asking for too much. Isn't it enough that we are all alive?"

He grips his beard as if gripping on to life. "What are you saying?"

She closes her eyes, praying for courage. "David, you know what I'm saying."

"No! No, I don't."

Scraping her chair back, she gets up and goes to the sink, where she starts to scrub down the already clean surfaces, swallowing her tears.

Then she feels her husband next to her. "Sarah, maybe you should go and meet Beauchamp. It might help you."

"Will you come?" She turns to him, wiping her eyes with the back of her hand.

"No. I couldn't bear to see him."

Chapter Eighty-Four

Paris, November 2, 1953

SARAH

After Sarah drops Sam off at the school gates, she can't stop thinking about it. Should she go to the prison? If she goes, she might gain some insight, something that will help her understand Sam. Something that will help her take the next step.

She knows where the prison is—in the 14th arrondissement, at Montparnasse. It will take about thirty minutes to get there. That's thirty minutes there, thirty back, and she has three hours before she has to pick Sam up for lunch. It should be enough time. But she's afraid, anxious about how she will feel toward Beauchamp, how he will feel toward her. He probably hates her.

But she wants to see her son through his eyes. From the photos they were shown, it was clear he was a happy, healthy child, full of the joys of life. She wants a glimpse of this boy.

The psychologist assigned to them advised them against bringing up the past. "I know Freudian theory would have you going through it all," she said, "but we believe the human brain suppresses certain memories for good reasons. It's a kind of survival instinct; life moves forward, never backward. Well, not yet anyway—we'll have to wait for time travel for that." And she laughed, a horrible shallow laugh.

Sarah hurries down to the Métro at Saint-Paul. When she gets off at Montparnasse and walks to Rue de la Santé, she realizes it's an area of Paris she's never visited before. The prison imposes itself on the narrow street, tall and gray. With a trembling hand, she knocks on the wooden doors.

She hears a latch being moved aside, and a man peers through a small square opening. "Yes?"

"I'm here to visit a prisoner."

"Visiting starts at ten." He stares at her.

She looks at her watch—it's 9:20.

"You can go in now and wait. You need to leave your ID here."

She feels herself break out in a cold sweat. With trembling hands she produces her identity card, reminding herself again that it's no longer a crime to be Jewish. He takes it from her and writes the number down. "Who are you visiting?"

"Monsieur Beauchamp."

"You have to be out by ten thirty. Go and wait inside."

She hurries over to the entrance.

A guard meets her there. He rifles through her handbag, then shows her to the waiting area. She sits down on a cold metal chair, a shiver running down the back of her neck. Dampness clings to the room, leaving it cold and humid. Auschwitz comes crashing into her mind. The freezing cold, the starvation, and the twelve-hour days of physical labor were hard enough to endure, but it was the fear of the unknown that was truly petrifying and soul-destroying. She shudders, attempting to dislodge the memories she's tried so hard to suppress, reminding herself that this isn't the same thing at all. And it's not. It's really not. It's just that the loss of freedom, loss of control over one's own destiny is there in the cold plain room, the unnatural hush, and the vinegary smell of stale sweat and fear seeping through the walls.

She tries to compose her thoughts, working out how best to

approach him. She wants to know what Sam was like at one, at two. What were his first words? What made him happy? What made him sad? What might comfort him?

"You can go through now." A guard interrupts her thoughts.

Taking a deep breath, she walks into a room containing scattered tables and chairs. She's shown to a small table at the back with a chair on each side. As she sits down, more visitors enter the room, shuffling to chairs at other tables.

A door opens. She glances up to see a line of handcuffed prisoners slouching through. The sound of the guards' boots and the odd barked order interrupt the soft pad of their open shoes shuffling along the floor. Will she recognize him? Will he know her? She's almost too scared to look.

"Beauchamp!" a guard shouts.

That can't be him! A thin, hunched man shuffles his way toward her. She thought he was taller, much taller. She holds her breath.

Then he looks up, stopping in his stride as their eyes meet. It is him! She sees the scar running down the side of his face.

"Hurry along now!" A guard pushes him in the back. "Your visitor is waiting."

Involuntarily she flinches, as though it were she who was pushed.

She stands up, not sure how she's supposed to greet him. Then he's right in front of her, stretching out his fingers from the handcuffs. Briefly, she touches them. They sit down opposite each other. She notices a bruise on his cheekbone. For a moment she wonders what it's like for him, here in prison. It's not what she wanted. She only wanted her son back.

"Is Sam okay?" His voice is hoarse, and she sees him swallow.

"No." The rest of her words stick in her throat. She looks away, blinking back tears.

"What's wrong?"

She watches his Adam's apple go up and down as he sticks his chin out. She sees Sam in this gesture, when he's trying to be brave, trying not to cry.

"He's been uprooted from the only family he's ever known." She sits up straight, trying to control her emotions. This wasn't how she wanted to start.

He bows his head, his eyes on the table now instead of on her.

"He doesn't know us. And we don't know him. For God's sake, we don't even speak the same language!"

He won't look at her. His silence goads her.

"It would have been better for you if we hadn't survived, wouldn't it? Certainly easier for Sam."

"No!" He looks up now. "I didn't want that! When I saw the photos... what happened in the camps, it was... it... I didn't see how anyone could have survived that. And I thought of you, I thought..."

"That they'd sent me straight to the gas chambers!" Her voice cracks. This wasn't what she wanted to talk about. The bitterness of her words makes her feel sick.

A guard strides over to their table, banging his baton down onto it.

Sarah jumps back, sweat breaking out on her brow, running down her ribs. She closes her eyes in an attempt to distance herself, to calm herself. She's making a total mess of it.

"Keep it quiet." He hits Jean-Luc on the shoulder with the baton. The thud makes Sarah cringe, but Jean-Luc doesn't flinch, though she sees a flash of light cross his eyes.

"Please. We're fine. It's my fault." She tries to quell the pity welling up inside her.

The guard walks away.

"Why didn't you look for us after the war?" she whispers across the space between them.

"I... I was scared."

"Scared? Why? They would have considered you a hero—saving a baby from Auschwitz."

"No...scared of losing Sam."

"How can you say that? Don't you think *I* was scared of losing him? Do you know how much courage it took for me to give him to you?"

"I know." He holds eye contact with her.

"Tell me about Sam, when he was little. What was he like?"

He smiles, a lopsided smile, and her heart jumps. It's Sam again.

"He was a quiet baby, hardly cried at all. But once he could walk, there was no stopping him. He wanted to explore everything, always sticking his fingers into things, pulling things apart. I was forever putting his toys back together for him. He'd watch me, fascinated."

"Just like my father. He always had to understand how things worked. Tell me something else."

"He's a great runner. He...he was going to run in the state championships."

"I didn't know that."

"Yes. You should get him to show you how fast he is. He's got the long limbs for it."

She shakes her head, thinking of Sam's legs, his awful skin rash. "Did he suffer from eczema before?"

"What?" His eyebrows come together in a frown.

"Eczema," she repeats. "A skin rash."

He doesn't speak for a moment, but she knows what he's thinking. The day she gave him to Jean-Luc, he had dry red patches on the inside of his thighs.

"When he was a baby, that day at the station..."

"Yes, I know." She swallows. "We didn't have any cream for him. It was awful. But it was just diaper rash." She stops, overcome by feelings of guilt and longing, a yearning to care for her baby.

"Don't worry. It soon cleared up. He's got great skin, he never gets sunburned, not like me." His cheeks redden. "But of course, there's no reason why he would take after me. I didn't mean to..."

"I know."

"He has your eyes. Most people think they're just brown, but if you look carefully, you can see there are specks of green too. It depends on the light and what mood he's in."

Her heart sinks. She's never seen the green in them.

"What about sleeping? When did he start sleeping through the night?"

"We moved around a lot when we first arrived in America, so it took awhile for us to get into a routine."

She imagines them as refugees, looking for a place to settle. She's not getting the picture of Sam she was hoping for, the one that will bring him closer to her.

"And walking?" she persists. "How old was he when he first walked?"

"I don't remember the dates so well. I'm sorry. Charlotte is better than me at those details."

"Charlotte..." She pauses, the thought of her being Sam's mother cutting into her like a knife. "What was she like as a mother?"

"She..." Sarah hears the crack in his voice. "She is...was a good mother." Tears gather in his eyes. Then he sticks his chin out again.

"Go on." Her voice comes out harsher than she intended.

"I don't know what else I can say."

"I...I don't know how to be a mother to him." The words come tumbling out. "You can't suddenly become a mother to a boy who doesn't know you, who doesn't even speak the same language."

The guard strides away, coughing loudly.

Sarah watches his back as he walks away. He's just a prison guard, but she hates him. They're bullies. All of them.

"You know, he's a wonderful kid," Beauchamp says abruptly.

Sarah brings her eyes back to him, grateful that he's talking, bringing her back to the present.

"He's such a happy kid, he was born with an easygoing disposition. You'll find a way to reach him. But he will need time."

"Time. Everyone talks about time, as if it was a friend. But it's not, is it? Time has been our enemy. If only we'd found him earlier, when he was two, three even, it would have been different."

"I know. It was wrong of me to keep him from you." He pauses. "On the other hand, he has been loved, and he is stable, well balanced. We love... we love him as if he were our own."

"Love him?" Her anger rises up again in a tidal wave. "I loved him too!"

"Loved?"

"I mean love. I love him."

"I'm sorry. I didn't mean—"

"You took away our chance to build that bond with him. And now you dare to question my love for him." Tears of rage sting her eyes. "I'd walk through fire for Samuel."

He stares at her, as though weighing her last statement. "Would you put his happiness before your own?"

"Yes! How dare you even ask me that?"

"How about your husband? Would he?"

"Of course he would!"

"Good."

She's fuming now. The audacity of the man! Taking a deep breath, she calms her indignation. "We love Sam more than life itself. If you'd loved him half as much, you would have looked for us after the war."

Beauchamp raises his chained fists to his eyes. Then he lowers them, shaking his head as if he can shake away his sorrow.

She watches him closely, noticing the slump of his shoulders, the deep regret in his eyes, his eyelashes flickering over them as he tries to make sense of it all. She's seen it before—in her son. That bewildered look, as though the world is just too complicated to comprehend. Compassion threatens to take over, but he is not a child, she reminds herself.

"What else can you tell me about my son?"

"What do you want to know?"

"What was his first word?"

He frowns. "I'm not sure. I can't remember." He looks uncomfortable, and she wonders if he's embarrassed that he can't remember these details.

Then suddenly she knows it as if he'd said it out loud.

"I think it was car," he mumbles. "He loves cars, knows all the models. He helped me choose our car; he came to the garages with me, checked out the engine capacities, the motor, everything."

She looks into his eyes and he tries to hold her gaze, but eventually he has to look away.

"It wasn't car, was it?" She blinks. "It was Mama."

Chapter Eighty-Five

Paris, November 2, 1953

SARAH

The school bell rings out just as she turns the corner into Rue Hospitalières-Saint-Gervais. The children come swarming out, some boys pretending to be fighter planes swooping down. They're noisy and hungry, eager to get home. All except Sam. Standing back from the mass of mothers and children, she waits for him to slouch out. But the playground is empty, suddenly quiet.

What if he's run away again? She runs through the gate, into the school and along the corridor to his classroom. Then she stops dead. He's there, standing next to the principal. He looks tiny, his shoulders slumped and his head hanging low. An overwhelming feeling of sorrow drowns her.

"Madame Laffitte." The principal looks at her. "I'm glad you came in. We need to talk. Let's go into my office."

"Yes, monsieur." She feels like a child again, a child in trouble. Following him down the corridor into his room, the silence is threatening. She reaches for Sam's hand, and he lets her take it for the first time. They are both in trouble. Once in the room, the principal sits at his desk, signaling for them to sit opposite. As Sarah takes her seat, she glances at Sam, hoping to make eye contact, but he stares blankly ahead.

"Madame Laffitte," he starts, "I know this isn't easy for anyone, least of all for Samuel. But we have to think of all our students. Look, I'll get straight to the point. We don't know what to do with Samuel, and it's not just a problem of language. He shows no interest in learning whatsoever. This is unusual in such a young child. He's sullen, uncooperative, and today he was caught fighting in the playground and—"

"Please stop," Sarah interrupts him, surprising herself as much as him. "I know he doesn't want to be here. He's homesick." She reaches out, touching a strand of Sam's hair. "I'm going to take him home now. He won't be coming back again."

"Madame Laffitte, this is not what I meant. You can't just withdraw him like that. He has to attend school."

"Don't worry. He'll attend a school. Come on, Sam." She holds out her hand, standing up, ready to leave.

He puts his hand in hers. She's careful not to apply any pressure, just lets herself feel its warmth. Together, in silence, they walk out of the school, down the street, around the corner, and up the stairs to the apartment. She takes him into the living room and sits next to him on the couch. Burying his head in his hands, he cries and cries. Sarah holds him as he sobs. "It'll be all right. Everything will be good again. I promise you."

She picks up the phone, twirling the coiled plastic around her finger. Slowly she dials the number of her husband's office. He picks up straightaway.

"David, can you come home early? We need to talk."

"Did you visit Beauchamp?"

"Yes, I went to see him. Please, David, can you come home?"

"What's the matter? What did he say?"

"Just come home."

She makes a sandwich for Sam and, breaking the rule in their home, takes it to him in the living room. She sits in the armchair watching him nibble at it. He's lost so much weight since he arrived, and his skin has turned paler. She wonders if it's possible for a child to die from sorrow, or would nature kick in, the survival instinct taking over?

"Sam."

He glances over at her, his eyes blank.

She feels like she's looking at Beauchamps' son, not her own. "I know how hard this has been for you. It's been hard for us too, to watch you suffer, to see how much you detest being here with us."

He's watching her, and she has the feeling he's following what she's saying. "We love you very much. Do you know that, Sam?"

He shrugs a shoulder and looks away.

"We want you to be happy. But we want you to know who you are too."

"I know who I am."

She stares at him in astonishment. His French is almost perfect. "I know you do, Sam."

How she longs to take him in her arms, to feel his proud, vulnerable heart beating near her own, to breathe in the smell of him. It's as though he's outgrowing his child's body, his thoughts and emotions too substantial to be contained in such a small, slight frame.

She leaves the living room, wandering back into the kitchen, waiting for David.

As soon as she hears the front door click open, she goes into the hall.

"What is it, Sarah? What did Beauchamp say?" David hasn't even taken his coat off yet.

"Come into the kitchen, please."

He follows her in. "What did he say?"

"Sit down first. Do you want something to eat?"

"Later. Tell me what he said."

"He didn't say much. It was more the way it made me feel."

David looks at her, his eyes searching hers.

"It was horrible. Him being there...in prison. He shouldn't be there. It reminded me of..."

He takes her hand, squeezing it softly. "I wish I'd never suggested you go."

She sees a frown grow across his forehead, and she pushes ahead before she loses her nerve. "He loves Samuel. He really does."

"I don't doubt that, Sarah. Of course he does. What were you expecting?"

"I don't know. Someone I could despise."

"That's not what you would have wanted for Samuel." He pulls on his beard. "What did he say to you?"

"He asked me if I would put Samuel's happiness before my own."

"Unbelievable! How dare he!"

"And he asked if you would too." She pauses, looking into David's eyes. "I told him that of course we would. I can't believe he asked me. He doesn't know what it means to give your child away." Her voice cracks.

"Maybe he knows now."

"But is it true?"

David raises an eyebrow, as though guessing at what's coming next.

"Would we really put his happiness before our own?"

"Sarah, don't torture yourself like this. He's our son and we love him. One day he'll love us back. He just needs time."

"Time," she repeats. "The intolerance of time."

"What?"

"Time stole him away from us."

"And time will give him back."

"No." Her throat feels thick; it's going to be hard to let out the words she really wants to say. "David, I can't do it...I can't do it anymore. When he ran away, I prayed to God." She wants to reach out, take David's hand, but she can feel a wall growing between them. "I made a promise to him. I promised to give Samuel up if he brought him back safely. That's all I want now. His safety and happiness. I don't care about the rest."

"What do you mean?"

"I can't stand by watching his despair, his misery. He's behaving like a prisoner who can't see a way out. He's losing his will, and he's only a child." Picking up a tea towel, she wipes away her tears.

"But Sarah, we can't give up now."

"David!" She swallows fresh tears. "We have to...we have to give up. Don't you see?"

"No, I don't." He moves toward her.

She pushes him back. "I can't do it anymore. Don't make me!"

He stands there, staring at her with wide disbelieving eyes. Then he turns away. "I'm going to visit Beauchamp myself."

Chapter Eighty-Six

Paris, November 3, 1953

JEAN-LUC

The worst thing about prison is the helplessness. He could put up with the terrible food, the cold nights, even the constant threat of violence. But the helplessness, that kills him. Sam is growing up without him, and Charlotte is having to manage in America all on her own. She writes to him almost every day, so he knows how she's had to sell the house, how she's had to move to a smaller apartment, nearer town, where she's found a job translating. Her grief pours out of the pages she writes. Sometimes he has to fold them up, to return to them later, when he's feeling stronger. But today he's not feeling strong.

"You have a visitor!" the guard shouts, tapping on the bars of his cell with a baton.

Oh God! He really doesn't feel like seeing Sarah Laffitte again.

He follows the guard along the corridor, through the double security doors into the waiting room. The guard points with his baton toward a dark-haired man with a long beard sitting at a visitor's table, gripping the edges as though he's holding on, afraid to fall off. It comes to him with a jolt. It's *him*! It must be him. David Laffitte.

Blood pulsing in his veins, he approaches the table. Tentatively he holds out his handcuffed wrists, expecting some modified version of a handshake, but Laffitte doesn't even stand up, and his hands don't leave the table.

"Monsieur Beauchamp." He stares at Jean-Luc from under thick dark eyebrows.

Sitting down, Jean-Luc inclines his head, acknowledging his name. He waits for Laffitte to say something, but the man just continues to stare, his eyes boring into him.

"I don't know what you want from me." Jean-Luc rubs his temples with his chained hands, trying to ease the headache pounding against his forehead.

"What we want from you?" Laffitte's eyes drill deeper. "The last nine years of our son's life."

Jean-Luc stretches his neck and closes his eyes. His headache is getting worse.

"Do you know what it does to a parent?" Laffitte's tone is harsh, his voice rising. "Not knowing whether your child is dead or alive. We didn't know whether to grieve or carry on the search."

"Listen. If it weren't for me, you wouldn't have a son. You've got him back now. Why don't you go home and take care of him? You have your revenge."

"Revenge! You think this is about revenge?" Laffitte's words burst out, louder than before.

"Well, what is it about then? What do you want from me?" Jean-Luc matches him in volume.

The guard appears. His baton hits the table with a thud. "I've told you before. Keep it quiet!" He puts the baton under Jean-Luc's chin, pushing it upward at a painful angle.

Suddenly Laffitte collapses onto the table, shuddering and shaking as though he's having a fit.

"What's wrong with him?" The guard lifts Laffitte's head. His face is gray, drops of sweat glistening. Naked fear shines out from his eyes.

"I think...I think you scared him."

"Me? I was just telling you to keep the noise down."

Laffitte sits quietly, as though numbed. Jean-Luc puts his chained hands on the table, reaching out toward him. Laffitte stares at him with wild eyes, then he grips Jean-Luc's wrists, his chest heaving with the effort of breathing.

The guard walks away, tutting loudly.

For a while they sit in silence, and Jean-Luc waits for Laffitte to calm himself.

"I'm sorry," Laffitte finally says. "It just...it brought it all back."

"It's okay. It's over now."

He looks up at Jean-Luc with dark eyes. "Is it? Is it over? It will never be over."

Jean-Luc knows what he means. He tries to change the subject. "How is your wife?"

"She...she was very upset after she came to see you."

"I'm sorry. I didn't mean to upset her."

"She wanted to find out more about Samuel, but instead she came away feeling unworthy in some way."

"I didn't intend to make her feel like that. She wanted me to give her details about Sam, but I couldn't remember everything she asked, like when he first walked, when he first slept through the night. These things aren't the things I remember."

"I see." Laffitte rubs his eyes again, as if he's tired of it all. "What are the things you remember then?"

Jean-Luc thinks for a minute, Sam's earnest face vivid in his mind. "His smile. The funny things he said. The way he stuck out his chin in determination or defiance. His long thin arms wrapped around me. The gentle strength he had when he hugged me. The sweet smell of his sweat. His way of looking at me with wide eyes when I'd read him a story—"

Laffitte's hand lands hard on the table. "That's enough." He shifts in his chair. "Why didn't you have children of your own?"

Jean-Luc frowns. "We wanted to." He pauses for a minute, wondering whether to go on. "But...well, it was difficult. Charlotte couldn't. They said it might be due to the deprivation she suffered during the occupation—at that sensitive age."

"Oh." Laffitte is embarrassed now, his gray cheeks regaining some color.

"The doctors said there was nothing they could do." The words roll off his tongue now, feeling like a release. "They said that with a proper diet and healthy lifestyle things should return to normal, but it just didn't happen." He looks at Laffitte and is surprised to see traces of Sam in his dark, intelligent eyes, and in the way he rubs them when confronted with a problem. "Can I ask you, if you don't mind...I know you don't have any other children either."

Laffitte stares down at the table, shaking his head. When he finally looks up, his eyes are watery and unfocused, as though he's lost in a memory.

"I'm sorry." Jean-Luc doesn't know where to take the conversation now. They've hit dangerous territory, and he scrambles around, trying to find a way out.

But then Laffitte blinks and starts talking, his eyes focused now on some distant point. "It was hard when we got back. The physical labor, the starvation, the brutality—it had all taken its toll on both of us. We'd changed; our bodies no longer felt like our own. We weren't the young couple we'd been. I think we both felt..." He looks straight at Jean-Luc with wide eyes, as though surprised at how much he's said already. "It took a long time to feel human again, like ourselves. And all the time we were still looking for Samuel. I wanted to try to have another child, but Sarah's heart wasn't in it. She used to cry...She just wanted her baby back."

"And now she's got him back."

"Well, he's not a baby anymore, is he? If only...if only you'd looked for us after the war. Everything would have been different." He sighs.

"Ten minutes!" the guard shouts.

"Tell me how he is now," Jean-Luc says. "Please. Your wife told me he was suffering from a skin rash...Is it better?"

Laffitte's eyes glaze over as if he's lost in thought. Then he replies, "No, it's not." He raises his eyes to meet Jean-Luc's. "Fine. You want to know? I'll tell you." He pulls on his beard, leaning forward. "The poor boy has been terribly disturbed. He refuses to speak French, he cries most nights, and he has developed a rash that is eating him up. Last week, he finally ran away. He was found up in Le Havre, trying to board a boat to America."

"No! Oh God, no!" Jean-Luc falls back in his chair, holding his chained hands up against his forehead. What have they done to Sam? Pain shoots through his stomach, like knives cutting him up from the inside. He can hardly breathe.

The guard approaches. "Five minutes."

"Sarah," Laffitte murmurs. "It's hard for her to see her child like this. It's hard for me too, but I make myself think of the long term, see the whole picture. But all Sarah sees is her little boy suffering." He shakes his head. "It's killing her."

Chapter Eighty-Seven

Paris, November 3, 1953

SARAH

While David is visiting Beauchamp, and Sam's in his room, Sarah takes out her special writing paper she keeps in a wooden box, a dried rose lying on the thick parchment. This will be the most important letter she will ever write. Carefully she fills her fountain pen with ink, thinking about David, knowing it will be impossible for him to accept her decision. But he won't be able to stop her, not now that she's told him about her promise to God. David's faith is like a rock, unmovable, and he wouldn't want Sarah to compromise hers by breaking a promise like that.

Dear Mrs. Beauchamp,
It is with a broken heart that I write this letter. Samuel isn't happy here. We are at a loss. His distress at being uprooted is too much for us to bear. I am appealing to you in desperation. He needs you. Can you come?
Sarah Laffitte

The front door clicks open. Sarah looks up from her letter. David stands there, his shoulders slumped, his face gray. Rubbing his eyes, he stares at her.

She doesn't move from her chair, but gazes at him, thinking how exhausted and weary he looks. She doesn't even want to ask him how the meeting with Beauchamp went, imagining it could only have been painful.

A silent tear slides down his cheek, followed by another. Still she doesn't move. How can she comfort him? She has nothing to offer him now, only her surrender. He wanted her to be tenacious, to hold on to their son with all her might, whatever the cost. But she loves Sam too much for that.

She doesn't notice the tears sliding down her own cheeks until they land on the letter, blurring the ink. As she looks down at the blue splotches, she feels David come and crouch down beside her, his wet cheek leaning into hers. She knows he's reading the letter. Holding her breath, she waits for his hurt, his anger to come flying out.

"Sarah," he murmurs. "Sarah." Then his arms are around her, pulling her into him.

She slips effortlessly into his embrace.

"Sarah, don't cry. Please don't cry."

"But you're crying."

Holding her face in his hands, he kisses her tears away. "Our son is alive. It is enough for me. It is enough, Sarah."

Chapter Eighty-Eight

Santa Cruz, November 9, 1953

CHARLOTTE

Another Monday morning. I drag myself out of bed and into the kitchen, put two large spoonfuls of coffee into the filter paper, and heat the water on the stove. Waiting for it to boil, I light up. I've never been a smoker, but now it calms my nerves and gives me something to do with my ever-fidgety fingers. I like the breathing too—a long deep breath in; hold it a second, then let it out slowly. I could give it up if I wanted to, and one day I probably will.

I have to be at the psychiatrist's at nine o'clock. When I enter his room with its bright white walls, I feel the same apprehension I do every week. It's hard work pretending to be someone I'm not. I sit on the rounded plastic chair opposite him, looking at him with a fake smile stretched across my mouth.

"Good morning, Charlotte. How are you today?"

"Very well, thank you. And yourself?" I look him in the eye, hoping to convince him that I'm sincere.

He smiles back at me. "What have you been doing this week?"

"I went to pottery class on Saturday."

He nods as though I've said something profound.

"The women there are such fun! We talk about everything."

I don't mention how I just sit there letting their conversation wash over me while I stroke the damp clay into the shape of a child's face, then squash it up to start again. I just can't get Sam's features right. I like listening to their chatter. It's soothing. Maybe it's the lack of a male presence that makes them feel free to talk. They talk about everything—children, education, their own childhoods, men, love, relationships. They excuse me from participating because I'm foreign and they don't think I follow everything they say. But I do. I've just found this is a good card to play. My foreignness. It stops people from trying to get too near.

"And have you seen any of them outside of the class?"

Damn! He's not as easy to fool as that. "Not yet," I say. "But I'm planning on inviting a few of them over next weekend."

"Good. Very good. You'll tell me how it goes at our next appointment then?"

"Of course," I say brightly, cursing myself for this little lie. Now I'm stuck. What if he checks up on me?

"And how are you sleeping now?"

"I'm still taking the pills you gave me."

"Yes, maybe it's time to wean you off those."

I nod, but I'm not sure if I'm ready. I can't go back to those weeks of insanity I lived after they took Sam away, sleeping only thirty minutes at a time, collapsing from mental exhaustion, to awaken again as though struck by lightning, a sinking feeling spreading through every cell in my body.

"Start by taking half the dose you're on now for a week, and we'll see how you get on."

I look at him, wondering if I can ask for more time, but quickly decide that I need to appear positive if I want him to give me a clean bill of health, so I nod again.

"And your thoughts on Sam? How are you managing them?"

"I try not to think about him." I pause, getting ready for the big lie. "I'm coming to terms with the fact that I was never his real mother, I was just standing in."

"Good. Good."

How could he know that I think about Sam every minute of every day, wondering what he's doing as the hours, the days, the weeks go by? I have no news from him, but I know how he must hate Paris. It will seem so alien to him. Is he learning French? Does his new father read to him at night like Jean-Luc used to? Does his new mother hold him tight when there's a thunderstorm? Does he let her? Do they allow him to leave a night-light on? Does he know how to ask for one? Does she make him crêpes for breakfast? How is he getting on at school? Are the other children kind to him? I torture myself with these questions.

"And your husband? How is he?" The psychiatrist interrupts my thoughts.

I think he must have forgotten his name. "Jean-Luc. It's hard for him to be in jail." I can't say any more. The irony of Sam and Jean-Luc being in Paris while I am here feels tragic. All three of us are prisoners now, lost to one another.

"Are you ready now to try for children of your own?"

I stare at him. How can he ask such a question?

"I mean, when your husband is released." He looks down at his notes. "I see he is only serving a short sentence."

"Two years." I'm not smiling now.

"Yes, that's right. But you are still young enough to start a family of your own."

"I can't. I can't have children."

"Hmm. Well, the reason for that was never very clear. You may find that once you've accepted that Sam is gone, it might free something up inside you."

I continue to stare at him. Is he mad?

"It could be psychological," he continues.

"I don't think so." I could tell him how my periods never came back after the war, but I think I'll spare him the details. I remind myself that I'm only here so he can declare me mentally stable and I can get my passport back. I can't afford to alienate the idiot.

Gritting my teeth, I nod. "Maybe you're right," I say sweetly. "I hadn't thought of it like that."

"Good. Good. And how is work going?"

"Fine. The people are friendly and I enjoy the work." It's an undemanding, quiet job—translating legal documents. The small wage covers the rent on my one-bedroom apartment, leaving a bit left over every month to put aside for my plane ticket to France—for when I get my passport back.

On my way back from work later that day, I distractedly open my mailbox. There's a letter sitting there in a white envelope. It has a French stamp, but it's not Jean-Luc's writing. I rip it open, my heart thudding, imagining it's from Sam.

But no. It begins: *Dear Mrs. Beauchamp*... My heart sinks. Then I read on, and my blood starts pulsating through my veins, fast and furious. They want me to go there!

I hold the letter against my heart. I'm going to see my son again. I read the words over and over again. Sarah Laffitte—she does love him. Tears stream down my face, blurring my vision. She has always loved him. Through all these years, she kept on searching. She never gave up.

Guilt cuts its way into my soul. We should have looked for them. We could have. It would have been the honest, decent thing to do. But no, we took the easy option, letting ourselves believe they had perished at Auschwitz. After all they've been through, and then this—finding their son nine years later to realize he's no longer their baby, that he doesn't even speak the same language. How can they get to know him now? We made it impossible for them.

With a heavy heart, I walk up the stairs to my apartment, clutching the letter, each word of it burning into me. *Samuel isn't happy here.* The quiet understatement tears into my heart. It's no worse than I imagined, but seeing it there on paper, written by his biological mother, brings it alive. It hits me in the stomach with its force. He's so distraught, his own mother doesn't know what to do. She's willing to do anything to make him happy, even let me see him. I thank God she loves him this much. But now what? Does she imagine I might move to Paris? That we would bring him up together? I doubt it. It would only hurt her to see him loving someone else as his mother. Is she ready to give him up? Would she really do that? Could a mother who had lost her child face losing him all over again?

Chapter Eighty-Nine

Santa Cruz, November 17, 1953

CHARLOTTE

It's still warm here in Santa Cruz, but I know it will be cold in Paris at this time of year. I've been wondering what to wear all week. Sam loves my yellow summer dress with poppies around the edges, but that will be no good in the French winter. Instead I put on a straight beige skirt and a cream blouse, carrying my woolen cardigan and jacket over my arm.

I stand in the kitchen, restless and ready to go, waiting for the taxi. Looking around at the white walls, I wonder if I'll ever come back to this apartment. I hope not; it's a lonely place. On the dot of seven, the doorbell rings. I pick up my suitcase and grab a light cashmere scarf from the hat stand.

"Airport?" The taxi driver looks at me in his rearview mirror.

"Yes, please."

"Where you flying to?"

"New York, then on to Paris."

"You got family there?"

"Yes."

"I thought I heard an accent. You French?"

"Yes."

He stares at me in the mirror as if trying to work out who I am. "Didn't get too badly bombed, did it? Paris?"

"No." I hesitate, not wanting to be rude, but not wanting this conversation either. "It didn't."

"Not like London. They really hit London, didn't they?"

"Yes," I say, deciding to tell him what he wants to hear. "Paris was occupied instead."

"Exactly. They didn't need to bomb it into submission."

I turn my head away and look out the window, hoping to make it clear that I'm not interested in this conversation. He taps the wheel as if in time to some song in his head. I watch the streets go by: houses with long front lawns, mailboxes standing on one wooden leg, waiting to receive their mail for the day. So different from Paris, but so familiar. It has begun to feel like home, and it makes me wonder if Paris will feel a little foreign to me now.

"They just marched right on into Paris, didn't they?"

I wish he'd shut up. I sigh loudly and hope he'll get the hint.

He goes back to tapping the wheel, and we drive the rest of the way in silence. I give him a whole dollar tip when I get out, to thank him for shutting up.

I'm relieved to get to the plane, to finally be going back to France. It's the first time I've flown, and I feel a little nervous when we accelerate so quickly for take-off. I grip the edges of my seat, wondering how Sam felt during his flight. Was he scared? Did someone hold his hand as he boarded the plane? The thought of him doing these things alone, without Jean-Luc or me, fills me with sadness.

"Would you like a drink?" The stewardess stops in front of me with a trolley laden with miniature bottles.

"No, thank you."

The man sitting next to me looks up from his paper. "A beer, please."

He pours his drink into a plastic cup. "Where are you going?" he asks.

"New York," I reply. "Then Paris." I don't want to talk, it's too complicated, so I close my eyes, feigning sleep. But I'm too excited to sleep, and too nervous. Sam. Sam. Will he be angry with me? Will he think I abandoned him? Will he have changed in four months? Four months. Is that all it's been? It feels like four years.

After the change at New York, we finally land in Paris and I go through customs. I realize I haven't brought any presents with me. I hesitate, wondering if I should get something, but gifts would feel superfluous and superficial, as if I were on some kind of social visit. I hurry through to the line of waiting taxis.

"*Rue des Rosiers, s'il vous plaît, dans Le Marais.*" The French words slide effortlessly off my tongue It's a relief to speak my own language again. It feels like coming home.

Staring out the window as we drive into the city, I wonder what the word "home" really means. Is it a place? Is it a language? Or is it wherever your family is? I suppose it's a mixture of all these things. But this is not a place Sam can call home. I wish we'd spoken French to him when he was small; we had no right to deny him that part of his identity. I wonder if he'll resent us when he grows up, when he realizes what we kept from him. But right now, all I want to do is hold his little body tight and tell him everything's going to be okay. I'll worry about the rest later.

The taxi drops me off right outside their apartment building. Two men with long beards and black hats walk past me, reminding me that I'm in the Jewish quarter. I'm shaking, and I suddenly realize how cold it is. Setting my case down, I put my cardigan and jacket on, but still I can't stop shivering. I wrap my arms around myself, my stomach tying itself in knots. I'm only a few meters away from him now. I look up at the windows, imagining him inside, knowing he must be waiting for me.

Taking a deep breath, excitement and trepidation pumping through my veins, I push open the heavy wooden doors, finding myself in a small courtyard. Their apartment is on the fourth floor, so I pick my bag up and heave it up the narrow winding staircase, my heart thumping hard against my ribs. Before I knock on the door, I take a moment to smooth my hair down and straighten my scarf, trying to calm my trembling.

Then I raise my hand. But before I have a chance to make contact with the door, it flies open and Sam jumps on me, almost knocking me over, his arms around my neck, his legs wrapped around my waist, gripping me tightly. I put my arms around him. I hold him. I breathe him in—the sweet, musky smell of him. We have no need for words. I feel the force of his love and I know he can feel mine.

Then I hear a cough. I stumble into the apartment, Sam still clinging to me. Slowly he loosens his grip and puts his feet back on the ground. I hold his face in my palms, staring into his brown eyes. He hugs me around the waist, burying his head in my chest. I stroke his hair. "It's okay, Sam. It's going to be all right."

I hear another cough and look up over his head. Mr. and Mrs. Laffitte are standing there, pale as ghosts, watching us with tears in their eyes. I see Mr. Laffitte reach out to his wife; she buries her face in his shoulder. With the other arm he gestures to a door at the end of the corridor. With Sam still hanging on to me, I follow them into the living room.

Mr. Laffitte helps his wife into an armchair, then stands behind her with his hand on her shoulder. "*S'il vous plaît.*" He indicates the couch for us to sit.

Sam squirms onto my lap, though he is too big. "Mommy," he says. "Can we go home now?"

I kiss his head.

"Please. Please. I promise I'll be good. I just wanna go home."

"I know. I know." I kiss him again.

Mr. Laffitte coughs again. "*C'est très difficile pour nous.*"

I look over at him. "*Je suis désolée. Pardonnez nous.*"

"Mommy!" Sam shouts, taking my cheeks in his hands. "Don't speak French!" Then the tears come, rolling down his cheeks. "Mommy! Please!"

"Sam, it's okay. It's still me. I'm not leaving you again." He hasn't behaved like this since he was five years old.

Mr. Laffitte takes his wife's hand and they stand together. "*Nous allons vous laisser.*" They're going to leave us alone. I nod in agreement. Before we can talk together properly, I need to spend some time with Sam.

They leave the room, and I hear the front door click open and then shut again. "They've gone out!" Sam throws his arms around my neck. "Can we go now? Can we? Can we go home?"

"Wait, Sam, please wait."

His eyes widen, the black pupils expanding. "When? When?"

"I need to talk to . . . to . . ." What should I call them? "To Monsieur and Madame Laffitte first."

He removes his arms from my neck. "But we will go home, won't we? Promise?"

"I'll do my best."

"No! You have to promise!" Fresh tears well up.

I run my hands over his wet cheeks. "I promise." Now I will have to make it happen.

By the time Mr. and Mrs. Laffitte return, a couple of hours later, Sam has fallen asleep, his head in my lap, exhausted from all the emotion. Gently Mr. Laffitte lifts him up, and I follow him as he carries Sam into his bedroom. He lays him on the bed, putting the cover over him so tenderly it makes my heart lurch. For a minute he stands there looking down at him. I wish I could put my arm around him, offer him some comfort. He bends down, kissing Sam on the head.

"Mommy," Sam murmurs.

Mr. Laffitte backs away, and I kneel down by the bed, stroking Sam's head. "It's okay. I'm here." I watch as he drifts off again.

When I stand up, I see Mr. Laffitte has left the room. Guilt fills my heart as I walk back to the living room. I sit in the armchair, looking at my feet. I can't bear to see the sorrow in their eyes. Mrs. Laffitte passes me a cup of coffee, and I glance at her as I thank her. She has the most remarkable green eyes, like Sam's but brighter. Sam's are only green in certain lights and depending on his mood. "Cat's eyes," a friend once called them.

Mr. Laffitte speaks up. "We want you to take Samuel back to America."

It's not what I was expecting. So direct. So clear-cut. "But..."

"It's too hard for all of us. Especially for him."

"It's too late." Mrs. Laffitte's voice is so soft I can hardly hear her. "He doesn't belong to us anymore."

I put my coffee down and stand up. Without thinking, I walk toward her. She moves along the couch, making room for me. I sit next to her, putting my hand on her knee. "Please forgive us."

She covers my hand with hers. "We forgive you. You saved our son." Her silent tears fall onto our joined hands. I lean toward her, holding her as she cries, wishing I could absorb her pain.

"I'll teach him French. He'll write to you. We'll talk about you. It's not over. Please don't think it's over."

Mr. Laffitte puts his hand on my shoulder. "We know you will. You've been a good mother to him." He pauses. "And Jean-Luc has been a good father. Sam was lucky that such a man saved him."

I can't stop the tears now from streaming down my face. Sarah and David love Sam more than themselves; they are putting his happiness before their own. It hits me like a dagger in my heart. They are his true parents. They always have been. The thought fills me with shame, and I promise myself to make sure he grows up knowing what they did for him.

* * *

The paperwork is completed in a week and, as the plane flies over the Atlantic, taking us home to California, I watch Sam sleep. His long eyelashes flutter on his pale cheeks and he clutches my arm as if afraid he'll wake up and I won't be there again.

I look out at the clouds and think about the Laffittes again and the sacrifice they made. About my husband—the bravest man I know—who will return to us. And about Samuel.

I offer up a silent prayer, grateful for this second chance.

Epilogue

One year later, as they were getting ready for bed, Sarah took David's hand, placing it on her abdomen. "David, I have something to tell you." She paused, watching him. "I'm expecting a baby." As she looked into his eyes, she saw them fill with tears.

Six months later, she gave birth to a baby boy they called Jérémie.

When Sam was thirteen, David, Sarah, and Jérémie went to visit him, and Sam met his little brother, but truth be told, it was a strained visit. He was shy about speaking French, and they struggled to make conversation. This time it was David who comforted Sarah. "He's thirteen, it's not an easy age. He's feeling awkward anyway, and he doesn't understand yet. One day he'll accept us, you'll see."

It was agreed that Charlotte and Jean-Luc would bring Sam over to Paris when he was eighteen. But somehow it never happened. They had to pay for college, and it took up all their funds. Money was tight all around, and his education had to come first, didn't it?

Through Sam's letters, David and Sarah heard how he had met someone special. How he hoped they would be happy for him.

Now, one sunny Saturday morning in the summer of 1968, David and Sarah sit in their kitchen, dipping croissants into bowls of coffee. Jérémie and his little sister, who is seven now, are at school. Sarah's hair has started to turn gray, and the lines of heartache around her eyes have deepened. David has kept his beard, though it too is turning gray.

Soon they'll finish their breakfast and go to the synagogue. David is looking over the paper. "They've actually banned student protests," he comments, raising his eyes to look at Sarah.

She's about to answer, something about de Gaulle needing to resign; after all, he's nearly eighty. Time to move over. But the doorbell interrupts her line of thought. "Who can that be?" she asks. "On a Saturday morning?"

"I'll go," David offers. He leaves the kitchen and walks down the stairs to the entrée. There's a young man standing there, looking around as though he's lost. David opens the glass door. "*Bonjour, monsieur.*"

The man stares at him. He's tall and handsome; a mop of straight dark hair flops over his forehead, and his skin is tanned. David is drawn to his eyes; they're chocolate brown, but specks of green twinkle as he opens his mouth. "*Bonjour.*"

David takes a step nearer.

"It's me, it's—"

"Sam-uel," David whispers. The name feels like pearls on his tongue, and he can't resist saying it again. "Sam-uel, Sam-uel."

The young man smiles a lopsided smile. "Yes, it's me." A tiny laugh escapes his lips. "Sam-uel." He walks toward his father, his arms open.

David finds himself enveloped by strong arms. As he lets himself be held, his limbs go limp. His energy saps away as he gives in to his tears.

The young man's arms wrapped around him tighten their grip. "I'm sorry, I'm sorry."

David is vaguely aware of Sarah's footsteps coming down the stairs. He feels the tight grip on him loosen as Samuel turns toward his mother. He watches as he takes Sarah's hand, bringing it to his lips to kiss.

"Samuel?" she murmurs softly. "Is it you?" Her hands smother his face, stroking, wrapping themselves around his cheeks. "Is it really you?"

He laughs, kissing her again.

David can see he's grown into a kind man, one who understands the pain of others. His heart fills with pride, and a feeling of peace spreads through him. This is all he ever wanted.

With Samuel holding on to them both, they make their way up the stairs. They sit down at the kitchen table, and David watches his son looking around, taking it all in, comparing his childhood memories with what he sees now.

"I'm so glad I came," he starts in flawless French. "I wasn't sure, but now that I'm here, I'm so glad."

"I always knew you'd come back." Sarah wipes her eyes. "We just had to wait till you were ready." Reaching out her hand, she puts it up against his cheek, as if she can't quite believe he's real.

"Is that one of my drawings?" Samuel asks, looking at the wall.

They all turn to look at the framed drawing. "Yes," David replies. "We like to look at it and think of you there in California."

"It's the Big Dipper. It actually looks like it." Samuel smiles another lopsided smile, then his face grows serious. "I want to thank you both for letting me go." He looks from one to the other. "I know what it must have cost you. How much you must have loved me."

"Still love you." Sarah smiles.

"Yes, your mother's right. We didn't stop loving you just because you weren't here."

"And I didn't forget you." He puts his hand into the inside pocket of his jacket and pulls out a small wooden box.

David recognizes it immediately. Reaching over, he undoes the tiny hook and looks inside. He takes out the small colored stones, rolling them between his fingers. "Do you know where I got these?" He looks at Samuel. "I found them on the ground at Auschwitz, one day when we were digging." He stops to wipe away a tear. "It was a sign from God. I knew that if I could find beauty like that among the dirt and the gravel, then I would find my son again."

"I have something to tell you." Samuel reaches his hands out to the middle of the table, palms up. Sarah and then David place their hands in his. He squeezes them tightly. "I know how much you loved me, because I know what it's like now. To be a parent. I have a daughter. She's three months old and she's outside, waiting in the car with her mother, Lucy. Do you want to meet them?"

"Want to meet them? Of course we do! Waiting outside indeed. Bring them in." David is already halfway out of the kitchen.

Samuel continues to talk as they walk down the stairs. "I couldn't let you know by letter. I needed to see you to tell you this."

"Thank you, Samuel." David puts his hand on his shoulder.

"We're not married either," he continues. "I wouldn't have gotten married, not without telling you."

"Well, you can get married now then." Sarah laughs, her heart overflowing with joy.

Lucy is blond, hair cascading over her shoulders in golden waves, and her eyes are a lively blue. How American she looks, Sarah can't help thinking; like a Hollywood film star.

With the baby in her arms, the young mother leans forward to kiss Sarah and then David. The warmth of the infant burns through Sarah as she brushes up against the bundle, but she doesn't look yet. She wants to save the moment for when they're inside, in the privacy of their apartment.

"I'm so pleased to meet you." Lucy is the first to speak. "Sam's always talking about his French parents."

Sarah pauses before answering, looking into the young woman's blue eyes, relieved to find that they are warm.

"Your French is excellent," David interrupts.

"Well, it should be," Lucy says. "Didn't Sam tell you? I'm half French."

"Which half?" David asks.

"My better half." She laughs. "My mother is French and my father is American. They met at the end of the war, here in Paris. But I've never lived here. I was brought up in San Francisco."

"Come on. Come on in." David puts his arm around Sarah, directing the little gathering back toward the apartment building.

The baby doesn't wake as they walk up the stairs. They go through to the kitchen and arrange themselves around the table. David, sitting next to Lucy, leans over to stroke the baby's cheek. "She has the same long eyelashes as Samuel."

Sarah, sitting on the other side of Lucy, is finally ready to look at her grandchild. Her heart beats hard as she gazes down, seeing eyelashes curling up onto soft cheeks, dark silky hair. She plants a kiss on the baby's forehead.

"I didn't realize," Samuel starts. He clears his throat. "I didn't know what you'd gone through. I was only a child, and I didn't understand, or I wasn't listening. I can't remember now. But I didn't know."

They both look up from the baby. "You were only a child. It was too much to ask of you."

"I'm sorry."

"Samuel, you have nothing to be sorry for. You came back."

"Well, we might be staying. We'd like to spend some time here. You know, experience both our cultures."

David's eyes glisten. "This is more than I ever dared to dream of."

"Thank you, both of you." Sarah smiles at the young mother. "May I?" She holds out her arms.

Lucy passes the baby over without the slightest hesitation.

The gesture, the handing-over of the infant, brings it all flooding back, and she's overcome with a feeling of protectiveness toward this new child. Quietly she starts to hum as she gently rocks the baby.

Samuel leans down over his daughter, placing a kiss on her silky head. Then he looks at his mother and whispers, "Her name is Sarah."

Acknowledgments

When I arrived in Paris in 1993, I had no inkling of the impact it would have on my life. As I wandered around the city in the first few months, I was surprised and moved by the large number of plaques and monuments in remembrance of those who were killed during World War II, with lists of names that went on and on, and sometimes even fresh flowers laid nearby. Outside a school in Le Marais (the Jewish quarter of Paris) there is a simple plaque, telling of the 260 pupils who were arrested during World War II. Not one of them survived.

It shocked me deeply and made me want to learn more about this dark time in our history. I began to ask anyone I met over the age of sixty what it was like to have lived through the occupation, and I began to read up on the subject.

One of the people I met was Dora Blaufoux, a wonderful, sprightly lady in her late eighties. Dora was only thirteen when she was deported to Auschwitz. When I wrote the chapters on Auschwitz, I used some of her memories, as well as personal accounts I took from books. I must admit, I felt like something of an impostor when I wrote these chapters. I don't know, and I can barely imagine the horror of Auschwitz. But that isn't what this story is about.

Writing this book has been an exciting, eventful journey, and along the way I have met many interesting, sometimes crazy, often wonderful people. Writing is essentially a solitary occupation, but I have found invaluable support in various writing groups here in Paris. One such group has been especially important to me—Scriptorium, founded by Hazel Manuel. Her positive criticism, gentle guidance, and enthusiasm kept me going when I doubted myself. Different writers have passed through and still attend this group, and my gratitude goes to you all, in particular Rachel, Carol, Nancy, Kass, Cris, Shelley, Connie, Anne, Melissa, and Deborah.

A special thanks goes to my friends Marilyn Smith, Ian Hobbs, and Hazel for being with me in La Loire, Les Alpes, and India, for sitting in the heat and the cold, listening to my chapters. Thanks for the laughs too! And then I would like to thank my friend Lucy for letting me do the rewrites in her beach shack, and Christian for checking my French.

When researching this book, I was lucky enough to have some guidance from Stefan Martens, Vice-Director of the German Historical Institute in Paris. His knowledge and dedication to the subject of World War II provided me with a wealth of information, and I would like to thank him for the time he spent helping me work through some of the finer details.

Finally, my deep gratitude goes to Abbie Greaves at Curtis Brown for making all this possible when she picked out my manuscript from the many she must have received. And then to my wonderful agent, Sheila Crowley, for believing in it and understanding what I was trying to do, and for helping me get there. I would also like to thank the lovely team at Headline for making it all such a wonderful experience: Nathaniel Alcaraz-Stapleton, Rebecca Folland, and Hannah Geranio in the translation and foreign rights department; copyeditor Jane Selley, for her attention to detail; and my editor Sherise Hobbs, who helped me add those vital, final touches. My thanks also go to Karen Kosztolnyik, editor-in-chief at Grand Central Publishing in the USA, for working so hard on getting it all just right.

My parents brought me up to believe anything was possible; all I had to do was put my mind to it, and for this I am eternally grateful.

If you are interested in this time in history, I have included a list of some of the books I read while doing my research:

Berr, Hélène, *Journal 1942–1944* (2008, Tallandier)

Haffner, Sebastian, *Defying Hitler—A Memoir* (2002, Weidenfeld and Nicolson)

Humbert, Agnès, *Résistance—Memoirs of Occupied France* (2008, Bloomsbury)

Moorehead, Caroline, *A Train in Winter* (2011, Chatto and Windus)

Ousby, Ian, *Occupation—The Ordeal of France* (1999, Pimlico)

Sebba, Anne, *Les Parisiennes* (2017, Weidenfeld and Nicolson)

Vinen, Richard, *The Unfree French—Life under the Occupation* (2007, Penguin)

Wiesel, Elie, *Night* (1958, Les Éditions de Minuit)

Poem for an Adopted Child

Not flesh of my flesh
nor bone of my bone
but still, miraculous,
my own.
Never forget
for a single moment,
you didn't grow under my heart
but in it.

Anon

About the Author

Ruth Druart grew up on the Isle of Wight, moving away at eighteen to study psychology at Leicester University. She has lived in Paris since 1993, where she has followed a career in teaching. She has recently taken a sabbatical, so that she can follow her dream of writing full-time.